Cover art by Lauren Patrick and AR Wise

PART ONE – A New Game

March 15th, 2012

"So you don't believe in ghosts?" asked Wendell.

Pierce groaned and shook his head. "Look man, we've been through this before. Sorry, but I don't believe in that sort of thing. Never have, never will."

"Even after all the stuff I sent you?" Wendell loaded his paper plate with the pizza that had just been delivered. He'd invited his friend over to drink beers and watch a bad movie, a tradition they'd shared ever since they were in high school.

"Those videos can be manipulated, bro," said Pierce. He was standing in front of the fridge, grabbing a couple of the beers he'd brought over. "You can't believe everything you see online."

"All right, all right," said Wendell as he licked sauce off his thumb after setting his paper plate down beside the pizza box. "Then I've got another one I want you to see." Wendell was determined to convince his friend. He grabbed his laptop and flipped it open.

Pierce sighed and then laughed as Wendell's computer booted. "There's no video you're going to show me that's going to convince me of anything, man. I mean, come on, that shit's all fake."

"Most of it," said Wendell as he nodded in agreement. "But not all of it."

"No, all of it is," said Pierce. "Those shows they've got on TV, with those jackasses running around haunted places, jumping every time the wind blows and saying it's proof of ghosts – you're really telling me you believe that shit."

"I'm saying there's more to life than we know," said Wendell. "That's all. You can go around pretending like you know everything, or whatever, but I'm just saying you should keep an open mind."

"An open mind's one thing," said Pierce as he used the bottle opener on his keychain to pop the tops off both beers. "Letting yourself get lied to is a whole other story."

Wendell just responded with a half-hearted "Sure," as he waited for his computer to boot.

Pierce set Wendell's beer down beside the computer and then walked around to the other side of the island in the kitchen, opposite his friend. Wendell's face was illuminated by the computer screen, and was changing color as he navigated the web.

"This is the site I wanted you to see," said Wendell.

"All right," said Pierce. "Let's get it over with."

"They've got a video on here where this hot chick is touring this old, abandoned place, and you can totally see a ghost in the background."

"Okay," said Pierce as he made his way back around to stand beside Wendell. "Let's see it."

"Yeah, hold on a sec," said Wendell, preoccupied as he read something else on the site. He pointed at the screen and said, "This is new. This just popped up. They haven't had anything new on the site in a while, but they just posted this video."

"Click it," said Pierce.

Wendell pressed play.

"Hi, my name's Rachel Knight," said the woman in the video.

"You were right," said Pierce. "She's hot."

Wendell hushed his friend.

Rachel continued, "We're recording this on March 13th, 2012, in the basement of a facility owned by a company named Cada E.I.B."

CHAPTER 1 – Suffer the Children

Widowsfield
March 14th, 1996

Ben was lost in the fog.

He cried out, but no one answered. He yelled his sister's name, but she didn't remember him anymore. He even tried to call for his father, but he knew Michael wouldn't come looking for him.

There was a constant din of metallic sound, like the grinding of gears as a great machine fell apart somewhere far off. Ben was walking through something wet, but he couldn't see the ground through the thick, swirling fog. For a moment he thought he saw the glow of a sunrise in the distance, but then, as if in response to his glance, the clamor of machines grew more intense and the fog swelled to block out the light.

The grind of metal revealed a sudden, familiar rhythm that might've been words. Ben tried to walk towards the noise, but he never seemed to get any closer. And every time he caught a glimpse of the warm glow of the sunrise, the fog would move to intercept him. He felt like he was tumbling through the ether, despite being able to feel the ground beneath his bare feet.

Again, the metallic grind came in the rhythm of speech, and this time he thought he heard his name. At the same moment, his face began to tingle, as if something wet and warm had fallen on it. He touched his cheek and felt a hot wetness that confused him. When he looked at the tip of his finger, he saw blood there.

"I'm hurt?" asked Ben, but his confusion quickly turned to fear as the pain came back. It wasn't just the pain that returned, but also his memory of what had happened. He felt his cheeks burning as blisters formed, and he tasted the caustic soup he'd poured into the tub to try and burn away the corpse of the woman his father told him he'd murdered.

Ben screamed in pain, but his voice was nearly lost, an echo from far off, barely heard through the fog that shrouded everything. His teeth began to chatter from the pain, and his hands were shaking as he watched the blisters form on his arms. As the pain grew worse, he began to see a break in the fog ahead. He ran to it, hoping for any sort of salvation from the agony he was being forced to endure.

At first, the only thing he could perceive within the fog was a square of darkness, but as he got closer he began to make out shapes. He was within a massive, rectangular room, but the edges were distorted by the fog. He could feel the cold wood beneath his feet, and he looked down to see that the mist had begun to dissipate. Far in the distance he saw what appeared to be a bed with a young boy sitting at the edge, and in front of him was a man.

The metallic grind finally formed words, "Would you bleed the lamb?"

A crash of metal silenced the scene and the fog swelled again, blinding Ben as he tried to run forward. It felt like he'd fallen face first into a fire pit and was struggling to push himself free as the flames licked at his eyes. The skin on his arms continued to bubble from the heat and he watched as the boils burst, leaking bloody pus that dripped down to his elbows. He clawed at his face, desperate to peel away the fire, desperate to be free of this agony.

"You must bind him," said the voice again, but this time it sounded closer than before.

Ben cried out, "Daddy, help!"

"Ben?" asked Michael Harper.

Ben tried again to call out for help, but this time a sudden crash of metal silenced him. The fog swept in and grasped at Ben, like a cold rush of air from a freezer on a scorching, summer day. The fog soothed his pain. It covered his face and pulled away the agony, giving Ben a reprieve from his torture.

Then the fog cleared again, but this time in a new direction. He couldn't see the bedroom anymore, but was instead staring out at rocky terrain that was dotted with scant, wiry brush. The white fog continued to dominate the area, as if intent on blocking out the sun's warmth, and as Ben walked, the fog stayed beneath him.

There was a path that led through the brown rocks that dotted the parched earth, and Ben followed it until he caught sight of something moving ahead. There was a lamb cowering in a bush ahead, and it stopped and stared down at Ben. The creature became taut, as if ready to flee, but stayed where it was and waited for Ben to make the first move.

Ben tried to comfort the frightened creature, but his words were lost within the fog.

Then he heard his own voice cry out from far off, "Daddy, no!" He looked up the hill and saw a man with a knife stabbing down at a bound shape on an altar. The man was at least fifty feet ahead of where the lamb was hiding, but the frightened animal reacted to the thrusts of the knife as if it were the one being stabbed. The creature yelped in pain, but stayed where it was in the bush. The man ahead stabbed back down a second time, and again the lamb reacted as if pained, but didn't flee. The creature stayed where it was, screaming in pain, and its off-white wool suddenly bloomed with bright red blood.

The lamb quaked where it stood as its body burst blood that quickly streamed across the dusty earth. Ahead, the man on the hill continued his sacrifice to appease his vengeful God.

Ben couldn't look away. He wanted to turn and flee, but he was trapped within the fog. He was forced to stare at the lamb as it continued to bleed. The creature's eyes locked on Ben, but then blood began to seep from its nostrils. Its glassy eyes were gushing fluid that started clear, but quickly turned to blood. The lamb's eyes bulged and popped forth from its skull. The bulbs dangled from the creature's head by white cords that suddenly snapped and let the eyes plop down into the blood that fed the thirsty dirt.

As if suddenly freed, the lamb finally began to walk. It shambled forth, weak and feeble, and its front legs crumpled, sending the creature's face slamming to the blood-wet dirt. It let forth a deep howl of pain as it pushed itself back to its knees and then tried to get back to a standing position. Its quivering legs finally found the strength to stand, but Ben noticed that the creature didn't have hooves; it had human hands. The bloodied hands looked like they belonged to a child. Then the animal collapsed again, but this time with its front legs stretched out in front of it. The tiny hands clawed at the ground and pulled the shambling mass of wool and flesh forward. As it moved, parts of the creature were being torn away and left behind, and as the wool was ripped away, Ben saw a naked, human boy pulling himself away from the corpse.

The child's head was down, and his dark hair was mopped with the blood of the creature he was crawling free of. Then the boy looked up at Ben, and revealed that his eyes were missing. He opened his mouth as if to speak, but his jaw continued to extend until he was a grotesque impression of a human face that had been warped and broken.

A child's voice whispered in Ben's ear, "Suffer the children."

The fog released Ben and he turned in shock and fear to try and see who it was that had spoken to him. As he turned, the fog swept back in, blinding him from everything but its presence. He tried to scream out, but his voice was barely audible.

A black cord pierced the fog ahead and shot out at him. It grasped his wrists and then quickly bound them together. He felt himself being pulled forward rapidly, and the fog zipped past him as he found himself suddenly sitting again on the edge of Terry's bed as his father wrapped the black wire around Ben's wrists.

"Bind the lamb," said Michael Harper as Ben was hoisted into the air.

All the pain and suffering returned as the fog abated. Ben was left staring at the smiling visage of his father. Ben was the lamb that was sacrificed that day, and Michael was absolved of sin. Ben's pain was his father's salvation.

"Suffer the children, for they know not yet of fear. We will teach them."

Branson
3:14 am
March 13th, 2012

Ben Harper wanted to boil his father alive. He wanted to peel his skin off and pour bleach in the wounds. He wanted to drown him in a tub of chemicals and blood. Michael Harper would pay for what he did. Through all the years he'd been stuck in The Watcher's prison, Ben Harper had dreamt of this moment.

"You left me to suffer," said Ben as he stood from his wheelchair. He was no longer bound by the frail prison he'd suffered within on the trip here. Michael had made the mistake of stepping into a place where The Skeleton Man held reign. "You cast me into Hell so that you could escape. But I've come back, and I've got so many things to teach you about pain. Before this is over, I'll murder you in a thousand different ways."

Ben felt his skin shedding as he walked, leaving the husk behind him. He was slick with his own blood, and he looked down in wonder at the musculature that emerged. Parts of him were sliding off, like skin off a boiled chicken. The muscles beneath looked like they were made of white thread, and blue veins snaked along his arm. He pinched one of the veins and pulled it away. When it snapped free, he tossed it to the ground at his father's feet. The vein writhed like a leech, growing long and suctioning one end to the floor so that it could pull its other half along in a looping motion.

Ben Harper's skeletal frame, formerly trapped in the wheelchair, too weak to move, now lunged forward. His skin hung from him like wet clothes from a line, and his yellowed teeth were bared as he screamed. His eyes were globes, with lumps of gelatinous pus and Vaseline around the lids. His pupils were pinpricks of black in the center, focused on his father as the wraith stampeded the space between them.

Michael tried to scream, but his voice was muffled.

Ben collided with his father, and he bore a strength that his weak body shouldn't have afforded. He threw the older man back, causing him to crash against the stove. Then Ben rose taller. He reared back, with his hands splayed like the claws of a beast, and he cried out in fury.

Michael reached back and gripped the handle of the pot of boiling water. He raised the pot, intent on flinging the contents at the monster, but the handle warped as if melting. As his arms swung forward, the pot lost its shape, as if he'd grasped a pot of clay that hadn't been fired. The boiling contents spilled out onto his arm, searing his flesh as he screamed in agony.

A bubble of air rose from Michael's mouth, as if they were both stuck at the bottom of pool. Michael stared at the bubble in shock and surprise, and then the sound of rushing water became suddenly louder, as if a flood was moments away from overcoming them both.

"No," said Ben as he clawed at his father. "Don't wake up!"

Michael burst from the tub, gasping and flailing. The water was still running, and he surged forward to shut it off. Water splashed over the side of the tub and to the towel that he'd spread out for a mat. He coughed up water and pulled himself to a seated position.

Ben was sitting in his wheelchair, still in the same spot where Michael had placed him – still staring in at his father. Michael realized that he'd fallen asleep in the tub, and that the nightmare hadn't been real. He struggled to erase the sense of fear that had gripped him, and sat heavily on the toilet as he pulled another towel off the rack behind him.

"Son of a bitch," he said between gasps as he wiped off his face. "I almost drowned." He laughed, more out of embarrassment than humor, and shook his head while looking at his son. "Did you see that, kid? Your dad almost drowned and there would've been nothing you could've done." He blew his nose into the towel. "Think of that, kid. You would've been fucked for sure. Who'd take care of you if something happened to me? Huh?"

Ben's tongue flopped in his open mouth. His wide eyes stared at Michael, and he was issuing a pained gurgle, as if trying to speak. His hands shook and his fingers tried in vain to grip his armrest.

"You all right?" asked Michael. "Were you scared?" He stood, nude and dripping, and tossed the wet towel into his son's lap. "Were you scared you were about to lose the only person in the world that gives a shit about you?"

Ben quivered. His Adam's apple rose and fell as his tongue flicked in his parched mouth. His gaze followed Michael as the meth addict walked past.

"That sure was a hell of a dream," said Michael as he fell heavily upon the bed, near the entrance to their suite. He perched himself up against the pillows and picked up the television remote to turn on the set on the dresser that faced the bed. His gun was also on the dresser, with the barrel pointed his way.

Ben turned his head and stared at his father, still clicking his tongue in a desperate attempt to speak.

"Oh, I'm sorry kid. You probably don't want to sit there staring at me all night." Michael got up and jiggled his exposed genitals. "I like to air dry." He laughed as if the two of them had shared a joke. Michael had found a nurse's smock in the back of the car he'd stolen from the lady in Widowsfield and was planning on wearing it once dry. The smock had a faint odor of gasoline on it, as if the nurse had an accident while filling her gas tank, but he didn't let that bother him. It would be nice to wear something clean instead of the dingy t-shirt he'd had on for days already.

Ben watched as his father came over to reposition the wheelchair. Michael wheeled his son so that the chair was beside the bed, with Ben facing the television. Then Michael flopped back down on the bed and started to click through the channels.

Ben stared at his father, ignoring the television. His right hand moved weakly to the side, and fell off the armrest of his chair to the bed beside him. He groaned as he reached out to his father.

Michael felt his son's fingertips brush against his arm and he looked over at the invalid. "Hey there, pal." He brushed his boy's hand away after giving him a smile.

Ben continued to try and grasp his father's arm.

"Ben, quit it," said Michael before moving further away, out of his son's reach. "Don't worry kiddo, I'm fine. I just fell asleep in the tub is all. Gave us both a good scare, didn't I? But I'm fine."

Ben grit his teeth and scowled as best he could. His fingers still reached out to touch his father, but Michael was too far away.

Inside Cada E.I.B.'s Compound
March 13th, 2012
2:30 AM

"I forgot you," said Alma. Her eyes were smeared with a mix of tears and the salve that the nurses put over the sleepers' eyes to keep them from drying out. She wiped away the sludge and blinked rapidly. Then she reached out and pulled Paul closer to the gurney she was laying on. "I lost you."

"I'm right here, babe," said Paul as he embraced her.

"Wait," said Rachel as she wiped her eyes. "Was that real? Was I dreaming?"

"We were in Widowsfield, in 1996," said Alma.

"Right," said Jacker as the group tried to get their bearings. "So we all had the same dream? How'd we end up here?"

"It wasn't a dream," said Alma.

"Some of it had to be," said Stephen. "I dreamed about some of you dying."

"Did we really drive off that cliff?" asked Rachel.
"No," said Paul. "We were in the cabin when some guards brought Jacker and Aubrey back. They had shotguns loaded with salt pellets, and hit us with them. I'm not sure what happened after that, but there was something in the cabin with us – it said it was Ben, but the guy here called him something different. He called him…"
"The Skeleton Man," said a stranger's voice. Paul turned to see that the door was open and a tall, black woman was watching them. Her hair was in dreadlocks, with what looked like twine interlaced within, and a purple handkerchief around her neck that covered several beaded necklaces. Her clothes looked handmade out of simple, one-color fabrics and thick thread. She was carrying a satchel that was partially open, revealing a thick pad of paper and several paintbrushes within. She had on black, leather gloves and was holding a Glock with both hands that she was pointing down at the ground. Her wrists were adorned with a plethora of beaded bracelets that were the same style as the necklaces she wore.
"Who are you?" asked Paul as he set his hand on the grip of the pistol tucked in his waistband.
The woman eased her stance, and holstered her weapon. "I'm a friend."
"Not my friend," said Paul, suspicious.
The woman ignored Paul and looked to Alma. "Did you meet the younger version of yourself? Is she the one that told you to drive off the cliff?" The stranger had obviously been eavesdropping.
"Yes," said Alma. "How do you know about the witch?"
"The witch?" asked the stranger.
"That's what the children called her," said Alma. "She said she created a lie about me dying."
"Yes, that was me. I didn't know the children had started calling me a witch though." She smirked. "I guess that's appropriate."

"Wait," said Paul as he began to understand who he was speaking with. "Are you Oliver's assistant? The one that drew the pictures in his book?"

"Yes. My real name's Rosemary, and I'm here to help put an end to what Oliver's done here."

One of the nurses in the other room, where the awakened sleepers were writhing, screamed, "We need help. Please!"

Rosemary looked back into the other room as Paul turned to Alma and said, "Stay here. I'll go see what they need."

Rosemary and Paul headed back into the large area where the female sleepers had suddenly and violently awoken. The women had been in a near-coma state for sixteen years, and their muscles had atrophied to the point of uselessness. When they'd rolled off their beds, they smashed onto the unforgiving floor, cracking their brittle bones and leaving them helpless and in pain. The women's faces lay against the tile, their mouths opening and closing as vomit and spittle leaked forth – all of their eyes were open and searching.

"Only the girls," said Rosemary as she walked to stand beside a male sleeper that still stared helplessly at the ceiling, lying on his bed and not writhing like his female counterparts.

The two nurses, Helen and Rachel, were hoisting a woman off the floor and onto one of the gurneys. The frail, thin sleeper's head rolled back and forth as she moaned. "Help us get them back on the beds," said Helen.

Paul and Rosemary went to the nearest fallen sleeper and began to gingerly lift her. As Paul situated himself at the fallen woman's upper half, he asked, "Why is it that only the girls woke up?"

"The Skeleton Man would use the boys in the town to help him create his lies," said Rosemary before they lifted the quivering sleeper to her bed. Then they latched her down with restraints that hadn't been used to hold the sleepers down in quite some time. "When I created a lie about…"

"Wait," said Paul as he shook his head in disbelief. "Sorry, but this is all a bit confusing. You created a lie?"

They moved to the next fallen sleeper and Rosemary tried to explain. "I don't understand all of it either, but I've spent the last five years trying to sort through the things I saw in this town."

"Oliver said you were a psychic of some sort," said Paul. "Where is he? Is he still in the facility?"

Paul looked over at Helen and Rachel and asked, "Where did Oliver go?"

The two nurses looked puzzled and then Helen answered, "I'm not sure. He couldn't have gotten far."

Paul grumbled and looked at Rosemary. "He was here. I put a bullet in his foot, so he shouldn't be hard to find."

"I can find him easily enough," said Rosemary, unconcerned. "I have a feeling I know where he went."

They moved to the next sleeper as Paul pressed the stranger for more information. "You still haven't explained what you meant by 'creating lies.'"

"This will be a bit hard to believe," said Rosemary.

"I've given up on disbelief, at least as far as this crazy fucking town goes."

"I think Oliver and his company discovered another dimension, and there's intelligent life there."

"You mean like aliens?" asked Paul, absently allowing a skeptical tone to infect his words.

"No green guys in flying saucers or anything," said Rosemary. "They're all around us, inside of inorganic objects." She rattled the edge of a sleeper's gurney. "Like this bed. They don't exist like you and I; they don't eat and breathe. They're entities that normally can't interact with us."

"And Cada E.I.B. figured out a way to talk to them?"

"No." Rosemary shook her head as the two of them walked over to another woman that was writhing on the floor. "Oliver and his company just discovered that they existed. I don't know how, or why, but they did something here sixteen years ago that brought the creature closer to us. It took control of the town, and the people in it."

"Is that The Skeleton Man?"

"I don't think so," said Rosemary. "I think The Skeleton Man was created by the other one, the one they call The Watcher."

"Why do they call it that?" asked Paul.

"Because it's always watching." Rosemary tapped another of the beds, clicking her nail on the metal railing. "The Watchers are in everything. They're in the walls, watching us, studying us. And Oliver figured out a way to bring them closer. I'm fairly certain of that part, but the rest is more conjecture than anything else."

"Well, clue me in," said Paul. "Because I haven't got even the slightest clue as to what the fuck is going on."

"I think The Watchers speak to us through dreams. When we're awake, we have no knowledge of their presence, but when we're asleep they can reach out to us. I don't think they have much of an influence over most of us, but whatever Oliver did here in Widowsfield gave one of The Watchers a tighter grip. All of the people in the town on March 14th, 1996 fell unconscious, and they were put into The Watcher's version of reality."

"Into his dream?"

"Yes," said Rosemary as the two paused. "Although, he was careful to trick them into thinking it was real. The dream only lasts about fifteen minutes, and it always starts just before 3:14 on March 14th, 1996. When he first started creating these dreams, he made them similar to how life would've normally played out for the people that lived here. Then he started changing things, just slightly, and turning the dream into a nightmare. With each new change he was able to twist their recollection, just like I did with Oliver's book. And that's where The Skeleton Man came in."

"You mean Ben, right?" asked Paul.

"Not exactly," said Rosemary. "But, speaking of Ben, we need to hurry up and find him. Hopefully he's here, with the other sleepers somewhere."

"No, he's not," said Paul.

Rosemary became concerned as she asked, "Do you know where he is? Is he dead?"

"No, Alma's dad showed up and took him."

Rosemary walked away from him, and headed back towards the room where Alma and the others were. She was clearly upset by Paul's revelation. He followed behind and asked, "What's wrong?"

"I'm not sure," said Rosemary as they made their way through the maze of gurneys and crying women. "I have to find out more about what happened to your friends."

They got back to the other room where Alma, Stephen, Rachel, and Jacker were standing by the bed that Aubrey was laying on. Alma looked up at Paul as they came back in the room and said, "She's gone. Aubrey's dead."

Paul nodded, having already come to the realization that Aubrey was gone. He didn't know the girl very well, but she didn't deserve to die in Widowsfield this way. No one did.

Rosemary was undeterred by Aubrey's death. "Alma, you need to tell me what happened to you. I need you to try and remember everything you can."

"It's…" Alma struggled to remember, and closed her eyes to try and bring the dreams back, but she shook her head and said, "It's all a jumble."

"Try harder," said Rosemary impatiently.

Alma appeared offended, but did what she could to recount what had happened while she was unconscious. "We kept appearing in the van, on our way into Widowsfield. Sometimes we would make it into town, but it was always in 1996, like we'd traveled back in time." She looked at Rosemary for approval.

"Go on," said Rosemary while motioning for Alma to continue.

"After being in the town for a few minutes, fog would roll in. It was thick, and slid across the ground like it was heavy."

Rachel interrupted, "And there were green lights flashing inside of the fog, almost like there was a storm in it."

"Right," said Alma in agreement. "And I think the children were in there too. They went in there to die."

Rosemary shook her head in disagreement. "No. The Skeleton Man tricked them into thinking he cared about them. They would go to him, hoping that he'd protect them from the red-haired woman."

"Terry," said Alma. "The red-haired woman was my father's girlfriend, a meth-addict named Terry. She owned the cabin, and she had a dog named Killer that she used to tell us was a werewolf."

"She's the one that died there?" Rosemary asked Alma, who nodded in response. "She got trapped while she was dying."

"What do you mean?" asked Jacker. "Like her soul got trapped?"

Rosemary nodded and said. "Yes. There was another woman that died right when the fog first swept over the town. Her name was Amelia Reven, but The Watcher and The Skeleton Man didn't trap her. She died before the fog got to her, before it blotted out the light. Terry, on the other hand, was stuck in the town with everyone else, but she wasn't controlled by The Watcher."

"Who's The Watcher?" asked Stephen.

"He's the one that controls everything that happened in your dreams," said Rosemary.

"I thought The Skeleton Man was," said Alma.

Rosemary shook her head. "No. He was just a guardian. I think The Watcher used your brother's experience at the cabin to create the nightmares that you saw, but then he kept changing things to make the dreams worse. I'm not sure I'm right, but I've had a lot of time to think about it. I'm a psychic, or more specifically I'm a psychometric. That means that I can pull memories out of physical objects, but I was never able to do it consistently until I came here to work with Oliver."

"Who's that?" asked Rachel.

"He's the one in charge of this place," said Paul.

"In the real world, right?" asked Jacker, which at first came off as a bizarre question, but which Paul then realized was astonishingly cogent.

"Yes," answered Rosemary, relieving Paul of the responsibility of discerning what was and wasn't real anymore. She continued, "I helped him recreate what happened here leading up to March 14th, 1996."

"So you're the reason there were mannequins everywhere," said Rachel as the rest of the group also began to understand Rosemary's role in what had happened in the town.

"Yes. He wanted my help putting the town back together, like the whole place was just a puzzle waiting to be finished."

"What happens when he finishes it?" asked Rachel.

"Let's hope we never find out," said Rosemary. "I did what I could to make sure he never put everything back together exactly as it was, but I don't think the inanimate things matter as much as…" she looked at Alma and added, "the living things."

"My brother and I?" asked Alma.

Rosemary nodded. "When I was at the house on Sycamore, I realized that The Skeleton Man was fixated on you. You distracted him, and you're the reason he started changing the dreams."

"How did I do that?" asked Alma.

"When your mother brought you back here, when you were ten; not long before she tried to kill you."

Alma shook her head. "She didn't try to kill me."

Rosemary looked warily at Alma, as if certain she were lying. "Yes she did."

"No," said Alma, eager to correct the stranger. "She brought me here, but then took me back to my grandmother's before she came back here and…" Alma stopped, unwilling to continue.

Rosemary was silent for a moment as she looked at Alma, and then said, "Our minds can play tricks on us sometimes, honey. When you want to know what really happened, just let me know and I'll…"

"I know what really happened," said Alma with obvious anger that she tried to mask with a laugh. She glanced at Paul, and her burgeoning fury subsided into embarrassment. She looked away and said, quieter, "I know what happened."

"Okay," said Rosemary, willing to leave the subject alone. "That part doesn't matter. What matters is what happened at the house."

"We broke in and that's when my mother wrote the numbers on the floor. That's when I remembered Ben."

"And that's when he remembered you as well," said Rosemary. "Until then, The Watcher had stolen you from him. But when you went back, you reminded your brother of what he'd lost. He saw you again, and The Watcher had to try and get rid of you. He did what The Skeleton Man didn't think was possible. He broke out of the dream and spoke through you. He threatened your mother, and that's what convinced The Skeleton Man that he could get out as well."

"When I talked to this thing," said Paul, "he was acting like he was Ben."

"He might think he is," said Rosemary. "Everything The Watcher created was inspired by what happened to Alma's brother. I was never able to see how things started; there're too many timelines laid out on top of one another that it was like picking through a thousand pieces of multiple puzzles that had all been thrown together. It wasn't until just before I left that I figured out this all started with some sort of fog or smoke that came from the reservoir."

"What happened to your brother?" asked Rachel of Alma.

"He got burned by chemicals and boiling water while trying to help my father kill Terry."

"Oh my God," said Jacker. "Seriously?"

"That was the part that I couldn't remember," said Alma. "Remember how I told you that I could recall everything up to when the fog showed up? And how the next thing I could remember was leaving the town?"

"Yeah," said Rachel.

"Well, I think I can remember some of it now. Although," she put her hand over her eyes as she tried to recall the dream that was slipping away. She could remember being at the sink, with Ben beside her, and how he was goading her into taking a pot of water up the stairs. "I'm not sure which parts are lies."

"Ben," said Paul, but then he corrected himself, "or I guess The Skeleton Man, showed me what happened. The red-haired girl was overdosing, and Ben walked in as it was happening. Then his father asked Ben for help, and went to get water when the girl fell unconscious. Your dad thought she was dead, and told Ben that he was the one that killed her. He made Ben go boil water and get cleaner so they could melt her down in the bathtub."

"Jesus," murmured Rachel as the group listened. "Is that even possible?"

"I don't know," said Paul. "They tried, but Terry wasn't dead. They put her in the tub and poured the cleaners in. Then Ben poured boiling water over her and she woke up. She grabbed him and pulled him face-first in with her."

"Right," said Rosemary, providing Paul with a sense of balance as he tried to determine if what he'd learned was true. "That's when Alma came up the stairs. She could hear Ben crying, and she got a knife to try and protect him. Terry was blinded by the chemicals in the tub, and she was trying to run out of the room when Alma came in."

"And I killed her," said Alma matter-of-factly.

"You stabbed her," said Rosemary, "but your father was the one that killed her. He gutted her."

"That's why the mannequin was on the floor in there," said Rachel. "But why were the two child-sized mannequins still on the couch?"

"Because I was trying to trick Oliver," said Rosemary. "I lied to him to change his perception of what had happened, the same way The Skeleton Man started to try and hide from The Watcher."

"How?" asked Stephen.

Rosemary tried to explain, "The Skeleton Man kept The Watcher's lies intact. All of the timeframes exist in the same short period of time, but The Watcher is the one creating the new ones. The Skeleton Man was the one that kept them in order. It's sort of hard to understand, but the best way I can explain it is to think of someone knitting one long scarf, and there's someone behind him carefully laying the scarf down and making sure the pattern stays correct. The Watcher is the one making the dreams, and The Skeleton Man was behind him, keeping the whole thing in order so The Watcher can change things if he wants to. Does that make sense?"

"Not really," said Jacker.

"I get it," said Stephen. "Instead of thinking of it like a scarf, think of it as a fifteen minute video clip. Pretend I've got the clip, and I keep making little changes to it and then sending you a copy. Your job is to keep all of the versions in order, so that if I ever need to go back and make a change I can do it easily." He looked at Rosemary and asked, "Is that right?"

She raised her brow and nodded in satisfaction. "Sure, if that makes more sense to you. The Skeleton Man started making changes of his own to what was happening in the town. He did it because he wanted to try and trick The Watcher into forgetting him."

"He wanted out," said Alma.

Rosemary looked at her and asked, "Are you sure?"

"Yes. He used his lies to hide, and then he tried to get me to take his place. I think it worked."

"Why do you say that?" asked Rosemary, her concern becoming more apparent.

"Because he made me switch places with him. I was the one that put the chemicals in the tub, and I was the one that Terry tried to grab. Then he stabbed her, and then The Watcher tried to catch me. I got away, and that's when I met you," she said as she motioned to Rosemary, "or some version of myself that you put there. You explained that I needed to get out by going over the cliff and into the reservoir so that I could go and bring The Skeleton Man back. Then we ended up back in the van, and we saw my father driving away with Ben sitting in the back seat instead of me."

"I remember that," said Rachel.

Stephen agreed and then Jacker added, "That's when you took the wheel and made me sit in the back with Aubrey."

"That's why you plowed over that cliff?" asked Rachel. "I thought you'd lost your damn mind."

"I'm not sure I didn't," said Alma with a quick laugh.

"Don't worry," said Rosemary. "I've been trying to make sense of this damn town for five years and I still don't understand most of it."

"I'm still confused about Ben," said Paul. "Are he and The Skeleton Man the same person or not?"

Rosemary shook her head and said, "No, but I don't think they exist separately either. I've always gotten the sense that The Skeleton Man is a jumble of a bunch of people."

"Well that makes sense," said Jacker sarcastically.

Rosemary wasn't amused. She continued like a teacher trying to ignore the class clown. "The Skeleton Man was created by The Watcher's twisting of Ben's fears. Without Ben, he wouldn't exist. That's what I mean by saying they can't exist separately."

"Then did my dad really kidnap Ben?" asked Alma. "Or did he take The Skeleton Man?"

"Both," said Rosemary. "And we have to get them back."

"Or what?"

Rosemary looked as if the answer should be easy, but then struggled to explain. She looked down and sighed before she finally said, "Honestly, I have no idea. I don't know what sort of things a creature like that would be capable of in the real world."

"Maybe he'll be just like those girls out there," said Paul as he motioned to the other room where the sleepers were. "If he's been in a coma for sixteen years then he'll be just like them. Right?"

"Physically, sure," said Rosemary. "But what can he do mentally?"

"You think he's a psychic or something?" asked Rachel.

"The Skeleton Man spent at least the past sixteen years creating nightmares. Now that he's out, there's no telling what he's capable of," said Rosemary.

"But he's in Ben's body," said Paul. "He won't have any of the abilities that he had in Widowsfield."

"Won't he?" asked Rosemary. "Before today, would you have ever believed in psychometry? No one's sure what the human brain is capable of. The Skeleton Man lived his entire life learning how to warp the world around him into nightmares. He's got no reason to believe he can't do the same thing in the real world. I'm scared to think of what The Skeleton Man can do now that he's out of Widowsfield."

pupils were hellish proof that they were anything but celestial. They all blinked independently, and they were glassy, as if tearful.

"Bind the lamb," said a deep, male voice from inside the room.

A black wire descended from the mass, followed by a second, and then a third. Lyle tried to move away from them, but they inched closer, unattached to the walls as opposed to the rest of the shadows. The wires came too close to avoid, and he tried to swat one away.

The black cord wrapped around his wrist, and then another snapped out like a whip to sting his other arm. The second cord gripped his other wrist, and then Lyle was pulled up. The wires dug into the flesh of his wrists, and his blood spurted forth as the cords continued to draw tighter. He cried out in pain as he was lifted. The third wire coiled around his neck, choking away his voice, and he was forced to stare up at the approaching gloom, all the while the crying eyes stared down.

Widowsfield
March 14th, 1996

Raymond was sitting alone in the Salt and Pepper Diner. He was at the table where he and his father normally ate, but Desmond wasn't where he was supposed to be. Nothing was as it had been, or ever would be again. The world was different now – lonely and desolate.

"Dad?" asked Raymond, desperately hoping for an answer. "Hello?"

Only the faint static from a distant radio could be heard. Other than that, the restaurant was silent.

Raymond got up from the plastic bench that was affixed to the floor. He looked down at the steel-rimmed tabletop and saw a set of silverware that was wrapped in a napkin. He unrolled the set, but knew there wouldn't be a steak knife. His father had brought him to this diner hundreds of times, and Raymond knew that the rolled napkin would have a spoon, fork, and butter knife in it, and that the steak knives were kept behind the counter for customers that ordered a meal that required a proper knife. He picked up the butter knife to defend himself with as he dared to explore the empty diner.

He looked out of the large window to Main Street and saw that it was also devoid of life. Raymond walked to the counter where the register sat beside a cake that was displayed on a covered, glass pedestal, but the cake inside was lopsided, as if it was slowly melting.

"Grace?" he called out loudly for the waitress, but no one answered.

Raymond took the opportunity to rush behind the counter and replace his butter knife with a serrated one that was kept in a cup under the register. He took two, holding one in each hand, and then moved to the white, swinging door that separated the dining area from the kitchen.

"Juan?" He looked for the cook, but the kitchen was deserted as well.

The cook's small radio sat on the counter and was turned on. Its antenna was stretched out at an awkward angle and it wasn't picking up anything but static.

"Hello?" called out the boy as his dread grew.

Raymond walked to the entrance of the Salt and Pepper Diner and opened the door, causing the bells tied above to jingle. He stepped outside, and looked around. The blue sky was marred only by a scant few wisps of clouds, but it was still oddly grey out. He looked around for any sign of the sun, but it was nowhere to be seen.

Raymond couldn't recall ever being more fearful. There were no signs of life in Widowsfield: No chatter of voices, no birds breaking the still pool of sky above. While Main Street was never congested with traffic, he'd also never seen it empty. There always seemed to be at least one or two people milling about, but today he was alone.

"Dad?" He screamed, but no one was there to hear him.

Raymond looked to his right, but saw no cars driving in the distance. He looked left and saw a UPS truck parked in front of the Anderson Used Book store. There were other cars parked along the road, but Raymond knew that if the UPS truck was still in front of Winnie Anderson's store that the delivery man was probably inside. He walked over to the store, which always looked closed due to how Winnie kept the lights off to conserve energy, and he gently eased the door open.

"Hello?"

No one answered him.

A staircase behind the counter led up to Winnie Anderson's apartment, and there was a light on up there. Raymond made his way around the counter, feeling like an invader as he did. He'd been to the book store many times, and his father often bought him Choose-Your-Own-Adventure books that Raymond eagerly read, but in all the time he'd spent in the store he'd never wandered behind the counter. It felt like an invasion to be back there.

"Miss Anderson?"

Raymond walked up the creaky, wooden stairs, his hand gripping the railing as if he might slip at any moment. He got to the top, uncertain if he wanted to find someone or not. He struggled to recall how he'd gotten to the diner, vaguely remembering a planned fishing trip with his father, but everything that led up to him sitting alone at the Salt and Pepper Diner felt like it was just a faint, distant memory.

The apartment above the book store was empty as well. There were signs of life: a half-eaten bowl of oatmeal on a tray table, a book set on the arm of the sofa, marking the reader's place, and the dishwasher was churning in the kitchen. But no soul survived to claim ownership of this place or its contents.

Raymond's heart began to beat faster, but he wasn't sure what he was frightened of. His palms became clammy, and his brow began to sweat, as if some part of him knew something bad was about to happen, but he had no idea what it was. He raced back down the stairs and out of the building, feeling safer outside, as if he'd suddenly realized that the building was haunted. When he got to the sidewalk he paused and took a breath, but there would be no respite.

A thunderous bang shook the world, causing the alarms of nearby vehicles to come alive. The rumble was sudden, but lasted for several seconds, causing the ground to tremble with its force. When the aftershock faded, Raymond looked north and saw a billowing cloud of white smoke rising above the trees in the distance. The cloud swelled, and began to mushroom over the woods before cascading down, as if the tree line was an edifice that the smoke flowed over. The fog fell to Main Street, and then surged forward like a tidal wave.

Raymond was hypnotized, gazing at the coming wave as if paralyzed by its magnificence. Then he saw the twisting shapes within. The fog was hiding something dark, and Raymond was reminded of staring through the glass door of a washing machine as a single black shirt tumbled with white clothes. The fog was a shroud, and the creature within was headed his way.

There was no escape, and even though Raymond tried to run, he knew he would never escape the God that bore down on him. Despite his cries for help, he understood there'd be none. When it caught up to him, there would be no pleading for safety. This wasn't an animal he ran from; it wasn't something that could be reasoned with. It had no concept of pity.

The thrashing of wire, that metallic grind, was the only sound Raymond could hear once the fog descended. Smoke swept under his feet, and the ground disappeared. The sound of The Watcher's approach was like that of a great machine breaking itself apart. The groan of metal, and the squeal of bending steel, the grinding of gears, the crash of breaking concrete, it was the cacophony of his existence. And as the chaotic noise persisted, a fateful sound pounded a maddening rhythm, steady and heavy, like a hammer striking a bell that had fallen to the ground, the vibration trapped within.

The tendrils snaked through the pavement, and up the walls of nearby buildings. They broke apart the concrete, shattered windows, and crumbled bricks, but the remnants of their destruction didn't fall. The pieces of Widowsfield that were torn apart by The Watcher's tentacles revealed themselves as part of the mass. The fragments turned black and eroded into dust that joined the tentacles themselves. As the world evaporated, the creature grew.

Raymond tried to swipe his knife down at the fog, but the parts of the blade that touched the smoke disappeared, as if he'd dipped it in acid. He dropped the weapon in fear, and it vanished beneath the mist.

Raymond was lifted off the ground, but felt no force pulling him skyward. It was as if the ground had disappeared, and he was left weightless in the fog. His clothes shredded, pulling away from him as if burning, the ash melding with the fog. His cries for help were lost, despite the pain in his throat as he tried to scream. The blackness overcame him as the tentacles blocked out the light. He was left in what felt like darkness, but when he looked down at his body he could still see himself as if it were the middle of the day.

Then the blackness revealed shapes. Bulging orbs swam through the black, as if he were staring down at eggs bobbing in a pool of oil. Then the shapes revealed themselves to be eyes when their lids split, showing the white beneath.

The Watcher studied Raymond.

The blackness rippled as the grinding metal noise tried to form words. Raymond saw that the tentacles had become thinner. The blackness that surrounded him now appeared like a mass of thin cords, as if he were trapped inside a ball of black yarn, but each strand traveled in a different direction, turning the sight into maddening chaos.

A voice broke through the mechanical grind. "Afraid…"

Raymond pushed at the darkness, but his fingers slid through the cords and he pulled away, fearing he might be harmed. The wires were cold and scaly, similar to what it must feel like to thrust your hand into a nest of snakes.

Again, the voice spoke to him. "Afraid of…"

The cords slid around the multiple eyes that watched him, but occasionally one of the wires would pass across an eyeball. The black cords would cut into the unblinking eye, causing black blood to ooze forth before the eye would finally close and retreat. Soon, another eye would appear to take the wounded one's place in the mass.

"What are you afraid of?" asked the voice as Raymond began to understand it.

The boy tried to answer, but The Watcher didn't need to listen.

A tentacle snaked away from the sphere of blackness that had formed around Raymond. The tentacle coiled, and its tip became smaller the more it moved. It approached, and slid along Raymond's cheek, toward his ear. The cord was thin now, and spun around his ear before the tip invaded the canal. Raymond felt the fullness in his ear as the wire forced its way inside. It felt like half of his head had been submerged, but then the cord burst in deeper and intense pain tortured the child. His left eye watered as the wire searched behind it, scraping its sharp edge against his tender eardrum, causing blood to drip along the cord's length.

"Let's build hell for you."

Widowsfield
October 13th, 1994

Raymond was in his sister's closet, praying she didn't open the accordion-style door. He'd been in her room, where she'd warned him not to go more than a few times, looking for a lighter. He'd found a packet of firecrackers in the garage, and wanted to go into the backyard to light them. He couldn't find a lighter anywhere in the house, but knew that his sister smoked. It was one of the many things that she fought with their father about.

He hadn't heard her until she was already coming down the hall, and he ducked into the closet to hide. He could see her through the slats in the door as she stood in front of her dresser.

Then he heard a stranger's voice, "You still live at home? How old are you?" The man walked into Terry's room and chuckled as he inspected it.

"I'm legal," said Terry as she opened her top drawer and started to pull out a stack of underwear to get something from deep inside. "I'm moving soon. My Dad and I fight all the time, so I told him I was going to move to California, but he begged me to stay around here in this dumpy shithole of a town. I told him I'm not living here with him and my brother forever, so he's going to get me my own place."

"Why stay in Widowsfield if you hate it here?"

"Would you turn down a free house?" asked Terry.

"No, I guess not," said the stranger as he plopped down heavily on the bed. He was facing the closet, and Raymond was certain he was about to be caught.

Raymond pushed himself back, terrified as he couldn't help but stare directly out at the man that Terry had brought home. He was thin, and was wearing what might've been proper work clothes, but they looked like he'd been wearing them for a long time. He hadn't shaved in days, and his hair was a haphazard mess. He was looking at the closet, and Raymond stared right back, realizing that he was about to be discovered. There was no way the man could be looking directly into his eyes like this and not have realized that Raymond was hiding there.

Terry took a glass pipe and a plastic bag out of her drawer. She set the drugs on the dresser and then went back into the drawer to get a pack of cigarettes. She took a lighter out of the pack, and then gathered up everything as she turned to face the stranger. "Let's go before my dad comes home."

"So you've got a little brother?" asked the dirty stranger as he continued to sit on the edge of the bed and stare into Raymond's eyes.

"Yeah, why?" asked Terry.

"Do you know where he's at?"

Raymond's heart thundered in his chest, and he felt his hands trembling as the stranger continued to stare at him. He'd surely been caught. This greasy, middle-aged man was certainly only seconds away from opening the closet and pulling Raymond out.

"He usually goes to our dad's shop after school. Why?"

"So we're alone?" asked the stranger.

"Yeah. Why?" asked Terry in a playful tone.

The stranger finally broke his gaze at the closet, and pulled Terry closer to him. She was standing between his legs and giggled as he nuzzled his face in her belly. She complained and tried to push him away, and then laughed as he continued to tickle her. "Stop it," she pleaded. "What if my dad comes home?"

"That's part of the fun," said the stranger as he unzipped Terry's jeans.

"You're terrible," said Terry as she shoved the stranger backward, onto the bed.

Raymond was relieved that he hadn't been caught, and chose not to question how the stranger had managed to lock eyes with him, but not see him. The darkness in the closet had shrouded Raymond, thankfully, but now he was being forced to watch as his sister grinded on the man on her bed. They pawed at one another, and kissed, and the man kept trying to take Terry's clothes off even though she insisted they should leave.

"Michael, stop it," said Terry. She pushed the stranger's hands away as he tried to unbuckle her bra from under her shirt.

"Come on, just a quickie."

Terry groaned in feigned annoyance, but was clearly enjoying his attention. She pulled her shirt off and tossed it off the bed. "Fine, but make it quick."

Raymond covered his eyes. He knew he shouldn't be seeing this, and felt equally terrified and enticed. He knew what a Peeping Tom was, but had never set out to become one. He knew he shouldn't watch, but he peered between his fingers anyhow.

Terry and the man named Michael flung one another around on the bed as if angry. It appeared as vicious as it was sensual as they bit and clawed at one another. Michael threw Raymond's sister to her back on the bed, and then pulled his shirt off before tugging at her jeans. She rose her waist up to help, and Michael whipped the jeans away before tossing them hard against the closet door. Then he stood straight as if admiring Terry's nearly nude body. He calmly took off his watch and set it on the nightstand as Terry took her underwear off.

Raymond again covered his eyes, momentarily shamed by his act. He tried to keep from looking, but curiosity soon got the better of him. He peered out, and saw that the stranger was now nude, and was thrusting his penis into Terry as she lay back on the bed. Michael's back was facing the closet as he stood there, thrusting again and again. Terry's legs were wrapped around the stranger's back, and she was using them to force him to push deeper into her as they continued.

Michael climbed onto the bed, and moved to the back, causing Terry to adjust her position. Then he looked at the closet and smiled before he raised Terry's legs and pushed his penis back into her.

Raymond's curiosity turned suddenly to intense fear. Why had the stranger looked at the closet that way? Did Michael know Raymond was hiding there? What other reason could there be for the way he'd smiled like that?

Terry and Michael continued, and the stranger seemed to once again be ignoring the closet. Raymond's momentary terror subsided as he continued to watch his sister have sex.

The pair moved to various positions, and then, finally, the stranger pulled out of Terry and ejaculated onto her stomach and breasts.

"Feeling better?" asked Terry with a lascivious grin as she toyed with the semen on her belly, poking at it and swirling it with the nail of her index finger.

"Yeah," said the stranger as he got off the bed and started gathering his clothes. "Let's go."

"Really?" asked Terry. "It's going to be like that, huh? You get yours and we call it a night?"

"Hurry up and get dressed," said Michael, his tone darker and uncaring, as if ejaculating had stolen every ounce of his former lust.

"Fine," said Terry, annoyed. "Throw me something to clean up with."

Michael picked up a bathrobe that was lying beside the dresser and tossed it to Terry. "Don't forget the meth," he said as he walked out of the room.

Raymond watched as his sister cleaned the semen off her stomach and then started to get dressed. He'd never seen her naked before, and knew that he shouldn't have the desire to see her like this, but he watched anyhow.

When she left, Raymond felt a sense of relief and complete sorrow. He knew what he'd done was bad, and the feelings that had dominated his thoughts as he watched the carnal act were devilish and contemptible. He'd heard of sex, and had even seen it on a video over at a friend's house, but this had been an awful way to be exposed to it. Never-the-less, he'd watched it happen. He couldn't help himself, and even as terrified as he'd been, the experience was arousing.

He wanted out. He just wanted to get out of his sister's room and pretend that none of this had ever happened, but he needed to wait until he was sure they were gone. Raymond listened for the front door to close, but then he heard heavy steps coming back down the hall.

"I forgot my watch," said Michael as he returned to Terry's bedroom.

Raymond held his breath.

The stranger named Michael walked to Terry's nightstand, retrieved his watch, and slipped it on. Then he turned to the closet, walked to it, and opened the accordion doors.

Raymond was caught. He gasped, and then held his breath again as he cowered on the floor, sitting on Terry's shoes.

The stranger stared down at the boy, silent, and unsurprised by his discovery.

"Was it a good show?" asked Michael.

Raymond didn't answer.

Michael stared, waiting for an answer. When Raymond refused to say anything, the stranger grew bored, and frowned. He looked oddly shamed, and then he closed the closet door and walked away, leaving Raymond alone to hide and cry.

Widowsfield
March 14th, 1996

"Hi," said Raymond to the boy that answered the door. Raymond's father was standing beside him. They'd come to Terry's house to get the keys to the cabin in Forsyth. They were planning a fishing trip, and Desmond had gotten his son out of school early for the short vacation.

The boy at the door appeared frightened as he looked back over his shoulder. Raymond could see an animal's crate on the floor of the kitchen, not far from the front door. The dog inside the cage was barking viciously, causing the plastic crate to clatter on the tile floor.

"I'm looking for my daughter, Terry," said Desmond. "Is she here?"

"Who is it?" asked a man that was descending the stairs behind Ben. Raymond could only see his legs as he came down the stairs, but he recognized the voice. His heart began to beat faster, and his hands trembled. Once the man was in full view, Raymond's fear was realized. This was the same man that had been in Terry's room, a couple years earlier, and had discovered Raymond hiding in the closet.

Raymond never told anyone about that experience, and had hoped to never be reminded of it. He was ashamed of himself for having been hiding there, and even more ashamed of how he'd been caught. Raymond had never been more terrified than he was that day, as Michael Harper stared down at him. Now his devil had returned.

Michael sounded annoyed when he saw who was at the door. He frowned when he saw Desmond and said, "Oh."

"Hello, Michael," said Raymond's father, his tone mired by anger.

"What do you want?" asked Michael of Desmond, but he looked down at Raymond, a glimmer of recognition that caused the boy to cower.

"I need to talk to Terry," said Desmond.

"Well, she's busy." Michael looked dirty, his white t-shirt sodden with sweat that had turned the pits yellow.

"I'm not trying to pester her, or you," said Desmond. "If you two want to rot away in this place, I just don't have the energy to care anymore. I need the keys to our cabin in Forsyth. I'm taking my boy out there for a fishing trip. We already paid the fees, but I'd rather not spend the money on a hotel if possible."

"Yeah, well…" Michael Harper's words started to linger, as if they were taking longer to exit his mouth than they should. His voice deepened, and his movements languished. "I think she's already…" his words slowed down too much to be understood, like a tape deck slowly losing power.

Raymond tried to tug at his father's hand, but discovered that his own body was caught in the slow flow of time that Michael seemed to be trapped in. Raymond had been focused on Michael, but then noticed a swirling blackness behind the man. The wall on the far side of Terry's cabin looked like a pool of black, and within was a single eye watching them.

Then Raymond heard The Watcher speak, "Michael Harper." The creature sounded pleased. "I like the nightmares you inspire."

CHAPTER 3 – Alma Harper

Philadelphia
June 13th, 1943

"Is that really him?" asked Lyle as he leaned against the railing overlooking the naval yard on the Delaware River. He was watching an older gentleman that was smoking a pipe while touring the destroyer escort anchored in the yard.

It was a bright, summer day, and the old, white-haired man on the ship was in shorts and sandals, appearing dramatically out of place among the host of smartly dressed Navy men that guided him. The gulls called as the water lapped against the concrete basin. The wind carried the scent of the water and oil, a mix of musty odor and industrial pollution – a confluence of nature and man's abuse of it.

The ships groaned in the harbor, as if their steel ached, as the water rose and fell against them. Lichen clung to their grey sides, waving in the water like tiny hairs on metal skin.

"Yes, that's him," said Vess, unimpressed.

"Wow," said Lyle with a beaming grin. He was young, impressionable, and enticed by the lure of fame. Lyle shook his head in disbelief as he gazed at the most famous person he'd ever seen in real life. "I can't believe it's really him."

Vess was unmoved, and stood with his back to the railing. He was taller than Lyle, and much thinner. While Lyle looked the epitome of fitness, his partner was a wraith by comparison. "You give him too much credit."

"I do, do I?" asked Lyle with a snort and a quick shake of his head. "I guess me and the rest of the world are fooled, aye? You're the only one that ain't been taken in?"

Vess ignored the baited question and just nodded.

Lyle waved off his employer's indifference. "Suit yourself. Me? I'm looking forward to shaking his hand. After all, ain't he the one who set this whole thing in motion? If what you said was true, and this experiment really could put an end to the war, then I figure I'd like to shake the hand of the man that made it possible."

"Then you'll be shaking hands with a corpse," said Vess.

Lyle glared over at his friend, expecting the tall, sickly man to elaborate. When Vess stayed quiet, Lyle prodded, "Well, out with it then. What's that supposed to mean?"

"The man that set this in motion has been dead for five months now."

"And who'd that be, then?" asked Lyle.

"Nikola Tesla," said Vess.

Lyle smirked, sucked in air through his teeth, and then said, "Nope, sorry, but that name's not ringing any bells."

Vess grimaced at the younger man, and then shook his head as if in disgust.

"What? I'm not a scientist or nothing," said Lyle. "Who the heck is this Tesla character?"

"Never mind," said Vess, appearing bored with the conversation. "It doesn't matter."

"Sure it does," said Lyle as he hooked his thumbs under his suspenders and leaned against the railing with his legs crossed, looking the part of a relaxing dockworker. "We ain't got nothing but time. Give me the skinny on this Tesla character. What's he got to do with all this?"

A harsh breeze swept up from the river, and Vess pinched the edge of his wide-brimmed fedora to keep it from flying off. His solid blue blazer fluttered and when the breeze had calmed he buttoned his coat.

"Come on, Vess," said Lyle. "Clue me in."

"Your friend up there owes a lot to Tesla, that's all," said Vess as he motioned back at the ship where the white-haired man was still touring with the naval officers following along. "We wouldn't be here if the FBI hadn't raided Nikola's hotel."

"So this guy was a scientist or something?" asked Lyle.

Again, Vess regarded his companion with disdain. "Yes, he was. Perhaps the single most important scientist in modern history, not that goons like you would ever know it."

"No need to be grumpy," said Lyle. "Why'd the FBI raid his place?"

"Because they're a bunch of jackbooted thugs. They illegally seized all of Nikola's belongings, including the notes from his experiments."

"Illegally?" asked Lyle. "How'd they get away with that?"

"They claimed he was an alien."

Lyle guffawed and said, "You mean like from the Flash Gordon serials? Like he was Ming or something?"

Vess sneered and shook his head, "No, you idiot. Not that sort of alien. Alien as in not a resident of the United States, even though he was. They had no right to his belongings, but that didn't even put a stutter in their step. They marched right in and seized the whole lot. That's the only reason your idol's up there now, gallivanting around like he's the one that came up with this idea. No doubt he's been studying Tesla's notes day and night."

"Looks like you'll get your chance to ask him," said Lyle as he straightened his posture. "He's headed back this way."

The white-haired scientist was puffing a briar pipe, holding the bowl with the black stem between his lips. His bushy hair and loose fitting clothes rustled in the breeze as he descended the plank from the Destroyer escort to the harbor. His sandals clopped against his bare feet, a stark contrast to the shined shoes of the General that followed behind him.

Lyle took off his dull brown newsboy cap and held it to his chest with his left hand as he extended his right in greeting. "Sir, it's a pleasure to meet you."

"Oh, oh," said the elderly scientist with a grin. He shook Lyle's hand and his words were flavored with a German accent, "Good to meet you." Then the older man's demeanor darkened as he looked past Lyle and at Vess. The scientist stared through the round spectacles that had drifted to the tip of his large nose, his pipe lowered, and then he nodded to Lyle's companion and spoke with a tone that teetered on disdain. "Vess."

Vess didn't bother taking off his hat to greet the famous scientist. He just nodded and spoke with an equal amount of disdain, "Einstein."

Inside Cada E.I.B.'s Compound
March 13th, 2012
2:45 AM

Paul had retrieved the older nurse, Helen, and brought her to the room with the others. He remembered that Helen said Michael had stolen her car when he took Ben, and the group needed to figure out a way to track him down. Helen had told Rachel that her car was a light blue, 2000 Ford Escort, but the reporter's next question confounded the nurse.

"Do I know my license plate number?" asked Helen as if what she'd been asked was ludicrous. "Of course not. Who in the heck memorizes their license plate number?"

"Do you have your license?" asked Rachel.

Helen nodded and then took a billfold out of her smock. As she handed it to Rachel she asked, "What do you need it for?"

"I can use a little reporter magic." Rachel took the license from the nurse. "I'll use the description of the car and the license to see if I can track down Michael."

"How will you do that?" asked Alma.

"I've got my ways," said Rachel with a devilish smirk. "If we can find a computer with an internet connection I can get this done a lot faster."

"That's no problem," said Helen. "My co-worker's always on her laptop. I'll go get it for you."

The older, rotund woman left to go get the other nurse's computer. Alma waited until she was gone and then asked again, "So how are you going to find him?"

"If we can get her license plate number then we can check with the State Police to see if he's been pulled over. There aren't any tolls nearby, unfortunately, otherwise we could use them. We can also start calling hotels in the area to see if anyone's checked in that matches his description. He might even have to give them his license plate number when checking in."

"Will they give out that sort of info?" asked Jacker, surprised that this was legal.

"Depends on who's asking for it," answered Stephen with a knowing smile. He was clearly familiar with Rachel's wile.

"How long do you think that'll take?" asked Rosemary.

Rachel shrugged. "Hard to say. Could be ten minutes, but it could take hours. We might not get any leads at all. Depends on how lucky we get."

"I don't usually rely on luck," said Rosemary. "That well ran dry years ago."

"What do you suggest we do?" asked Paul.

Rosemary considered the situation and then came up with a solution. "We need to split up. One group will stay here and try and find Michael and Ben with your friend here," she motioned to Rachel. "And the other will go with Alma and me to track them down in my security van."

"In a van?" asked Paul. "They could've headed over to 65 and be down in Arkansas by now. Or they could be headed north to Springfield. We've got no clue where he went."

"Wait," said Rachel in concern. She looked at Rosemary and said, "I thought you just wanted help finding Michael and Ben. I didn't know you wanted any of us to go chasing after him with you. I'm not sure that's a good idea."

The nurse returned with a laptop, interrupting Rachel as she handed the computer to her. Rosemary turned to the nurse and said, "Thanks for your help, Helen. Do you think you could show me where you were parked before he stole your car?"

Helen nodded and said, "Sure, I guess."

"Alma, you come with me," said Rosemary, commanding the group as if they'd all agreed she had the right. "Who else is coming with us to go track down Michael and Ben?"

"Guys, this is a bad idea," said Rachel, but her soft voice was overwhelmed by Paul's.

"Wait." Paul was frustrated with the stranger. "You didn't answer my question. How in the hell are we going to know where to go?"

"Trust me," said Rosemary. "I've got my ways."

"I'll go," said Jacker.

"I'll stay and help Rachel," said Stephen.

"Paul?" asked Rosemary as the others accepted their assignments.

"I'll go wherever Alma's going."

"Okay, then you're with us," said Rosemary. "I trust you guys have cell phones to keep in touch with one another?" She pointed between the various members of the group, and they nodded in agreement. "Good. Rachel, call us with any details you're able to find out. But you can't tell anyone about what's going on here. Okay? I can't stress that enough."

"Fine," said Rachel, but she was flustered by how the group was making decisions without listening to her input. "But I really think this is a mistake…"

Rosemary interrupted her, "We need to hurry."

"Hold on," said Jacker. "Let me get my stuff." He lifted a cardboard box onto one of the gurneys and began to pick through the contents until he found his wallet and keys. Then he paused before picking up the purple sobriety coin that Paul had given him back in Chicago, the night before they left for Widowsfield. He lifted the coin and muttered, "Damn, look at this."

"What about it?" asked Rosemary, oddly intrigued.

"Paul gave this to me."

"Does it have significance to you?" asked Rosemary.

Jacker looked over at Paul when he answered, "Damn straight it does."

"Then give it to me," said Rosemary.

Jacker looked perplexed and clasped the coin in his palm. "No, that's all right. I think I'll hold onto this."

"I'm not going to steal it," said Rosemary as if chastising a child. "In fact, it would be in everyone's best interest to figure out something you're carrying that has some sort of significance to you, something that you think is important, and give it to me."

"Why?" asked Alma.

"Because we're going to be fighting something that can use your worst fears against you," said Rosemary.

"Fighting it?" asked Rachel, incredulous as she looked around at the others. She was becoming exasperated as she realized that she was the only one that wasn't fully on board with their plan. "Look, lady, I'll help you track down Michael and Ben if I can, but that's as far as I go with this. I'm not fighting any demon or whatever."

"We'll help," said Stephen as he moved to stand closer to Rachel. He started to take off his wedding band to hand over to Rosemary. "Will this work?"

Rosemary nodded and said, "That should be fine."

"Wait a minute." Rachel was surprised and annoyed by her husband's acquiescence to the stranger's request. "I'm not planning on fighting anything." She looked at Alma and said, "I'm going to help you guys find your dad, and then I'm out of here."

"Isn't this the biggest story of your life?" asked Stephen. "How are you not at least a little intrigued about what's going on here?"

"I don't give a fuck about a story," said Rachel, emphasizing her curse as if telling a joke. "Whatever happened to us in this town, in that dream, or nightmare, or whatever... Whatever it was, it's enough for me. I want out!"

"Just give her your wedding ring," said Stephen as if he were bored with Rachel's argument.

"No, I'm not giving some stranger my ring," said Rachel. "That's crazy."

"Don't worry," said Stephen with a grin. "It's not worth as much as you think it is."

Rachel was flustered. "Well, that's great." She closed her eyes and shook her head while waving her hands in front of her face, an expression of her annoyance and frustration.

"Look, guys, I'm not trying to be a pain in the ass here or anything. I'm trying to be the sensible one. Whatever the hell it is that we just went through…" She motioned to the gurneys and then over at Aubrey's corpse, "Whatever it is, it just killed that girl. She's dead. How am I the only one that thinks we shouldn't be screwing around with stuff we don't understand?"

"We're the only ones that can stop The Watcher and The Skeleton Man from getting out," said Rosemary.

"He's already out," said Rachel. "Too late."

"Then we have to put him back in," said Rosemary.

"What about calling the cops?" asked Rachel. "Has anyone given that a thought?"

"And tell them what?" asked Stephen. "That some inter-dimensional demon is fucking with our heads, knocking people out, and killing them in their dreams?"

"We've got a goddamn room full of fucking coma patients in there," Rachel pointed at the door that led to the sleepers' room. "It's not like we'll be going to the cops empty handed."

"We can't go to the police," said Rosemary. "There's no guarantee they're not in on it."

"Oh come on," said Rachel. "Don't tell me you think every police officer in the area is in on this whole cover-up thing."

"Maybe not all of them, but at least a few must be," said Jacker.

Rachel turned to face the big man, frustrated that he'd spoken against her. "We all know why you don't want the police showing up."

"Hey," said Jacker, annoyed at her insinuation. "I already tried to give myself up to the cops to save your ass. I don't need you…"

"Cool it," said Paul as he stepped between them. "Both of you."

"If you call the cops," said Rosemary, "then they'll be dredging your corpse out of the reservoir in a week or two, just like all the others. You can check the records yourself. There're an awful lot of supposed boating accidents out here all the time – far more here than any other county in the area. That's no coincidence."

Paul took a key off its ring and handed it to Rosemary. "That's the key to my bike."

"What does giving that to her do exactly?" asked Rachel, still trying to force the issue. She looked at Rosemary and asked, "What are you going to do with this stuff?"

"Like I said, I'm a psychometric. That means I can take information from objects. When you were unconscious, you saw how The Watcher and The Skeleton Man were able to warp the world around you, and confuse you. Hopefully I can keep them from doing that. If I can get to know you, through these things," she held up Paul's key, "then hopefully I can stop them from tricking you."

"Guys, please tell me I'm not the only one that thinks this whole thing is insane," said Rachel, pleading for someone to agree with her.

"This whole town is insane," said Alma as she reluctantly handed over her teddy bear keychain that Paul had bought her on their first date.

Rachel sighed, but pulled at her wedding ring. Her engagement ring and wedding band had been fitted together as part of their design, and it caused them to be difficult to separate. She struggled to get the ring off, but then begrudgingly gave both the band and the engagement ring counterpart to Rosemary. "Fine, fine," said Rachel. "But I still think we should all consider leaving this place and forgetting we were ever here."

"We're the only ones that can put the devil back in Hell," said Rosemary. "And I'm going to do whatever it takes to get the job done."

CHAPTER 4 – No Such Thing as Truth

Philadelphia
June 13th, 1943

"Personal demons?" asked Lyle as he followed Vess across the deck of the ship. Young men in Navy uniforms passed them, never once stopping to question why they were there. Vess was an important man, but if he was well-respected then no one was displaying the proper reverence. He was admitted wherever he chose to go on the USS Eldridge, a Navy Destroyer escort. Everyone seemed to understand that the tall scientist and his assistant were allowed access to every part of the massive ship, but none of the sailors seemed fond enough of Vess to acknowledge him.

"Is that what you said?" asked Lyle, uncertain he'd heard his employer correctly.

"Yes," said Vess as he led the way. "What sort of personal demons are hiding up here?" He tapped the brim of his fedora and smiled down at his companion. The call of seagulls above threatened to drown them out. The birds flocked at the yard, drawn here by the families that often crowded the dock to welcome their husbands and sons home, or to send them away. The anxious family members were subjected to long waits, as it often took hours for the Marines to exit the ship after docking. To ply the children, mothers would bring stale bread that the kids could throw to the gulls. Today, however, there were no families present, and the seabirds voiced their frustration.

"Demons?" Lyle chuckled and nodded knowingly, "Oh I get it, you're talking about that Austrian chap, right? Freud?"

"Depends," said Vess as if toying with his new assistant. "Do you want to bed your mother?"

"Quit with that nonsense," said Lyle, perturbed. "I'm not a mental-case, if that's what you're after."

"Liar," said Vess, still smirking. "We've all got skeletons in our closets; those little demons we try to keep quiet as we pretend to be normal. Did you used to fantasize about having sex with your mother? Is that what you're hiding up there?"

"That's enough, Vess," said Lyle, more fervent now. "Back off with the Mom-talk, I'm serious." He glared at his new employer, and Vess halted. The pale scientist smirked and nodded, but didn't say anything. "What is it? Why are you looking at me that way?"

"It's just that I've always found people's fears fascinating, that's all. Most people's issues can be traced back to their parents. It's part of the human condition, I guess. What about your father? What was he like?"

Lyle cringed and shook his head. "Nothing special." He hadn't been close to his father, but he would never forget the man's final few weeks as the formerly tall, robust man had succumbed to polio. He'd been forced to lie in an iron lung for several tortuous months before he passed. Lyle was haunted by how his father had gone into the machine looking strong and thick, but when they pulled his body out he'd wasted away to nearly a skeleton. In his casket, his father had been draped in an old suit of his that had once been snug, but now hung from his skeletal shoulders. "He died when I was young. Why? What's it matter?"

"Nothing to be concerned about, my good man. Nothing at all," said Vess.

"You're a peculiar sort," said Lyle as he stuck his thumbs beneath his suspenders and wandered to the edge of the ship. The ledge was high, but he was able to look out into the greenish water of the bay. "Before today, I thought you were all hot air."

"Did you?" asked Vess. An emerging tickle turned into a cough, and made his question sound malicious, though he hadn't intended it to be. He hacked, the force causing his back to arch, and then wiped his lips with a handkerchief pulled from an inside pocket of his blazer. "Then why did you accept the job?" he asked after recovering from his fit.

"I'm not the sort of guy that can afford to turn down a paycheck. Especially now that I'm not gambling no more."

Vess leaned against the rail, his arms draped over the edge as he watched the gulls spinning above the bay. "I wouldn't think an able-bodied chap like you would have trouble getting work, what with most gents at war and all."

"Able-bodied?" asked Lyle with a laugh. "Why do you think I'm not fighting Japs in the Guadalcanal?"

Vess glanced at Lyle curiously. The stout man was shorter than Vess, but sturdy, with strong arms and a thick chest. He bore no visible signs of illness or anything that would make it obvious why he would've avoided conscription. "I thought you were an immigrant."

"Me? No, sir. Born and bred in the fields of Kansas. My parents were immigrants, but I'm American-made."

"Then how'd you dodge a trip overseas with the rest of them?"

Lyle tapped his barrel chest. "Got tuberculosis when I was a kid. Damn near killed me and drove my parents into poverty. My lungs ain't never been the same. When I registered, they told me I'd never be allowed in with the rest of the boys, but that they'd stick me in with some pencil-pushing unit. Never got the call, though. Guess I lucked out. What about you? How come they didn't snatch you up?"

"Who said they didn't?" asked Vess with a smirk.

"You went to war? How'd you make it out?"

Vess shook his head and explained, "I'm not the sort of soldier that gets a gun put in his hands. There are other ways of killing people."

Lyle became uncomfortable, and he started to try and figure out what Vess meant. "Science and stuff? Is that how you knew old crazy-hair back there?" He thumbed back at where they'd boarded the ship.

"You know the interesting thing about science?" asked Vess, as if almost entirely ignoring or avoiding Lyle's question. "It's just an attempt to explain the unexplainable. Science is like an adult, standing over our shoulders, reaching past us to help put a puzzle together that we can't quite figure out. Trick is, no one's sure about anything."

Lyle expected Vess to continue, but the sickly man seemed content to stop there. "What's that supposed to mean?" asked Lyle.

"Everything you believe to be true is just one discovery away from being proven wrong."

Lyle stared at Vess and snorted in amusement. "If the military hired you to try and confuse folks, then they're getting their money's worth. You scientist fellows speak above my pay grade."

Vess chuckled and pat Lyle on the back. "I'm no scientist, my friend. Not by any conventional definition at least."

"No? I thought you were a science guy," said Lyle, confused. "The way you were talking about that Tesla fellow earlier, I figured you were an egghead just like he was."

"An egghead?" asked Vess, amused but mildly offended.

"No disrespect or nothing. I just don't come from that stock."

"Yes you do," said Vess. "We all do. You can't opt out of science, my man. It's as much a part of you as the blood in your veins."

Lyle snickered and shook his head, "You sound like the Baptist friends of mine, preaching your 'truths' and whatnot."

Vess stared out at the gulls and said, "There's no such thing as truth."

"Well, you're an odd chap, that's a truth if ever there were one."

Vess didn't offer a retort.

"If you're not a scientist, then what in the blazes are you? What are we doing here?"

The tall man looked down at his hands in contemplation for a few moments, and then glanced sideways at his companion. "I study other things," said Vess. "Darker things." Vess reached into his coat and pulled out a folded cloth that he handed to Lyle. "Be careful with that," said Vess.

"What is it?" asked Lyle after taking it.

"Open it up," said Vess as he reached back into his coat for something else. He pulled out what looked like the hilt of an ancient dagger, but the blade had long ago broken off.

Lyle opened the folded cloth and found a few pieces of jewelry. They were gold figurines that looked like they might once have fit on something larger. One of the smaller pieces was connected to a bracelet, and it was clear that it had been meant as a depiction of a pagan God of some sort. It had the body of a human and the head of a snake. Its arms were long, and it was holding a staff that had been bent and misshapen over time.

"What are these?" asked Lyle.

"Those were given to a young boy as a gift," said Vess. "Be careful with them. They're quite old. They were given to the boy as a way of honoring him for his sacrifice."

"His sacrifice?" asked Lyle.

"Yes, that's part of what I used to study. Not necessarily just human sacrifice, but all the ways mankind used to try and contact their deities." Vess regarded the bladeless knife, turning the old thing over in his hand to inspect the twine that wrapped the handle and the decorative skull on its pommel.

"So why'd you bring this stuff with you?" asked Lyle.

"It's symbolic," said Vess as he put the bladeless hilt back into his coat and then reached out to take back the jewelry. "They're special to me."

Widowsfield
March 13th, 2012
2:55 AM

"Oliver's still here somewhere," said Rosemary as they looked at the blood trail that he'd left behind after Paul had shot his foot.

"My assistant is going to try and follow his tracks," said the nurse, Helen, who they'd been following out of the facility. "He needs to be bandaged up. I don't think his injury was life-threatening or anything, but still, he can't run around bleeding like that." She motioned down to the trail that headed off deeper into the facility.

"Where do you suppose he went?" asked Jacker as he stared down the dark hallway.

Helen shook her head. "Beats me. I doubt I've seen even half of this place. My days are spent with the sleepers."

"How long have you worked here?" asked Alma.

Helen sighed and raised her brows. "Too long."

"Since 1996?" asked Paul.

"No, no," said Helen, as if worried the others would think poorly of her had she been an employee at the time of the event. She looked over at Rosemary, and then back at the others, and her discomfort was apparent. "They hired me several years after that. Well after the first sleepers started to die."

"How many died?" asked Paul.

"In my time?" Helen considered the question for a moment and then said, "A couple hundred or so."

"Christ," said Jacker as he ran his hands through his curly, shoulder length hair in exasperation. "How come you never went to the cops or anything?"

Helen was hesitant to answer, but the scrutiny of the group only intensified with her silence. "I made some mistakes here, for sure. I'm not claiming total ignorance. I knew what they were doing was messed up, but I was hired to try and help the people in there be comfortable, not to question what caused all this. The reason they kept me on for so long is because I don't ask questions."

"I guess that's one way to live a guilt-free life," said Paul, clearly discontent with her answer.

"Everyone makes bad choices from time to time," said Rosemary, surprising the others by coming to Helen's defense. "Trust me. I know better than most."

"Should we try to find Oliver?" asked Paul.

Rosemary shook her head. "Not yet. He's not leaving town, I guarantee it. For now, the most important thing for us to do is to find Ben and get him back here."

"What happens if we do manage to get him back here?" asked Alma. "What do we do then?"

Rosemary didn't have an answer. Everyone was waiting for one, so she just offered something she hoped would placate them. "The Watcher will take care of him."

"I'm not going to hand my brother over to be killed," said Alma.

"We can do whatever it takes to save Ben, but we've got to do whatever we can to keep The Skeleton Man out of the real world. He's too dangerous. Now let's stop wasting time." She put her hand on the nurse's shoulder and said, "Helen, show me where your car was parked."

Helen led the way through the hallway to the door of the parking lot. Rosemary went out first, eager to track Michael down. The darkness was prevalent, shrouding most of their surroundings save what the moon revealed. The lot was nearly silent, devoid of even the chirp of crickets. Cada E.I.B. was fenced off from the rest of the world, a prison of concrete, steel, and glass. All around them lived The Watchers, who Rosemary was acutely aware existed in the dead things that stole the world from nature. The walls, windows, and floors were anything but innocuous. They were the playground of the creatures that Oliver had awoken.

There were tire tracks on the pavement. In Michael's haste to escape Widowsfield, he'd hit the gas too hard, leaving behind the tracks; like a signature he hadn't meant to write. Rosemary gingerly removed the glove on her right hand, and then reached out to lay her fingertips on the black skid mark.

Paul, Alma, and Jacker stood with Helen, beside the door that led back into Cada E.I.B.'s facility. They watched as the psychometric worked.

Rosemary closed her eyes and waited for the past to be revealed to her. Over the past five years she'd gotten better at practicing her gift, although she still hated doing it. Every time she focused on drawing information out of the world around her that she had no business knowing, her mind struggled to maintain sanity. She'd developed a strong appreciation of what was and what wasn't the truth about her own life, since it was so easy to accept that some of the things she remembered to be true hadn't actually happened to her at all. There were too many instances in her life when she was certain that she'd done something in the past that had actually been done by someone else. Discovering that your memories don't belong to you is something that the human brain doesn't handle very well.

She took her hand away, and then nodded over to Alma. "He had the nurses help him load Ben in, and then took off."

"Do you know where to?" asked Alma.

Rosemary shook her head, and then looked out toward the gate. "We can go up there and see if we can find another track."

"What about the gurney?" asked Jacker. "Maybe you could use that to…"

"No," said Rosemary as she regarded the empty bed on wheels that sat beside her. "Not if that's the bed that Ben's been laying on for years. No way in hell."

"What are you planning on doing then?" asked Jacker. "Walking the whole way and touching the ground?"

Rosemary pointed to a security van that was parked near the entrance. "I've got the keys to that van. We can take that and drive out to each intersection. I can get out and try to touch the road to track them down. Not too many vehicles drive around this area, so it won't be hard to follow him – at least until we get out of town."

Paul grimaced and shook his head. "That trick of yours is going to be pretty hard to do if he gets on the highway."

"Hopefully your friend in there can find him before that happens," said Rosemary in reference to Rachel's attempt to use Helen's license plate number to track Michael down.

"All right then," said Paul as if he was giving in to something he didn't want to do. "Let's get moving." They were all tired, but Paul seemed wearier than the others. Rosemary realized that he'd woken up earlier from the forced sleep the group had fallen into, and hadn't rested the way the others had. Paul met The Skeleton Man, and had learned about what happened at Terry's cabin, but Rosemary also understood that the creature had either lied to Paul about some of the details – either that, or The Skeleton Man had lost some of the facts to The Watcher's lies as well.

As they headed for the van, Rosemary couldn't decipher which parts of her recollection about Paul's time with The Skeleton Man he'd told her, and which she'd gleaned from the key he'd given her. Trying to pick apart the difference caused a headache to begin to torture her, and she decided not to worry about it. Before long, the lives of these strangers would be laid bare to her as their personal belongings poisoned her mind with their memories. She would be quickly overwhelmed if she tried too hard to organize them.

Rosemary lived her life teetering on the edge of insanity, or so she hoped. It was entirely possible that she'd fallen off that ledge long ago. Sometimes the secrets she kept felt like they belonged to someone else, as if all the bad things she knew she'd done might not have been her own sins.

"You drive," she said to Jacker as she handed him the keys she'd stolen from the security guard named Alex that had confronted her by the reservoir.

Paul and Alma happily sat in the back as Rosemary walked to the passenger seat and started to adjust her plan on how to put an end to the Widowsfield nightmare.

CHAPTER 5 – Fewer Players

Widowsfield
Free of The Watcher's Lies

Grace Love heard the boy call out for his father. She was getting her order pad from under the counter, although she knew she wouldn't need it. Desmond and his son, Raymond, always ordered the same thing: A Salisbury steak for Desmond and a BLT for Raymond. It was an endearing trait of the pair, and their consistent habits had become a comforting part of her job.

Grace knelt down, and her knee pushed up on the underside of her apron, causing her red, polka-dotted sunglasses to fall out of the pocket. She picked them up and put them in her bouffant as she stood back up.

She turned to walk toward the only populated table in the restaurant, but saw that it was empty. Her patrons had vanished, leaving no trace they'd ever been there.

"Well I'll be a monkey's uncle," said Grace with a confused chuckle as she looked toward the bathroom, guessing that the two had a sudden emergency to attend to in there. She was surprised to see that an 'Out of Order' sign had been hung up over the men's room. She grimaced when she guessed that the cook had plugged up the toilet and just stuck the sign up instead of plunging it.

"Juan," said Grace with an angry flair to her voice. "Did you much up the toilet again?"

No one answered.

"Juan?"

Grace glanced through the window that breached the separation between the dining area and the kitchen, but Juan was missing. She started to lean through the window to search for the cook, but when she placed her fingers on the metal shelf she recoiled, expecting pain. The heat lamps always turned the shelf blisteringly hot, but despite having worked here for years, Grace continually made the mistake of touching the metal. However, this time the shelf's heat didn't sting her. Curious, she tapped her finger on it again to see if it was hot, but found that it was barely warm at all. She resolved to change the bulbs, deciding that even though they were still on, there was something wrong with the heating filament inside of them.

"Juan, where'd you disappear to? Is this some sort of joke?"

Grace went to the swinging door and shouldered it open, but there was no one in the back of the restaurant. She walked through the empty space to the walk-in refrigerator and pulled the hefty handle, but found the door was locked from the outside. If Juan was in there, then someone had locked him in.

She started to get nervous, and called out again, "Juan?" She pulled the thin metal bar out of the hole that prevented the handle from opening and let it hang from its chain. She pulled the handle and felt the rubber seal break as she tugged the heavy door open. Cold air pushed out at her, but she didn't feel the sensation that she expected. The fans inside of the cooler were on, and she could feel the air hitting her skin, but the temperature was lost. There was frost on the zinc oxide shelves inside, and she could tell the freezer was still working properly, but she couldn't distinguish the temperature, as if her skin had lost the ability to tell a difference.

"Grace," said a male's voice.

She spun, startled, but there was no one in the kitchen with her.

"Who said that?" her question was labored by her encroaching fear.

"I'm here," said the man again.

Grace turned in a circle, leaving the freezer door standing open, the mist drifted out of it and disappeared as it cascaded across the greasy floor. There was no one else in the kitchen with her.

"Desmond?" she asked as she recognized the man's voice.

"Yes."

"Where?" She stuttered as she continued to search for him. "Where in the blazes are you hiding? What sort of joke are you guys pulling on me?" She tried to find the humor in it, although her fear refused to subside.

"I'm right here." Desmond put his hand on Grace's shoulder, and she twirled in shock to find him standing behind her.

"Son of a…" she nearly cursed as she clasped her breast. "Desmond. How'd you do that? Where… Desmond?" She could see his familiar face, but also recognized that he wasn't completely there. It was as if he were an illusion, or a hologram. She could see him, but could also see through him to the door behind.

Grace reached out to touch Desmond, but her hand slid through his chest as if he weren't there. A stinging cold bit her fingers and she pulled them back. Then she began to back away, as if fearful Desmond might attack, but she was simply trying to comprehend what was happening. Her brain struggled to make sense of what her senses promised was real.

"No…" Grace blinked rapidly and then she began to touch her own skin, an inexplicable reaction that she needed to do, as if it was necessary to ensure she was really there. "How?"

"Grace, I'm so sorry," said Desmond as he took a step closer.

"Stay away!" Grace staggered back, terrified of the approaching phantom.

Desmond's visage faded away.

Grace's sneakers hit a slick patch of grease and the sole of her shoe squeaked as it slid out from beneath her. She nearly avoided a fall, but then her clumsiness interceded and sent her flailing backward. She bashed into a stack of hefty cardboard boxes that were used to tote vegetables. The sturdy stack of boxes did little to soften her fall, and she tumbled to the floor, smacking her hip against the tile. Her sunglasses fell out of her hair and the delicate, plastic frame cracked when they bounced off the greasy, black and white tile.

She was crying out in fear as she tried to recover from her stumble. Grace pressed her hands on the slick floor, a week's worth of gunk beneath her that Juan should've mopped, but he was never concerned much about cleanliness. As she slipped again, she cursed the cook.

"Grace," said Desmond, although his voice was the only proof of his existence.

"No!" Grace got to her knees, her hip pulsing from the impact with the floor. "Stay away from me." She gave up trying to get to her feet, and crawled to the back door that led to the alley. The fire station was just behind the diner, and she planned to escape there and plead for help.

Grace gripped the door handle and used it to help herself up. Then she pushed the back door open without daring to glance backward. A blinding flash of yellow light greeted her, and she instinctually raised her arm to shield her eyes.

The light was warm, but pleasantly so, its heat a soothing influence on her addled senses. Once she experienced the warmth of the rays hitting her, Grace's fear subsided. She lowered her arm, unafraid of the light that greeted her outside of the building. Despite its intensity, the light didn't hurt her eyes. She gazed out, and felt her eyes begin to produce tears. Within the glow she caught sight of human shapes moving, casting shadows that the rays burst past, like crepuscular, heavenly light piercing clouds.

"Dezzy," said Grace, but she couldn't look away. "Are you seeing this?"

"Yes," said Desmond as he approached from behind Grace.

She wasn't afraid of him anymore. As the glow warmed her, she realized she wasn't afraid of anything. The rays caressed her skin, as tactile as anything that had ever touched her before. It felt like the warmth was seeping into her, and slowly pulling her in, piece by piece. Dots of sparkling white floated away from her, and up along the path the rays cut through the sky. She felt like a budding flower that was feeling the first rays of a sunrise as it burned away the fog.

"I'm dead, aren't I?" asked Grace, but not with trepidation. Unlike any moment in her entire life, she was fully aware that death was not something to be afraid of. The realization was equally invigorating and tranquilizing, a sensation unequaled in all of her years on Earth. Human beings live with a constant dread of creeping death – that specter looming large over every other facet of life. Despite any promise that religion holds, or assurance that a pastor gives, an uncertainty about mortality rests deep within. Once that fear was allayed, Grace experienced a burst of joy that could only be rivaled by the deepest love.

"Yes," said Desmond. "I think we've been dead for a long time."

Grace recognized sadness in Desmond's voice, and she turned to him, hoping to carry him into the light with her. He was standing in the kitchen, out of the rays that reached down.

"Come with me," said Grace as she held out her hand.

Desmond shook his head. "Not yet, Gracie. Not without my boy."

"Are you sure he's not up here already?" asked Grace.

"I heard him here, somewhere. I know he's still stuck down here, and I'm not leaving without him."

"You've always been such a good father to that boy, Dezzy."

"Thanks," said Desmond with sorrow in his voice. "Hey Grace, I want to tell you something. If this is the last time we ever see each other, there's something I want to say."

"It won't be the last time we see each other," said Grace. "I've never been surer of anything in my whole life."

Desmond smiled. "Even so, I just want to say thanks. You were always so good to Ray and me. I always…" he looked down, embarrassed, but forced himself to continue. "I guess

I've always had a crush on you. You're the prettiest girl I know."

"Thank you, Dezzy," said Grace. She wasn't embarrassed by his admission, and realized that her appreciation was influenced by the sense of enlightenment that flooded her. In life, Grace would've been uncertain how to react to an admission of attraction of the sort that Desmond had given. She was married, and was not attracted to Desmond. His declaration would've made their relationship difficult, and she would've been tempted to change the way she interacted with him. Now, however, she felt wholly appreciative of his love, and wanted nothing but to give him happiness. "I'll be waiting for you up here."

"Bye Gracie," said Desmond as he waved from the cover of the Salt and Pepper Diner, out of the light.

Elsewhere in Widowsfield, similar events were taking place. At the Emergency Services Building across the street, Nancy walked back in to tell Claire and Darryl about the blooming light descending from the heavens. Darryl was slow to rise from his seat, as he normally was, but when the golden hue reached in through the windows he joined his coworkers as well.

They stood at the door, hesitant to leave until the light touched them. One by one, they each accepted their fate. Darryl wept, and Claire embraced him, neither feeling any sense of sorrow – only joy. They had no fear of death, and no concern about leaving loved ones behind. As the rays warmed them, it was clear that life was a stumbling block on a much longer journey. There was no sense that a heavenly father was guiding them on, but rather that they had only temporarily forgotten their place in the fabric of existence, and the connection they each shared. The sparks of their souls danced together in the light, free of inhibition and concern, trauma or pain.

Winnie Anderson was with the UPS driver, Walter, watching from the windows of the used book store as the light finally broke through the shroud of fog that had hidden the occupants of Widowsfield for sixteen years. They were both scared at first, but then Walter dared to reach out to the rays and felt its warm embrace. He pulled Winnie in to share a kiss he'd been meaning to give her for months. As the glow grew brighter and cast the shadows of Walter and Winnie over the wood floor of the book store, they held one another tighter.

Their nightmare was finally over. But not all of Widowsfield had been set free.

Widowsfield let the souls of the dead leave, but only because The Watcher had discovered new horrors left in the minds of the residents that still slept. The new Widowsfield had lost the girls that the witch led into the water, and now The Watcher released the souls of those who'd died years earlier. The fog was less crowded, but The Watcher was delighted by the fear it clung to – those souls in the mist, anchored to Widowsfield by the husks that slept at the Cada E.I.B. facility.

In the sixteen years after the event in Widowsfield that traumatized the residents of the town, several of them passed on. Some of the sleepers died of natural causes, from things like heart attacks and aneurisms. The Watcher and The Skeleton Man had caught their energy, what a religious person would refer to as their souls, in the web of lies that they'd created out of Widowsfield, and used them to help create the nightmare. They'd hidden away the light of heaven with the fog of nightmares.

The Widowsfield where The Watcher lurked existed between two worlds, a layer between heaven and earth. In one world, the denizens of Widowsfield had fallen unconscious, and were kept at the Cada E.I.B. facility; they were the sleepers. The other world was where the souls of the dead tried to reach, but The Watcher's web caught them, forcing them to exist in his nightmare. Now that The Watcher had been forced to retrace his steps, and to recreate a new nightmare, he released the souls of the sleepers that had already died on Earth.

The girls of Widowsfield that followed the witch to the Jackson Reservoir and leapt in were thrust back into their bodies on the gurneys inside Cada E.I.B.s facility. Their souls were free, but still trapped by their living shell. The sleepers that hadn't awoken were the ones that were still anchored to earth, but existed in The Watcher's grasp.

Raymond was among the sleepers that still clung to life, and The Watcher focused on the boy's worst moments. The Watcher craved the fear the boy felt when he was discovered in Terry's closet by Michael Harper.

The Watcher in the Walls longed to know Michael again. He was creating new terrors based on the phantom of Michael, and he fantasized about what nightmares he could weave if Michael returned. The Watcher craved new sacrifices to torture, but he only had another day to wait. Vess would come back soon to turn on his machine. Then new souls would be sent back into The Watcher's hell.

Widowsfield
March 13th, 2012
3:10 AM

Alma Harper stared at Widowsfield through the tinted windows of the Cada E.I.B. security van. Paul was sitting beside her on the long, single seat. He held her hand, but neither of them seemed capable of expressing emotion of any sort. Paul was exhausted, and Alma's time in the clutches of The Watcher had left her mentally and emotionally drained. Too many thoughts clouded her mind, and it was impossible to settle on a single thing to worry about.

She whispered, "I wish I never came back here," as she looked out at the dead town.

Paul squeezed her hand and scooted closer to her. He put his arm around her and said, "You had to."

"No I didn't," said Alma. "I avoided this place for most of my life. I should've kept avoiding it."

"There's nothing wrong with trying to face the skeletons in your closet," said Paul. "And there's no way you could've known what was actually going on here."

"I don't know," said Alma. "I think I should've expected this."

"Why do you say that?" asked Rosemary from the passenger-side seat.

Jacker stopped the van at an intersection to give Rosemary a chance to get out and touch the pavement ahead, like they'd been doing since leaving Cada E.I.B., but Rosemary was interested in what Alma was saying. She didn't get out.

"I've always been afraid of this place," said Alma.

"Right, of course," said Rosemary, disinterested with Alma's fear of Widowsfield. "But you said you should've expected this. Why would you say that?"

Alma felt like she was being put on the spot, and glanced helplessly over at Paul. "I don't know. The things I remembered about this place were awful. I should've known not to try and come back here."

Rosemary continued to stare at Alma, causing her to become increasingly uncomfortable.

"What? Why are you looking at me like that?"

Rosemary shook her head slowly and then said, "I just had a horrible thought."

"Great," said Jacker as he sunk down into his seat. He sighed and put his hand over his face as he groaned. "What's your horrible thought?" He was clearly sick of horrible thoughts.

"That we're all stuck in a different Watcher's lies," said Rosemary. The rest of the occupants of the van stiffened.

"What's that supposed to mean?" asked Paul.

"It's sort of pointless to worry about," said Rosemary as she glanced away in thought. "But what if we've always been stuck in an illusion a Watcher created?"

Paul leaned his head back and groaned loudly, and then he started to laugh. He shook his head, sighed, and said, "Then tell the mother fucker I want out."

Jacker chuckled in agreement. "Amen, brother."

"You're right," said Rosemary as she started to open the door. "It's silly to worry about…"

"Wait," said Alma. She was the only one in the car that was still taking the conversation seriously. "I used to dream about him."

Rosemary sat back in her seat, and closed the door again. "About who?" she asked as she turned to Alma.

"I thought it was Ben," said Alma as she became increasingly concerned. "But now I'm not so sure."

"What were the dreams?" asked Rosemary.

"I have this recurring dream about my teeth falling out, and children laughing at me. And sometimes I'd hear the teeth chattering."

"The Skeleton Man," said Paul, apparently recalling how the creature's teeth would constantly clack against one another.

"But there were also black wires in the dreams," said Alma. "I never really thought about them before, but in all of those recurring dreams there were these black wires around. Sometimes they just made up the strings on a harp, and other times entire walls were made up of them."

"The Watcher in the Walls," said Rosemary. "I've only ever gotten glimpses of him."

"I met him," said Alma. "He was a mass of tentacles or wires, all coiled up and turned into the shape of a man. He was part of the fog, but he was also connected to the cabin. Does that make sense?"

"The Watchers live inside the walls," said Rosemary before she slapped the headrest beside her. "They live in these inanimate things. I think my gift, the psychometry, is just an ability to tap into what they know. Like they're allowing me to see the things they remember."

"Maybe that's what my dreams were," said Alma. "Maybe they were trying to talk to me?" She phrased the statement like a question.

Rosemary nodded, and bit her lip as she considered what Alma had said. "I just don't understand why The Watchers everywhere else are so docile, while the one here in Widowsfield is so malicious."

"Maybe he's an insane one," said Jacker. "Like a serial killer or some mental case like that."

"Well, we know that Oliver's company had something to do with it," said Paul. "Right?"

"Yes," said Rosemary. "But I still don't know how or why. It had something to do with a warship that was in the reservoir on March 14th, 1996. I looked into it, but all I could find out was that a replica of a Greek ship had been built in the reservoir to attract tourism."

"Wait," said Alma as she sat up straighter. "I've heard of that before. I used to get all sorts of insane conspiracy theorists calling me each year about what happened here. I remember someone talking about a boat before. They mentioned specifically about it being a Greek boat."

"Maybe Stephen and Rachel could find out more," said Paul. "Let's give them a call and see if they can start using their reporter tricks to snoop around the net a little."

Rosemary agreed, but said, "The most important thing is to find Michael and Ben, let's not put their focus on something else until after that."

"Hey guys," said Jacker with a tone of uncertain humor. "Not to be a jackass or anything, but check out the time."

It was, of course, 3:14.

CHAPTER 6 – Practice Makes Perfect

Philadelphia
June 13th, 1943

"Vess," said a deep voice from behind them, interrupting the discussion Lyle had been having with his new employer. They turned to see a large man, both in stature and width, in a beige Army uniform that distinguished him from the rest of the Marines on the ship. The man stood as tall as Vess, and a smile of greeting came easily to his face, but disappeared just as quick. He had a full head of hair that was greased with an ample amount of Pomade that caused the silver streaks to gleam, just as the grey whiskers did in his mustache. He wasn't a thin man, and wore his belt high over his belly, squeezing his girth in an almost comical manner, like a sausage tie that had come undone and allowed the link to slowly expand.

"Leslie," said Vess when he turned and recognized the man. "How are things in New York going?" The two men shook hands.

The man named Leslie grimaced and grunted as he shook his head. "I haven't been back to the office for a few weeks, and I think I'd be safer staying away for a few weeks more. I'm on my way back to Washington, coming back from New Mexico."

"Setting up the project?" asked Vess.

"Doing more than that," said the gruff man. "We're full-steam ahead now. Oppenheimer's getting about ten times the staff, and we've been struggling to keep the spies out. Easier said than done."

Vess smirked wryly and said, "I can't believe you've got a Communist working on the project. I don't imagine Byrnes is too happy to hear that."

"He's the right man for the job. Byrnes will have to bite his tongue and pout for a bit. If Oppenheimer can get the job done, then I'll be damned if he's not the one heading it up." Leslie had a clear New York accent, but his speech was languid and easy, similar to how a southerner spoke, taking time to savor the words. "Unfortunately, the guy's got Commie friends all over the damn place. There's a rumor he's got some teaching buddy who's been trying to get him to send information over to Stalin about what we're up to out in the desert. God forbid that ends up being true." Leslie grunted and shrugged his shoulders. "But we're not dropping bombs on the Soviets – at least not yet."

"Give us time," said Vess, but the other man was clearly uncertain how to respond.

Leslie took a deep breath, his massive chest expanding and testing the soundness of his buttons, and then he expelled his next sentence with plenty of air, "But who am I to judge Oppenheimer? Here I am spilling national secrets in front of a man whose name I haven't even bothered to ask."

Vess regarded Lyle and said, "My apologies, let me introduce my new assistant, Lyle Everman. Lyle, this is Major Leslie Groves, he's the man in charge of our little outing today."

The Major gripped Lyle's hand tight, easily swallowing the smaller man's hand within his own. "Pleasure to meet you."

Lyle meekly said, "Pleasure's all mine, sir."

"Lyle scored higher than any previous applicant on the Cording Exams," said Vess.

"Glad to hear it," said Groves. "We've been waiting for a man like you."

Lyle laughed uncomfortably and looked back and forth between the two, taller men. He felt like a child being lauded by a parent and a teacher for something he didn't quite understand. "Happy to help the war effort any way I can, although I have to admit, I'm not sure what that exam has to do with anything. It was just a bunch of silly questions about my childhood while men in white coats played around with wires and machines."

"It was important," said Groves. "You can be sure of that. We've been looking for someone like you for quite some time."

Vess spoke before Lyle had a chance to. "Why's Einstein leaving? I thought he was going to be observing today's test."

"He is," said Groves. "I'm going to be joining him on a second ship."

Vess appeared surprised and a little concerned. "A second ship? I know I said I wanted this room empty of onlookers, but there's no need to leave the ship."

"We'll have a couple tugs out there, just in case," said Groves. "I'll be on one of them with Al."

"Is he concerned about the machine?"

"Concerned isn't the right word," said Groves. "I'd say cautious better explains it."

"Should I be 'cautious' as well?" asked Vess.

"Don't take it too seriously," said Groves. "I've just got to be extra careful about everything these days. For crying out loud, I was told to draft up a letter to Oppenheimer about how he should consider not flying or driving long distances anymore. With as much money as they're throwing at these projects, we've got to be mighty careful with the lives of the men running things."

"I guess it's good to know my place then," said Vess, his sarcasm evident.

"Don't go being sensitive, Vess," said the Major as he clopped his mighty hand on the frail man's shoulder. "You know as well as anyone how hard your brand of, uh, 'science' is to get the folks in D.C. to take seriously."

"That's comforting," said Vess, again with thick sarcasm.

Major Groves ignored the frail man's chagrined response. "Have you been down to see the set-up yet?"

"No, we were waiting for you," said Vess.

"All right then," Groves smiled wide. "Your wait's over. Let's get moving. We're burning daylight."

Branson
Shortly before 3:00 AM
March 13th, 2012

Charles Dunbar pulled into a hotel parking lot far later than he'd anticipated. Unfortunately for him, Branson was hosting a music festival this weekend, and several out-of-towners had filled up the majority of local hotels. He'd never had much trouble finding a place to stay in this part of the state before, but on this trip his poor planning skills had finally caught up with him. It took him a couple hours of calling various hotels to finally find one with a vacancy.

"Christ," he muttered as he started to gather his papers. He was an outside sales rep for a hunting apparel company based out of California, and his regional manager required nightly reports on each salesperson's activity while on the road. Charles had always turned in his reports in a timely fashion, but tonight he resolved to wait until morning, hoping that his manager would be reasonable.

As he was gathering his things, a blue Ford Escort pulled into the roundabout outside of the hotel's entrance. "Goddamn it," said Charles as he watched the driver of the Escort jump out and rush inside. Charles had already called this hotel to reserve a room, but was annoyed that now he would have to wait in line. He was exhausted, and just wanted to eat a quick snack, jerk off, and go to bed.

Charles got out of his Expedition, clicked his fob to lock it and set the alarm, and then headed for the hotel's entrance, past the still-running Escort in the roundabout. He casually glanced into the car, curious to spy the contents. What he saw in the backseat shocked Charles enough to cause him to curse and step back.

A thin, skeletal man was lying on the back seat, his arms folded across his chest like a vampire plucked from a coffin. The man's mouth was open, and his dark red tongue was flicking behind his yellow teeth. His eyes were also open, but there was clear gel smeared over them. The living corpse caught sight of Charles, and he seemed to become agitated or excited. He began to shake, and his tongue flicked faster. Charles walked away briskly, disturbed and frightened by what he'd seen.

As he approached the hotel doors, the owner of the Escort appeared with a hotel staff member beside him. The young staff member was pushing a wheelchair.

"Evening," said the dirty, unwashed stranger to Charles as they neared one another. "Or morning I guess. Right?"

"Morning," said Charles as he nodded to the haggard man with the blisters on his lips.

They passed one another, and the automatic doors closed between them. The cool, morning air outside was replaced by the strong scent of floor cleaner. His shoes squeaked on the newly polished floor, and he saw a large waxing machine plugged in and leaning against the wall. Charles paused and spied through the entrance as the hotel staff helped the invalid move from the back seat of the car to the wheelchair.

"Hello, sir," said the concierge, stealing Charles' attention away from the door. "Will you be staying with us tonight?"

"Hopefully," said Charles as he walked to the counter. "I called about an hour ago to book a room. Name's Charles Dunbar."

The young employee searched his computer and found Charles's name. They started to go through the check-in process and Charles stole glances outside to watch as the other staff member got the helpless, skeletal man into the wheelchair.

"City sure is busy tonight," said Charles. "I had a hell of a time finding a room."

"Music festival," answered the staffer. "We were booked solid, but a bus that was headed out here broke down on the way, which freed up a bunch of rooms."

"Lucky for me," said Charles with a grin as he took a mint from a glass dish on the counter. He pulled the cellophane off the red and white candy and then left the wrapper on the counter. The concierge reached over and retrieved the garbage, disposing of it in a bin nearby beside him.

The concierge asked for Charles's driver's license, and he complied, sliding the card across the counter as he kept an eye on what was going on outside. Then the man across the counter handed over a pen and card that he asked Charles to fill out.

"Is it okay if I don't know my license plate?" asked Charles as he reviewed the information he was being asked to provide.

"That's fine," said the concierge. "Just leave a description of the car."

Charles did as he was asked, and shortly after he was given a plastic cardkey. The only rooms available were suites that were located on the side of the building, requiring Charles to walk around the outside of the hotel.

By the time he was done with the concierge, the Ford Escort was gone. Charles could hear the squeak of the wheelchair as it was pushed along somewhere nearby, although he couldn't see the source.

The entrances to the suites were located along a row that drew a square around an outdoor pool. The pool was still covered with a green tarp for the season. Leaves had collected in the dimpled portions of the tarp, and the shape of the hotel caused the wind to spin them, creating a scratching noise that sounded like animals clawing at canvas. Charles pulled his wheeled overnight bag behind him as he made his way around the pool, and then saw that the other man that had arrived late was in the room beside his. It seemed that whoever had rented the rooms before their bus broke down had asked that they be placed together. Charles cursed his luck, and hoped to avoid a conversation with the odd man.

The stranger had his door open, and the staffer that had assisted in bringing the wheelchair over was leaving as Charles approached. The unlaundered man stepped out of his room to say, 'Thanks' to the staffer, and then saw Charles entering the room next to him.

"Howdy neighbor," said the thin, grizzled man as he waved.

Charles smiled and nodded, but offered nothing more than that in an attempt to allay a conversation.

"How come you're getting in so late?" The stranger took a step towards Charles.

"Long day of working on the road." Charles dropped the keycard in and pulled it out, but red lights flashed on the electronic lock and the door wouldn't open.

"Oh yeah?" asked the stranger. "You travel a lot for business?"

"Too much," said Charles with a smile as he tried to be cordial. He could smell the stranger's body odor, and wanted to end their pleasantries as quickly as possible. He slipped the card in again and this time was met with a pleasant chirp and a row of green lights signaling that it worked. "There we go. Well, good to meet you. I'm off to bed."

"Have a good one," said the stranger as Charles hurried inside.

He closed the door and then flipped the latch to lock it. He muttered, "Weirdo," as he tossed his overnight bag onto the bed.

Charles had stayed at a hundred different hotels in his years as a field rep, and this one was neither one of the best, nor one of the worst. He rarely stayed in suites, preferring to keep his expenses down to avoid the always-vigilant eye of the company's CFO, but these were the only rooms available when he called, and his days of sleeping in the car to appease the accounting department's miserliness were long over.

He explored the space, but was chagrined that he wouldn't even utilize half of it. In the morning he would be headed out to St. Louis for a conference, and then all the way to Springfield, Illinois to meet with a distributor that the company was courting. He wouldn't end up getting any use out of the full-size refrigerator or stove in his room. He simply didn't have time for much else but sleep.

Something in the wall rumbled, and Charles grimaced at the loud noise. It sounded like running water, but he was surprised by how much the noise bled through the walls. He placed his hand against the flower-print wallpaper and realized that his neighbor's bathroom was located just behind the headboard of the bed. It seemed the foul-smelling man was finally taking a bath, but the sound of the running water was frustratingly loud.

Charles went through his normal hotel procedure, unpacking only essentials, and then started to get ready for bed. He texted his wife, choosing not to wake her with a call, and then started to run through his emails, but the swell of work-related messages quickly antagonized him. He was tired of the debates that consumed the time of everyone at the corporate office, and didn't want to get bogged down reading through the multiple, strongly-worded replies about the necessity for a minimum sale price limit for online retailers or the quality of fabric being used on pocket linings. He was too tired to care about any of that at the moment.

His neighbor had stopped running the water, and Charles flipped on the television to make sure he drowned out any further disturbances. As he was searching channels, he passed the adult pay-per-view, and considered purchasing one, but ultimately decided he was too tired.

"You're getting old, Charlie," he said to himself as he continued clicking through channels. He stopped on a rerun of Buffy the Vampire Slayer, a show that he never thought he would enjoy, but that his daughter had convinced him to watch a few months earlier. Remarkably, he found that he liked it a lot more than he would've ever expected, although he still hadn't admitted that to his daughter.

He struggled to get comfortable on the annoyingly plump and fluffy pillows. Despite how most people seemed to enjoy large, thick pillows, Charles liked his flat and nearly devoid of filling. He kept meaning to bring a pillow from home along with him on his trips, but always forgot to while preparing to leave.

Despite his minor annoyance with the bed, he soon drifted to sleep, but was rudely awakened by a commotion in his neighbor's room. It sounded like someone was thrashing in the tub, and then he could hear the bass of the man's voice bleeding through the wall. Charles cursed, and tried to go back to sleep. He could hear the man in the room beside him blather on, but he eventually calmed, and things were quiet enough for Charles to doze off again.

He would only be asleep for little more than an hour, but that was plenty of time for the lies to sink in.

Branson
3:45 AM
March 13th, 2012

The Skeleton Man was alive, but he was trapped in the incapacitated body of Ben Harper. The boy had grown much more than The Skeleton Man had expected, and he realized that his perception of the flow of time was warped by The Watcher's lies. For years, The Skeleton Man had searched Widowsfield for Alma Harper after she appeared with her mother at Terry's cabin. He thought he was looking for a young girl, certainly no older than high school-age, but he was proven wrong when Alma appeared at the cabin again, this time as a woman in her mid-twenties.

"Michael," said Ben Harper as he stared at the man on the bed beside him. Ben was in a wheelchair, and was leaning over the bed in an attempt to grasp the man that had been the cause of all his feelings of hatred, betrayal, and sorrow. "Michael."

"That's good, buddy," said Michael Harper before he yawned. He'd moved to the far side of the bed, out of his son's grasp. Ben continued to try and reach out to him, his fingers uselessly scratching at the bed sheet. "I'm happy you're starting to be able to talk again, but it's getting late. You should try and get some sleep."

"Michael Har…" Ben choked on the name.

"You need a pillow or something?" asked Michael. "Or do you want me to lay you down on the sofa? Would that be more comfortable?" Michael started to sit up, but then settled back down and said, "Nah, I bet you're sick of lying down. I bet it feels good to be sitting up like that, watching some TV instead of staring at the ceiling all day and night."

"Michael Harper," said Ben, his voice a hoarse whisper.

"You've got to quit doing that, kid," said Michael as he relaxed. "You're going to drive me nuts."

Several minutes passed, and Ben continued to try to reach out to his father while repeating the man's name. Michael grew increasingly upset and kept pleading with his son to stop, each time becoming more frustrated than the last.

After this continued for nearly fifteen minutes, Michael finally lost his patience. He bounded from the other side of the bed, visibly agitated as he glared over at his son. "Now I warned you, buddy. I warned you over and over. Didn't I? How the fuck am I supposed to get any sleep with you grabbing at me and talking all night?"

He picked his belt up off the floor where he'd thrown it earlier.

Ben Harper held his breath. The child that still resided behind The Skeleton Man's consciousness was suddenly dominant over the other souls within the human shell that sat in the wheelchair. The boy recalled the beatings his father used to inflict with a similar belt, and all those memories came rushing back. The time he'd been whipped for breaking the vacuum while cleaning his room; the time he'd been beaten for crying too loud; the time he'd been spanked for seemingly no reason except that his father had accused him of giving him a 'snide' look at dinner.

"You did this to yourself," said Michael as Ben watched, frozen by both terror as well as the mortal prison he was stuck within.

Michael Harper took a pocket knife out of his jeans. Ben watched as his father approached with the belt and the knife, frightened of what was about to occur, but helpless to defend himself. He tried to move his body to block his father, but his arm just flopped off the side of the bed and down into his lap when he moved.

"Michael Harper," said Ben as he stared glassy-eyed at his father.

Michael reached out with the belt and strapped it over Ben's mouth, and then looped it behind his head. Ben gnawed at the belt, and saliva dripped over his lip and down his chin as he tried to say his father's name. Michael tightened the belt, and then used the knife to cut a mark in it where the buckle would latch. He pulled the belt away, leaving his son to gasp and lick at his raw lips.

Michael dug the tip of the knife into the leather belt, spinning it until a hole emerged. Next, he set the knife and the belt on the bed before taking off his sweat-stained t-shirt.

"Michael Harper," said Ben, his voice maligned by the pain in his lips that the belt had caused.

"Keep it up," said Michael with a snicker as he shook his head.

Ben's father stuffed his sweaty, unwashed shirt into his son's mouth. He pushed hard, as if eager to cause pain, and then he wrapped the belt around his boy's head, forcing the buckle through the hole he'd made and tying the shirt to Ben's face like a ball-gag.

"That should do it," said Michael, pleased with himself.

Ben struggled to breathe. The belt had pushed part of the shirt high up against his nose, and he felt as if he were hyperventilating. He shook his head and moaned, and tried to raise his arms, but his body was a prison. He scratched at his legs and writhed as best he could.

Michael sighed, and for a moment Ben thought he was going to apologize. Ben hoped his father would untie him.

"Looks like you're sleeping in the bathroom tonight, kid," said Michael as he unlocked the wheels on his son's chair before pushing him across the room. He put Ben in the bathroom, facing the tub with his back to the door, and then shut off the light.

"Goodnight," said Michael before he closed the door, leaving Ben alone in the dark.

Every breath of air was laden with the stench of Michael's shirt. He could taste the sweat as his tongue was pressed hard against the balled up fabric.

Ben Harper's fingers clawed as his arms tried their best to move. He had just enough strength to raise his arms up to the armrests, but not up to his face. He shook as best he could, but was never able to do anything more than rattle the chair a little. As he struggled, his left hand touched the cold wall beside him. His pinky finger brushed against the coarse stucco.

The walls of the hotel slowly spilled their secrets, as if Ben had spent a lifetime studying the architectural plans of the building. He knew what the room on the other side of the wall looked like, and how it was connected to another suite that also looked the same. He could sense the electrical wires that snaked through the thin walls, protected by a metal sheathe. He could feel the bed in their neighbor's room as it succumbed to the weight of a tossing occupant. As the night went on, and The Skeleton Man lingered alone in the dark bathroom of Michael Harper's hotel room, new possibilities presented themselves. He began to comprehend weaving in and out of the world The Watcher had come from, and the one where Michael Harper lived. He knew that once Michael fell asleep, he would be susceptible to The Skeleton Man's power, but Ben needed to practice first.

On the other side of the wall, snoring as Buffy the Vampire Slayer played on his television, was a man named Charles Dunbar. The Skeleton Man would test his powers on this stranger as he waited for Michael Harper to fall asleep again. The Skeleton Man perfected his lies.

CHAPTER 7 – The CORD

Philadelphia
June 15th, 1943

Two pillars rose to twice the height of a man on either side of a large, steel box. Lyle, Vess, and Major Groves were in a cavernous bay of the USS Eldridge. Lyle would've never guessed the ship housed such a large room, and he marveled at the space as Groves led them across the catwalk that looked down on the area of interest.

"There she is," said Groves as he motioned over the side of the railing. They stood on a walkway about twenty feet up, and Lyle could look through the grated metal that they walked across to see the floor beneath, causing his stomach to churn. Groves and Vess were focused on the spectacular machine that was the only thing housed within the gigantic space. "Your Charged Oscillating Radiation Distributor." Then Groves looked at Lyle and said, "Or CORD for short."

"It's magnificent," said Vess, unwilling to look at anything other than the machine below. His face was alight, like a child staring in through a Macy's window during the holidays. "I can't believe I'm here, looking at it." His voice was tempered by reverence, as if he were daring to whisper in church. "I've studied Tesla's drawings a thousand times, but seeing it in person..." he grinned as he looked at Groves. "It's magnificent."

"Well, let's not spend any more time dithering about up here," said Groves. "Let's go have a look."

Vess and Lyle followed behind Groves as he walked down a circular staircase to the solid floor beneath. Lyle could feel the gentle sway of the ship, although it wasn't as severe as he'd feared. He wasn't much of a seaman, having thrown up as a child while fishing and never giving it another chance. This ship, however, seemed too large to be affected much by the water around it. The USS Eldridge was like an island unto itself.

Vess approached the CORD as if drawing near a fragile masterpiece. Lyle got a better chance to study the monstrosity. The pillars on the side rose higher than the unit in the center, and four rings were independently mounted by a rod that stuck out of apertures on the pillar they haloed. The rods were each different sizes, with the largest on the bottom and the smallest on top, and a foot-sized gap separated each. The pillars were both adorned with massive globes on top that cast shadows down over the center box. Thick wires littered the floor, crawling out from the pillars and connecting to the square hub, which was fitted with various levers, switches, and gauges that Lyle was certain he'd never understand even given a course on their function.

"It's perfect," said Groves with certainty. He stood stoic, his arms clasped behind his back as he watched Vess inspect the machine. "Down to every last detail."

"They're silver?" asked Vess as he approached the rings of one of the two pillars. "You didn't lace this with copper to save money?"

"No expense spared," said Groves. "You're looking at a machine that's worth more than the GDP of some small countries." He chuckled, but neither Lyle nor Vess reciprocated.

"Damn," said Lyle, trying to add to the conversation. "That's quite a machine you fellows built. But, forgive me for asking, why the hell'd you build it? What's it do?"

"That, my good man," said Groves as he walked to stand beside Lyle. He put his huge arm on Lyle's shoulders, making him feel like a child at his father's side. "Is a mighty good question. Care to answer it, Vess? Because we haven't been able to get it to do a damn thing."

"You turned it on?" asked Vess, perturbed.

"We had to make sure it worked."

"And?"

"It turns on," said Groves. "I can tell you that much. But other than being a light-show straight out of a Lon Chaney film, it didn't impress."

"There's more to it than flicking a switch," said Vess with dismissive venom in his words.

"I'd feel more comfortable if you let me bring Dr. Felcher in for…" Groves was interrupted by Vess.

"No, no, no. We've been over this before. We have to limit the number of people present in the room. For crying out loud, Groves, I'm surprised you were even able to turn it on considering how little attention you paid to Tesla's work. You have to follow everything down to the very last detail."

"We did," said Groves, a sternness returning to his mannerism as he stood straighter and spoke a little harsher. It was clear that he didn't enjoy being questioned by the likes of Vess. "I just don't feel comfortable leaving this up to the two of you, with no one else observing."

"You'll get over it," said Vess as he went on inspecting the CORD, ignoring Groves' apparent displeasure.

Leslie Groves muttered something under his breath, and then frowned as he glanced over at Lyle. "I don't know how men like us put up with guys like him."

Lyle snickered and nodded in agreement, more out of nervousness than concurrence.

"I'd give anything to be with a squad in the Balkans than here arguing with his type," said Groves for only Lyle's benefit. Then he raised his voice so that Vess could hear, "I'll leave you to it then. We set sail in about thirty minutes. Will that be enough time?"

Vess was knelt down beside the CORD, inspecting one of the multitudes of wires that wound their way across the floor. He rose his hand and waved without looking back. "That should be fine."

"We'll keep in contact with the radio over there," said Groves as he pointed to a table set off to the side with a single chair beside it and a large radio and microphone on top.

"Fine," said Vess, still not giving Groves his full attention. "We'll be ready. Right, Lyle?"

Lyle chuckled and shrugged, "Whatever you say, boss."

Vess finally looked back at Groves and said with assurance, "We'll be ready. It'll only take ten or fifteen minutes for the CORD to charge."

"Make sure to wait for us to raise the anchor before turning it on," said Groves.

Vess grinned back at him, smug as he said, "So you did read Tesla's notes."

Branson
Shortly before 4:00 AM
March 13th, 2012

Charles Dunbar was at a bar that he didn't recognize, but it felt oddly familiar. He'd been to hundreds of bars over the years, and the patrons here could've been transplanted from any number of them. The bar had a southwestern theme, with too much wood and too many dead animals staring down from plaques hanging on the walls. The barstool was plush and comfortable, and he swiveled on it as he waited for the bartender.

"What's yer poison?" asked the husky man behind the counter as he washed a beer mug with a dirty rag. He had dark black hair that was cut short and a twirled mustache that made him look like a caricature from a different age. The man could've posed for the poster of a western and nothing about his countenance would've given him away.

"Whiskey sour," said Charles, ordering his tried-and-true favorite.

"You got it," said the bartender as he started to make the drink.

Charles reached for his pocket to retrieve his cellphone, but found it missing. "Son of a bitch," he said, although his voice was drowned out by the southern rock that dominated the bar. He'd meant to bring his phone so that he could call home, but must've forgotten it at the hotel.

A gunshot startled him.

Charles spun in his seat to see what had happened, but the crowded bar seemed ignorant of the noise. When he turned back around, the bartender was dropping down a coaster in front of him before setting his drink on it.

"Did you hear that?" asked Charles of the bartender. "It sounded like a gunshot."

"Oh, that's just the weasels. Don't worry about it."

"The weasels?" asked Charles, confounded and amused.

"Yep, we've got them in here all the time. Best way to deal with them is one in the head." The bartender made a gun with his right hand and then set his fingers to the side of his own head. "You've got to get them right here. Right behind the ear. Pow." He mimed a gunshot and smiled wide.

"Weasels?" asked Charles as if he were hearing a joke that he didn't want to admit to not understanding. "Like the rodent?"

The bartender shrugged.

Charles wasn't content letting the conversation end. He was fearful, as if the bartender had somehow threatened him. "You mean the rodents, right? Like those little weasels that kill chickens?"

The bartender ignored Charles, and started talking with another patron. Charles got up from his seat and moved down the bar, desperate to get an answer. "You're not talking about people, right? You mean animals. You're shooting animals, right?"

"Settle down, Mr. Dunbar," said a fat woman sitting at the bar. She was in a biker outfit, with a leather vest and gloves, and her grey hair was pulled back in a ponytail. Flies buzzed around her as she swiveled on her seat to face Charles. She lifted a cell phone off the bar and offered it to him. "Your wife's been calling."

Charles took his phone, and didn't question why the stranger had it. He saw that he'd missed a number of calls, and then noticed that his wife had texted him. His hands were shaking as he read the text.

"Charlie, Amber called. She told me everything. You weasel."

He looked up and saw that the bartender had his hand shaped like a gun again, but this time he was pointing at Charles. The bartender had one eye closed, as if he were aiming down a gun's sight, and he was grinning wide.

Charles started to shake his head as he backed away. "It was a mistake. She found out years ago. We moved on. We got past it."

"I see you, Charles Dunbar," said the bartender as he continued to look at him as if staring down the barrel of a gun.

"That was years ago!" Charles backed away in the direction of an exit.

He bumped into someone as he was moving to the exit, and the person grabbed his shoulder before spitting in his ear. Charles recoiled, and then pushed himself away as he wiped the spit from his ear canal. The man that had done it was short, but thick, with a grey and white beard and sunglasses.

"Weasel!" said the man before spitting again.

Then the rest of the patrons began to chide Charles as well, screaming, "Weasel," and spitting at him.

"Sixteen years!" screamed the woman at the bar that had given him back his phone. "We were married for sixteen years and he was willing to throw it all away for some cunt with big tits." The obese woman grasped her breasts and shook them.

"You're not my wife," said Charles, but his defense was overwhelmed by the jeers of the crowd.

They pushed and tugged, kicked and punched, and Charles found himself in a desperate attempt to flee. He covered his face, and stared at the floor as he tried to push his way out. As he started to fear that he'd be pushed to the ground and trampled, he saw that he'd miraculously made his way to the entrance of the bar. He pulled the door open and rushed outside, expecting to be chased.

The door slammed shut behind him hard enough to rattle the walls, and none of the patrons followed him out. He was panting, alone in the gravel parking lot of the seedy bar. It was the middle of the night, but there were no stars in the sky. Only the moon sat above in the bleak night, a Cheshire cat smile on a black canvas.

He inspected his injuries, but was pleased to discover that he was mostly unharmed. He cursed as he wiped the spit from his cheeks.

"Charles," said a familiar voice.

He looked up and saw Amber, the girl from corporate that he'd cheated on his wife with after getting drunk at a conference a few years back. "Amber, what are you doing here?" asked Charles.

"I just wanted to see you," said Amber as she stayed far away. She was in her mid-twenties, cute but slightly overweight, with long blonde hair and brown eyes. When she smiled, he was reminded of his wife when she was her age.

"I'm sorry, Amber, but I really can't. I'm sorry, but I can't."

"I see you now, Charles Dunbar."

Charles stared at her as if she'd threatened him. "Why do people keep saying that?"

Amber smiled, but her teeth were chattering as if she were cold. Then she put her finger to her lips, and he noticed that her eyes were glassy, as if covered in gel. She pushed her hand to her jaw in an attempt to stop her chattering teeth, but it didn't help.

"Amber, are you okay?"

She pressed both hands against her jaw, and when she spoke it was as if she were in pain. Her words came slow, and between clenched teeth. "Will…" Her body quivered. "You…" Blood dripped from her lips as if she were crushing her own head. "Help?"

Charles staggered back. "What the hell's wrong with you?"

Amber twisted her head, causing a sharp crack as if she were trying to break her own neck. She didn't succeed, and then twisted her head in the opposite direction, harder this time, causing a similar crack of bone. Blood fell in thick strands down her arms as her teeth rattled. She released her head, but continued to violently shake it back and forth. Streams of blood cascaded away from her mouth, striking the gravel near Charles's feet.

Then suddenly, as if the world had been frozen, she stopped and stared directly at him.

"I like it when the daddies scream."

Charles tried to run, but the gravel slipped out beneath him as if he were trying to climb a hill. He fell to his knees and clawed at the ground, trying to find a handhold to pull himself forward. The entire world seemed to be flipped on its side, and the gravel slid out from his grip, tumbling backward at the slightest provocation. He screamed, and dug his fingers in, but he couldn't help but slide towards Amber.

When he looked back, the girl was standing where she'd been, unaffected by the tilting world around them. Her body looked thinner now, and taller, as if she were being stretched. The skin on her face looked as if it was being pulled downward, and her eyes sagged until her cheeks ripped. The skeleton within her was growing beyond the space her skin allowed, and it was bursting forth like a seedling from soil. The chattering monster pulled the remnants of her flesh and hair from his head and threw it to the side.

Charles screamed, and The Skeleton Man laughed.

"Yes, daddy, let's see how loud you can scream tonight."

The creature advanced, stepping forth from the husk it had inhabited. He was tall, thin, and wearing a suit that hung limply on his frame. His bones were held together by white and black sinew, and the white bone peaked through Amber's bright red blood that covered his entire body.

Charles screamed for help, but no one came. No matter how hard he struggled to move away from the creature that stalked him, he was sliding back.

The Skeleton Man knelt beside Charles, and thrust his hand into the man's back. Charles felt the skeleton's fingers pierce his body like knives, and he gasped in agony as the creature wiggled within him.

The Skeleton Man saddled his victim, and as Charles tried to reach back to fight him off, the creature swiped at his hands, cutting him as if his fingers were blades.

"Please, let me go. Please."

"No," said The Skeleton Man through chattering teeth.

"This is a nightmare," said Charles as he clenched his eyes shut, hoping it would all end.

"What difference does it make," asked The Skeleton Man, "if the dreamer never wakes?" He twisted his fingers inside of Charles's back, causing the man to convulse in agony.

"Keep screaming," said The Skeleton Man. "Call The Watchers. Let them watch us play."

CHAPTER 8 – The Ship

Widowsfield
In The Watcher's new nightmare

Desmond cowered from the light. While the other residents of Widowsfield happily accepted their demise, and allowed themselves to dissolve in the warmth of a heavenly light, Desmond stuck to the shadows. He knew there were still children here, caught like flies in the web of Widowsfield. He'd heard his son, and the cries of other boys, all of them scared and pleading for help. He wouldn't leave Raymond behind.

Was this rapture? Had Widowsfield been a purgatory for the sinful to waste away in? Had God finally forgiven them, but forgot about the children? Desmond wasn't sure what had happened, or why the gates of Heaven had opened. He was vaguely aware that he'd been participating in a sort of mock-existence, and that a long time had passed since March 14th, 1996. He also knew, although it was maddening to admit, that he was dead. He had no expectation of old age, or to watch his boy grow up, or to reconcile with his daughter, at least not on Earth. However, he refused to pass on without first finding his beloved Raymond.

The streets of Widowsfield were glimmering from the rays that escaped the clouds above, but the shadows that Desmond clung to were growing colder every minute. He was moving down Main Street, yelling out for his lost child, but only the vague cries of frightened children drew him forward. It was like the distant howl of coyotes, but he heard the boys weeping in the web of Widowsfield, stuck and unable to climb into the light.

Desmond dared to glance into the sky, and saw the shadows of men and women dancing in the clouds, as if angels were welcoming the souls home. He felt a longing to be with them; to give in and walk out into the street to feel the warmth of heaven's glow. He'd been pressed to the brick wall of a building, hiding in the shadows afforded by an awning above, but now he found himself coming closer to the golden hued pavement that was awash in the heavenly light.

Then he heard the cries of a child, and he clenched his eyes shut to avoid the spell the angels cast upon him.

"No," said Desmond as he slunk back into the shade. "I'm not leaving without him."

He clung to the wall, and stared down, refusing to allow himself the comfort the light offered. As he stood there, shivering in the cold absence of grace, the light began to dissipate. There was a fog rising, blocking out the glow above. The streets darkened as the fog grew, closing Widowsfield in like the glass of a snow globe.

As the final sliver of light was swallowed up, Desmond heard the voice of a child.

"Hello?"

He searched for the source, and saw an unfamiliar boy, no older than ten, wandering Main Street. Desmond ran to him, startling the child who was already on the verge of tears.

"I'm here," said Desmond as he approached the frightened, cowering boy. He got on his knees and was careful to be gentle with the child. "What's your name?"

"Jeremy," said the boy. "I lost him."

"Lost who?" asked Desmond.

The boy looked at Desmond, frightened and untrusting. "The Skeleton Man."

Desmond felt a pang of fear and recognition when the boy uttered the name.

Jeremy backed away from Desmond and shook his head. Desmond stood, and took a step towards the boy, his hands out as if pleading for Jeremy's trust.

"I can't reach the fog," said Jeremy, his trembling voice revealing his terror. "He used to hide us in the fog, but now it's way up there." He pointed to the sky. "No one's here to save us."

"I can help," said Desmond, although he wasn't sure how. "Let me help you."

"No you can't," said Jeremy. "None of the daddies can."

Desmond was going to chase the boy as Jeremy ran, but then he heard a grinding, metallic sound behind him. He turned and discovered that Main Street no longer drew a line through downtown Widowsfield, but now it went straight through knots of black wires that feigned shapes similar to the buildings that had once been there. The cords moved, like earthworms bought at a bait shop and stuffed into a cup for a fishing trip. Then, between the wires, white globes began to emerge. The balls spun, revealing pupils that stared at Desmond.

He was too terrified to move, and only managed to take meager steps backward, as if hypnotized by what he saw. A flash of lightning crackled above, green and powerful, and caused the hair on Desmond's neck and arms to stand straight.

The grinding of metal got louder, and then the steady cadence of a hammer's strike, one each second, came closer, like the pounding of an approaching soldier's boots. Desmond finally tried to flee, but found that his feet were caught in a web of wires beneath him. He sunk into the road as the wires moved to let him fall. He cried out, and grasped at the cords, but they slithered through his grip, growing thinner or wider as needed.

"Suffer not the aged men," said a deep voice amid the clamor of the chaos. "For their fear has dulled with time."

"Where's my boy?" screamed Desmond as the wires drew tighter around him, constricting him until they caused pain. "Where's Raymond."

"Suffer not the mothers, for they have no fear for self."

"Give me my boy!" Desmond's voice croaked as the cords drew tighter. He was being pulled further down, and the wires grasped him like arms, dragging him into their depths and tightening around his limbs. Once his chest sank into the mire, he felt the bones in his legs begin to twist. The pain was excruciating, and he screamed in agony as the twisting cords pulled his flesh off his bones. The cords' black color was now tinted red with his blood, and the grinding never ceased.

"Suffer the children, for they know not yet of fear."

Desmond was crushed in the grip of Widowsfield. His skin, meat, and bones were grinded within the churn of wire, swallowed into the black as the world around him came alive. The Watchers preferred the sacrifice of children above all else, but every creature's suffering brought them pleasure. The Watchers cursed the living, and wanted nothing more than to give them something to fear. The Watchers had existed as envious creatures, forced to gaze upon the lives of those oblivious to the eyes that studied them. However, The Watcher in Widowsfield had been given a sacrifice, but now his grip had loosened. Hundreds of souls had slipped through his web, which only made him hold tighter to the ones that were left.

The survivors of Widowsfield would learn the true extent of suffering. He would mold a world devoted to ruining them in every way he could conceive.

"No one mourns for the ones lost here."

Inside Cada E.I.B.'s Compound
March 13th, 2012
3:45 AM

"We found him." Rachel had called Alma and spoke with a mix of satisfaction and weariness. Stephen and Rachel had been calling various hotels around the area, pretending to be dispatchers from a police station who were hunting for a suspected kidnapper. They used Helen's description of the car that Michael had stolen, as well as a description of Michael, to see if he'd checked in. They also suggested that the man they were looking for might be traveling with an emaciated man, most likely confined to a wheelchair or otherwise barely mobile.

"That's great," said Alma on the other line.

Rachel gave her the address of the hotel in Branson, and explained that she'd told the concierge not to alert the guest, and that they'd be sending a squad car over. Alma was concerned that the hotel might call the police to make sure it wasn't a prank.

"I doubt it," said Rachel. "The kid sounded pretty scared. Just hurry up and get there."

"We're not too far," said Alma. "Thanks for the help, but we need something else from you too."

"Sure, what is it?" asked Rachel.

"Can you check into the rumors about a Greek ship being in Widowsfield in 1996?"

"Hold on," said Rachel. "You should check with Stephen. He knows more about that stuff." She handed the phone to her husband, who was standing beside her in the cramped room where they'd formerly been tied down to gurneys. "She's asking about a Greek boat."

Stephen frowned and shrugged, but took the phone anyhow. "Hey Alma, what's up?"

He heard Alma giving the name of the hotel to someone else in the van, and then she returned her attention to the phone. "Stephen, I need you to check into something for me."

"What is it?"

"I remember getting a call a few years back from a conspiracy theorist that wanted to ask me questions about Widowsfield. He was talking about a Greek boat, but I didn't pay any attention to him. I used to get a hundred calls from goofballs like him, talking about Bigfoot and aliens and that sort of stuff. But now I think the boat theory might have some weight to it. In the dream, or whatever it was, I saw a boat out in the Jackson Reservoir. We think that's where this all started. Something happened on that boat that caused everything."

"I can look into it," said Stephen. "I never ran across anything about a ship before you brought it up the other day, but I'll search around for whatever I can find."

"Okay, thanks."

"Hey," said Stephen before Alma could hang up. "What are you guys planning on doing once you find your dad?"

She didn't answer immediately, and then gave a tired chuckle. "I don't really know."

"He's dangerous," said Stephen. "You guys need to be careful."

"We will be. You too," said Alma.

Stephen was surprised and asked, "What do we need to be careful about?"

"Well, for starters, you're still in Widowsfield," said Alma. "And second, that guy that Paul shot in the foot is still wandering around there somewhere."

"Oh yeah," said Stephen. "I forgot about that guy. One of the nurses was going to go look for him. I guess he left a trail of blood."

"Just be careful," said Alma. "I'll call back after we find my brother."

Stephen said goodbye, and then walked warily over to one of the doors to their room. The door he was beside led to the hallway, and another door was connected to the sleepers' room beside them. He locked the door to the hall, and then went to do the same at the other side of the room.

"What's wrong?" asked Rachel.

"Nothing," said Stephen, trying to persuade his wife that he wasn't concerned when he plainly was.

"Why are you locking the doors?"

Stephen paused at the second door. The upper half of the door consisted of a large reinforced window, with black, crisscrossed wire within the glass. Beyond the door he could see the writhing bodies of the women that had woken up, but the male sleepers still lay silent and were staring at the ceiling. Helen was busy assisting the female sleepers, attempting to sedate them as they continued to cause themselves harm.

There was no lock on the door that led to the sleepers' room, so Stephen pushed one of the gurneys in front of it before locking its wheels.

"Stephen, what's wrong?" Rachel was concerned by her husband's behavior.

"Nothing, I just think we need to be careful. I don't know if we should trust that nurse, and Paul said there's a guy named Oliver running around."

"Do you know what Alma was talking about?" asked Rachel. "About a boat in the reservoir?"

Stephen shook his head. "No, but we can look around online and see what we can find."

Rachel let Stephen sit in front of the laptop, and shadowed him as he began perusing his usual conspiracy sites. He'd always had a fascination with the conspiracy community, while Rachel had been the one to often discount the bizarre theories he uncovered. Now, after everything she'd experienced in Widowsfield, she was willing to reconsider her prejudice about the conspiracies Stephen often babbled on about.

Rachel yawned, her weariness finally catching up with her as Stephen searched various sites.

"If you're sleepy, I've got my energy pills. There should be some in that box where they put our stuff."

"The diet pills?" asked Rachel. "Are you still taking those?"

Stephen nodded and answered with an unconcerned, "Uh-huh."

"Why?"

"I don't know," said Stephen as if annoyed. "I like them."

"But you don't need them. You're already skinny."

"I take them for the energy," said Stephen, his frustration with the debate growing. "Look, you can take one if you want, or don't. I don't care. I was just trying to help."

"Geeze, calm down," said Rachel. "I wasn't trying to start a fight. I just didn't know you were still taking that stuff. You should quit."

Stephen groaned and then said, "Do you have to lecture me about that now? Who gives a shit? It's not like they're illegal or anything. Don't we have bigger things to worry about right now?"

"Fine, fine," said Rachel as she put her hands up in defeat. "I'm sorry." She was too tired to argue any longer, but she decided against looking for the pills out of spite. Instead, she crawled back up onto one of the gurneys to lie down while waiting for Stephen to find something. After several minutes of silence, she closed her eyes and felt herself nearly drifting to sleep. Despite how bizarre and terrifying the day had been, she was still exhausted. Her lack of sleep caused her to feel like she was lying on a boat, with the waves gently rolling beneath her. However, the fact that the gurney was on wheels kept her in constant fear that the illusion of movement was real, and that the bed was rolling. That kept her from falling all the way to sleep, and she jolted up in fear several times after feeling like the bed was about to roll out from beneath her.

After the third time she jolted awake, she cursed and said, "Have you found anything yet?"

Stephen was reading an article online, and held up his finger to tell her to give him a minute. After a little while longer, he said, "That's weird."

"What's weird?" asked Rachel.

"That can't be a coincidence."

"What can't be?" asked Rachel, feeling as if her husband was purposefully ignoring her.

"It looks like people have been finding evidence of ships being built all over the place. Usually at abandoned military sites. They're not finding the actual ships, but… here, look." He moved aside so that Rachel could see the computer screen.

She sat up carefully, still unsettled by the gurney's mobility, and looked at the picture that Stephen had found. It looked like a patch of dry earth but there was a clear indentation in the ground that resembled the shape of a battleship. It also appeared as if there were dirt roads leading to the area, as well as a large square that might've once been a building. Everything that had been built there was now gone, but the footprint hadn't been erased.

"What am I looking at?"

"This is a picture someone found using Google Earth. This one's at White Sands Missile Range in New Mexico. And there are others, all similar, as if someone built a huge ship out in the middle of nowhere and then disassembled it."

"Is that what happened here?" asked Rachel.

"I don't know," said Stephen as he studied the picture. "Maybe."

"But I thought Alma said the ship had been in the reservoir. Why are the others on dry land?"

"I don't know," said Stephen. "I'm not sure it's even related, but it's still weird. The official explanation for this one is that they were digging up dirt to build a berm to protect people from missile tests, but why did they dig it in the exact shape of a battleship?"

"Yeah, that doesn't make much sense," said Rachel. "Have any of the sites mentioned them being Greek boats?"

"No, not that I've found."

"Do you think we should call Alma?"

Stephen shook his head. "No, not yet. There's not much to tell her. I'll keep looking for something else."

After a moment's contemplation, Rachel said, "I can't help but feel like we're being really stupid here."

"What do you mean?"

She looked around the room and shook her head. "Don't you think we should've called the cops by now?"

"Absolutely not," said Stephen with conviction. "They're not going to take our side. I promise you that."

"But there's a room full of prisoners over there," she pointed to the sleepers' room. "And they did something to us too. Back at home, when I was beating Alma at Scrabble the other night, you said that this Cada E.I.B. company brokered weapons between the US and other countries. Right?"

"Yeah," said Stephen.

"Well, maybe that's all this is. Maybe they developed some nerve toxin that screws with your head, and gives you nightmares."

"I don't think they manufactured weapons," said Stephen. "From what I read, they just brokered deals between countries."

"Well, they're also in the business of hiding hundreds of victims," said Rachel. "So I don't think it's a stretch to think that maybe they're doing more than just brokering deals."

"Yeah, you might be right," said Stephen. "But there's still no way I'm calling the cops."

"Why the hell not?" asked Rachel.

"Because this shit's been going on here for sixteen years, and no one's done anything about it as of yet. I know it's crazy to think that the entire police force all around this area is in on it, but it's also crazy to think that none of them ever investigated everything that happened here in '96. Every resident of this town vanished, and I never saw anything about a massive investigation. That's not the sort of thing that should happen without a lot of people asking a bunch of questions, but here in Widowsfield it was just swept under the carpet with some bullshit excuse about the people here being in a meth ring. Someone up high in the chain of command of the police had to have been in on keeping this quiet."

"Maybe the FBI or the military took over the investigation," said Rachel.

"Yeah, maybe. And maybe if we call the cops now, they'll hang up with us and then get right on the phone with the FBI or the military to let them know that people are snooping around in the town again. Fuck that. We'll deal with this ourselves."

Rachel laughed, and then she saw that Stephen wasn't joking and she started to laugh harder. "We're going to deal with it ourselves? What are you talking about? What are we going to do?"

Stephen smirked and gave his wife a demeaning look of disapproval. "How can you claim to be a reporter and still have no concept of the weapon we've got on our side?"

"What are you talking about?"

Stephen pointed over to the box that had their belongings in it. "My camera is in that box. They already erased the footage I had of Widowsfield from before, but the camera still works." Then he pointed at the computer that Helen had provided them with. "And we've got a computer right here."

"You want to broadcast what's happening here?" asked Rachel as his plan dawned on her.

He nodded in satisfaction. "Damn straight."

Rachel's expression turned from intrigued to concerned. "Don't you think they'd find out and come shut us down immediately?"

"We don't have to do it live."

"But then how can we be sure the info gets out?" asked Rachel. "What if someone gets to us first?"

"We can do it in segments, and then put them on our site with a delay on publishing," said Stephen. "It's not hard to do that. We can start by recording that horror-show in the next room, and upload the video with it set to publish a couple nights from now, like on the 15th. Then, as long as we get out of this alive, we can stop the video from publishing and figure out how we want to handle everything. But, if something does end up happening to us, then at least we know that the information will get out. And if we end up unconscious and strapped to a gurney again, if the video gets out then we'll have a shot at someone coming to rescue us."

Rachel grinned and said, “Stephen Knight, I was wrong about you.”

“What about?”

“You’re not as stupid as you look.”

“Ha ha,” said Stephen with a sideways grin. “You should get your makeup and do yourself up. You’ve still got bedhead.”

Rachel grimaced as she patted her hair down. “Are we doing this now?”

“Might as well,” said Stephen. “Who knows what this place has in store for us next.”

CHAPTER 9 – The Right Door

Philadelphia
June 15th, 1943

Lyle felt the immediate surge of electricity after Vess turned the CORD on. The ample hair on Lyle's arms stood up as blue arcs of electricity crackled across the silver rings of both pillars. Then the machine began to make a grinding sound as the rings spun, controlled by a motor hidden within the pillar. Each ring spun opposite its neighbors, and lightning streaked between them with more intensity as the machine sped up.

"Holy hell!" Lyle had to shout over the crackling bursts.

Vess was grinning as if he couldn't help himself. He pointed at the pillars and screamed, "Watch it. Watch the electricity. It should change color."

Lyle stared at the machine, but had to shield his eyes from the intensity of the light. The walls of the massive bay of the USS Eldridge flashed blue as the electricity intensified, but then Lyle saw that the color was changing. Slowly, the hue turned green.

Then Vess pulled several of the levers on the control panel of the CORD. When he did, the electricity died, and the rings began to slow down. The explosive noise calmed as Vess cheered.

"It works! I can't believe they did it. Groves and his men actually did it. The CORD works, Lyle!"

"Fine, great," said Lyle as he ran his hand over his arm to see if his hair would still stand on its own again. "But, what the hell does it do?"

Vess moved to the side, away from the control panel that he'd been operating. His tall, slender frame was dwarfed by the size of the monstrous contraption Leslie Groves had built. Lyle wasn't an uneducated man, although he knew he wasn't on the same level as the men he'd been surrounded with that day. From the talk of Tesla, to shaking the hand of the world's most famous living scientist, Lyle felt like an ant among giants. He'd discounted Vess as a well-funded lunatic when they first met, and had only agreed to the job for the ample pay the man promised. Today, however, his previous impressions had been proven incorrect. As he and Vess stood within the bowels of a massive navy vessel, staring at a machine that seemed plucked from a Frankenstein set, Lyle knew he'd been thrust into the center of what might be a world-changing experiment. Unfortunately, he didn't understand any of it.

Lyle Everman had answered an ad in the paper requesting the assistance of people who believed that they possessed some level of psychic power. Lyle had never taken much stock in the world of psychics, believing the majority of them to be charlatans in dark rooms with tricks up their sleeves and bells on their boots. However, his mother had always told him that he possessed unnatural gifts, and that she'd witnessed his abilities manifest shortly after his bout with tuberculosis. Instead of being intrigued by her son's newfound abilities, Lyle's mother was terrified of them. She called it his 'curse' and insisted that he keep quiet about his unnatural powers. Those abilities, combined with how the combination of his illness and his father's polio had bankrupted their family, led the Mrs. Everman to shun her child. He left home at a young age, and had been wandering the country ever since, doing whatever he needed to survive.

Lyle wasn't certain how his abilities worked, but there was no denying that he had a better chance of guessing another player's hand in poker than any other person he knew. His card playing ability had been the reason he'd been able to forego a proper job for most of his life, only recently having to give up gambling after having a run-in with mobsters that were certain he was a cheater, but just couldn't prove it. He'd fled New York, and settled in Philadelphia, where he saw the ad asking for psychics to come participate in a test. All applicants would receive a small amount of pay, and anyone that could prove ability would be paid handsomely for their service.

How a simple card trick had earned Lyle a spot on the Eldridge, observing this experiment, was a mystery to him.

Vess lifted a latch on the side of the square that seemed to have no function. Then he pulled on it, revealing it was attached to a door that was otherwise imperceptible. He pulled the door wide, and then motioned inside.

"This is where you come in, Mr. Everman," said Vess. "Figuratively and literally," Vess grinned, which caused him to look more maniacal than usual.

"What are you on about?" asked Lyle as if Vess was fooling him. "I'm not going in there."

"Don't worry, it's insulated," said Vess. "You won't be harmed."

"Even so," Lyle laughed as he shook his head, "I think I'd rather stay out here."

"Look, here," said Vess as he positioned the door to reveal that the inside of it was filled with a black layer of rubber. "The inside is insulated. You won't be in any danger. In fact, inside here is the safest place in the room."

"Are we both getting in?" asked Lyle.

"No, I have to stay outside to operate the CORD."

"Then I'm not going in neither."

"I think you'll change your mind when I tell you what this machine is for," said Vess.

"Maybe, but unless Rita Hayworth's in there with her top off, I ain't going in." He crossed his arms and grinned as if the two of them were sharing a laugh.

"Through this door, Mr. Everman, you're going to play a part in the greatest experiment in the history of man. Your name will go down as the single most important explorer to ever live."

"Explorer of what? A big, empty death trap?"

"An explorer of other worlds."

Lyle frowned and looked suspiciously at the machine. "I'm not following."

"You have a gift, Lyle," said Vess as he stepped closer. "You showed me that during your test. It's undeniable. You have an ability that's one in a million, or even one in a billion. And it's because of that ability that you're here. It's the reason that you might be able to help us put an end to this damnable war; maybe even an end to all war."

"How's that exactly?"

"Tesla had a theory that he was working on in secret for the last couple of decades before his death. This," Vess stepped back over to the CORD and slapped his hand against the metal side, "is the result of his research. You see, he theorized that our dimension, the very world around us, is actually just one of several layers of existence."

"You're losing me," said Lyle. "What's that supposed to mean?"

"Imagine a stack of paper," said Vess. "Now imagine that one of the pages in that stack represents our world. On that single page exists everything you know of as reality. As human beings, we only exist on that page, but our energy isn't confined to it."

"Our energy?"

"Our souls," said Vess. "Some people call them souls, others say spirits, but scientists refer to it as energy. Believe me, most scientists would love nothing more than to disregard spirits as nothing but unsubstantiated nonsense. But they can't. In 1901, a man named MacDougall proved that the human body loses 21 grams upon the moment of their death."

Vess gazed at Lyle with wild, excited eyes, but Lyle shook his head and said, "I'm not following. What's that prove?"

"That's the weight of our soul, of our energy, leaving and moving on once we die, but they've never been able to figure out what the weight change is caused by, or where that energy goes." Vess tapped his index finger to his temple and said, "But I know, and so did Tesla."

"Where's it go then?"

"To the next page," said Vess in satisfaction.

"Next page of what?" asked Lyle.

"Of our stack of paper," said Vess, frustrated that Lyle wasn't following along with the metaphor. "It moves beyond our existence and into another dimension. That's what we're here for. We're going to prove the existence of another dimension beyond our own. But what Tesla understood was that if this were true, and that energy was being passed between the dimensions, then these dimensions have to be inexorably linked. The energy that escapes from our dead bodies must somehow be able to pass into the other dimension, and eventually make it back here again. A sort of spiritual resurrection, or reincarnation, if you will. Otherwise, the energy around us would eventually be sapped away, slowly but surely, every time someone passed. That was the inspiration for this machine. This," he slapped his palm on the CORD again, "is the doorway in and out of this other dimension. This machine uses electromagnetic radiation to affect gravity, and brings our dimension, or our page, closer to the next, making the leap through easier to achieve."

"So why's the military involved? And how's this going to help us stop war?"

"Remember that I told you how the FBI seized Tesla's work?"

"Yes."

"They did it because they're desperate to prove to the world that the United States is the ultimate power on Earth. That's the only reason we're at war, Lyle, because if we let the Russians save Europe from Hitler, then it'll only be a matter of time before Communism sweeps through all the continents and puts an end to our beloved capitalism." Vess couldn't hide the sarcasm in his voice when he mentioned 'beloved' capitalism.

"How would this help end the war? Is it a weapon?" asked Lyle.

"No, not exactly," said Vess. "But if we can knock on the door to heaven, it might be God that answers."

"So you're saying this thing's supposed to help us talk to God?" Lyle couldn't quite believe what he was being told.

Vess cringed at the question and said, "More than likely not the God you've been raised to believe in, that's for sure, but a God none-the-less. It's my theory that a large percentage of the religions on Earth are inspired by whatever lies beyond that door." He pointed at the door that led inside of the CORD.

Vess paused, and Lyle scowled as he looked at the CORD, trying to figure out how he felt about what Vess had said. "I'm not too religious, Vess." Lyle's God-fearing mother, and her insistence that Lyle's abilities were a gift of the devil, had guaranteed her son would stray from the flock.

"Neither am I."

"But you said…"

"God is just a word we use to explain something about our world that we haven't figured out yet."

"Then, why are you saying you want to use this thing to talk to God? You're not making a lick of sense."

"Because I'm confident that this machine can connect us with a layer of existence that we've only hypothesized exists. And if we're right, then there are entities in this other dimension that are playing a role in the very fabric of our own existence. Our theory is that people like you, people with extrasensory perception, are tapping into the knowledge of this other dimension. In other words, you're closer to the door than the rest of us. That's why we need someone like you to be the first to step through, because you're already halfway there."

"And you think there's going to be something there? Something alive?"

"All we have are theories," said Vess. "It's reasonable to think that, if we can live here, then something else can live there." Vess pointed at the box.

"And how can doing this help with the war?" asked Lyle.

Vess looked saddened and apprehensive, but explained. "There are things going on in this country that I'm loathe to admit, Lyle."

"Like what things?"

Vess looked as stern and serious as Lyle had ever seen him. "Like the development of the strongest weapon mankind has ever dreamed of. You heard the major talking about what Oppenheimer is doing in New Mexico, right?"

"Some of it," said Lyle. "Why? What's he got going on out there?"

"A man by the name of Jean Joliet-Curie discovered something six years ago that could destroy the planet. And I'm hoping to keep that from happening."

"What did he discover?" asked Lyle.

"He created a nuclear reactor."

"What in the devil is that?"

"It's the first step in the creation of a bomb that might very well end life as we know it on this planet. Roosevelt was convinced by Einstein and another scientist named Leo Szilárd to begin production on an atomic bomb. Oppenheimer is heading the project, and there's no limit to what Roosevelt is willing to spend on it. He's been listening to a fellow by the name of James Byrnes, who's set on proving that the United States is a global power. Rumors have even started flying around Washington that F.D.R. is considering dumping Wallace to take Byrnes on as a running mate next election."

"Next election?" asked Lyle with a smirk. "I thought we started this country to get away from monarchies. How many times does this guy plan on running?"

Vess shook his head, disinterested. "I've never cared much for politics, but now that our government is in the business of world wars and atomic energy, I'm worried we might be getting ourselves into a fight that no one can win."

"And how is this machine supposed to help?" asked Lyle.

"If my theories are correct, and we're able to send you to another plane of existence, then we'll usher in a new age of science. Byrnes and F.D.R. won't need to prove our might to the world with bombs, because we'll have a direct line to God." Vess walked over to Lyle and put his arm around the man's shoulder so that they could both admire the CORD together. "That, my friend, is the only doorway to heaven that's not a one way trip. And you're going to be the first person to walk through it."

"I don't know about this," said Lyle, still concerned.

"You can walk away now," said Vess. "I can't stop you. But you'll be walking away from becoming the richest, most famous man on the entire planet. You'll be walking away from having your name in every history book as the most important explorer ever to grace the Earth."

Lyle looked over at the machine and took a deep breath. He imagined how his mother, who had shunned him because of her adherence to scripture, would feel when she found out how her son had been the man that proved, or disproved, the existence of her God. "And you're sure it's safe?" asked Lyle.

"Like I showed you, the box is insulated. It's the safest place on this whole ship."

"What am I supposed to see on the inside? Will it be like a door popping open with a white-bearded guy smiling on the other side or something?"

Vess shook his head and said, "No one knows. That's what being an explorer is all about. You're the one that gets to be the first to find out. Are you ready to take your place in history, Mr. Everman?"

Lyle snickered and said, "I guess so."

"Fantastic, Lyle! Fantastic! Now, go get in there so we can open the door to heaven."

Lyle took a wary step towards the machine. He inspected the door, and the rubber lining within, and then he looked back at Vess and said, "Just make sure you don't turn this thing the wrong direction and open the door to hell by mistake."

In a Chicago Suburb
April, 2006

Alma Harper sat on the burgundy couch that was pressed up against the wall beneath the picture window in the den of her grandparents' home. She was wearing her new, light purple dress that her grandmother had made for her. It was long, but well-fitted, and shimmering thread was laced randomly through it to make the dress sparkle. She was wearing her hair up, which was a rarity for her. Alma had a bad habit of rushing out wherever she was going, never bothering to take the time to look pretty. Today was different. Today, Alma was going on her third date with a popular boy from school named Paul.

Alma had never fared well in the social world of high school, and had resigned herself to being unpopular and forgotten amongst her peers. She'd been content alone, silent and unassuming, but then Paul Keller, a football player and a member of the popular crowd, had started paying attention to her. They were both seniors, and had a couple classes together. Throughout most of high school, Paul had been content ignoring her, but a few weeks ago that changed, and he started a relentless pursuit to charm her into going on a date with him.

On their first date he took her to a carnival, and did his best to win a stuffed animal for her from one of the booth games. Unfortunately, all he'd been able to win was a small stuffed teddy bear on a keychain, but she happily attached it to her keys and promised to keep it forever.

Paul took her to a movie for their second date, but the entire time she'd been obsessed with proper date-etiquette. Despite being eighteen, Paul was the first boy to ever ask Alma on a date, and she knew that she should be more willing to kiss him, but just holding his hand caused her enough anxiety as it was. She tried to convince herself to give him a goodnight kiss after that date, but when he dropped her off she chickened out, and dashed from his truck. She'd regretted it since, and had been sure Paul would give up trying to date her.

She was overjoyed when he asked her out again, although she was determined not to make the same mistake a second time. Tonight, she was going to kiss him as soon as she saw him, to get it over with.

Paul finally arrived in his battered Dodge Ram. He wasn't from a wealthy family, which Alma liked about him. They both came from meager beginnings, and it helped her feel more comfortable with him. Despite how they existed in different social circles at school, she'd been pleasantly surprised by how much they had in common. He honked once, but Alma was already getting her things to go. She turned to yell up the stairs that she was leaving, but saw that her grandmother was already standing at the top.

"I'm going," said Alma.

Her grandmother stayed silent.

"I'll be back by ten," said Alma.

Still, her grandmother said nothing. Instead, she just turned and walked away. Alma's grandmother had become quiet and forlorn over the past six months, after her husband had passed. Alma had spent months trying to help her grandmother, but the old woman insisted she would never be happy again – not after losing her grandson, her daughter, and her husband. No matter what Alma did for her, the woman never smiled anymore. It was hard for Alma not to feel like her grandmother blamed her somehow, as if the deaths in the family had been Alma's fault all along.

Alma yelled up the stairs, "I made a plate of spaghetti for you. It's in the fridge."

No answer.

She clenched her jaw in frustration, and then shook her head as she reminded herself that she'd promised not to let her grandmother's foul mood affect her anymore. Alma was going to leave the house and forget her grandmother's morbidity, if only for a couple hours.

Alma left her grandmother's home, and used her key to lock the door, the teddy bear keychain dangling from the ring. Paul had gotten out of the truck and was standing by the passenger side door, holding it open. He was wearing his letterman jacket, a simple t-shirt, and a pair of jeans. Alma felt immediately foolish for wearing a dress, and felt herself blushing. When he said he wanted to take her to dinner, she'd assumed they'd be going someplace fancy, but he was still wearing what he'd worn to school. She felt her cheeks begin to burn with embarrassment.

"You look incredible," said Paul as he held the door open for her. "Gosh, I feel like a tool. I should've worn something nicer."

"No, that's okay," said Alma. "I'm a dork for getting dolled up." She thought about kissing him, but was too nervous. She got into the truck, and he shut the door before going around to his side.

She repeated to herself over and over, 'Kiss him, Alma. Just do it. Kiss him.'

Paul got into the truck and smiled at her. She smiled back, but then slid across the gap between them and pecked him on the cheek. She'd meant to kiss him on the lips, but became too nervous at the last second. Alma slid back over to her side.

"Thanks," said Paul, a wide grin on his face.

Branson
March 13th, 2012
3:50 AM

Rosemary held Alma's keys, with the teddy bear keychain in the center of her palm. She rubbed her thumb over the aged fur, and allowed Alma's treasured past to sneak into her subconscious. She was a spy to the life the refugee of Widowsfield had lived outside the reach of The Watcher in the Walls.

"We're almost there," said Jacker. A billboard on the side of the highway directed travelers to the exit that they could take to get to the hotel where Rachel said a man fitting Michael Harper's description had checked in. "How are we going to do this?"

"Let me handle it," said Rosemary. "Just pull into the parking lot and I'll go in."

"What are you going to do?" asked Alma from the back seat. She was sitting beside Paul as he draped his arm over her shoulder.

"I'll figure out a way to get his room number," said Rosemary. "And then we'll get in there and surprise him."

"How are you going to get them to give you the number?" asked Paul.

"Don't worry, I can be pretty persuasive," said Rosemary.

"You're not planning on hurting anyone, are you?" asked Alma as she sat up straighter.

"No, of course not." Rosemary turned in her seat so that she was facing the back. Her seatbelt restricted her, so she unbuckled it to be more comfortable. An incessant beep began to sound from the dash, warning that the person sitting in the passenger seat wasn't wearing a seatbelt while the van was moving. Rosemary grumbled and slid the seatbelt behind her before buckling it back in to stop the alarm. She looked back at Alma and Paul and said, "I'm not going to risk drawing any attention to us or Widowsfield by hurting anyone. You have to trust me."

"Then tell us how you're planning on convincing them to help you," said Paul. "They'll usually call the room instead of giving out room numbers or keys or anything like that."

"Like I said, you've got to trust me."

"No," said Paul bluntly. "Sorry, but you've got to earn my trust, and I haven't even known you for an hour."

"I'm the only one trying to help you," said Rosemary. "If you don't trust me and do what I tell you, then it'll only be a matter of time before Oliver and his people track you down. You need to trust me."

"But why can't you just tell us how you're planning on getting the room number?" asked Paul, his frustration beginning to turn to anger.

"I can get the information from whoever's at the desk the same way I know about how Alma kissed you for the first time on your third date together. And how she was wearing a purple dress, with her hair up, but you just wore a t-shirt and jeans."

No one spoke for a long moment before Paul uttered, "That's crazy. How did you know that?"

"I told you, I'm a psychometric. That's why I took those things from you. I need to know your history so that when we meet The Skeleton Man you're not seduced by his lies."

"So you're using those things to steal our memories?" asked Paul.

"Stealing is a strong word," said Rosemary. "I'm sharing them. The Skeleton Man and The Watcher can warp your memories. That's why Alma forgot about Ben. I'm going to try and keep that from happening again."

"You're sort of like our back-up drive," said Jacker. "Keeping a record of our memories?"

"Right," said Rosemary, but her uncertainty was apparent. "I guess so. Sorry, I'm not much of a computer person. My family never had enough money for a computer, and the school I went to had a computer lab with two computers in it, and one of them didn't work. I don't have a great relationship with technology. Too much information gets passed around in those damn machines anyhow, and it jumbles up my thoughts. Ever since Widowsfield jacked up my powers, I've stayed pretty far away from computers and back-up drives, or whatever."

"A back-up drive is just a way to save information from being corrupted. So, wait though, you can, like, remember everything we do?" asked Jacker.

"No, but every minute I hold onto the things you gave me I start to learn more about you. To be more specific, I remember more about the things that you did while you were holding onto these things."

"Wait," said Jacker with sudden alarm. "Are you saying you remember me taking a crap and stuff like that too?"

Rosemary wasn't sure how to answer, but then started to laugh.

"What's so funny?" asked Jacker, but he was beginning to smile as Rosemary's laughter got louder. "That's crazy. You're remembering me peeing and pooping and jerking off and everything like that?"

Alma started to laugh as well, and Paul said, "Jacker, I just gave that coin to you the other day. How much crapping and jerking off did you do in that time?"

"I don't know," Jacker smirked. "A lot."

Alma and Paul laughed along with Rosemary. "I'm sorry," said Rosemary as she calmed. "I don't mean to laugh. I think I'm just so tired that I'm getting goofy. In all my years of being cursed with this damn psychometric stuff, I've never had anyone ask me if I can remember them pooping or masturbating."

"Well, it seems like a pretty important question," said Jacker, partially in jest but also somewhat serious.

Rosemary was still chuckling as Jacker pulled into the parking lot of the hotel. He had to pull around the side of building, away from the entrance, to find an empty parking spot. Once he did, Rosemary opened her door and then turned to look at the two in the back seat. "Paul, do you trust me?"

Alma put her hand on Paul's thigh and squeezed. He sighed and said, "For now."

"Good enough," said Rosemary as she took her bag with her. "I'll be right back."

She waited until she'd turned the corner and was out of sight before she took one her pistols out of her bag to check and make sure it was loaded. There were people in this hotel that had come in contact with Michael and Ben Harper. Whoever they were, Rosemary had to silence them.

CHAPTER 10 – A Gift

Philadelphia
June 15th, 1943

Despite the insulated walls, Vess could still hear Lyle screaming from within the CORD, but Vess wasn't concerned with the man's discomfort. After all, Vess was confident that agony and suffering wouldn't follow the traveler into a new dimension. Pain is a symptom of this world, tied to the nervous system of our physical bodies.

The green electricity crackled through the air, snapping at the walls like whips, but was never able to linger anywhere for long except within the rings that spun on either side of Tesla's machine. The USS Eldridge had set sail, and now they were floating somewhere in the Delaware, away from prying eyes. Groves and Einstein were on a tugboat, far from the battleship, and only a skeleton crew had remained with Vess. It was important to limit the number of people that were aware of the experiment happening below deck. The United Sates government feigned fear of the Japanese, but the Red menace was what kept the men in power on edge. Stalin's spies stretched nearly as wide as his ambitions.

Vess watched one of the various gauges on the side of the CORD, waiting for it to reach its limit. The machine roared, pounded, and ground as the rings spun. The walls of the ship flashed, and the display caused an array of stark shadows to dance. Vess ignored the shapes around him, and focused only on the gauge that was slowly reaching its zenith. Once the black hand touched the final notch, Vess would experience what Tesla had merely fathomed.

All those shadows, once rigid reflections of the metal bones of the ship, were now swirling. Eventually, Vess was no longer able to ignore them. The electricity was burning shapes into the walls, as if the light cast by the CORD was staining the metal around him. But then the charred shade quivered, revealing that it was more than a simple effect of the light. The shadows cast upon the walls weren't the result of any structure Vess could see. The rounded edges of a living creature revealed itself from the flat surfaces of the shadows, like a sea monster rising above still water.

The black tentacles circled him, confined to the second dimension projection against the ship's walls. They wrapped around the room, like the twigs of a bird's nest, slowly trapping him within. He spun in an equal amount of shock and astonishment as the otherworldly creature revealed its existence.

Where fear should've crippled him, Vess discovered joy. He raised his arms as the arcs of green lightning zapped around him, and he began to laugh.

"I've done it!"

His laughter and words were lost amid the screech of metal. Then the world seemed to take a deep breath, sucking in sound instead of air, and all was silent. The chaos of electricity and swirling shadows continued, but it did so in a vacuum. Vess tried to cry out, but his voice was lost along with every other sound. He turned to look at the CORD and saw that white smoke rose from the center, as if something within had caught fire. He rushed to inspect the various gauges, concerned that the pressure within had dropped, or that the radiation had spiked.

When he got to the CORD he saw that the gauges were missing their black hands. He tapped at the glass, but it achieved nothing. Then he unlocked the door and pulled the handle, causing the gap to emerge. The door was hard to open, and when he got it slightly ajar, the air around him began to rush inside. The suction pulled the metal door out of his grip, and slammed it shut, but there was still no sound other than the distant hum of electricity.

Vess stood in the void of noise as the chaos around him continued. He watched the door handle move by itself, and then it was thrown open hard enough to cause the side to warp. Despite the violent action, he still heard no noise other than the crackle of the green lightning.

White smoke seeped out of the entrance of the box, as if made of liquid. Vess knelt to inspect it, and pushed his hand into the chilling vapor. The cold burned him, and he retracted his hand like a child upon first touching fire. He glanced into the box, expecting to see Lyle within, but found it empty. He didn't dare walk into the mist, having already learned of its bite.

"Looking for me?" asked Lyle from behind, his voice like thunder in the silence.

Vess was startled, both by the sudden emergence of his assistant and by the return of his hearing. He'd assumed his eardrums had been damaged by the pressure the machine inflicted upon the room, but Lyle's voice had been clearly audible. When he turned, he saw Mr. Everman standing far across the room, beside the wall. Shadows of black tentacles swam on the wall behind him, swirling as if attracted to his presence. He stayed where he was, his hands pressed to the wall as if tied there.

"Lyle," said Vess, daring to take a step closer. "Tell me what you saw. Tell me what happened."

Lyle Everman looked taller and thinner than he had before, and his clothes were hanging loosely from his body. He appeared like a man succumbing to disease, wasting away on a hospital bed. There were dark circles under his eyes, and his skin had a greyish appearance. His hair was thinner, and mottled with grey, and it flapped as his head jerked back and forth as if he were searching the room for something. He opened his mouth, and blood gushed out, quickly covering his torso and then down to the ground, but Vess couldn't hear the liquid splash.

"I see everything," said Lyle's voice, independent of the vessel it had once inhabited. Blood was still pouring from Lyle Everman's open mouth, and the pool was growing beneath him, sneaking closer to Vess every second, but the man's voice was speaking as if from another person's body.

"Who are you?" asked Vess as he backed away from the blood that continued to pool beneath Lyle. He watched as the shadows took shape, pulling away from the wall. The shadows seemed to be of giant tentacles, but the black forms that stretched forth were mere strands; just thin wires that reached out and wrapped around Lyle's body, drawing him in until he was wrapped like a spider's meal.

"I'm the only God you've got left," said the creature with Lyle's voice. "Watch how I cherish you."

The physical body of Lyle Everman began to scream. Vess stared at the man that had been cocooned in the black wires that sprouted from the wall. The cords were separating, revealing glimpses of Lyle's flesh beneath. They pulled away even more, giving Vess a better view of the man trapped within. Finally, his psychic assistant's face was revealed enough that Vess could see his agony evident in his expression. The cords were still in his mouth, curled over his lips and disappearing within his throat, leaving only his flapping tongue visible. One by one, the cords slid away and retreated back to the wall, dripping with blood and saliva as they went.

Once Lyle could finally speak, he cried out, "It burns! Oh God, it burns. Help me, please."

Vess took a step forward, intent on helping, but then stayed his hand. He was too frightened, and the cords that emerged from the wall acted as if sentient, writhing and taunting him, giving him false hope that he might be able to help free Lyle from their grip. He stepped back again, shaking his head but unable to look away. The cords constricted Lyle as if vengeful that Vess hadn't come closer. They slid back and forth across his skin in a variety of directions, and as he cried out in pain the cords slit him to shreds; but he never stopped crying out. Even as the cords sawed through bone, and chunks of his body were slipping out of their grasp to splash in the blood, he continued to feel the torture. Death never claimed him.

Then the sound of Lyle's hell was silenced once again. It proceeded in front of Vess, but he couldn't hear any of it.

He covered his eyes, but when he did he saw the flash of other eyes staring back at him.

"Tell us what evil means to you," said Lyle's voice, though deeper and with a more malicious tone than Vess had ever heard his assistant use. "We'll surpass your expectation."

The wires finally released Lyle, but the man seemed only vaguely human now. His skin had been pulled away, as had most of his fat and muscle. Strips of pink flesh clung to the cords as they slithered at his feet, and though there was no way he could still be alive, he was standing and staring at Vess. He was a skeleton, tied together by the wires that reached out from the wall, but the demon had left him his lidless eyes to watch with. The globes darted back and forth as the creature's mouth opened to reveal a shredded tongue within.

Lyle Everman's risen corpse focused on Vess, and then took a step forward. The black cords that surrounded him expanded around his feet, and with every step he was pulling them forward, as if the darkness couldn't exist except where he'd walked. Lyle reached out, his arm a mess of black wire and hanging strips of flesh, and his bone finger beckoned Vess forward.

"You can burn too," said the corpse as it advanced.

"Wait," said Vess as he cowered and stepped back. "Wait, I can help you."

Lyle didn't pause his shuffling gait. He reached out with his bony arm as the worms of cords slid around between his bones and flesh.

"I can bring you more."

"Bring me more?" asked Lyle's voice from somewhere in the room.

"Yes," said Vess, sensing that his offer had intrigued the inter-dimensional entity. "I can bring you more like him." He pointed with a trembling hand at Lyle Everman.

"More sacrifices?" asked the creature whose shadows dominated the walls.

"Yes," said Vess. "We built this machine to offer you a sacrifice. That's what you wanted, right? I gave Lyle to you."

Lyle Everman's shattered corpse cocked its head like a confounded dog. "You..." he sputtered a word from his blood soaked mouth.

The creature that appeared as only shadows and wires spoke with Lyle's voice, "What would I need more for? I can toy with him for ages." The wires rose and fell through Lyle's mangled body, sliding in and out of his exposed ribs.

"You'll get bored of him."

"But then I'll have you," said the creature, cherishing Vess's fear. "And all the other men aboard this ship. Together, we can explore your fears."

"You have the whole ship?" asked Vess, but he continued before the creature could respond. "It doesn't matter. You'll want more."

Lyle Everman's corpse took a step forward, and the wires sprouted from the ground beneath him like blades of grass. Vess continued to move back, but then bumped into the CORD as it continued to function silently; the only sound Vess could hear was what the creature that dominated the room wanted him to.

"You need me," said Vess, feeling insignificant and vulnerable as the shadows loomed around him. He looked down and saw that he was standing in the bitterly cold fog that had come out of the machine's opened door, but he couldn't get out of it. Lyle Everman's corpse was too close now, and the black cords had begun to sprout from all around him. There was no escape.

Vess cringed as Lyle reached his skeletal hand out to him. The creature touched his cheek, leaving a smear of hot blood behind.

"We might consider your offer," said Lyle. This time his voice didn't emanate ethereally from the room, but rather directly from the corpse in front of him. The shambling mess of bone, flesh, and wire spoke to him as blood fell over his exposed teeth and down a strip of flesh that had once been a lip, but was now dangling under his chin. "But let's play first."

The wires thrust forward, piercing Vess in a hundred places, and snaked beneath his flesh to pull his bones away from one another. Vess experienced a level of torture that few humans had ever known, but he wouldn't be the last.

The Watcher in the Walls had seen a million souls pass through his domain over the years. Their spirits were flashes of light streaking across his existence, never pausing or recognizing his presence. Only the sacrificed ever passed slowly enough for The Watcher to catch, and often they eluded him as well. He was merely the shadow that the blinding light of a new world held at bay, but no longer. Now these souls lingered, and he would make the most of their visit.

Vess had used the CORD to breach the barrier between heaven and earth, but The Watchers laid between. This Watcher took the opportunity to gather more souls, and it would keep the door open as long as it could.

Branson
March 13th, 2012
4:00 AM

"Hello," said the clerk with a smile as Rosemary walked in.

She looked around the lobby of the hotel in search of cameras. There was one mounted in the corner, just behind the front desk, as she'd expected. She pulled at the front of her shirt to be certain her pistol, which was tucked under her belt, was hidden.

She walked up to the counter and offered the young man a weary smile. He smiled back, but she recognized nervous energy in his gestures. She surmised that he was the one that Rachel had contacted about the police looking for someone staying at his hotel. He was young, she guessed around twenty-five, with a thin face and blue eyes that were amplified by his glasses. He had a goatee, and his hair was thinning despite his youth, promising that he'd be bald by his mid-thirties.

"I hope you're having a better night than I am," said Rosemary, feigning an exhausted attempt at humor.

"Uh oh," said the concierge. "Is something wrong?"

"My car broke down out on the road. It's pouring smoke all over the damn place."

"Sorry to hear that," said the young man with honest empathy.

"I was hoping to use your phone," said Rosemary as she pointed over the edge of the counter to the shelf on the other side where the staff's computer and phone sat.

"Of course," said the young man. He lifted the phone's base and set it on the higher counter, just in front of Rosemary. "You have to dial 9 for an outside line."

"Thanks," said Rosemary as she picked up the receiver and dialed a random number. She walked away from the desk as far as the phone cord would allow and then started a fake conversation. She pretended to be speaking with a friend, and recounted how her car had stalled on the road. She kept an eye on the concierge to make sure he wasn't becoming suspicious. All the while, she was recalling the moment when Michael Harper walked into the hotel looking for a room. She could remember the concierge swiping an electronic keycard through the activator and then setting it in a paper envelope where he jotted down a room number. Then she recalled the other staff member that went out to help Michael get Ben out of his car just before another guest arrived, and she cursed her bad luck. There would be more people to deal with than just this single concierge, but she was resolved in her decision that no one could be allowed to remember that Michael and Ben Harper came to this hotel. She had to erase any trail they left of their passing as best she could.

"Thanks," said Rosemary to the concierge again after she hung up the phone.

"Did you find someone that can help?" asked the kind young man.

"Yes, they're going to come here in a little while. Is it okay if I wait here in the lobby?"

"Of course. No problem, as long as you don't mind the elevator music they play in here."

"No, that's fine," said Rosemary with a pained smile. She wished the young man had been mean to her, that way she wouldn't regret what she was going to have to do next. "Do you have a restroom?"

"Right around the corner there," said the young man as he pointed to the left. "Just past the vending machines."

Rosemary thanked him and then walked in the direction he'd pointed. She went to the women's restroom as details about the young man's life flooded her memories.

His name was Jim Broadbent. He was twenty-three, with a new girlfriend that he was certain he loved more than any other girl he'd ever met. They'd been dating for six months, but he was already considering asking her to marry him. He'd even gone to a jewelry shop to check how expensive a ring would be. Last weekend he went to…

"Stop it," said Rosemary to herself as she went into the bathroom. She pressed her hands to her temples and clenched her eyes shut. "Stop it," she repeated over and over as she stood in front of the mirror. "You can't do that. This isn't your fault. They've all gotta go."

Her hands were shaking as she took the pistol out. The gun trembled in her grip.

Rosemary stared at her reflection in the mirror, and lamented how tired she appeared. Physical weariness was one thing, but the weight Rosemary bore had sapped her of more than just that. She was exhausted both mentally and physically, and the toll her gift imparted threatened to break her. It had been five very long years since she fled Widowsfield, and these annual trips back threatened to break her each time. This year, however, promised to be the last.

She'd already put into motion things that she hoped would end what Oliver and his boss had done.

Rosemary found her resolve, and stood straighter as she looked for a place to hide the gun. The bathroom had an automatic hand drier, with a paper towel dispenser on the wall beside it. She unlatched the top of the dispenser and saw that the white box was filled with folded, brown paper. She took a stack out, and set it on the counter before placing the handgun inside. She carefully closed the case, threw the stack of unused paper towels in the trash, and then headed back out into the lobby.

Jim Broadbent was standing behind the counter, and he smiled at her as she walked back into the lobby. She grinned back, and then sat on a bench near the entrance. As she sat, she fiddled with one of her bracelets. It was made of plastic beads that were designed to resemble wood. She thumbed at the individual beads as she closed her eyes and concentrated.

After several minutes, she stood up and walked over to the counter. Jim had been sitting down, and he stood when he saw her coming closer. He set down the book he'd been reading and asked, "Can I help with something?"

"Actually," said Rosemary as she slipped the bracelet off. "I wanted to thank you for being so nice."

"Oh, it's no problem," said Jim with a shake of his head and a smile. "All I did was let you use our phone."

"Yeah, well, a lot of folks might've sent me out without offering help. I wanted to thank you by giving you this." She handed him the bracelet.

"Oh no, that's okay," said Jim.

"I insist. I make jewelry for a living. Giving that to you is my way of saying thanks."

"Well, thank you," said Jim as he accepted the gift. "I appreciate that." He examined it as Rosemary watched, and then he started to put it in his pocket.

"Try it on," said Rosemary.

Jim did as he was asked, and slipped the bracelet on. The central band was elastic, allowing the bracelet to conform easily to the width of his knuckles before the beads snapped back together once around his wrist. "It's pretty, but I think it'd look better on my girlfriend."

"Maybe," said Rosemary. "But just promise me you'll wear it for a little while. Okay?"

"Sure," said Jim, happy to comply. He certainly didn't suspect any malice evident in the gift. "I'd be happy to."

Widowsfield
March 13th, 2012
4:00 AM

"Oliver," called out the nurse that had gone looking for the wounded man. After the strangers had left to go find Michael and Ben, Helen had told her assistant to go find Oliver while she went up to check his office. The events of the night had shaken the younger nurse, and her hands were still trembling.

Oliver's foot had been shot by the man named Paul. The wound had caused blood to seep through a hole in the bottom of his shoe, leaving a trail that was easy to follow. It led deep into the facility, far from anywhere that she'd ever been before. She'd always known the Cada E.I.B. building was large, but never knew it stretched this far. Oliver's tracks led to an elevator, and the young, blonde nurse stepped inside and knew that she would have to check each floor. The elevator had four buttons, but the level marked 'B3' was only accessible by inserting a key. She took the elevator to each floor, but then realized that Oliver must've used a key to access the restricted area. She debated going back to tell Helen that she'd been unable to follow their employer, but then she had an idea.

Helen had hit an alarm after the man that claimed to be Michael Harper left with a sleeper. The alarms in the facility caused several of the automatic locks in the facility to disengage, helping to prevent people from being trapped in the event of a fire or gas leak. She stepped out of the elevator on floor B2 and then walked over to a nearby staircase to check if it was unlocked. It was, and she went down one more level to check the door that would grant her access to the floor where she was certain Oliver must've gone.

It was open, and she went out into the hallway to find that she'd been right. Oliver's bloody tracks led away from the elevator door and down the dark hall. The lights on this level weren't functioning, so the nurse pulled out her cellphone to use its flashlight function. She stared down the long hall, searching its shadows for the wounded man.

"Oliver," she called out. "I just want to help."

She moved cautiously forward, following the trail of blood. She had no reason to suspect what was about to happen. When she saw the bloody, abandoned shoe in the middle of the hall in front of her, she paused in confusion.

She couldn't have guessed that Oliver had taken his shoe off in the elevator and wrapped his wounded foot with his shirt. She had no reason to suspect that he would've used the bloody shoe to create a false track, and then hid in a room along the way to wait for someone to dare and chase after him.

Oliver approached from behind, and then bashed the young nurse in the back of the head with a fire extinguisher. She fell immediately to her knees, but he hadn't hit her hard enough to knock her out. Her red glasses bounced off the floor as she cried out in shock and pain before he hit her again, this time with enough force to drop her.

Oliver lifted the young, thin nurse into his arms, and groaned in pain as he tried to walk on his damaged foot. Her head was bleeding, and he did his best to keep the blood from dripping to the floor as he retraced the false trail he'd left. He carried the nurse deeper into the facility, and finally to a locked room. He struggled to get his key out while still holding the unconscious girl, but managed to finally get the door open.

He started to flip the multiple switches that turned on the lights in the massive room. One by one, the rows of lights hanging far above burst to life, revealing the cavernous room that held the secret that Vess had left Oliver in charge of.

Oliver approached the CORD with the nurse still in his arms. The machine was dormant, for now. But once he got the young woman inside, he would start the process of powering the monstrous machine.

Despite how The Accord had ordered that the machine be disassembled and taken to a new location, and that the facility in Widowsfield be abandoned, Oliver was intent on meeting the entity that had come to be known as The Watcher in the Walls.

PART TWO – With New Rules

CHAPTER 11 – All in the Name

Widowsfield
March 14th, 1998

Alma Harper was only ten years old when her mother tried to kill her. Amanda had strapped her unconscious daughter into the car seat after they'd left the home of the woman that Michael had been sleeping with. Amanda knew the truth now, and realized that the only way to save Ben was to kill herself, and Alma along with her. She was prepared to plunge off the cliff that overlooked the Jackson Reservoir. When Alma awoke, she told the girl her plan, and then drove them both through the guardrail at the edge of the cliff.

That lurching feeling that surged in Alma's gut as the car fell off the cliff would haunt her for the rest of her life.

How she'd managed to get out of the car after it crashed and started to sink was nothing less than miraculous. Her mother had been knocked unconscious when the airbags deployed, but Alma only had the wind knocked out of her. She screamed as the water rushed in, and tried to open her door, but the pressure exerted on the sinking car kept the doors shut tight.

The car's lights were still on, revealing some of the murky depths of the reservoir. She could see the movement of catfish as they swam out of the way of the sinking car, just flashes of shadows in the soupy green. Alma rolled down her window and allowed the water to rush in. After taking a final gulp of fleeting air, she hoped to swim out of the open window.

The incoming water woke Amanda, and she saw that Alma was trying to escape. She grabbed at the girl's ankles, desperate to keep her in the grave. She clawed at her, but Alma kicked and struggled as the water swallowed her up.

Finally, Amanda lost her grip, and Alma tried to swim to what she thought was the surface.

A bloom of light hung above, all but hidden by the dark water. Catfish swam between Alma and the surface, like monsters through mist, but Alma moved past them in a desperate attempt to reach safety.

Now she was on the shore, crawling across the grass in an attempt to reach the road ahead. She wailed as best she could, though her body offered barely enough strength to cry. When she got to the pavement, she collapsed.

Ben found her. He held his sister in his lap and wept for her. Alma opened her eyes and looked up at the brother she'd thought was lost. She felt his arms around her, and she reached up to touch his cheek. "Ben?" Was he alive? Was she dead?

"Hi Alma," said the boy that held her. "I missed you so much."

"Ben, I'm so sorry. I forgot about you. I'm so sorry, but I remember now."

"It's going to be okay, Alma," said Ben. "Someone's going to come and help you."

"Mom tried to kill me," said Alma. "She drove us off the cliff. Why would she do that?" She quaked with sorrow and her brother held her tighter.

"I don't know, Alma. They hated us. Both of them." The malice in his words was startling. "Forget them, Alma. You've got to forget what they did, otherwise it'll make you hate everything."

"Why would she try to kill me? Why didn't she love me?" asked Alma as she wept. "Why does everyone hate me?"

Ben hushed her and said, "I love you, Alma. I'll always love you."

"Why would she do that?" Alma could only focus on her mother's betrayal.

"Close your eyes, Alma. Just imagine you're headed back home. Okay? Imagine she's driving you back to Chicago to stay with Nana. Just forget about this. Pretend like Mommy loved you."

Widowsfield
March 13th, 1996

"It's good to finally meet you," said Oliver as he was introduced to the man that had been the architect of the CORD project.

Vess's appearance was a shock. He didn't look as old as Oliver had expected, but there was certainly something terribly wrong with the man's health. He was tall, and so thin that his clothes hung on him as if his shoulders were a hanger. He had a gaunt face and skin that was plagued by a grey pallor. His white hair was thinning, and he had dark bags under his eyes, but his face wasn't as beset with wrinkles as it should've been for a man that had participated in the first CORD experiment, over fifty years earlier. The sparse fat on Vess's face drooped, giving him the appearance of a hound, and the edges of his eyes slunk. He reminded Oliver of a wax figure that had begun to melt.

"You must be Oliver," said Vess as he struggled to move forward, relying heavily upon his walker. He was frail, but it appeared a result of illness rather than age.

Oliver wasn't sure if he should offer help. The two large, barrel-chested men that had escorted Vess to the dam stood on either side of the old man, each dressed in similar attire: Suit jackets with matching slacks. Each of them was equipped with an earpiece that had a looping cord that stretched out from beneath their coats. Neither of the members of Vess's security team seemed concerned with their employer's ability to walk, so Oliver decided not to offer help either. Instead, he matched Vess's slow but steady pace as they headed toward the railed stairs that led up to the dam's observation area.

Vess and his entourage had arrived in a line of black Lincoln town cars, as if a funeral procession had paused here. The majority of his group lingered back at the cars, taking the opportunity to smoke and chat, while Vess and his two bodyguards walked over to meet with Oliver. Vess and the others had driven here from New York, stopping at other Cada E.I.B. facilities along the way. However, the Widowsfield endeavor had become a top priority for the company, and Vess's arrival signaled that the board had agreed it was time to begin what they all hoped would be a successful experiment.

This was Vess's personal project, and one that he'd been attempting to duplicate since what happened in Philadelphia over a half century earlier. Oliver was honored to be involved.

"There she is," said Oliver as they went up the slight hill that led from the road up to the concrete side of the Jackson Reservoir. The battleship that had been meticulously rebuilt to match the ship where the original experiment had taken place was floating before them. "The Leon," said Oliver with pride.

Vess paused and looked at Oliver. "That's what the Greeks called her." He looked back at the ship in reverence. "But that's not who she really is."

"No?" asked Oliver.

Vess handed his four-legged walker back to one of the two men that walked with them. Then he grabbed the stair's railing to steady himself. He carefully stepped up, and Oliver noticed that the man's leg wobbled. "No, Oliver. Didn't anyone tell you why we bought this ship from Greece?"

"No sir," said Oliver. "I was just privy to the details about the psychic we needed to get."

Vess nodded and explained, "We didn't buy just any boat. That ship might've lived the past fifty years with the name 'Leon' painted on its side, but she'll never stop being the Eldridge."

Oliver looked back at the massive battleship with new respect. "Really? That's the same boat?"

"Yes. That's why we bought her back. The Navy sold her after removing the CORD. No one expected that the ship itself had anything to do with the experiment. Since then, we've developed new theories about how the device works. We're trying to do everything we can to replicate the Philadelphia experiment."

"And the ship ties into it?"

Vess nodded as they walked along the edge of the dam that separated the reservoir from the lake that rested sixty feet below on the other side. When opened, the dam would spill water and create a manmade waterfall that could be viewed from the observation deck where Vess and Oliver were walking, but the area had been closed during Cada E.I.B.s construction of the Greek battleship, the Leon.

The town of Widowsfield had agreed to allow the company to close off the normally public land in exchange for Cada E.I.B.'s promise to build a plant on the outskirts of the town. Widowsfield was attempting to capitalize on the sudden popularity of nearby Branson, and thought it would be smart to woo in large businesses to the area with the promise of relaxed regulation and low county taxes. By the time the ship was built, Cada E.I.B. had already proven to the city council of their intent to invest a large amount of money into the town. They'd purchased a sizeable amount of land on the north side of town, and had already constructed a massive office building. They were promising to hire a minimum of 500 employees, which would draw in families from other states that were looking for work and interested in living near Branson.

Cada E.I.B. had explained that they needed to use the reservoir to build a replica of a World War 2 era battleship that would eventually be attached to a visitor's center and museum. The town happily agreed, never suspecting that the European investment group was actually a front for a group of scientists that were experimenting with a potentially world-changing device.

"The theory is that the walls of the ship itself have something to do with how the CORD works. Something to do with harmonic resonance." Vess tapped a ring on his finger against the metal railing, causing the rail to hum. "I guess we'll find out tomorrow."

"Pi day," said Oliver as they neared the bridge that crossed the gap between the dam's observation area and the Eldridge.

"Yes," said Vess. "Are you privy to the reason for that?"

"I thought it was just for symbolism's sake," said Oliver. "That's what the engineer they sent out to build the CORD said."

"He's right," said Vess. "But I doubt he understands the significance."

The bridge that led to the deck of the ship was inclined, and Vess struggled to get up. Oliver reached over to assist him, but Vess pushed his hand away. "I'm fine. I can do it myself."

Oliver meekly apologized and glanced back at the two men that walked behind them. The one carrying the old man's walker nodded to Oliver with empathy. He understood that the reason the two guards never offered to help Vess was because the elderly man was too proud to accept it.

They got to the bridge, and Vess took his walker back. He paused and admired the ship before saying, "It's like stepping back in time. It looks exactly like it did back in 1943."

"The engineers brought along pictures that they referred to so that they could get every detail as close as possible," said Oliver.

"Then let's not waste any more time," said Vess. "Take me to see the CORD."

"This way," said Oliver as he led Vess along. As they were walking, Oliver asked, "What did you mean about the significance of the symbolism?"

"They want to own the date."

Oliver was confounded and asked, "What do you mean?"

"Symbolism makes a much bigger difference than you might expect. It's the sort of thing that gives power to the powerless. Symbolism sneaks into our brains and cements itself there whether we realize it or not."

"And they want to take advantage of that? Why are they so concerned about symbolism?" asked Oliver.

"You're surrounded by symbols every day of your life. Whether it's the stop sign on the side of the road, or the hidden Free Mason messages on every dollar in your pocket, symbols control you more than you're aware."

"Stop signs are symbols?" asked Oliver with a chuckle.

Vess wasn't similarly amused. "Of course they are. You abide a shape and a color without even having to stop and think about what it means. With just a flash of a red octagon with a white border you immediately stop what you're doing. You don't even need to be made aware of why you need to stop. It's become an instinct for you. That's the way symbols work. They convey messages without needing explanation."

"And March 14th has something to do with that?"

"Yes," said Vess. "Many people already know about pi. They were taught that number in school, and it's lodged in their heads. It's been used by architects and mathematicians throughout the ages. If you ever want to see proof, just look into the Egyptian pyramids and you'll see how people have communicated with likeminded people through the symbol. Also, it's one of the only dates on a calendar that can be represented by a symbol."

"The symbol for pi?" asked Oliver.

They reached the door that would allow them access to the lower deck and Oliver pulled the heavy latch that released the seal while Vess continued his explanation. "Yes. You see, corporations learned a long time ago how important symbols are. That's why they work tirelessly to ingrain their logos into your brain with advertisements. When they do their job well enough, just the image of their logo can switch a trigger in your head that makes you desire what they're selling. It's not exclusive to just companies selling things though. Why do you think countries have flags? A flag is just a symbol, but soldiers are taught to regard them as if they're some sort of holy relic. And don't get me started on the church. They've been using the power of symbology ever since they started. It's all about controlling another person's mind without even having to say a single word to them."

"Mind control?"

Vess nodded as he cautiously made his way down the metal stairs that led to the holding bay in the bowels of the ship. "Yes, in every sense of the word. You see, it's more than simple recognition of the symbol that is happening in a person's brain. They've proven that there are chemical reactions that can be triggered by simply seeing a symbol. For instance, the brain of a devout Christian can release endorphins just by looking at a cross. That's a powerful effect."

"So why does Cada E.I.B. want to use pi as a symbol?" asked Oliver.

"Because if you're the one that opens the door to Heaven, you damn well want people to remember your name."

Branson
March 13th, 2012
4:15 AM

Charles Dunbar was covering his face as the bar patrons spit at him. He was desperate to get out, but the crush of the crowd had spun him in circles. They were grabbing at him, and pulling at his arm, trying to get a clear view of his face to spit on him. They laughed and cried out, "Weasel," as they pushed him. Then their hands gripped harder, and some of them began to punch and kick at him. He hid his face as best he could, but the crowd continued to tear at him, and he could feel their nails digging into him as their fervor intensified.

"Please, please," he begged, "just let me go."

As he spun, he caught quick glimpses of the crowd. Most of them were around his age and almost all of them were overweight. The men had beards that were a mix of brown, grey, and white, and the women had stringy hair and double chins that bounced as they cackled. Then, hidden within the crowd, he caught sight of other things moving that shouldn't be there. Some of the people near the bar were hoisting a white shape above them, like a reveler at a concert surfing on the hands of the crowd, but it wasn't human. He saw legs and what looked like wool, and then he heard the tell-tale "Baah" of a lamb just as he saw a glint of metal.

The crowd spun him again, and continued to spit at him, but he was intent on seeing what was happening to the animal. By the time he caught sight of the lamb again, the crowd had stabbed a knife into its side, causing blood to gush out over them. They opened their mouths and accepted the fluid as if lustful of it, like they were hoisting a barrel of whiskey with the cork pulled free.The lamb stared at Charles and opened its mouth, but the creature no longer had the voice it should. Instead, Charles heard the pained cries of a child as the lamb's eyes bled.

"Weasel," said a woman beside him, and Charles felt her press her body against him. He felt her warm flesh against his hand and realized that she was nude. He glanced down at her in surprise and saw that she was old and obese, and she was licking at him as she pressed herself to his side. He tried to push her away, but the crowd was too dense for him to move. They held him tight as the nude stranger rubbed herself on him, laughing and licking at him as he squirmed.

The lamb's blood made the hands of the crowd grow slick, and when Charles heard something heavy fall to the floor and splash he thought they'd dropped the animal. He saw that they were still hoisting the carcass, but then he realized it was just the pelt, now covered in blood, that they held aloft.

"Charles," said a child's voice from nearby.

He tried to find the source, but the nude old woman was still forcing her body against him and she was wet with the blood of the lamb even though they were standing at least ten feet from the dead animal. She was grinding against Charles's leg and moaning as the rest of the patrons continued to spit at them both.

The child's hand found Charles, and gripped him. He felt himself being pulled away.

"Don't go, weasel," said the nude woman that had been pressing against him.

"Charlie!" The bartender shouted and drew Charles's attention to the bar. The man with the curled mustache was standing atop the bar, high above the throng of people, and he was holding a six shooter with a long, silver barrel. "Gotta get them right behind the ear." He placed the gun to the back of his head and then pulled the trigger.

The crowd cheered as the gunshot rang out, and the bartender's brains splattered across the already bloody crowd. They grasped at the pieces of the suicidal man's head that had stuck to the faces around them, and they all started to shove the brains, skull pieces, and hair into their mouths.

"You've got to come this way," said the child, but Charles still couldn't see the boy. The crowd was too thick, and he could only see an arm sprouting forth between fat bodies.

A door opened, and Charles could finally see the exit. He was wet with saliva and blood, and he was slipping through the crowd easier, but there were several people barring the exit. The nude woman was there beside a bearded man that had apparently been eating pieces of the bartender. Bits of flesh and blood were stuck in his beard and he was picking at his teeth with what looked like a pocket knife. Charles had lost his grip on the child's hand, and he desperately searched for it.

The child's arm was sprouting from between the two people, but Charles still couldn't see him. The boy yelled, "Come on."

Charles pushed his way between the final two patrons and the woman tried to grab at him, but he was too wet with blood and saliva for her to get a grip. He slid through them and out into the freezing cold night.

"Are you okay?" asked the child.

Charles was finally able to see the boy, and he was shocked by the sight. The child looked to be about ten, but he'd been horrifically burned. His skin was blistering as Charles watched, and his teeth were chattering. He was cold and shivered as he held himself, and his clothes were wet. Worst of all was his face, which had been scarred and was bright red, as if a layer of skin had been peeled off. His eyes never blinked, and stayed wide as he stared at Charles.

"Mr. Dunbar, are you okay?" asked the boy again. "I keep having to save you."

Gravel shifted under Charles's feet, and for a moment it felt like the world was moving without him. Then he focused on the boy and he regained his balance.

"He's right," said a second stranger that Charles hadn't seen at first. A stout man was lounging against the side of the bar with his thumbs tucked behind his suspenders. He was wearing a newsboy's cap and had a strong chin that was dotted with black whiskers. "Kid's saved you more times than I can count."

"We should keep going," said the boy as he continued to shiver. The boy's breath came forth as thick, white steam in the cold.

"What happened?" asked Charles as he looked back at the entrance to the bar.

"Ben saved you, that's what happened," said the man by the door. "Like always."

"Who? Ben? I don't..."

"My name's Ben," said the child. He pointed to the man in the suspenders and said, "And that's Lyle." Next the boy pointed out towards the road that ran along the side of the bar's gravel parking lot. "And out there is Fidaa and John, but they don't come out much anymore."

Charles thought he saw someone tall and thin hiding behind a tree in the distance, but the figure slunk back and disappeared again. "Where are we?"

"At the hotel," said Ben. "Come on, we have to hurry."

"The hotel?" asked Charles, confused.

"I'd listen to the kid," said Lyle. "He's saved your ass more than a few times."

"He has?" asked Charles, although it felt like he knew that already. This all seemed so familiar, as if they'd done this before. The boy was special to Charles, even though he couldn't explain why.

"Damn straight. I'd do as he asks if I were you, otherwise he's not going to be around to save you next time."

"I need your help," said Ben as he walked through the gravel parking lot to the edge of the building.

"All right," said Charles as he followed. He heard a noise that sounded like chattering teeth. Then he saw that there was a pool on the side of the bar and that leaves were cascading across the tarp that covered it, causing the sound he'd mistaken for teeth. There was a tall, wire fence that drew a square around the pool. The building that housed the bar stretched around the edges of the pool. There were multiple doors on the walls, and Charles realized that they were at a hotel that he'd stayed at recently.

"I know this place," said Charles.

"Of course you do," said Lyle as he followed behind. "How many times do we gotta do this before you know what the deal is?"

"Sorry," said Charles, although he wasn't sure why he was apologizing.

Ben reached a door and stopped. He motioned for the others to hurry and then said, "This is where my friend is. His name's Ben too, Ben Harper, and he's in trouble. There are people breaking into his room tonight and they've got weapons. You're the only one that can save Ben. Okay? Do you understand me?"

"Sure," said Charles.

"Do you really?" asked Ben.

"Well..." Charles looked back at Lyle and then to Ben again. "I guess so."

"He doesn't get it," said Lyle, frustrated.

"He's got to," said Ben. "We're running out of time."

"No, I get it," said Charles. "I understand. Your friend is in there, and he needs my help."

"Ben's in there," said the boy, accentuating the name. "And if you don't save him, then the people at the bar are going to kill you for cheating on your wife. Don't let that happen, Charles. You can't let that happen."

Branson
March 13th, 2012
4:15 AM

Michael Harper was nearly asleep when someone lightly tapped on the door. He wasn't certain what he'd heard at first, and looked hastily around. The television was on, but he'd turned it down to where it was only a whisper. The movie he'd been watching was still playing, although he'd lost sense of the plot. He rubbed his eyes and sat up before saying, "Ben?"

He heard his son's wheelchair rattling in the bathroom, and assumed that the tapping he'd heard had been coming from there.

"Go to sleep." He started to lie back down, but then there was another succession of taps and this time he was certain it hadn't come from the bathroom. He started to curse quietly as he slipped his jeans back on. Then he went to the bathroom door and whispered, "Be quiet in there. You hear me?" The metal chair continued to rattle.

Michael debated his options, and considered not answering the door, but then the tapping started again and that spurred him to action. He went to the door and peered through the peephole. There was a black woman with dreadlocks standing outside. She was watching the peephole, waiting for a shadow to pass over to reveal someone was looking through.

She waved and smiled before saying, "I'm sorry to bother you. I work with the hotel."

Michael opened the door, but left the chain lock still attached. "What do you need?"

"Sorry, to bother you," said the woman, "but we had a gas leak in one of the rooms and we have to check each of them. I'm so sorry for the intrusion."

"We're fine," said Michael groggily. He started to close the door, but the woman stuck her foot in the gap. "Hey…"

"I have to insist."

"Screw you, lady," said Michael, his temper flaring.

"No, screw you," said a male's voice from outside.

Michael didn't have a chance to react before a large man with curly black hair thrust his weight into the door, causing the chain to clang in its brace, but not snap. The lock held steady, and the man on the other side of the door cursed in pain and frustration. Michael ran from the door and picked up his jeans, believing his pistol would be with them. It wasn't, and he suddenly recalled that he'd placed it on the dresser where the television sat.

"Hold on, I'll get it this time," said the man outside before thrusting his ample weight into the door a second time. He managed to snap the chain, and then came tumbling in just as Michael got his pistol.

"Don't shoot," said the black woman that had been at the door. Michael turned and saw that she was pointing a shotgun at him. His hand was on his gun, but he wasn't sure he had time to turn and fire.

"Michael Harper, I'll shoot if you don't put that gun down," said the stranger as she walked carefully into the room. "And I've already got too many souls on my conscious as it is. Don't go adding another."

"He's mine," said Michael, his hand still on the pistol.

"Ben's dead," said the stranger. "The person you've got in that bathroom isn't your son."

"Bullshit," said Michael as he slipped his index finger into the trigger guard, but left the pistol still sitting where it was.

The stranger raised her shotgun in a menacing gesture as another person entered the room behind her. Michael recognized him as Alma's boyfriend, who he'd fought with at his daughter's apartment a couple days earlier. The big man glared at Michael from behind the black woman.

"Your son died sixteen years ago," said the woman with the shotgun.

"No he…"

She interrupted, "He died at the cabin after you forced him to pour boiling water on Terry. He died that day, and the thing you have in the bathroom is just using his body."

Michael was shocked by how much the woman knew; not only about his past, but also about how Ben was in the bathroom. It was as if the stranger had been spying on him. "You're crazy."

"Dad," said Alma as she walked in beside her boyfriend. "Please put the gun down. No one needs to get hurt."

Michael grimaced at his only daughter, and remembered how much he wanted to kill her for daring to go back to Widowsfield. He didn't want her to unleash the secrets that had been buried there, but now it was too late. "Alma," he said her name in both anger and regret. "I wish you would've listened to me. Goddamn it. Why didn't you just listen to me? Why'd you have to go back there?"

"I had to," said Alma. "I'm through running away from what happened."

"Are you sure?" asked Michael with a wicked grin. "Life's better when you ain't looking back on it, kid."

"Don't make me kill you," said the black woman as she took a step closer to Michael.

Michael took his hand away from the gun and stepped back. "I just wanted my boy back," said Michael. "I wanted a chance to start over is all. You can't fault me for that."

"Sure we can, psycho," said Alma's boyfriend.

"So who are you?" asked Michael as he stared at the stranger with the shotgun. "Are you working with those fuckers that put Ben in that prison?"

"I'm the one trying to put a stop to all this," said the woman.

"And how do you plan to do that?" asked Michael.

"I'm going to start by bringing him," she motioned towards the bathroom, "back to Widowsfield."

"So you are working with them," said Michael.

She shook her head. "No. I just know where he belongs. And it sure the fuck isn't at a hotel in Branson with you."

"He's my son," said Michael as he stepped around to the other side of the bed, away from the others.

Alma closed the hotel room door as her boyfriend said, "You sure turned out to be a hell of a Dad."

"Shut the fuck up," said Michael. "You don't know anything about me, or about what happened. Who are you to say…"

Alma's boyfriend shouted over him, "I know enough."

"Stop it," said the black woman. "Both of you. Just calm down and get his things together. We've made enough noise as it is. Be careful not to leave anything. We can't leave any evidence they were here."

"Why?" asked Michael.

"I wasn't talking to you," said the woman with the shotgun.

"You trying to erase me or something?" asked Michael. "Is that it? You planning on getting rid of me?"

"We don't want people following us back to Widowsfield," said the stranger. "Did you tell anyone you were here?"

"Yeah, I called a bunch of people," said Michael. "I called them and told them where I was, and who I was with, and to call the cops if I didn't call them back tomorrow. So, you're shit out of luck, bitch."

The black woman walked over to the phone that was sitting beside the bed. "Did you call from here?"

Michael nodded, uncertain why the woman would ask that. She placed her hand on the receiver, and then looked back at him with a devilish grin. "He's lying. He didn't call anyone."

"Bullshit," said Michael. "I called lots of people. How the fuck are you supposed to know if I did or not?"

"Trust me, I know," said the woman confidently.

"The guy at the front desk has my name. He knows I'm here. And they're going to see what you did to that door tomorrow. You're going to have people looking for me."

"I'm not worried about that," said the woman. "Now let's get Ben and get out of here. We don't have much time. One of the other guests might've called the cops already."

As she pointed to the bathroom, someone knocked on the door to the room.

"Fuck," said the big man that had busted the chain. "Do you think that's the cops?"

"No, they're not that fast. I'll take care of it," said the black woman as she went to the door. She looked through the peephole and then turned to look back at the others. "I don't think it's anything to worry about. It just looks like one of the people staying at the hotel coming to check on us."

She set the shotgun down against the wall so that when she opened the door it would be out of sight. She looked at Michael and said, "Keep your mouth shut."

The woman feigned a smile for the newcomer as she opened the door and said, "I'm sorry for the noise…"

Before she could finish, the man pushed his way in and screamed, "I'm not going to let you hurt Ben!"

CHAPTER 12 - Sacrifices

South Side of Chicago
July 13th, 2007

Rosemary had called her mother to tell her that she was coming over. Rosemary had only spoken with her mother a few times since she'd left to go with Oliver to Widowsfield, and this was only the second time that she'd visited since then. Rosemary had lied to her mother about where she'd been, thinking it would be better for her to know as little as possible.

Her mother was ecstatic to see her daughter, but they had a large family, and the eldest children would often disappear for several weeks or months at a time, so Glenda hadn't been concerned about Rosemary's disappearance. Meanwhile, Rosemary's mother was busy with her grandchildren, and several of them were running around the small apartment while Rosemary visited.

"I swear to God, Rose," said Glenda as two of Rosemary's nephews tore through the kitchen. She had her hands up in the air, holding a wooden spoon that was covered in sticky cookie dough out of the children's reach. The boys ran off to another part of the apartment, screaming the entire time. "These kids are going to be the death of me." Being a grandmother had changed Glenda, and Rosemary liked the way her mother was smiling more often than not these days. It was a drastic change since the days they'd spent living with Rosemary's father.

The sweltering summer heat was barely eased by the box fan in the window, and Rosemary felt herself beginning to sweat as she sat at the kitchen table. Her mother was in the middle of preparing cookies for a church bake sale, and insisted that she needed to keep working while Rosemary visited. The oven's heat made the sweltering afternoon even worse.

"How's the money situation been?" asked Rosemary.

"You know what? It hasn't been that bad, honestly. I'm a business owner now. Can you believe that?"

"A business owner?" asked Rosemary in shock and disbelief. "What are you talking about?"

"That's right. No need to look at me like that. It's the truth."

"What sort of business."

"An internet one," said Glenda as she started to mix the dough after adding in more butter.

Rosemary gave her mother a queer look and asked, "What sort of internet business? And since when are you a computer person?"

"I'm not the one with the computer. Someone else is handling that for me. You know I've got no use for technology."

"What are you selling?"

"Jewelry. You know how I used to always like making those beaded necklaces, right? Well, Pauline at church said that her niece sold that sort of thing on the internet, and that she was making loads of cash."

"No kidding?"

"Mmm hmm," said Glenda as she stuck her pinkie finger into the dough and then into her mouth. She seemed satisfied with the taste and started to stir again. "Before you know it, I'm going to be making millions. You just wait and see. And you know what, speaking of jewelry, you just wait there a minute. I'll be right back. Make sure the boys don't get into that cookie dough."

Rosemary's mother left the room, and no sooner had she walked out than the two boys reappeared, standing on the tips of their toes to stare into the bowl. "No," said Rosemary sharply as she pointed back into the living room. "You two get on out of here."

They groaned complaints, but obeyed. Rosemary waited until they were gone before she reached into her satchel and took out an envelope filled with cash. She'd finally cashed all of the checks that she'd gotten from Oliver in Widowsfield, and she was planning on leaving the area to hide out somewhere in Indiana for a while. However, she wanted to leave her mother some cash before she left.

Rosemary lifted a stack of bills that were on the table and set the envelope beneath them. She didn't put her name on the envelope, but drew a rose on it so that her mother would understand where it had come from. She heard her mother's heavy footsteps returning and she quickly spread the rest of the mail out over the money she'd left.

"Here we go," said Glenda as she brought back a wooden, beaded necklace. "What do you think? Do you like it?"

"It's gorgeous," said Rosemary as she inspected the jewelry.

"Well then, don't just look at it, go ahead and try it on."

Rosemary put the necklace on and smiled up at her mother. "I love it. Thank you."

"You're welcome baby. I've been saving it just for you. But you've got to promise me you'll keep it on. Okay? Don't ever take it off. That way a piece of me can always be with you. Then, next time I see you, I'll give you a new one. Sound good? That'll be like a new tradition for us."

"Sounds good," said Rosemary with a wide smile.

Widowsfield
March 13th, 1996

"Heaven?" asked Oliver in surprise. "You don't really believe that, do you?"

Vess walked slowly down the stairs, with Oliver just ahead, as they went down to where the CORD was being kept. "What else would you call it? This entire project is based around trying to explore the place our energy goes when we die. Don't let yourself get caught up in terminology. In Norse mythology it was Valhalla, the Great Hall in Asgard; the ancient Greeks longed to reach Elysium; and Buddhists refer to it as Nirvana, where we give up our desire to own material things. Most cultures developed some version of the same thing. All we're trying to do is use science to explain what people think God is responsible for. That is, after all, what all the various sciences have been doing since they began."

"But if we prove that heaven, or whatever you want to call it, is real? Wouldn't that prove God exists?"

"No, of course not," said Vess as if Oliver's reasoning was ludicrous. "It does the exact opposite. Mankind has spent too much time creating Gods to explain what they didn't understand. Finding heaven's no different than proving the sun isn't Apollo's chariot streaking through the sky."

Vess took each step cautiously as they traversed the skinny halls within the belly of the Eldridge. Oliver took advantage of their time together to learn more about Cada E.I.B.'s goal. "Is that what we're trying to do? Put a knife in God?"

Vess enjoyed Oliver's phrasing. "That's an interesting way to put it."

"Am I right?"

"In a way, yes," said Vess. "Although, it's not as diabolical as you make it sound. Giving up faith is a step forward for the human race. Just like we stopped believing in Hades, or Zeus, or Odin, or any number of the old Gods, the current deities people cling to will die in time. We're not suffering any delusion that we can eradicate all belief in God around the world, but if science is able to provide us with an explanation about what happens when we die…" He shook his head and smiled before saying, "It doesn't take a scientist to recognize what sort of affect that might have on society."

"So why March 14th?" asked Oliver. "What does doing it on that date, at 3:14, do for us?"

"It's just marketing," said Vess. "Most people are familiar with the numbers because of their relationship to basic math, but the history books don't have much regard for the date. When you hear the number, it doesn't immediately conjure up any recollection about an important event. But we're going to change all of that. Soon, whenever someone hears the numbers three-fourteen, they'll think of what we accomplished. The name of our company, and the date and time that we performed our experiment will create instant immortality for us. Mankind will never forget us."

"Wow," said Oliver. They were moving slowly through the ship on account of Vess's disability. "Were you the one that came up with the idea to use the date?"

"No," said Vess. "Oddly, it was Einstein that suggested it. As much as the man tried my patience, I'm willing to give him proper due. Three-fourteen was his idea."

"I didn't know he had a mind for marketing," said Oliver as he opened the door that led into the loading bay where the CORD was located.

"Don't give him too much credit," said Vess with a snort. "March 14th is his birthday after all."

Oliver laughed and asked, "Is it really? I had no idea."

Vess snickered as he nodded. "The wily old bastard was intent on figuring out a way to make sure people remembered it."

"I would've thought he grew up with the dates switched around," said Oliver. "Wouldn't he have written March 14th as 14-3?"

"Yes, but back in those days he was keen on considering himself an American. Plus, he loved the mathematical significance of his birthday when written down in our style. Also, good luck finding the 3rd day of the 14th month, or the 31st of April. If you want to turn 314 into a date, then March 14th is your only option."

Oliver allowed Vess to enter the room first. The door opened to a catwalk that looked down on the bay where the CORD was kept. Oliver expected the old man to be pleased, but Vess turned to him with a scowl.

"This isn't right," said Vess.

"What's not right?"

"This," Vess motioned down to the level below. "All of this. What is that curtain?" He pointed at an enormous curtain that was currently bunched up and tied, but could be guided around a half-moon rail to shroud the CORD during the experiment. "And what is that box there?" Vess was referring to a stopgap measure that had been installed to regulate the flow of radioactive material. The original CORD hadn't implemented such cautions, because people at the time weren't familiar with the damaging effects that radiation could have on the human body. The stopgap was simply a container that could keep anyone on the ship safe from the uranium. When the stopgap was cut off, the CORD would be fed the radioactive material, a process that Oliver and the engineers at Cada E.I.B. began to refer to as 'Cutting the CORD.'

"We followed the directions that we…"

"I don't care," said Vess. "You have to fix this. We have to try and make the room look as much like it did as possible."

"We can't," said Oliver. "The stopgap measure can't be replaced. I can have the curtains taken down, but the…"

"Who authorized these changes?" asked Vess, incensed.

"The Accord," said Oliver, referring to the board of scientists that he'd assumed Vess was a member of. They were the collection of scientists that decided which projects Cada E.I.B. funded. "We built everything according to their plans."

"Those idiots," said Vess, seething with anger as he grinded his grip on the railing. "They ignored everything I told them. They don't understand. Goddamn it!" Vess made a fist and slammed it down, causing the hollow rail to hum.

"I can take the curtain down," said Oliver. "But there's nothing I can do about the stopgap mechanism." He glanced at the orange box that was positioned to the left of the CORD. It was about two feet high, and rectangular shaped, with black hazard stickers on each side. The reinforced box was an integral part of the CORD, and removing it couldn't be done before the experiment was meant to begin.

Vess pointed to the corners of the room, where cameras had been set up. "And those have to go."

"Sir, The Accord is going to want to be able to…"

"I don't care," said Vess definitively. "I'm here, and this is my project. You work for me. Do you understand?"

"Yes sir," said Oliver as he avoided looking into the old man's eyes.

"I was there the first time the CORD was activated," said Vess. "I'm the only one that's ever seen this thing work, and I'll be damned if they think they're going to tell me how to do things. We don't need these safety measures. I'm the only one that's felt the effects, and I'm not dying of cancer. I'm as healthy as I ever was." He looked at Oliver, as if expecting the young man to nod in agreement, but his new assistant just continued to avoid his gaze. "Look at me."

Oliver did as he was told.

"How old do you think I am?"

"I…" Oliver stammered. "I honestly don't know."

"I'm ninety-three."

Oliver was surprised, and couldn't help but scowl in disbelief.

"Yes, that's right." Vess was amused by Oliver's reaction. "Ninety-three." He raised his arms out to the side to present himself. "I don't look that bad for being so old, do I?"

"Ninety-three?" asked Oliver in surprise. "How is that possible? I wouldn't have guessed you were more than seventy."

"Seventy?" asked Vess as if offended. "Do I look that old?" He glanced at his hands, which weren't as wrinkled as a man of seventy would have. Then he poked at his cheek, which drooped. "I guess my skin's been pulled down a bit, and my joints are suffering more and more by the day, but you can thank gravity for that."

Oliver didn't say anything, but just continued to gape at the man. He couldn't fathom that Vess was as old as he claimed.

Vess sensed Oliver's disbelief. "Hard to believe, I know, but it's the truth. I was forty when I took part in the first CORD experiment. No one's certain what happened that day, and despite my best efforts I can only remember bits and pieces of it, but the experiment stopped the aging process in me. I was the subject of an awful lot of studies over the years, but it was only recently that they've come even close to figuring out what got triggered inside of me that day. Apparently, my body started producing an excess amount of an enzyme called telomerase, which is how cellular structures can prevent themselves from dying."

"That's incredible," said Oliver.

"Yes, it is, and we've never been able to recreate what happened that day. And if you don't do as I say, then we won't be able to recreate it today either."

"Ninety-three?" asked Oliver again in awe.

Vess laughed and nodded. "Yes. For most of the time I looked like any other forty year old, but my skin eventually gave in to gravity, and the cartilage in my joints continued to wear away. There's no getting around that part of aging. But beneath this drooping exterior is the mind and spirit of a forty-year-old, I assure you."

"Did you make it to heaven?" asked Oliver with reverence, like a former atheist that had suddenly found God.

"I don't know," said Vess. "I can remember everything leading up to the moment we turned the machine on, but then there was a span of time that's lost to me. The next thing I remember is waking up as the machine was powering down. I've spent my entire life trying to recreate what happened that day, and I'm not going to put up with anyone standing in my way."

"I'll do what I can to help," said Oliver. "I can have the curtain taken down, but there's nothing I can do about the stopgap. The CORD won't work without it. It's designed to prevent radiation from leaking. They even made us use an external power supply for it in case the battery fails."

"Do whatever you need to," said Vess. "When we set sail tomorrow, I want this room to be as close to perfect as you can get it. Understand?"

"Yes sir," said Oliver. "I'll do what I can."

Branson
March 13th, 2012
4:20 AM

Charles Dunbar awoke with the knowledge that a child by the name of Ben Harper was in the room next to him, and that Ben was in danger. A group of people had forced their way into the room, and were planning on hurting the helpless child.

Charles leapt from his bed, convinced that he was the only one that could save Ben. He put his ear to the wall and listened to the commotion next door, and was certain he was right. He could hear a slew of people yelling in the next room, but also heard the gentle scratching of Ben's fingers against the wall between them.

"You sons of bitches!" Charles was about to run out of his room, but then he went back to the kitchen to find a knife. He was in only a pair of boxer shorts and a t-shirt, but there wasn't time to get dressed. He rifled through the drawers of the small kitchen before settling on a dull steak knife. It would have to do.

On his way back out, he walked along the side of his bed to reach the wall that separated him from Ben. He put his hand on the wall and said, "Don't worry buddy, I'm on my way."

It was chilly out, and the hair on his arms stood tall as the wind struck him once he opened the door. For a moment, he considered how crazy the situation was, but he didn't give himself time to debate. He knew that Ben's life was in danger.

He walked over to the room beside his, and thought about what the best way to handle the group inside was. Charles wasn't sure how he knew about the people in the room, or why he was certain they had weapons, but it was an infallible truth. He raised his hand to knock, but then paused and wondered to himself if he'd taken a sleeping pill. A few years back he'd been prescribed a sleep aid, but had reacted poorly to it. His wife found him sleeping on the kitchen floor one night, and he had no recollection of how he'd gotten there.

Charles shook his head, confident that this wasn't the result of a bad reaction to any medication. Ben Harper was in the bathroom in this room, terrified and hoping that Charles would save him. Charles had never been more certain of anything in his life.

He knocked on the door, and waited with the knife behind his back. He was sure they had weapons, so he needed them to open the door without any expectation of being attacked. His heart was thudding, and he felt the knife's handle grow slick in his sweating palms. He smiled at the peephole as he swallowed hard, nervous and jittery.

A black woman opened the door. She looked to be in her early to mid-thirties, with dreadlocks and wearing several necklaces made of wooden beads. She smiled and said, "I'm sorry for the noise."

She didn't have a gun, so Charles decided this was his best chance to attack. He needed to surprise the group and get to Ben.

"I'm not going to let you hurt Ben!"

Charles charged at the stranger, knocking her back as he plunged his knife deep into her belly. She gasped and tried to fight back, but Charles easily pushed her toward the bed inside. A thin, white woman with bobbed black hair was also in the room, and she screamed out, "What are you doing?" Charles pushed past her, still gripping the handle of the steak knife that was now inside the black woman's gut. He forced the woman to the bed, and she fell backward while trying to claw at him. He tugged at the knife, desperate to pull it free, but it was slick and the serrated edge caused it to stick inside of her.

One of the large men in the room cursed as he grabbed Charles' shoulders and started to pull him back. Charles struck the man's ample gut with his elbow, causing him to exhale, but not retreat. The bushy haired, bearded man with the glasses was intent on stopping Charles, and wrapped his arm around his neck. Charles gasped as the big man squeezed, and then he finally released the knife as he tried to get his fingers beneath the fat man's arm.

"Hold him still," said one of the other two men in the room.

"I'm trying," said the fat one as Charles thrashed in an attempt to get free.

Charles saw the second man standing in front of him. He had a shaved head, and there was a tattoo of a snake near his ear. The man clenched Charles' shirt, and then reached back to strike him. Before Charles could react, the man hit him hard enough to knock him out.

"Aw fuck," said Jacker. "You hit him so hard he bashed the back of his head into my lip." He dropped the unconscious attacker and the stranger slumped to the floor. Then he put his hand over his bleeding lip as he winced.

"He stabbed Rosemary," said Paul, unconcerned with Jacker's minor injury.

"What?" asked Jacker. "Holy shit. I didn't even realize. Oh fuck."

"No!" Alma shouted in reaction to something Michael had done.

Paul and Jacker looked over at her, uncertain what had happened. They saw that Alma had grabbed the pistol off the dresser, and Paul realized that Michael had tried to get to it during the commotion.

"You stay there," said Alma as she pointed the gun at her father.

Rosemary was on her back, on the bed, with her hands gripping the knife that was lodged in her stomach. She was breathing hard, and groaning in pain as she cried. Michael was on the other side of the bed with a wicked grin as he looked at his daughter. Paul wasn't certain what to deal with first, so he tapped Jacker's arm and then pointed at Rosemary. "Help her. Wrap the wound, but don't pull the knife out."

"Oh fuck, dude. No," said Jacker. "I'm not..." He was blinking rapidly and shaking his head. "I'm not good with blood."

Paul slapped his friend and then snapped his fingers in front of his face. "Get over it. She needs your help."

Jacker took several deep breaths and nodded before moving to Rosemary's side. He had to step over the unconscious man on the floor as Paul closed the door and then focused on Michael. Paul walked over to Alma, who was still pointing the pistol at her father. He reached out, expecting her to hand over the gun, but she kept it gripped tightly with both hands. Her knuckles were turning white as she squeezed, and the barrel was wobbling as she pointed it at the man that had caused her so much pain.

"I'll take the gun, babe," said Paul, but she didn't hand it over.

Alma slipped her finger over the trigger, and stared down the quivering barrel. "You piece of shit."

Michael had his hands up, and his grin had faded. He scowled, and shook his head while saying, "You don't want to do this, kid." He looked at Paul, desperate, and said, "Take the gun from her, man. Take the fucking gun from her."

"Babe, give me the gun," said Paul as he put his hand over hers.

She jerked her hand away from him and sneered as she aimed. "I kept my mouth shut all these years, you piece of shit."

"Baby," said Michael. "Alma, sweetie, come on. Put the gun down."

"All those things you did..." Alma's words were accented by a lifetime of pain and anger. Her eyes were wet with tears, and she stared at her father with intense hatred. Her pupils were pinpricks, each focused solely on the man she'd fantasized about kicking out of her life in whatever way she could.

"I never wanted to hurt you, kid. I never wanted to..."

"Alma, give me the gun," said Paul as Michael pleaded for his daughter's mercy.

Alma ignored Paul as she focused on her father. She asked, "You never wanted to what? Go ahead and finish. Go ahead and tell them what you did."

"I never hurt you," said Michael. "I loved you."

Alma let out a quick laugh just as a tear fell down her cheek. "Is that right?"

"Alma," said Paul, "please give me the gun."

"Don't kill him," said Rosemary. Her voice was plagued by her pain, and she spoke through clenched teeth. Jacker was standing over her with his head turned to the side as he breathed in and out quickly. The large man's face had turned pale, and his brow was dotted with emerging beads of sweat. It was clear that he was fighting off unconsciousness as Rosemary's wound continued to pump blood. Jacker had taken the cover off one of the pillows and wrapped it around the blade that was stuck in Rosemary's gut, but the formerly white fabric had become sodden with brilliant red blood.

"Not here," said Rosemary. Paul noticed that she'd taken off one of her beaded necklaces and was gripping it like a dying Catholic might clutch a rosary. "You can't kill him here."

"Why not?" asked Alma, never taking her eyes off the man she was considering murdering.

"You need him." Rosemary was forced to speak in quick gasps as the pain from her wound gripped her. "Take him with us."

"I don't need him."

"Yes you do," said Rosemary. "As a sacri…" she groaned in pain as Jacker pulled the pillowcase away to replace it with a new one. He apologized profusely as he slung the bloodied case to the side.

"As a what?" asked Paul of Rosemary. "Why do we need him?"

"As a sacrifice," said Rosemary.

CHAPTER 13 – Skeletons

Widowsfield
March 14th, 1996

Oliver did his best to alter the room so that it resembled how it had looked 53 years earlier. The lead curtain had been removed, as well as the metal track that it had hung from. He expected to get contacted by angry members of The Accord that had been remotely monitoring the experiment after he took down the cameras, but no emails were sent, and no calls received. Oliver hoped that Vess had spoken directly with The Accord, and that he wasn't doing this against their wishes.

As he'd warned Vess, the stopgap mechanism that contained the radioactive material couldn't be moved. Oliver had spoken with their lead engineer, who laughed off the request before explaining that it would be impossible to change without several months of work, and that even if it could be done, he wouldn't do it. Exposing anyone to those levels of radiation would certainly kill them. Oliver decided not to argue that Vess hadn't succumbed to radiation poisoning. It wouldn't have mattered even if he convinced the engineer to do as he requested. They didn't have time to make the necessary changes.

It had been a long night, and Oliver hadn't gotten more than a couple hours of sleep. He was too excited to slow down, and too nervous to relax. He'd been working for Cada E.I.B. for almost a decade, and had been chosen for this project based on his experience managing other, less important projects for the company. His expertise wasn't in science, or engineering, or any other skill that would seem to be of importance for this position. Instead, Oliver was chosen based on his ability to follow directions and to manage other people.

The process of securing his job had been a lengthy one. It began with a simple application for a project lead position that was offered to all of the managers in Cada E.I.B. throughout the world. Hundreds applied, and those selected were advanced to the next stage of the hiring process. Oliver and those that advanced were given extensive written and oral tests to determine personality identifiers, and this helped to whittle the group down further. After an interview process, Oliver and a select few other managers were flown to Spain to meet with members of the board, also known as The Accord.

The Accord was made up of acclaimed scientists and scholars. They met quarterly and were presented with project reports and proposals from the various arms of the company. During this process, The Accord decided which projects would be ceased or continued, as well as what new projects would be funded. They also chose the managers for each of the projects, and Oliver was asked to perform an interview with the group to prove he was the right person for the upcoming job. He'd never been more nervous in his life.

Apparently he impressed them, because a month after coming home he was contacted about taking over the Widowsfield project. However, the offer came with a high cost. When they revealed what he would have to do to earn the position, he understood why so many of the previous tests in the interview process had included such personal information. The representative of The Accord explained that Oliver would have to leave his entire life behind if he was going to take on the Widowsfield project. He would never be allowed to communicate with his family again. It was as if he was being placed in a Witness Protection Program. While Oliver didn't mind leaving most of his life behind, he was given the chance to go visit his family before making any decision.

His final visit home had been predictably disastrous. His mother had been an uncaring, distant woman his entire life. She was petty and vindictive, and never had a nice thing to say about anyone. Her self-worth seemed to come from demeaning others, which she did with aplomb. His father had left years ago, and hadn't bothered keeping in touch with his children other than hit-or-miss holiday calls. Oliver's only regret was leaving his little brother, Frank, behind. But Frank had a family of his own, and was doing well for himself. He didn't need Oliver looking after him anymore. Oliver stayed at Frank's house the final night of his trip, and the brothers shared beers on the porch, recalling the scant good memories of their time under the watch of their domineering mother. When Oliver said goodbye, he knew he would never see Frank again, but he was confident his brother would be fine without him.

After Oliver agreed to take the job as the manager of the Widowsfield Project, The Accord provided him with tickets to Utah for another vacation. He would never go, and was instead sent to Missouri to start work. His family received the unfortunate news that Oliver's small, two-seat Cessna had crashed in a Utah state park, and that his remains had been savaged by animals before authorities were able to retrieve them.

Oliver watched the news reports about his death, and marveled at the length to which The Accord had gone to make it believable. While the majority of Oliver's body was reportedly charred or missing, authorities had been able to retrieve enough personal effects to declare him dead.

That had been three years earlier, and since then Oliver worked tirelessly to appease The Accord. Now the result of his labor was at hand, and his heart raced as he continually checked his watch while enduring the excruciatingly long wait until 3:00.

The sound of the door opening startled him, and he looked up in excitement. Vess came in alone and waved down to him as he said, "Hello, Oliver."

"Hi," said Oliver before he motioned around the room. "We worked all night to get this place looking as close as possible to how it did in 1943."

"I see," said Vess as he began the arduous trip along the catwalk and to the stairs.

"We couldn't do anything about the stopgap," said Oliver as he pointed to the orange box that sat beside the CORD. "I asked Jim if he could remove it, but he said it'd take months. He also said that the stopgap is tied to the flow of electricity, to make sure the CORD doesn't cut out if something happens to its power source. So there's no getting rid of that thing."

"That's disappointing," said Vess. "But we've run out of time to argue about it now." He took each step slow and carefully. "But there's something else in this room that will need to get out before we get started."

"What's that?" asked Oliver as he looked around the room. He thought they'd been thorough, and was curious what else Vess wanted to be taken out.

The elderly man pointed at Oliver and said, "You."

"Me? Why?" Oliver asked as if offended. "I thought that I…"

"You thought wrong," said Vess as he reached the bottom of the stairs. "There'll only be two people in this room when we activate the device, and it'll be the same two people that were here the first time."

"Wait," said Oliver. He was both confused and frustrated as he learned that he wouldn't be there to witness the result of the work he'd been a part of for the past few years. "Who else will be here?"

"The CORD is a magnificent machine," said Vess as he approached, relying heavily upon a cane. "But there's a cog missing in your monster, Oliver."

"I don't understand."

Vess passed Oliver and got to the CORD. He placed his hand against the smooth metal where the door was hidden, and then lifted the latch to open it. Oliver had known of the compartment within, but had assumed it was only meant as an access area for the mechanical components within the walls. Vess smiled as he opened the door and then motioned inside as if offering its contents to Oliver. "Your monster has no heart, Dr. Frankenstein." He knocked on the side of the machine, causing a hollow thump. Oliver looked within, but saw nothing.

"Vess, I'm sorry," said Oliver as he shook his head. "I don't understand what you're talking about."

"I never told you why I was chosen to participate in the original experiment," said Vess. "It certainly wasn't for my scientific acumen." He chuckled and shook his head. "I was no fan of what science was up to back then, at least not the conventional sort. Men were obsessed with bombs, and guns, and all manner of things to kill one another with. My work, on the other hand, was of an all-together different nature."

Vess stared into the CORD, studying its belly for a moment before continuing, "I was the successor of a man whose name has been criminally forgotten over the years: Dr. Duncan MacDougall. He proved that when we die, we lose approximately 21 grams of weight."

"I've heard of that before," said Oliver. "You worked on that study?"

"No," said Vess. "I was only a child when he was doing his work. I was involved in experiments that sought to expand upon what MacDougall had discovered. We were trying to find what caused the weight loss. Our best theory was that it was an unidentified energy of some sort."

"A soul?" asked Oliver.

"If that's the term you want to use, yes. I spent several years studying how cultures around the world regarded death, and the soul. And one thing that I continued to come upon, time and again, was the act of human sacrifice being a part of religious ceremonies. I developed a theory about this, and it got me a lot more attention than I ever anticipated. And not the sort of attention anyone would want."

"What was your theory?" asked Oliver.

"It's complicated, but the basic premise was that since MacDougall had proven that energy left the human body at the moment of death, it stood to reason that the energy must either dissipate or be transported someplace else. Since we were never able to find a way to identify the energy that was leaving the body, then there were only two options: either we hadn't yet discovered a way to identify the energy, or it was disappearing from this dimension."

"To heaven?" asked Oliver as he looked at the CORD.

"Perhaps," said Vess. "But wherever it went, the mere fact that we'd proven there was such a thing as a 'soul' was monumental. That's how I was introduced to a group of religious historians that had been cataloging examples of human sacrifice and how nearly every culture in history had become obsessed with it in some form or another. They read my paper and asked to meet with me to compare notes. Their work focused on how human sacrifice had been tied to religious zealotry. They were fascinated with how cultures all across the world had been obsessed with the same idea: That sacrificing a living creature, and oftentimes a human, could appease their Gods. These beliefs were so similar that it was reasonable to believe that it was an integral part of the human experience. Combined with my studies on the energy of the soul, it wasn't hard to come to the conclusion that sacrifice might actually play some part in the appeasement of a deity."

"You can't be serious," said Oliver.

"Oh I am, and I also understand your disbelief. All the greatest evolutions of science have been met with intense skepticism. This is just another example. Humans have been obsessed with murdering one another since the dawn of man. Whether it's a virginal girl being sacrificed on an altar, or a million young men shipped across seas with guns, we'll never stop trying to kill one another. Once you accept that every human death results in the disappearance of energy, it becomes reasonable to suspect that this energy is a resource to some other place, or some other being."

"God?" asked Oliver. "Are you saying that God needs our energy? Like we're some sort of Earth-dwelling battery or something?" He couldn't help but snicker at the thought. It seemed beyond outlandish.

"Perhaps," said Vess. "We know, without question, that mankind has been murdering one another in the name of their creator for centuries, and we know that cultures all across the world have parroted the idea that human sacrifice can be used to appease their God. Would it be so unfathomable that there's some truth to a belief that so many unrelated cultures have shared? After all, we're more than happy to accept the more tangible things those cultures gave to us, like agriculture and medicine. Why shouldn't we pay closer attention to their beliefs about other things?"

"You said it yourself yesterday," said Oliver as he started to become argumentative. "We proved that the sun is a ball of gas and not a chariot. Right? Same thing is true here. Agriculture and medicine have tangible results. Science relies on that. It relies on evidence."

"And I've given you evidence," said Vess. "We proved that human beings have souls, and that those souls vanish upon death. The next step is finding where that energy goes. And that's all this is," he slapped his hand against the CORD. "This is our attempt to open a door to where our souls go. This device could explain why mankind is obsessed with war. If we discover that there's a need for our energy past this gateway, in whatever dimension lies beyond it, then we might be able to explain the darkest part of the human experience. We might finally know why humans are so desperate to kill one another."

"Because God wants us to?"

"Could be," said Vess. "Wouldn't that be something? To discover the desire to kill is divine." He laughed, but Oliver was too stunned to laugh with him.

"I had no idea that's what this was about," said Oliver as he looked at the CORD.

"Our theory was outlandish, certainly, but it had enough of a foundation in fact to get us noticed. I never expected the attention the paper would receive. We started getting contacted by other groups, some of which had dubious intent to say the least. Some of them wanted to discuss our findings, and others wanted to provide evidence they'd uncovered. An archaeologist got in touch with us and even sent out some items he'd dug up at a ritual sacrifice site in South America. Then, suddenly, the military was knocking on my door because of how 'dangerous' they thought my ideas were. And while they never confirmed my suspicions, I'd heard from other sources that Hitler himself had become interested in my theory. From that point forward, all research related to my work ceased to exist; at least in the public eye."

Oliver looked at the open door of the CORD and suddenly comprehended what Vess had meant when he said there had been two people present during the first experiment. "Wait, are you going to put someone in there as a…" he couldn't finish his sentence.

"As a sacrifice?" Vess finished the sentence for Oliver, and then nodded. "Yes. But not just anyone. This machine requires someone with a special talent: A psychic."

"You're joking."

"I'm not, I assure you," said Vess. "The government was obsessed with competing with Germany and Russia in every way they could back when they recruited me. It wasn't just the atom bomb, and the CORD that they were interested in. Rumors swirled that Hitler was obsessed with psychic phenomenon, and so the United States government began funding studies into it as well. While it was rare, they were able to find people that exhibited enhanced senses. Of the various types of extra-sensory perception they encountered, the ones that were the most dramatic were the ones known as psychometrics. That's the ability to pull information out of inanimate objects."

"And there are really people that can do that?" asked Oliver.

"Oh yes," said Vess. "And they can do quite a bit more than just that, when trained properly."

Oliver was stunned. "That's incredible. I've never believed in any of that. I remember watching a show about a skeptic that was offering to pay someone a million dollars if they could prove that they had that sort of ability. He debunked all of them."

"Of course he did," said Vess. "He worked for us." He snickered as he put one hand on Oliver's shoulder. He massaged him for a moment before continuing, "Back when the government was in charge, they went about their search for psychics in a horribly inefficient way. Surprise, surprise," Vess smirked and rolled his eyes. "But once The Accord took over research of this project, they came up with a far more efficient way to find subjects. It was unbelievably easy to stage events like the one you mentioned. People who claimed they had special powers flocked to those studios in droves, each promising that they could claim the million dollars. The majority of them were frauds, but the ones that demonstrated actual ability were given the chance to do it in front of an audience. The event was staged so that they couldn't win, of course, and they were shocked when they were debunked on live television. After that, they disappeared from public view, and no one ever cared what happened to them."

"And what did happen to them?" asked Oliver, concerned that he knew the answer.

"They came to work for us," said Vess. "But don't worry, the ones that proved their abilities earned a lot more than a million dollars in their time. We reward talent. The Accord has employed many psychometrics, and has worked hard to find out how best to unlock their abilities. The most powerful psychometrics have even learned how to control other people's minds merely through touch. Take a gander through some of the more famous assassinations in recent history. You might be surprised how many assassins out there have no idea why they set out to kill their victims, as if during the act they were performing someone else's will. Not that the man I'm bringing here today was ever that powerful though. He barely understood his own abilities by the time I put him in the machine."

"So the person you're bringing here was with you back in 1943?"

"Yes, he was," said Vess.

"Does he remember what happened during the time frame that you forgot?"

"If he does, he's not talking about it," said Vess.

They heard the clang of metal from above, and both looked to see that the door was opening. The two guards that traveled with Vess entered slowly, with a stretcher between them. They maneuvered along the thin catwalk and then down the stairs. Oliver could see that a man was lying on the stretcher, but a blanket had been pulled over his entire body, including his face, as if they were carrying a corpse.

"Here's the very first true psychic I ever met," said Vess as the guards brought the stretcher over to them. The old man lifted the sheet to reveal a horrific sight.

The man on the stretcher looked skeletal. His eyes were open and bugged out due to the lack of fat puffing up his facial features. His skin sagged, similar to Vess's, but it was clear that he'd been laying on his back for the majority of his life, causing his loose skin to pool at his sides as if he were a wax figure melting away. His lips drooped as well, and saliva fell from the corners of his mouth, which it had been doing long enough to cause severe, inflamed wounds. His jaw jutted forth, accentuated by how his flesh sagged, and his teeth were yellow and long, the gums having receded back far enough to reveal the beginnings of roots.

What first appeared to be a corpse then revealed itself to be alive. The man on the stretcher was breathing, a throaty, wet gasp that came in quick succession, and his tongue was moving, causing a slopping sound as if a snake were writhing in a bucket of water. His eyes were open, and a clear gel had been smeared over them.

"Oliver," said Vess, "meet Lyle Everman."

Branson
March 13th, 2012
4:30 AM

"A sacrifice?" asked Alma, though she didn't take her eyes off the man they were speaking about.

Michael Harper had his hands in the air, and Paul was still trying to convince Alma to give up the gun. She had the trigger pulled partially back, a mere centimeter from firing.

"Yes," said Rosemary as she struggled to speak between pained gasps. "Trust me. You have to trust me."

"Alma, honey," said Paul, "give me the gun. He's not worth it."

"Sure he is," said Alma with dark humor as she continued to point the gun at her father.

"No, he's not. Think of what you'd be giving up. Think of the kids back home that are waiting for Miss Harper to teach them guitar in that new music room. Alma, think of us. If you shoot him, you're putting an end to what we just got started again. Come on, babe, I'm looking forward to the rest of our lives together. The last thing I want is to have to go to a prison to see you." He put his hand on hers, and this time she didn't pull away. "Give me the gun."

She relented, and let Paul take the gun from her. She apologized, and then went over to the bed to relieve Jacker, who looked like he was about to pass out on top of Rosemary.

"What the fuck do you mean by sacrifice?" Michael started to walk toward them, but Paul quickly halted his progress by pushing him back with one hand while pointing the gun at him with the other.

"The town wants you back," said Rosemary. "It wants you and Ben. It's up to me…" She grimaced as Alma pulled aside the wrapping that Jacker had bunched up around the blade. "It's up to us to get you back there."

"And kill me?" asked Michael. "So you're just a bunch of murderers?"

"I'm not killing anyone," said Jacker.

"Neither am I," said Paul, but then he smirked at Michael. "If I can help it."

"We're going to have to take her to the hospital," said Alma after examining Rosemary's wound.

"No, no," said Rosemary. "We have to get back to Widowsfield. The nurse there can help me. Take me to Helen."

"That's a bad idea," said Alma. "You're bleeding too…"

"We can't risk it," said Rosemary. "We have to keep it a secret that we were here. And we have to leave as soon as we can."

"I'm not going anywhere with you people," said Michael.

"You'll go wherever I damn well tell you to." Paul waved the gun in Michael's direction.

"So that you can use me as a sacrifice or something? You think I'm just going to get in a car with you and go back to that fucked up place? No way."

"This guy's an ass," said Jacker, "but he's right. I don't want to go back to that place either. This whole trip has been a nightmare. The last thing I want to do is willingly jump back into it. We should count ourselves lucky and just get the hell out of here."

"What about Rachel and Stephen?" asked Paul.

"Let's call them and tell them to get out of there too," said Jacker.

"You'll never get away," said Rosemary. "None of us will. Right Alma?"

They all looked at the young woman tending to Rosemary's wound, and she shrugged in response. "I don't know what you mean."

"You never got away," said Rosemary. "You ran and ran, but here you are, back in the nightmare you never left."

"She got away," said Jacker. "It was sixteen years ago, right? Fuck it. I'm game for getting the hell away from here now and coming back in a decade or two. Sounds like a good deal to me."

"It never leaves you," said Rosemary. "Widowsfield will haunt you for the rest of your life. You'll dream of it, and of the creature that lives there. You'll always feel him reaching out to you. Alma, tell them about your nightmares."

"What nightmares?" asked Alma.

Rosemary looked up at her as if her question was tiresome and annoying. "The teeth. The black wires. I know all about them, Alma. I know how The Watcher's been in your head all these years."

"How do you know about those?" asked Alma.

"You gave me your bear, remember? I'm a psychometric. Every minute I hold onto that thing I learn more about you."

"I can deal with nightmares," said Jacker.

"We have to go back," said Rosemary. "We have to get Ben and Michael back there too. Then we can put an end to this. If Michael's there, then Ben won't be able to help himself. He'll want to try and get to Michael through The Watcher's lies, and that's how we can trap him back in there. We're the only ones that can stop it."

"Stop what?" asked Paul as he got more and more flustered.

"We have to stop The Watcher from getting out," said Rosemary. "And we have to get Ben back there. We can't let him escape either."

"Why not? What does it matter?" asked Jacker.

"Look at the man on the floor," said Rosemary. "He came in here screaming about protecting your brother, but have any of you seen him before?"

"I have," said Michael. "He was staying in the room next door."

"The Skeleton Man hasn't been here for more than a couple hours and he's already affecting the guests." Rosemary moved Alma away as she gripped the steak knife that was lodged in her stomach. She clenched her jaw and breathed in as she tried to pull the knife free, but it was lodged in too deep.

"Don't," said Alma. "You're supposed to leave it in. They taught us that at a first-aid training we had to take at my school, in case one of the kids got hurt. You're supposed to leave it in and go to a hospital."

"No," said Rosemary. "I'll be fine. I just have to make it till tomorrow. Just get me back to Widowsfield so that Helen can patch me up."

"What happens tomorrow?" asked Paul.

Rosemary looked over at him, and then at the others who were waiting for an answer. "We end this."

"How?" asked Alma.

"We go back to Terry's house," said Rosemary as Alma helped push the blanket against her wound. "And then we force our way into The Watcher's world."

"Wait, what?" asked Jacker. "You mean back into that nightmare? No way, lady."

"I don't need you," said Rosemary. "I just need Alma, Ben, and Michael."

"No," said Paul. "Not a chance."

"If we don't put an end to this, then The Watcher and The Skeleton Man will come for each of you. They'll start with you, and then they'll move on to the people you love. They'll take pleasure in torturing them. You saw what they were doing to the souls that were stuck in that town. Just look at how Ben was able to take over this guy's mind. If we don't get him out of here now, and back to Widowsfield where he belongs, then by this time tomorrow he'll have an army on his side."

"You're all crazy," said Michael. "If you think you're getting me back into that house, you're dumber than you look, sweetheart."

"I'm not planning on giving you a choice," said Rosemary with no patience for Alma's abusive, drug-addicted father. "I'll have my friends break every bone in your body and then drag you into that place if I have to." She lay back down on the bed and took several breaths as she held a wadded pillowcase over her wound. "We don't have time to argue. Go get Ben, and get him in the van. We have to get out of here. We're running out of time."

"She's right," said Paul.

"What?" Jacker looked at his friend in disbelief.

"We can argue about it in the van," said Paul. "But we can't stay here. With all the noise we've made, they've probably already called the cops on us. The last thing we need is to have to try and explain all this shit to the police. Especially you, Jacker. They'll haul you in."

"I don't know how much I care about that at this point," said Jacker. "Christ, man, this is fucked up."

"Listen," said Rosemary. "If you take me to a hospital, then the police are going to get involved. We can't let that happen. The more people we get involved in this the more lives we're risking. Everyone that learns about what's happening in Widowsfield will become a target. Our only shot is to put an end to it, once and for all."

Jacker groaned and ran his hands through his shaggy head of hair. "How the hell did I get mixed up in this shit? All right, damn it, all right. Let's get that freak out of the bathroom and get the hell out of here. I'm too damn pretty for jail."

The group glanced around at each other, knowing that one of them would have to accept the responsibility of opening the bathroom door and facing the man in there. No one wanted to do it.

"I'll do it," said Paul as he motioned to Jacker to come take the gun and keep an eye on Michael.

"No," said Alma. "He's my brother. I'll get him."

"Alma," said Rosemary. Her voice had become weary and lethargic, a result of blood loss. "He's not your brother. You have to remember that. Ben might be in there somewhere, but the man in that bathroom is a twisted mass of souls. He's The Skeleton Man."

Alma nodded, and then went to the bathroom door. She paused with her hand on the cold metal handle, and then took a deep breath to calm herself.

The hinges squealed as the door slowly opened, and a spear of light invaded the darkness, illuminating the stark white tile floor and wall. Ben was revealed, shriveled in his chair with his right hand pressed to the wall. His glassy eyes stared out at his sister as his mouth was open wide with what looked like a t-shirt stuffed inside. Michael's belt was tied around Ben's head, keeping the gag in place.

Ben and his sister stared at one another, and Alma weakly said, "Ben, what did he do to you?"

CHAPTER 14 – Rest in Peace

Widowsfield
March 14th, 1996

"What's wrong with him?" asked Oliver as he stared down at the crippled man on the stretcher.

Lyle Everman's skin had sagged to the point that he appeared more like a rotting corpse than a living man. The skin on his face was so thin that Oliver could see the ridges of the skull beneath, as if only a silk sheet had been set over the skeleton. He stared directly up, and if not for the noises coming from his mouth and chattering teeth, he could've easily been mistaken for dead.

"We're not sure," said Vess. "After the original experiment, he fell into this state. It's some sort of coma, although his eyes are always open and he experiences frequent muscle twitches."

"Is that what's happening in his mouth?" asked Oliver, unable to hide his disgust with the way the man's tongue was slopping around.

"Yes, although he doesn't do that often. He's having a particularly bad episode today." Vess put his hand on the side of Lyle's face and thrust his thumb under his left eye hard enough to cause the lower lid to move and reveal a good amount of the bloodshot globe. The jelly that covered Lyle's eyes got on Vess's thumb, and the old man wiped it off on the cripple's shirt. "After the experiment, he aged like normal, but then around forty his aging seemed to slow down, just like mine. He's a freak of nature."

"I won't argue with that," said Oliver as he stared down at Lyle. "He's definitely a freak."

"He might be," said Vess, as if he'd taken offense. "But he's also the key that makes this machine work. Without him, we can forget all about opening the door to the next dimension."

"How can you be sure?"

"This isn't the first time we've tried to do the experiment again," said Vess. "The first couple attempts were absolute failures. We got new psychics, and they often ended up in the same condition as Lyle here, but we were never able to repeat our results."

"And you think putting him back in there will do the trick?" asked Oliver.

Vess looked around the room, admiring the work that Oliver's team had done to make it look like it had so many years earlier. "I think it's our best shot, for the same reason we had you design the room like this; for the same reason we convinced Greece to sell us this boat. We want to do everything we can to recreate the original experiment."

"Is there any chance I can get you to reconsider letting me stay here to watch the experiment?" asked Oliver.

"I'm afraid not," said Vess. "But don't worry, you'll be taking the place of Einstein. I want you to observe from a boat out near the Eldridge. We have Einstein's reports about what he and Major Groves saw during the first experiment, and I'm hoping you'll see the same. If you do, then there's a good chance the experiment has been a success. And if that's the case, I might not remember what happened."

"Don't you think we should at least put a couple cameras in here?" asked Oliver.

"No," said Vess with insistence. "The Accord has forced me to do this their way for years. Now it's my turn to say how things are supposed to go. No cameras."

"And The Accord is okay with this?" asked Oliver. Vess didn't answer, so Oliver asked, "You did speak with them, right? They know about what's going on here, don't they?"

"As far as you're concerned," said Vess with a grin and a wink, "I'm the only member of The Accord that matters." He looked at the guards and then motioned toward the open door of the CORD. "Put Mr. Everman on the floor in there."

"This is a bad idea," said Oliver as he began to get frantic.

"No it's not," said Vess. "Now tell me about this stopgap mechanism. Show me how to use it." He walked over to the orange box beside the CORD. His two guards carried Lyle into the machine and set the stretcher down. Then one of the guards opened the backpack he'd been carrying and started to pull out folded clothes that were sealed in plastic. He opened them while the second guard carefully slid Lyle off the stretcher before beginning to disrobe him.

Vess snapped his fingers, "Oliver, pay attention. We don't have much time."

"What're they doing?" asked Oliver.

Vess looked in on the two guards and said, "They're getting Lyle ready. We have the clothes he was wearing on the day of the experiment. I, unfortunately, never thought to keep mine. Hopefully that won't matter. Now, tell me about the stopgap please. You said something before about it controlling the power to the CORD."

"Not entirely," said Oliver. "It's just a failsafe. It's running on its own power source, and if the CORD is unable to sustain itself, then it can draw power from here."

"So it's just a battery?" asked Vess.

Oliver shook his head and then pointed at a black, coiled tube, about three inches wide, that snaked out from behind the stopgap and into the CORD. "It's also where the uranium is stored. When you power up the CORD, you also have to cut it."

"Cut it?"

"It's just the phrase we use for flipping this switch," Oliver knelt down and put his finger on a red switch on the face of the box. "The stopgap will regulate the flow of radiation, to prevent the machine from getting too much at once. That's why we call it 'cutting it.'"

"I don't understand the reference," said Vess.

"It's a drug thing," said Oliver, slightly embarrassed. "Like cutting cocaine."

"Oh," said Vess with a disappointed frown. "So I need to flip that switch just after powering the CORD?"

"Yes."

"Easy enough," said Vess. "You're going to go with my two friends here. They'll lead you out to the tugboat we have waiting for you. Stay about twenty or thirty yards away from the Eldridge, for your own safety."

"What am I supposed to be looking for?" asked Oliver. "I never read about what Einstein saw."

"He and Groves both claimed that the ship crackled with green electricity, and then," he snapped his finger and continued, "disappeared."

Oliver gave a puzzled look.

"Then, just as suddenly, it reappeared in a burst of white smoke. But several of the crew members weren't so lucky."

"What happened to them?" asked Oliver.

"Some fell into a sleep-like state, just like Lyle here. But others were found fused to parts of the ship, with their faces halfway in and halfway out of the ship itself."

"Seriously?"

Vess nodded and then laughed. "Sitting in a boat out of danger doesn't sound so bad now, does it?"

Branson
March 13th, 2012
Just before 5:00 AM

Alma felt dizzy as she stared at the brother she'd lost sixteen years earlier. His condition was horrifying. His eyes were open wide, the lower lids drooping as if having long ago lost the strength to close, and the whites blazing with red veins from dryness. His cheekbones jutted forth, easily defining his features as the thin, pale skin seemed to hang from his skull. Despite his appearance, she still recognized her brother.

"Ben."

"He's not your brother," said Rosemary from the bed. "Don't let him fool you, Alma."

Jacker glanced in at Ben and cursed, "Fucking hell." Then he glared over at Michael and asked, "Did you stuff that shit in his mouth, you sick fuck?"

Alma quickly moved to release the make-shift gag that had been wrapped around her brother's head. She was shaking as she did it, and felt her stomach lurch. She pulled the dirty t-shirt out of his mouth and then stepped back again.

Ben uttered his sister's name, "Alma."

She fell to her knees before him. The same sensation that had flooded her in the cabin when her mother had taken her there now came again. It was a wave of emotion that debilitated her. The skeletal man in the wheelchair, locked away in the dark bathroom by their abusive father, was unquestionably Ben. She'd never been more certain of anything.

"Give that to me," said Paul to Jacker. "Let's shove it in his dad's mouth to see how he likes it. I'm sick of listening to the fucker whine." Jacker retrieved the belt and t-shirt from the floor behind Alma and brought it over to Paul.

Alma reached out and put her hands on Ben's legs. She felt his knobby knees and began to sob. "Oh God, Ben. What did they do to you?"

"Alma," he said again.

His odor was distinct, a mix of decay and the antibacterial soap they used back at Cada E.I.B . She ignored the smell and pulled his chair closer to her. "I won't let them hurt you anymore, Ben."

"Alma," said Ben again, but this time he continued. "Kill him."

She didn't need to ask who he meant. She glanced over at the others, wondering if they'd heard. Paul and Jacker were in the process of gagging Michael. They were planning on loading him into the van first, and talked about cutting the cord on the blinds to tie his wrist with. He was struggling with them, but both Paul and Jacker were far larger than he was, and they had little trouble forcing their will upon him.

"Kill him." Ben's words were quiet, but filled with venom. He repeated himself, "Kill him."

Alma hushed her brother, and then shook her head. "I can't, Ben. I'm sorry, but I can't."

"Remember," said Ben. Each word was a chore for him to say, but he was intent on convincing his sister to do as he asked.

"Remember what?" asked Alma.

"What Daddy did."

Alma looked over at her father, who was being forced to stand up after having his hands tied behind his back. Paul and Jacker were focused on Michael, and weren't paying attention to what Ben was telling Alma.

"What do you mean?" asked Alma.

Ben's unblinking eyes stared at Alma as he put his hands onto hers. "Remember."

A lost memory began to return to her as Ben touched her hand.

Alma remembered coming home one night when she was very young, and feeling the wet carpet on her way down the hall. She'd found her father lying nude on her bed, having just showered. He beckoned her to him, and then…

"Alma!" Rosemary screamed from the bed.

Paul and Jacker had left with Michael, and Rosemary managed to turn herself so that she was facing the bathroom. Blood covered her face and hands, and she was clearly in pain as she pulled herself to the edge of the bed. Alma realized that at least a few minutes had passed as she knelt before Ben, but the time had passed without her knowing it, as if she'd fallen asleep. She took her hands off of Ben's knees as if they'd been burned, and then stared at her brother in shock.

His teeth were chattering as he glared at her.

"He's lying, Alma," said Rosemary.

Alma backed away from Ben and shook her head in confusion. "What happened?"

"I've been yelling your name, but you wouldn't answer," said Rosemary. "What did he do to you? What did he say?"

"He told me…" Alma didn't want to admit it. She didn't want to dredge up the awful memory of what her father had done. The image of his nude body on the bed was clear and detailed, as if it had happened minutes earlier. She could feel his hands on her, and his promise that, 'This is what Daddies do.'

"What, Alma?" asked Rosemary. "I can't protect you if you don't tell me what he said."

"He reminded me about what my dad did to me."

"No," said Rosemary. "No, that's not necessarily true. What did he say? What are you remembering that you didn't remember before?"

"He…" It was painful to admit. "He hurt me." That was as much as she was willing to say.

"It's not true, Alma." Rosemary winced as she sat up. She had a sheet tied around her waist, and continued to put pressure on her wound to stem the bleeding.

"I remember it."

"He's forcing you to think that way. Come here. Let me help you."

"I don't want your help forgetting," said Alma. "The whole reason I wanted to come back to Widowsfield is because I need help remembering these things. I don't know what happened to me, but I forgot about so much. I forgot about Ben, and I forgot about what that bastard did to me." She pointed in the direction of the parking lot where Paul and Jacker had taken her father.

"Listen to me, Alma," said Rosemary. "This is what The Skeleton Man does. He twists your memories to get you to do what he wants. That's why I had you give me this." She took the teddy bear keychain out of her pocket. It was wet with her blood as it dangled from its ring. "You have to trust me."

"No, I remember it now. I remember walking down the hall and seeing him on the bed, and I remember him holding me down." The painful memory brought tears to her eyes.

"You remember it exactly as he wants you to, Alma. This is what he does. This is how he made this stranger," she pointed at the man that was unconscious on the floor, "come in here to try and kill us. You can't trust anything he says to you."

"He wants me to kill our dad."

"Of course he does," said Rosemary. "He'll do anything to stop us."

"Why?" asked Alma. "Why would he try to hurt me like that? He's my brother."

"No, Alma, he's not," said Rosemary. "He's so much more than just one soul now. He's one of The Watcher's creatures, and he knows that we're taking him back. He's going to try and kill every one of us if he can. That's why you have to trust me. I'm the only one you can trust."

"I don't even know you," said Alma.

"But I know you," said Rosemary as the teddy bear dangled from her finger. "I know everything about you, and that's why you have to trust me."

Alma looked at Ben as she backed further away. Then she turned back to Rosemary and asked, "What are you planning on doing? At least tell me how you're going to end this."

Rosemary pointed in the direction of the bathroom, although she couldn't see Ben from her vantage on the bed. "We're going to put that thing back where it belongs. And then we're going to do whatever it takes to make sure he never gets out again."

"And how are we going to do that?"

"That's what we have to figure out."

Alma sighed and then let out a quick laugh. "You don't know? You're leading us back into hell and you don't have any clue if it's going to do us any good?"

"I know that you were able to do what Oliver and his boss have been trying to do again for sixteen years. You went into that cabin and you opened up the doorway back into The Watcher's world. For whatever reason, you're tied to his world, and together we can go back there and end this. You're the only one that can."

"Why me?" asked Alma.

"The Watcher used you," said Rosemary. "He used you to help control Ben."

"How?"

"I'm not entirely sure," said Rosemary. "But one thing I always understood about The Skeleton Man was that he felt unloved. He had a hatred of fathers, and felt like no one cared about him. The Watcher needed him to feel that way. He needed him to feel helpless and alone, but when your mother used Chaos Magick to give you back your memories, Ben saw that you loved him. The Watcher tried to use you to help drive your mother insane. He wanted you both dead, but it didn't work out that way."

"Mom took me back to Chicago," said Alma.

Rosemary looked weary as she shook her head. "No she didn't, Alma. You've repressed the memory. Your mother drove you off that cliff."

"No she didn't," said Alma, but her conviction was nearly lost. "She took me to my grandparent's house."

"You went into the reservoir with her," said Rosemary. "But somehow you managed to get out. You swam to shore, and that's where the police found you."

"No, that's not true," said Alma, but again her tone revealed how uncertain she was.

Rosemary continued without acknowledging Alma's disagreement. "I used the accident to convince Oliver that you were dead."

"How?" asked Alma.

"I messed with his head a little," said Rosemary as if proud of the fact. "He hired me to help him put Widowsfield back together the way it was in 1996, but there's no doubt in my mind that he was never planning on letting me leave. If I hadn't screwed with his head, then I bet he would've killed me for real."

"So you can screw with people's heads too?" asked Alma. "Just like Ben."

"It's not the same thing," said Rosemary.

"How can we be sure you're not lying to us?" asked Alma as she eyed the woman in suspicion. "How do we know you're not manipulating us to get what you want, just like how Ben was messing with me?"

Rosemary rolled her eyes and then regarded her bleeding wound. "I'm the only one that's been stabbed so far. If this is all part of some master plan of mine, then I suck at planning."

Alma laughed and nodded in agreement. "I guess that's true."

Rosemary held out the beaded, wooden necklace that she'd been holding. "Here, do me a favor and put this on our friend." She pointed at the hotel guest that had stabbed her.

"What for?"

"Hopefully this will help him forget we were ever here. We need to cover our tracks."

Alma took the necklace and then did as Rosemary asked. She lifted the unconscious man's head and slipped the necklace over him.

"Tuck it in, under his shirt," said Rosemary.

Alma did as she was asked. "How does that work?"

"Hopefully he gets up with a hell of a headache and believes that he was mugged by a girl that he brought back here from a local bar. That's all."

Alma smiled, but she wasn't sure if she should trust the gifted stranger or be frightened of her.

CHAPTER 15 - Liars

Widowsfield
March 14th, 1996

Oliver had been escorted to one of the two Z-Drive tugboats that were floating beside the Eldridge. He was in the rear tug, with the second only ten yards ahead. Each of the tugs were connected to the Eldridge by a winched cord that was fitted with a hook that looped through a hold on the battleship's side. Oliver had been assured that two of these tugs would be plenty to pull the battleship where it needed to be. Apparently these little, single-operator tugs were very powerful.

"We'll get him out to the middle and then detach," said the fat captain. He was a short, round man that looked to be in his mid to late fifties, with pure white stubble and wearing a camouflage hat. He was smoking a pipe, and the smell of his tobacco was thick but aromatic. "Might want to grab hold of something. It can get a bit bumpy when we first start her up."

Oliver complied, although he had to search for something to hold onto. He was in the small cabin of the tug, and the captain's girth left little room to maneuver.

The crew aboard the Eldridge was sparse, but there had to be at least five on there with Vess. Oliver wasn't sure if he was jealous of the men that were required to man the ship or if he pitied them.

The reservoir wasn't very deep, and the massive chain of the anchor on the Eldridge didn't have long to turn before the ship was ready to move out. Men lined the edge on the dam's side, ensuring that the boat was moving away from the fragile wooden observation deck as it got going.

"I think I'm going to go outside," said Oliver, frustrated with the cramped space.

"All right, but don't say I didn't warn you. Grab a ring, just in case you get knocked off the back. I sure the hell won't hear you screaming once the motors get going."

"A ring?"

"A life preserver," said the captain without turning and with a tone that insinuated that Oliver was an idiot.

"Oh, okay." He opened the cabin's door and was greeted with the cacophonous groan of the Eldridge's anchor settling in place after being hoisted. It was a unique sound, like a broken gear within a mighty machine that was clanking and grinding itself to death.

Oliver was carrying a notebook where he would record every detail about the experiment from his point of view. He'd always been a fan of bringing along notebooks to keep track of daily events. They proved to be a trustworthy journal when memory failed, which it often did.

He retrieved one of the life preservers from the rubber side of the tug to appease the captain, although Oliver was fairly certain the fat man didn't care whether his only passenger swam to shore or not.

In the distance, the Jackson Reservoir was as still as a pane of glass. But the raising of the anchor had caused ripples in the water to stretch out ahead of them, and Oliver watched as they grew more and more faint. The ripples seemed to stretch to nearly the center of the reservoir before they fell out of sight, and he took in the beautiful serenity of the area. Despite being stuck in the Ozarks, Widowsfield was actually a gem of a town, hidden away from the populace at large. Avid outdoorsman had known about this area for years, and took advantage of the lakes that carved their way through the rocky landscape. However, the recent upsurge of popularity of nearby Branson had brought more tourists this way, and none of the locals seemed too pleased about it.

Oliver looked at a cliff-face on the other side of the reservoir, above which was a scenic overlook where tourists could park and take pictures. All of the roads that led to the reservoir had been temporarily closed, so Oliver wasn't concerned about being spied on by any hapless tourists. Instead, he marveled at the shape of the cliff, and began to discern faces in the jagged outcroppings. It wouldn't take a leap of imagination to think that the rocks had been carved to look like faces, but Oliver knew that was an example of simple pareidolia. That was the scientific name for seeing faces in things, which he'd learned while studying about conspiracy theories that had once convinced people to believe in faces on Mars.

However, despite how he knew that those jagged rock faces were certainly just natural formations, it was stunning how much they resembled human faces. It was almost as if the world was staring back at him.

The z-boat's engine kicked on, and Oliver was quick to grab hold of something. Within a few seconds, the small craft thrust forward, causing Oliver to stagger back, and the wire that had been slack moments earlier to snap taut with frightening strength. The front of the boat kicked up, causing the entire vessel to slope backward at a dangerous angle, and the water behind them seemed to boil as the underwater motors roared. The boat ahead of them moved without restraint, and Oliver realized that the cord on its pulley was mounted to the opposite side of the Eldridge to prevent them from causing the ship to turn at an angle. After a few moments of churning water, the Eldridge began a slow and steady crawl out into the middle of the Jackson Reservoir, but it didn't go quietly.

The enormous vessel groaned and banged, as if being torn apart. Oliver's heart raced as he feared that he was listening to several months' worth of work being literally torn asunder. He wondered about the welds, and the cheap labor they'd employed. He tortured himself with thoughts of water spewing into the belly of the ship from cracks in the hull. But, as they moved forward, the Eldridge didn't show any signs of breaking apart.

The tug finally settled, and the front end came to a rest back on the water, its engines faithfully pulling the Eldridge along. They moved at a snail's pace, but the gigantic battleship was making its journey to the center of the reservoir.

Oliver glanced down at the water, and saw something moving beneath them.

It was hard to discern anything beyond the churning water that the engines sent up, so Oliver moved to the side of the boat where he could get a better look. He'd heard rumors that the reservoir had been stocked with catfish, a common occurrence in the area that helped keep the bottom of the lakes and reservoirs clean, and that the fish could reach enormous size. He wondered if the movement of the ship had attracted or upset one of the larger fish. He watched the water for any sign of the underwater denizens.

He saw something again, but this time he didn't mistake it for a fish. Below them stretched a long, thick, black cable, like the tentacle of an enormous squid. He followed the shape for as far as he could, and saw that it stretched out beneath the Eldridge. Oliver moved to the other side of the tug and stared down where he again saw the long cord. It was drawing a straight line from the ship out to the shore, and that's when the mystery was solved.

He was looking at the insulated, underwater power cable that had been connected through the hull of the ship to the stopgap mechanism that was attached to the CORD. On the shore was a shed that housed a connection to the local power grid. This cable was meant to ensure that the experiment was able to continue even if the Eldridge experienced a power failure.

Oliver remembered telling Vess that the stopgap was independently powered, but then he realized that he hadn't mentioned it was connected externally. Vess had said something about the stopgap operating like a battery, and Oliver had been too preoccupied with other matters to correct him. He shrugged off the omission, convinced it wouldn't matter.

The cable had been built to allow the Eldridge to go out into the center of the reservoir but still be connected to a consistent power source. Oliver didn't see why that would be a problem.

Branson
March 13th, 2012
Shortly after 5:00 AM

Alma was sitting in the second row of the security van that they'd stolen from Widowsfield. Jacker was driving, and Rosemary was in the passenger seat beside him, still clutching her stomach. Despite their attempts to stem the flow of blood, it still seeped out from under the multiple wrappings. She kept insisting that she was fine, but her formerly chocolate skin had paled, and her breathing had slowed to a worryingly lethargic pace. The only thing that convinced Alma that the strange woman was still alive was how she would occasionally groan in discomfort.

Paul was in the back row, beside Michael. They'd secured Michael as best they could, but he still continued to struggle and Paul thought it would be a bad idea to leave him in the back seat without someone to watch over him.

The seating arrangement meant that Ben had to sit beside Alma. The seat was wide enough that she was able to avoid his prying fingers, and they tied his arms to his side with another blind cord that had been cut from the hotel room, but that didn't stop the emaciated monster from staring at his sister. His mouth was frequently open, his tongue lashing within, and when he closed his mouth his teeth would chatter. Over and over, he whispered her name, "Alma."

She looked out the window, away from her brother. They were headed out of Branson, and onto 65 to head back to Widowsfield. She stared at the variety of restaurants and hotels that clustered at the exits. The sun had yet to rise, but the city was already beginning to wake. Early morning risers were on their way to their jobs, and garbage trucks were starting their routes. To most people, it was just another Tuesday, but for Alma it was the eve of what promised to be her worst day. The first time she'd decided to return to Widowsfield she'd been prepared for the possibility of facing her past, but now it was a promise; now they were charging knowingly back into hell.

"…remember…" said Ben, although it seemed to be just one word in a sentence that he was otherwise unable to say.

"Shut up," said Alma.

"Don't listen to him," said Rosemary.

Paul reached out from the seat behind and put his hands on her shoulders. She reached up and gripped one of them as she set her cheek against his knuckles. It felt good to have him there, and she wanted nothing more than to curl up in his big, strong arms. She needed his strength.

"Paul lies," said Ben.

Alma looked over at the skeletal man beside her, and he grinned back as he nodded. She hissed at him, "Shut up."

"Why…" Ben tried to speak, but each word took great effort to say. "Did he…" Ben choked and coughed as his fingers scratched at the plastic seat cushion beneath him. "Get fired?"

"Do what she says," said Paul. "Shut the fuck up."

"Why did he get fired?" asked Ben.

Alma let go of Paul's hand, and then turned to ask him, "What's he talking about?"

"Ignore him, Alma," said Rosemary. "He'll do anything to turn you against everyone else here."

"I won't lie," said Ben. He struggled to continue speaking even though it clearly pained him. "Not to you."

"Why did you get fired?" asked Alma of Paul, ignoring Rosemary's warning. She remembered hearing that Paul had lost his job, but had never asked why.

"It's not important," said Paul.

"Liar," said Ben.

Paul sighed and admitted, "I got caught fooling around with the boss's daughter."

"Fucking her," said Ben, as if to injure Alma with the harshness of the word.

Alma closed her eyes, and then shook her head as she sighed. She looked over at Ben, who was smiling back at her. "I don't care. We weren't together at the time, so I've got no reason to be mad about that."

"Lacey loves," said Ben as he stared at his sister. He was trying to say more, but his voice turned to a croak.

"Someone put a fucking gag on him," said Jacker in frustration.

"Who's Lacey?" asked Alma.

"Tell her," said Ben.

"Fuck you," said Paul in frustration.

"Just tell me, Paul," said Alma.

"Lacey is the girl I got caught with. We were together for a while. She's been…" He shook his head and sighed before deciding to get it over with and admit the truth. "She's been living with me. That's why my place was so damn clean."

"Oh," said Alma. She wasn't certain how to take the news. "And, does she know about us? Did you break things off with her?"

"Not yet," said Paul. He was quick to add, "But I will."

"Was she the one outside of your place the other night?" asked Alma. "The one you were talking to right before you followed me back to my place?"

"Yes," said Paul quietly, like a solemn whisper at a funeral.

Alma nodded, and remembered the buxom, young girl that had been outside of the tattoo parlor that Paul lived above. "She was pretty," said Alma, attempting to hide the fact that she was hurt. Unfortunately, the pain was evident in her voice.

"Alma, she never meant much to me. We never had anything like what I've got with you."

"It's okay, Paul," said Alma, but the tears had already started to fall. "I don't have any reason to be mad. You didn't do anything wrong." No matter how many times she said it, she couldn't convince herself it was true. She'd already known that Paul had been sleeping with someone the night they got back together, the evidence had been floating in his toilet. But the fact that the girl had been living with him, and that she was the reason his apartment had been so clean, was hard to deal with.

"I should've told you," said Paul. He reached back over the seat to touch her shoulder, but she moved away from him. "Alma, I'm sorry."

"Liar," said Ben. "He's a liar."

"Everyone lies," said Alma.

"Not me," said Ben. "I won't lie to you."

Alma looked out the window, but could see her brother's reflection staring back at her. She closed her eyes, and started to hum a quiet tune.

CHAPTER 16 – Back Again

Widowsfield
March 14th, 1996
3:14

Vess cut the CORD.

The Eldridge had been towed out to the middle of the reservoir, and Lyle had been put inside of Tesla's machine. Vess started powering the machine fourteen minutes earlier, at 3:00, and precisely at 3:14 he flipped the switch on the stopgap that would allow the radiation to be introduced. This was different than it had been when he performed the experiment over a half century earlier, but he was more confident than ever that he could replicate the results.

Vess had spent every day since that first experiment determined to find his way back to the doorway he'd opened once before. Einstein's reports about how the Eldridge had disappeared, along with the corpses that had been fused to the ship's walls, convinced Vess that the experiment had been a success, but Groves hadn't shared his enthusiasm. Major Leslie Groves halted the CORD project a few months later, explaining that it was too dangerous to continue without further study. Whatever he'd seen that day had frightened him, and Oppenheimer's success in New Mexico with the Manhattan Project drew all the funds that Groves had been splitting amongst the various endeavors. The CORD project was left to die, but Vess was determined to do whatever he needed to resurrect it.

Albert Einstein had been the one that was able to draw interest from fellow scientists around the world about what had come to be known as the Philadelphia Experiment. After the development of the atomic bomb, it became clear to the scientific community that their work could become more than the arbiter of war; it became the harbinger of it. Nations clamored to match the might of the United States, and that led to the dawn of a terrifying age. War profiteering had begun. The desire to crush Hitler's ambition with atomic might had seemed noble once, but the folly of their ambition became all too clear as more and more nations declared their intention to follow suit.

The final insult that had driven Einstein and his fellow scientists to form The Accord had been the revelation that German scientists were being given amnesty after the end of the war. The monsters that had slaughtered millions were pardoned so that they could bring their secrets to the United States. Any former belief they'd shared about America's honor had been dashed. A growing sense of unease began to grow among the scientists about how their discoveries had been handed over to a corrupt nation of power-hungry capitalists. Now that money could be made by waging war, there would be no end to death and destruction.

In 1961, Eisenhower voiced his concern about the military-industrial complex, but The Accord had been conscious of it for over a decade already. The march to war, that carrion call of irrationally angry old men in suits, would bleat on until the last soldier found his grave. That was why, after their first meeting, The Accord decided to revisit the experiment that promised to let man know God. Tesla's machine was unearthed, and Vess found himself connected to the most powerful minds of the age. At the time, The Accord was just a fledgling of what it would become, but their collected intelligence and wisdom allowed them to quickly gain power and funding.

However, as with many enterprises, what had started with the best of intentions got warped by the lure of money. The high-minded elite among The Accord began to die off, and the younger generation that replaced them wasn't saddled with the fear instilled by witnessing a World War. Soon, The Accord found themselves embroiled in the very military-industrial complex that their forefathers had fought against. They reasoned this by explaining that they weren't designing new weapons, but simply shuffling them around to different countries. They convinced themselves that brokering weapon contracts between countries didn't go against the wishes of The Accord's founders.

The first couple decades of continued research on the CORD project had met with little to no results. They were never able to recreate the events of that summer day in Philadelphia, and funding for the project was all but cut. Vess was given a salary that allowed him to focus his time on research, but little funding was provided for the experiments themselves. It wasn't until his lack of aging became apparent that The Accord took greater notice of him again.

Einstein and several of the founders of The Accord had since passed, and the younger generation was intent on focusing their efforts on discoveries that would not only be seen as revolutionary, but could literally alter the human experience. Their goal was to exceed what any scientist had done before them, and to make The Accord as powerful as a nation. It was an ambitious goal, but the arms race that dominated headlines through the post-war era convinced them that mankind was destined to eradicate itself without proper guidance. The Accord hoped to use science as a method of stripping the power away from the politicians and corporate warriors, and usher the world into an era of science and reason.

At first, The Accord hoped to capitalize upon what Vess's decelerated aging had revealed, and they focused their efforts on studying the enzyme, telomerase, that was abundant in Vess. This proved fruitless though, and despite heavy supplementation, none of the subjects in their studies showed signs of anti-aging effects that came close to duplicating what had occurred in Vess and Lyle. Chagrined, The Accord refused to abandon their interest in Vess. Shortly after, he was allowed to continue with his CORD experiments.

Unfortunately, the early results had been similar to what had happened when they first tried to recreate the experiment. The CORD never resulted in any contact with any other dimension, but Vess had amassed a slew of theories during the time The Accord had paid him to study Tesla's notes. This led him to eventually propose that harmonic resonance might have something to do with their lack of success. In each of their attempts to recreate the experiment, they'd done so in a closed facility and not within the bowels of a ship at sea.

Vess's lack of results made it difficult to garner unanimous support from all members of The Accord, and he was forced to be patient as the group funded various other experiments. Brokering weapons deals had become the group's primary focus, and had made the members of The Accord extremely wealthy. Cada E.I.B., which had originally been meant only as a revenue generating arm of The Accord, now dominated the majority of their time. Knowing this, Vess capitalized upon The Accord's ties to military interests, and resubmitted his proposal about the CORD project, but with a different focus. He used Einstein and Groves' own notes on what they witnessed during the original experiment to suggest that the CORD might be able to provide battleships with a cloaking mechanism. This, of course, put the project back at the top of their pile.

Securing an appropriate ship was a challenge, but The Accord funded the purchase of a battleship similar to the Eldridge. The Eldridge herself was unavailable, having been sold to Greece years earlier. Vess had been forced to accept a variety of petty alterations, but when the experiment failed he insisted that they allow him to proceed without their interference. They'd agreed, although he was still required to submit his plans to them so that they could pass it on to the project lead.

Vess had been keeping track of the Eldridge, and learned that Greece had decommissioned the ship and were planning on scrapping it. Vess influenced The Accord into having Cada E.I.B. make a bid for the ship. Greece officials had initially been leery of dealing with the brokerage, but Cada E.I.B. had a good relationship with a variety of countries. Greece agreed, and the Eldridge was bought back at an extremely reasonable price. The ship was torn apart, and the pieces shipped to a small town in Missouri.

That was how the Widowsfield project had begun. Now, after decades of preparation and failed attempts, Vess would regain the knowledge he'd lost. Those forgotten minutes, after the initial experiment had succeeded, had plagued Vess through the half-century since it occurred.

He watched the arcs of blue lightning that zapped along the circulating rings as they began to turn green. The sight ignited his memory and he cried out, "Yes, this is how it was. This is right!"

The electricity caused the hair on his arms to stand up, and he saw the dance of shadows flicker on the walls around him. Within the CORD he heard Lyle shriek. The man hadn't spoken in decades, but Vess heard the distinct wail as the psychic was tortured within.

Vess raised his arms, and wobbled on his decrepit knees. He laughed as the CORD came alive. He knew that he was moments away from learning the truth that had been stolen from him so many years earlier.

The shadows that were cast upon the walls stopped dancing in accordance to the light emitted from the machine. Instead, the shadows now seemed to writhe on their own, independent of any source. Vess remembered that this had happened also, and he watched as the shadows changed their shape, quickly revealing themselves to be ropes, or tentacles. The shadows undulated and spun, and Vess cried out in excitement at the sight.

An unnerving, metallic grinding overwhelmed him, erasing the zapping noise caused by the CORD. Vess covered his ears, but it did little to stop the pervasive sound.

The tentacles massed, a swirl of shadows that seemed to be growing behind the confines of the wall itself. Vess watched as the shadows gave birth to black wires that whipped out at the ground, lashing like the feelers of some deep-sea life form. They clawed at the floor, and were strong enough to dig into the steel. The wires pulled themselves forward, and the further they came forth from the wall the thicker their bases became. Then, from within the black, stepped a human figure. Vess recognized that the shape was an amalgamation of the various cords that had spun together to form the mere shape of a man, and that it wasn't in truth a human at all. The corded man stepped forward, though his legs were constantly affixed to the shadows on the floor as the cords stretched to allow his movement.

The grinding and clanging of metal grew louder, but it was apparent that the noise was forming a purposeful rhythm. The noise altered until Vess recognized that a voice was breaking through, like a note of music discerned from radio static.

"You remember," said the demon, but it was as much a command as it was a question.

Vess did. Now, as he stood before the creature he'd unleashed once before, he remembered everything.

Vess collapsed to his knees as sorrow overwhelmed him. He muttered, "What have I done?"

The creature approached, its wired hand a mockery of compassion as he reached out like the Madonna hoping to grace the devout. "I've been waiting in these walls for you, Vess."

"Why couldn't you have just let me die?" asked Vess as he stared down at the ground. The creature had been waiting in the walls of the ship, which was why they'd never been successful in any previous attempt to activate the CORD. Now that his memory had been returned, Vess remembered what it was the creature had asked for.

"Did you bring us a new sacrifice?" asked The Watcher in the Walls as his cords snaked a circle around the man that had been tasked with supplying a sacrifice.

The CORD's door banged open, and white smoke poured out from it. From within the fog stepped a skeletal man, adorned with the flesh of the victim he'd shredded within. He was tall and thin, and the cords of black wire that covered the ground rose up his legs like vines along the trunk of a tree.

Vess was about to speak, but then he saw that the fog that shrouded The Skeleton Man had begun to flow toward the side of the CORD. Vess had no recollection of something like this occurring during the first experiment, and then he saw the source of the aberration. The fog was flowing into the stopgap mechanism. The white cloud was disappearing within the orange box as if it were water falling down a drain.

The Skeleton Man pointed to the box and said, "There. He gave us a way out. I can hear the screams of children from out there."

The black cords followed the fog, and they searched the stopgap with interest, as if each wire was a sentient creature. Then the cords plunged into the box, disappearing within it without causing any visible damage to the mechanism itself.

"Good," said The Watcher. "All I hoped for was another man inside your monster." The Watcher's wires tapped against the side of the CORD before retreating back to the stopgap. "But you've given us so much more than that." The Watcher and The Skeleton Man approached the orange box.

"Wait," said Vess. "Where are you going?"

"We're following the cord you left for us," said The Watcher. "We'll find plenty of souls to torture out there. But don't worry, Vess, I'll make sure you suffer too."

The black wires shot forth from beneath The Watcher, and they pierced Vess like the tips of a hundred needles. He felt the cords sliding within him, wrapping around his bones and tearing through his organs. Every nerve ending in his body exploded in agony as the cords tore him apart, but he wasn't allowed the release of death. Instead, The Watcher and The Skeleton Man savored his pain. Together, they would explore the extent of human suffering. Vess would escape their hell, but his memory of the event would be stolen. All he would be left with was a desire to continue his experiments. He would obsess about the moments that were lost to him, and would work hard to recreate it. The Watcher in the Walls had found a way to collect human souls, and he didn't want that door to close.

Widowsfield
March 13th, 2012
Shortly after 5:30 AM

The horizon bore no hint of sunrise. Daylight savings time had started the previous Sunday, which meant that the sun wouldn't rise until around 7:30. The birds hadn't even begun to stir when Jacker crested the hill that preceded their final descent into Widowsfield.

Alma experienced the familiar, dreaded lurch of her stomach as they headed down the hill. This was the sensation that had plagued her for so many years. She'd assumed it was because the feeling reminded her of traveling to this cursed town with her father, but now she considered a new possibility. Perhaps the reason she hated the sensation was because she was repressing a memory of being driven over a cliff by her mother.

She continued to hum as they passed through the dark woods where she'd once seen the hands of demons reaching out from the mist. Alma closed her eyes and tried to imagine happier times, but the first thought that entered her mind was of the woman that Paul had spoken with outside of his apartment a few nights earlier. Now the bitch had a name: Lacey.

Alma wished she wasn't the jealous type, and that seeing the woman that had been living with Paul wouldn't fill her with self-doubt, but Alma had spent the majority of her life being an introverted, quiet, plain-looking girl. She'd suffered the vicious mocks of prettier girls throughout high school, and had torn more than a few pictures of llamas off of her locker. She could still hear their jeers, "How's it going, Llama Harper?"

Lacey, was young, buxom, and the type of girl you'd expect to see on the arm of a man like Paul. Alma had only seen her for a moment, smoking on the corner outside of the tattoo parlor, but knew instantly that the girl was a welcome member of that crowd. Where Alma always struggled to fit in with Paul's rough-and-tumble group of friends, she had no doubt that Lacey was the life of the party. Alma couldn't help but imagine Paul and Lacey together, laughing and drinking with their friends at the parlor. If things did work out between Paul and herself, Alma dreaded the thought of returning to the parlor where she'd struggled to fit in before. Now, after they'd gotten to know and love Lacey, Alma would be an outcast.

Alma had no way of knowing if any of this was true. She'd only caught a glimpse of the woman that she was now obsessing over, but that didn't change how she felt. It was petty, pathetic, and reprehensible of her to feel the way she did, and she reminded herself of that over and over in an attempt to move on. It didn't work.

She wondered if perhaps, after this nightmare in Widowsfield was over, she should break things off with Paul. After all, their past together had proven that they were more likely to break up eventually than stay together anyhow. Why should she steal him away from Lacey, from a chance at happiness? Was her love for him just an example of her own greed and possessiveness? She remembered how painful it had been to see that his apartment was clean after so much time apart, as if she felt like he should be broken without her. That's not the sort of thing a loving person feels. Is it?

Alma wiped away her tears and then reached instinctually to her pocket to hold onto the teddy bear keychain that Paul had given her on their first date. She panicked when she discovered it was missing, but then remembered that she'd given it to Rosemary.

They were past the woods, and Widowsfield stretched out before them. The long road led to the gate that was still left open after they'd left earlier in the night. As they approached, Alma was reminded of a gaping maw, as if the road was leading them down the gullet of a patient beast whose skin was made of the crisscrossed wire of the fence. It was a fitting thought.

"Last place on Earth I want to be right now," said Jacker as they drove past the gate and back into the town they all wanted to flee.

"Amen, brother," said Paul.

Michael gurgled beneath his gag, and rustled in his seat.

"How are you feeling, Rosemary?" asked Jacker as he reached out and set his hand on the black woman's shoulder. He shook her when she didn't respond. "Rosemary?" he asked again, more concerned this time.

"I'm alive," said Rosemary, although her voice was weak. "I don't think I'll be strong enough to walk when we get there."

"It's okay," said Alma. "We'll go in and bring out a stretcher or a wheelchair. We'll get the nurses to come and help."

Rosemary nodded, and started to thank Alma, but her voice trailed off into a murmur. The only word that came forth was the name of the nurse at the facility, "Helen."

"Jacker, hurry," said Alma as she scooted forward in her seat.

"On it," said Jacker as he sped up.

The tires squealed as they turned sharp corners on their way back to Cada E.I.B.'s facility on the north side of Widowsfield. Jacker wasn't concerned with stop signs, and within minutes they were pulling into the only place in Widowsfield that showed any signs of life other than the eerie silhouettes of mannequins staring out of other buildings in town. He parked beside the side entrance where Michael had taken Ben through earlier and then Alma quickly jumped out, explaining that she'd run inside to get help and that Paul and Jacker should stay with the van. She was more than happy to get away from Ben the first chance she got.

Alma felt relieved to be leaving Ben, but as soon as she entered the quiet, dead building, she wasn't sure how confident she was that it was better inside. The emergency lights were on, bathing the halls in red light, but it was eerily silent. She'd been groggy when they'd left, and had trouble remembering how to get back to where Rachel and Stephen were at.

She did her best to find her way, but then she heard a woman call out, "Rachel?"

Alma turned and saw the portly nurse that worked for Cada E.I.B. leaning out from one of the rooms. "Oh," she said when she recognized Alma. "In this light you looked like someone else."

"Where is Rachel?" asked Alma. "Isn't she with you?"

"No," said the older nurse. "She went looking for Oliver."

"She did?" asked Alma, surprised. "Did Stephen go with her?"

"Oh no," said the nurse as she approached. "I'm sorry, I thought you meant the other Rachel. The nurse that I was working with is named Rachel too. Your friends are in the room to the right, just down the hall."

"Oh, okay," said Alma. "We need your help outside."

"Me?" asked Helen. "Why?"

"One of our friends was stabbed. She's in the van outside and needs your help. She's bleeding badly."

"Oh my gosh," said Helen. "Are you parked in the lot?"

Alma nodded and said, "Do you have a wheelchair or something?"

"We can use one of the gurneys. Come with me."

"Let me go tell Rachel and Stephen what's going on," said Alma.

"Don't bother. They've got the door locked," said Helen. "I went in to check on them a little while ago and it looked like they were filming something."

Alma imagined that Stephen and Rachel were filming something for their internet show, and was mildly annoyed that they would still be thinking about that venture in the midst of everything that had happened to them. She shrugged off the concern and went to help Helen with one of the gurneys from the sleepers' room.

They hurried back to the exit that led to the parking lot. Jacker was waiting with the exit door propped open. He waved at them to hurry and said, "She's fading fast. Come on."

Alma and Helen guided the gurney over the threshold of the door, causing the metal bed to rattle before its wheels grinded on the concrete sidewalk outside. They were under a humming external light and large, flying shadows were cast from it by the moths that spun above.

Rosemary's door was open, and Paul was standing beside her, doing his best to help although his expression revealed his helplessness. His hands were covered in Rosemary's blood.

Helen was quick to command the group on how they could help. Her years as an ER nurse were evident as she calmly and decidedly dealt with the situation. Within only a couple minutes, Rosemary had been transferred to the gurney and Helen had her hands pressed against the wound, the blade still protruding forth. Paul and Alma took opposite sides of the gurney to push it along as Helen insisted that they get back down to the sleepers' room, where her supplies were at.

Alma and Paul both realized that they would be leaving Jacker alone to stay with Michael and Ben. They looked at him in concern, but he was quick to say, "It's okay, just go. I'll stay with the psychos. Don't worry about me."

"Don't listen to him," said Alma. "Whatever Ben says, just ignore him."

"Don't worry," said Jacker. "I'm shutting the two of them in that van alone. I'll wait out here. Fuck those freaks."

Ben overheard Hank Waxman say that he would leave the van's occupants alone, and his heart fluttered at the prospect of being left with Michael. He stayed silent and waited for the fat man to close the doors. He locked eyes with Jacker, and smiled at him. Jacker flipped Ben off, and then slammed the van's door shut, leaving Ben alone with his father.

"Daddy," said Ben, his voice a menacing hiss. "I'm feeling stronger."

Michael Harper was bound and gagged, and the noises he made were pitiful. Ben turned, and set his hands on the seat that separated him from his father. The Skeleton Man stared at his prey, and laughed through his chattering teeth.

CHAPTER 17 – No Witnesses

Widowsfield
March 1st, 1996
7:00 PM

Helen parked outside of the abandoned Salt and Pepper Diner. She was whistling as she got out of her car and went around to the back. She glanced around, making certain no one was near, but Widowsfield was a ghost town, just like it'd been for years. She opened her trunk, convinced no one was watching.

Inside was a stack of firewood that had been wrapped in oiled rags. The dingy rags were tied to the pieces of wood, and the kindling was placed inside of a large blue, plastic bag that her friend had brought back from an Ikea trip. On top of the bag was a hammer and a sign that read 'Out of Order'. Helen hoisted the heavy back up and over her shoulder, and then picked up the jerry can that was full of gasoline from the trunk as well.

The spout on the can of gas was open, and the liquid splashed out onto her smock. "Son of a gun," she muttered as she saw the liquid soaking into her shirt. Luckily, she always had a spare smock in her car. As a nurse, she'd quickly learned the value of a change of clothes. There was no telling what sort of horrific things could dirty up a smock during a day of work.

Helen carried the firewood and gas into the diner and then headed for the men's bathroom. It seemed as good a place as any to hide the tinder.

She wondered if she'd get to watch Widowsfield burn. She'd always hoped to see that.

Widowsfield
March 14th, 1996
3:13 PM

The tugboat that Oliver was on had been detached from the Eldridge, and was floating about fifty yards away from the battleship. Oliver was standing on the back of the tug, and kept checking his watch in anticipation of the time when he knew that Vess would cut the cord.

The tug captain was leaning back in his seat, his feet on the dash. He had a folded newspaper in one hand and a pencil in the other and he was mulling over a crossword, ignorant of the important event that was about to occur.

3:14 arrived, and Oliver anxiously glanced up at the ship. He knew that Vess's watch would be set to the same time. Cada E.I.B. and The Accord were very particular about their employees all sticking to the same time. Before Oliver had known about the significance of 3:14, he'd assumed this was a discipline issue. Now he knew the reason they'd been so stringent about everyone keeping to the same time schedule was because of the importance they placed on the number 314. He wondered how many other project leads had been instructed to activate their experiments at precisely 3:14 in whatever time zone they were located.

A hollow bang came from the Eldridge the moment that Oliver's watch displayed 3:14. Ripples appeared along the side of the boat and chased away from it, revealing that the entire ship was vibrating. Then a flash of green light reflected off the surface of the water and Oliver looked up in time to see another arc of lighting emit from the ship's bow. It was like watching a storm cloud, except that the lightning was distinctly green.

The captain of the tug had swiveled in his seat so that he was facing the back of the cabin. He kicked the door open while remaining seated and screamed out, "Did you see that?"

Oliver nodded as he lowered his notebook. He didn't dare look away to write down what he was seeing.

"What the fuck's going on?" asked the captain. "Do we need to get out of here?"

"No, keep us right here," said Oliver.

"Ain't too smart to be on a boat when there're Goddamned bolts of lightning shooting around."

Oliver turned to look at the captain and yelled, "Stay here!"

A crack of thunder exploded from the Eldridge, but when Oliver turned to look back at the boat, it was gone. The battleship had vanished, and in its place was just a faint, white smoke.

"What the fuck?" asked the captain as he forced his wide frame out of his seat and gazed at where the ship had been. He made the sign of the cross and kissed his knuckle before staring in wide-eyed fear at Oliver. "What did you insane pricks do? What happened to that boat?"

Oliver shook his head and blinked as if coming out of a daze. He murmured an answer, "I don't know."

Something caught Oliver's attention in the water. He glanced down and saw a flash of green light coming from deep below them. He went to the edge of the boat to investigate and saw that the cord that had formerly been attached to the underside of the Eldridge, and was used to feed electricity to the stopgap mechanism on the CORD, was still floating where it had been, as if it was still attached to the boat. The thick wire was crackling with the same green lightning that the Eldridge had been, and the light was pushing its way toward the shore.

Oliver looked up at the small building on shore that the cord led to. The green energy flowed into the building, and the cord that it traveled across vanished as soon as it had passed, as if Oliver was watching a bomb's wick receding. He didn't know what would happen, and he braced himself as if expecting the shack to explode. It didn't, and both Oliver and the captain were left staring at the building in wonderment.

Then the water near the shore splashed as the cord that the green energy had followed suddenly reappeared. At the same moment, a groan of steel echoed out over the reservoir and the water around the tugboat was pushed upward. Oliver and the captain struggled to stay standing, and then turned to see that the Eldridge was back where it had been. The only evidence of its disappearance were the waves it created when it had appeared again. Then a thick white smoke began to pour over the edge of the ship. The mist was growing at a shocking rate, and flooded the sky above them like the canopy of a tree or a mushroom cloud. Then the fog pressed forward out over the reservoir and in the direction of Widowsfield.

"What the fuck?" asked the captain as he waddled back into the cabin. "I'm getting the hell out of here."

"No, wait," said Oliver. "Take me back to the Eldridge."

"Hell no," said the captain with a roar of laughter. "You must be out of your damn mind."

"I'm serious," said Oliver as he went to the cabin to argue with the portly man. "Get me over there or…" He paused and then said with emphasis, "Or you're fired."

"Go ahead," said the captain as he turned on the boat. "Fire my ass. I don't give a shit."

The fog was coming their way, skirting the surface of the water as it reached out for them.

The tugboat shot forward, knocking Oliver back. He fell to his rear in the back of the boat. He debated going to shore with the captain, but he realized that the man owned the tugboat, and he probably wouldn't be willing to allow Oliver to drive it back to the Eldridge. There weren't any other boats on the reservoir except for the Eldridge and the two tugs, which meant Oliver would either have to swim back to the Eldridge or go down to a nearby lake and try to rent a boat that he could haul back here.

After weighing his options, Oliver decided that he needed to get onto the Eldridge as quick as possible. He grabbed the life preserver that the captain had ordered him to get earlier, and then dove off the side of the tugboat.

Hitting the water was more painful than he'd anticipated, and Oliver struggled to breathe as he swam over the waves left by the tug. He grasped the preserver, and then pulled himself onto it so that he could catch him breath. After cursing at the captain of the tug a few more times, he started to swim in the direction of the Eldridge. The fog that had bloomed from the ship sat a foot higher than the water, giving Oliver enough room to swim without touching it. From within the fog he saw the flash of green electricity.

After an exhausting swim, he finally reached the ladder that he'd taken down when he boarded the tugboat. The rope ladder was arduous to ascend, and he took each wrung slowly until he was finally pulling himself onto the deck. By the time he made it to the boat, the fog had moved on. The cloud was headed towards town, leaving the boat behind.

"Hello?" he called out but got no response.

Oliver wiped his face and then tried to shake off some of the water from his clothes, but it didn't do much good. His shoes squished as he walked, but he ignored the discomfort as he made his way across the deck to the door that he had to go through to get down to where the CORD was located. As he approached the door, he caught sight of something sticking out of the wall. The shape made no sense to Oliver at first. The steel wall was grey and smooth, with only the occasional rivet marring its surface, but then there was an odd series of lumps sticking out of it that he was certain hadn't been there before. It looked like cloth.

He reached the odd mass and cautiously reached out to touch it. It was a triangular shape that stuck out of the wall, and it seemed to be made of a white, cotton fabric. He gripped the top of the triangular expulsion, unsure what he expected to discover, and was horrified when it squished in his hand.

He backed away in surprise and stared at the lump in disgust. The base of the triangle, where the fabric looked to be fused with the steel wall, became wet with a red liquid. That's when Oliver realized what he was looking at. This triangular shape protruding from the wall was a man's elbow, covered in the white sleeve of his shirt. It was exactly as Vess said had happened in 1943, where sailors were fused to the Eldridge itself, as if their skin were a part of its hull. The red liquid gushing from the quivering mass was blood, and it was dripping down the side of the wall as Oliver watched.

Oliver rushed to the door and wound the crank that would open it. He pulled the massive door open and passed through the half-foot wide threshold. To his left, sticking out of the thick wall, was the head of one of the unfortunate men that had been on the ship when Vess cut the cord. The man seemed to be dead already, but there was no blood dripping down from where his neck was sticking out of the ship. He realized that the reason the man's elbow outside had started bleeding was because Oliver had ripped the skin away from the hull when he touched it.

Oliver gawked at the bizarre sight. The sailor's other arm was hanging limply from the wall, as was one of his legs. The rest of his body was lost within the wall itself.

Then a pathetic whine came from deep within the ship, and Oliver realized that someone was in pain nearby. He cautiously slid along the opposite wall from where the dead sailor sprouted, fearful that the man might suddenly wake and give Oliver new fuel for the nightmares this would certainly inspire. After passing the grotesque sailor, Oliver ran down the hall and to the stairs. The sound of the crying man grew louder as he went. Then, as Oliver turned the last corner that would lead to the door to the CORD's room, he saw who it was that had been crying.

One of Vess's guards was fused to the floor from the waist down. It was clear that he'd been trying to free himself, but his movement had ripped his skin away from the steel, causing him to bleed profusely. The blood pooled at his waist, and he was crying in pain and helplessness when Oliver found him.

"Help me!" The man reached out to Oliver. His pale face was contorted in agony as he held out his arms.

Oliver halted and offered no help. He just stared in horror at the doomed man.

"You have to help me. I don't know what happened. It hurts. It hurts." He continued to repeat himself as Oliver stood helplessly before him. The guard was blocking Oliver's way.

"I can feel my legs," said the guard. "Does that make any sense? How's that possible?" He pushed his hands against the floor, raising himself up again and causing his skin to rip further. "It hurts!"

"Stop…" Oliver felt his stomach turn at the sight. "Stop moving."

"Help me get out!" The guard reached out to Oliver again, but received no aid. "It hurts, but I think we could pull me out. Help me, Goddamn it!"

Oliver shook his head.

The guard groaned in pain and anger as he planted his hands on the floor again. He pushed, and then screamed as more blood gushed out. A flap of pink intestine emerged from under him, and he grabbed it as he said, "How…"

The guard was dazed from pain and blood loss. Oliver wasn't certain if the man knew what he was holding, or if he pulled on it in confusion, but either way, the man was eviscerating himself. Then the guard coughed, and blood spurted out over his chin.

He looked up at Oliver and said, "It hurts."

With that, the hulking guard slumped backward as he finally fell unconscious. The force of his body leaning back caused his stomach to rip further, and his intestines spilled out in front of Oliver like a bag of cooked spaghetti that had been slit open. The red blood and pink intestines stretched out as Oliver jumped backward in disgust.

Oliver had no choice but to wade through the gore as he made his way to where Vess and the CORD were at. He stared at the ceiling as he passed the dead guard, and then ran the rest of the way without looking back.

He didn't know what to expect when he got to Vess, and he hoped that the CORD's founding scientist wasn't partially fused to a wall somewhere. He opened the door that led to the catwalk above the bay, and saw Vess lying on the ground.

"Vess!"

He ran down the stairs while watching the CORD as its silver rings spun. The device was still on, but it wasn't creating electricity anymore.

Oliver was scared that Vess was partially fused to the floor, so he didn't grasp the old man as he got on his knees to inspect him. He kept saying the man's name and asking if he was all right.

Finally, Vess opened his eyes and tried to speak, but he sputtered and coughed instead.

Oliver watched as Vess moved, and felt confident that the old man wasn't stuck to the floor. He leaned over him and started to help Vess sit up, but the injured man grabbed Oliver's wet shirt, causing water to roll down his shaking arms and drip from his elbows. He coughed again, but was then able to force out his question.

"Did it work?"

Branson
March 13th, 2012
Shortly after 5:30 AM

Jim Broadbent whistled as he walked across the lobby of the hotel to the small dining area where guests would soon begin staggering into, looking for the complimentary breakfast that came with their room. He twirled his keys around his finger as he walked, and the beaded bracelet that the black woman whose car had broken down had given him, spun around his wrist. He got to the counter where the breakfast items would be displayed, and knelt to unlock the cabinet below. There were already boxes of cereal in a plastic case on top of the counter, but he pulled out the Styrofoam bowls and plastic silverware that was locked below.

Jim had worked the midnight shift at the hotel for long enough to be used to this routine. Setting up the breakfast buffet wasn't difficult, but if he didn't have everything ready by 6:00, there would undoubtedly be an early-riser groaning in frustration. However, Jim knew what the most important part of the process was, and that's why he always came to the cabinet first: coffee. He took out the plastic jug of coffee grinds and hoisted it to the counter before pulling down the old carafes.

The automatic doors at the entrance hissed open almost perfectly on schedule. Jim only turned as a courtesy, because he knew exactly who had arrived.

Elvis Jaurez came in with blustered cheeks and his normal wide smile. He didn't speak much English, but he was generous with his nods and grins. He was the newspaper delivery man, and he had two stacks of bound papers in his arms.

"Morning, Mr. Jim," said Elvis as he smiled.

"Morning Elvis."

The short, stocky man waddled over to the wire basket next to the breakfast counter and dropped his load of papers down into it. Then he pulled a box cutter from his jacket's front pocket and swiftly cut the plastic tie on the top stack. He whipped the plastic out, and then knelt to get the second. After finishing, he nodded to Jim and said, "Goodbye, Mr. Jim."

"Bye, Elvis." Jim smiled back at the man and watched him leave. The automatic door hissed closed, and Jim glanced up at the camera above. He looked for the red light that would indicate it was recording and saw that it was off, just as he wanted it to be. Jim had spent the last half-hour erasing the security footage of the previous night, and had made sure to turn off the cameras for the time being.

He left the coffee behind and went over to the front desk. Kyle should've come up already to help with setting up breakfast, but if he had it would've been the first time in months that he'd done it. Despite having the midnight shift for almost a year longer than Jim, Kyle still hadn't gotten used to the odd hours. Jim knew that Kyle would be asleep in the break room, so he called the phone that was in the room with him, rudely waking Kyle from his nap.

"Yeah," said Kyle's weary voice when he answered.

"Get up. I need you to get the sausages from the fridge and bring them up to the front."

"Yeah, okay," said Kyle, but his yawn didn't inspire confidence in Jim.

"Do it, Kyle. Your review is coming up."

"Yeah, yeah, bro. Chill." With that, Kyle hung up and Jim walked out from behind the front desk and back into the hallway. He looked in the direction of the break room, which was about fifty feet away, and waited until he saw Kyle emerge. The irresponsible employee flipped Jim off, to which Jim smiled and waved.

Next, Jim went to the door of the ladies room. He knocked gently as a courtesy, but was fairly certain it wasn't occupied. He looked back down the hall at Kyle and watched as he walked over to the storage room to retrieve the breakfast sausages from the freezer. All of the hot components of the complimentary breakfast were frozen. Even the biscuits that were for the biscuits and gravy came frozen in a package of six that were simply tossed into a microwave for three minutes and then transferred over to the hot plate that was warmed by a sterno placed below it. Once Kyle was out of sight, Jim opened the door to the ladies room.

Without any hesitation, he went to the paper towel dispenser and unlatched it. A pistol was resting on top of the folded brown paper, and he took it out so that he could do as he'd been told.

Jim walked back out of the bathroom and saw that Kyle had already brought out the plastic bag of sausages and was transferring a batch into the microwave. He looked tired, as always, and even though he glanced in Jim's direction, he didn't see the pistol in his hand.

Jim Broadbent raised the gun, and without a moment's thought, he pulled the trigger. Kyle's head burst open like a ripe watermelon dropped on a sharp rock. Blood and brains splattered the plastic case where the miniature cereal boxes were kept, and Jim saw a chunk of hairy scalp hanging from the edge of a Styrofoam bowl.

Jim vomited into his hand and then flung the liquid off to the side as he ran out of the hotel. He still had to kill someone else before he killed himself. There was just one person left that had been present when Michael Harper arrived. Tonight, they all had to die.

He could feel the gift that the black stranger had given him rattling against his wrist as he ran to the room where Charles Dunbar was staying. He had to hurry. The other guests would certainly discover Kyle soon, and the police station was only five blocks away.

The hotel had a central tower where the standard rooms were located, but also had suites that ringed the outdoor pool. These rooms were larger than the others, and featured a small kitchen. Mr. Dunbar had been given one of the suites because none of the other rooms were available when he called.

It was a cool March night, and Jim's breath turned to mist as he jogged along the sidewalk that led to the suites. He smelled gasoline before he even turned the corner.

There was a man wearing only a t-shirt and boxer shorts walking ahead, and he was carrying something, but Jim couldn't see what it was from his vantage. Jim thought this was the man he was looking for, but wasn't certain. He hid the gun behind his back before asking, "Mr. Dunbar?"

Charles turned and Jim saw that the guest was carrying one of the hotel's ice buckets in his arms. Liquid sloshed inside of the bucket as Charles turned in response to his name being called.

Jim raised the gun.

"Wait, I'm with Rosemary," said Charles. "She needs us to finish one other thing before we die."

Jim was confused, but the man's use of the name 'Rosemary' gave him pause. "I'm supposed to kill you."

"I know," said Charles. "She gave me a gift too." He raised his head, straining his neck so that Jim would see the necklace he was wearing. "She needs me to burn down the evidence in Michael's room. When she gave you your bracelet, she didn't know she'd need to do that. It took me longer than I expected to syphon the gas out of my truck."

Jim nodded and said, "Okay, we have to hurry. The cops will be here soon." Jim used the pistol to point at the room where Michael Harper had been staying. Charles went first, and Jim followed behind.

When they got in the room, Jim understood why it had to be burned. There was blood everywhere. "What happened?" asked Jim.

"I stabbed her," said Charles as he began dumping gas onto the bed. The room already stank from the fluid that had been spread on the carpet, and Jim guessed that this was Charles' second trip back to the room with a bucket of gasoline.

"Why'd you stab her?" asked Jim, concerned that he was being tricked. He kept the gun at the ready just in case.

"I don't know. I don't remember," said Charles as he splashed the gas over the blood soaked sheets. "It's all a blur. I just know we've got to burn the place down."

They heard police sirens in the distance.

"Oh shit," said Charles. "We have to burn this place down."

"What about the sprinklers?" asked Jim.

Charles pointed up and said, "I've already taken care of the one in here."

Jim saw that Charles had tied a towel around the sprinkler on the ceiling. The towel hung down, and Charles had placed a bucket on the bed under it. Jim realized that the towel wouldn't stop the flow of water, but would direct it down to the bucket, allowing the fire in the room time to spread and burn away the evidence before the sprinkler could put it out.

"Do you think we've got enough gas in here?" asked Charles.

"It'll have to be," said Jim. "I already took care of the computer's record of who was here, so if we kill ourselves and burn the blood then there shouldn't be any trace of Michael or Rosemary."

The flashing red and blue lights of the approaching squad cars lit up the room. Jim closed the door, and Charles tried to find the cord to the blinds to shut them as well, but the cord seemed to be missing. He pulled the curtain shut, hiding them from the police that had started to fill the parking lot.

"Let's move the dresser against the door," said Jim, and the two worked together to make sure it wouldn't be easy for any firemen to get into the room. Jim hoped that the police would be preoccupied with the murder scene, but he hadn't thought about the trail of gasoline that Charles had left behind. Two officers followed the trail, and by the time Charles and Jim had moved the dresser, the police were already at their door.

They pounded on the door and commanded, "Open up."

Charles cursed and backed away.

"You've got a lighter, right?" asked Jim.

Charles nodded. The color had faded from his face, leaving him looking ghost-like as he stared at Jim. There were tears in his eyes.

"Do it. You've got to light it. Now."

The police knocked again, harder this time.

Charles picked up a lighter from the nightstand. His breath came in sharp succession as he held the lighter over the bed.

"Do it!" Jim pointed the gun at the frightened stranger.

Charles rolled the thumbwheel, sparking the flint. Jim expected Charles to have to lower the flame to the bed to ignite the gas, but the fumes burst into fire immediately, engulfing Rosemary's arsonist. Charles screamed out in shock and pain, and his arms flailed as he spun. The police outside stopped knocking, and started to force their way in. They kicked at the door, and the frame cracked. The dresser was pushed forward as Charles continued to spin in pain and fear, igniting the puddles of gasoline on the floor and the bed in the process.

Jim tried to aim, but Charles was moving too fast. Jim's first shot grazed Charles' face, but didn't kill him. Jim shot two more times, this time aiming for the other man's chest. Charles fell, but didn't die. He was still screaming and swiping at his burning face until Jim shot him dead.

The police were screaming outside as Jim retreated to the bathroom. The room was already filling with black smoke as Jim closed the door and climbed into the tub. He felt his legs growing numb, as if they threatened to stop carrying him any further even if he wanted to run. He lay flat as the fire continued to grow, engulfing the room outside of the bathroom door.

He heard the fire alarm trip, and the sprinkler in the bathroom turned on, raining water down on him as he put the gun in his mouth.

Jim Broadbent pulled the trigger, and ended his servitude to Rosemary Arborton. The witch had won. No one would ever know that Rosemary, Michael, or Ben had ever been to this hotel.

CHAPTER 18 – An Offering

Widowsfield
March 14th, 1996

"Yes, it worked," said Oliver as he helped Vess up. "I saw the whole ship disappear. There was a burst of green electricity, and then I watched as it followed the underwater cord back to shore…"

"The what?" asked Vess.

Oliver pointed over to the stopgap mechanism and said, "That device is connected to an external power source."

Vess glanced over at the orange box, and then back at Oliver. His eyes were growing wider and his grip on Oliver's arms got tighter. "It's connected to shore? Physically connected?"

"Yes. It's hooked into the local power grid to make sure the CORD doesn't lose power if…"

"You idiot!" Vess shook Oliver. The old man's face contorted in anger as his ears turned red. "You didn't follow Tesla's notes."

"I did exactly what The Accord told me to. We followed their directions exactly."

"The notes said not to allow the device to be connected to anything. That's why we wanted it in the water, you idiot!"

"It's not my fault," said Oliver. "I followed The Accord's notes."

"And you saw the energy source itself?" asked Vess.

"Yes," said Oliver. "After the Eldridge vanished, we saw the cord beneath the water glowing green. It was vanishing too, just like the boat, but then it got to shore. That's when the ship reappeared."

Vess stopped squeezing Oliver's arms, but his jowl was still contorted in anger, as if he were forcing himself not to scream. Then he pointed at the CORD and said, "See if Lyle's okay."

Oliver made sure that Vess could stand on his own, and then he went to the machine where he unlocked the door and opened it to reveal Lyle within. The elderly psychic was on the floor, in the same position that he'd been when the guards placed him there. He was staring up with unblinking eyes, as if he were seeing things that his mind couldn't comprehend.

Oliver knelt beside the invalid and lifted the man's head, making sure he wasn't fused to the floor. "He's alive," said Oliver, uncertain that saying the man was 'fine' would be appropriate.

"Okay, leave him there," said Vess. "We have to get to shore. You have to take me to where you saw the energy go."

Oliver warned Vess about the dead men in the hall, and how they were fused to the ship, and Vess explained that this was what had happened after the initial experiment also. They made their way to the bridge where they discovered two other sailors that had both fallen into the same semi-unconscious state that Lyle Everman had been in for the past half century. Oliver commented on how lucky the men were that they hadn't been fused to the ship like the other victims, but Vess didn't concur. He shook his head and said, "There's no telling what's happening to those men right now. I think the ones that died are the lucky ones."

Oliver shivered at Vess's grim statement. He radioed one of the tugboat captains to come back and pick them up, but received no response. He could see the tugs docked on the other side of the reservoir, but either the captains had left or they were ignoring Oliver's call.

"I don't know why they're not answering."

"I think I do," said Vess. "It's the same reason none of our men on shore are coming to get us."

"Why's that?" asked Oliver.

"Because they're in the same state that these men are." Vess pointed at the sailors lying on the floor. "They're catatonic."

"How do you know?" asked Oliver as he walked to the window and gazed out at the tugboats on the shore far off.

"Because I was afraid this could happen," said Vess as he made his way over to one of the swiveling chairs on the bridge. He sat down and closed his eyes as if settling in for a nap. "We let it out."

"Let what out?" asked Oliver.

"Whatever it is we woke up when we started the experiment in 1943. The thing that watches us."

"And what's that? What the fuck are you talking about?"

"When we set up the first experiment, I brought along a few items that had been sent to me. I never thought much about them at the time, they were just good luck charms to me. I had a bracelet, and a necklace that was used in ceremonial Incan sacrifices, and the hilt of a sacrificial dagger found in the Middle East." Vess reached into his pocket and produced the hilt. It looked like it was made of metal that had long ago rusted, and there was thin twine wrapped tightly around its grip. The base was shaped like a skull, and a dull spike protruded from its head. "I don't have the jewelry anymore, but I still have this. For a long time I thought the entity we contacted in Philadelphia lived inside of one of those items, but we were never able to contact it again. Now I think I know why. When we activated the CORD, we allowed the creature to transfer from one of my items and into the ship itself. Now we've made it worse. Now it's out of the ship, and God only knows where it's gone."

Oliver looked at the wall with newfound fear. "What is it?"

"I don't know," said Vess. "But I think I dream about it. Ever since the first experiment, I've had dreams about black wires reaching out from the walls to grab at me. I've been haunted by those dreams, just as I've been endlessly pulled back to this experiment, and this ship. It won't leave me alone. I think that's the only reason I'm still alive. Because this creature that's watching us from these walls doesn't want me to die. I'm tied to it somehow."

"And you think we let it out?" asked Oliver.

Vess nodded and then stood from his seat. He walked back to the window that looked out over the bow of the ship. Oliver followed behind, and they both gazed out at the shore. "That's why we were supposed to be floating, unanchored, out in the reservoir. The water acts as a barrier to keep the energy in. But you and The Accord let it out."

"Let it out where? Onto the shore?"

Vess stared solemnly out at the tugboats floating in the distance. "I don't know what we're going to find out there, but it's going to be bad. There's no telling how far the creature managed to get before the CORD shut itself down."

"What should we do?" asked Oliver.

"Call The Accord, and then the army."

Oliver thought the old man was joking, but then realized he was serious. "The army?"

Vess nodded. "Yes. We're going to need help containing this. The Accord won't be happy about this, but we're going to have to tell the military about our experiment. It's our only chance of stopping this from getting any worse. But first, we need to discuss what we will and what we will not be telling them."

Widowsfield
March 15th, 1996

Oliver had never expected the CORD experiment to have such an impact on the area around the reservoir. Vess and Oliver had used a lifeboat on the Eldridge to get back to shore, and the devastation they encountered was vast. All of the Cada E.I.B. employees that had escorted Vess to the town were unconscious, lying in the same catatonic state that Lyle was suffering, staring blankly at the sky.

Other people, all throughout the town, were in a similar state. One odd occurrence that they discovered was that cars and trucks had stopped on the road or pulled over, and the passengers were lying on the ground outside of the vehicle.

Oliver and Vess had debated the possible reasons for this, and it was Vess that theorized the motorists had initially been protected from the CORD's effect by the rubber tires of their vehicles. But the moment they stepped out, and made contact with the ground, they were connected to the creature that had swarmed the town.

The Accord handled discussion with the military about the event in Widowsfield, and Oliver wasn't privy to what was decided. However, the National Guard arrived within an hour, but they didn't venture into the town. Instead, the National Guard investigated the extent of the damage, and it was discovered that whatever had happened in the area had been isolated to the town of Widowsfield. There were rural homes on the border of the town that hadn't been affected, and the residents were swept off after being given vague information about an event occurring within the town that might be dangerous. The National Guard then set up blockades around the town, preventing anyone from entering or leaving.

All traffic coming into town was stopped, and the occupants interviewed. Anyone that owned land within the town, or had family or friends there, were taken into custody. It was important that all public information about the event be marginalized.

Oliver and Vess were interviewed at length, but both refused to cooperate until representatives from The Accord arrived. Eventually, both Oliver and Vess were brought into an office inside of Cada E.I.B.'s facility and a conference call was set up. They were joined by several high ranking members of the military. Members of The Accord were also on the call, and once everyone was settled, they began the meeting.

The Accord recounted details about the experiment to the members of the military, but they didn't reveal Vess's theory about the entity that had escaped into the town. The Accord's explanation about the experiment was centered on the CORD's use as a cloaking device for ships, as well as potentially for large aircraft.

What had started as a contentious debate turned more civil as The Accord offered to hand over all data about the CORD to the military in exchange for their help dealing with what had happened in Widowsfield. Unbeknownst to Oliver, The Accord and the military were already working together on other projects. Cada E.I.B.'s work as a broker between the military and other countries had gave them a lot of clout. Everyone understood that if word got out about Cada E.I.B.'s involvement with what happened in Widowsfield, then their ties to the military would be revealed as well. That wouldn't be good for any of them.

That's how the process of covering up the Widowsfield incident began.

The catatonic victims of Widowsfield were collected, and several bodies were discovered fused to the walls of homes, or to the pavement, as if their legs had sunk into the concrete, leaving them twisting and screaming until they suffered a fate similar to the guard on the ship. Oliver and Vess had been left at Cada E.I.B's facility to collect their notes on the experiment, but they were retrieved by an Army general who explained they needed to see something.

They were brought to a house on the north side of Widowsfield. Along the way, Oliver marveled at how dead the town felt. The only activity he witnessed was at the high school, where several jeeps were parked and soldiers were pulling bodies out. The clean-up of Widowsfield had been limited to a small group of men to help avoid information leaking out about the event.

The general parked, and then turned to look back at his two passengers. He motioned at the plain looking house with his thumb and said, "Go on in."

"You're not coming?" asked Oliver.

"Nope. You two go see for yourselves. I've seen enough of the nightmares in this damn town to last a lifetime."

"Is it a body stuck in something?" asked Oliver. "We saw people stuck to the…"

"Nope," said the general. "I've seen those too. This one's different. Just go in and see for yourself."

Oliver got out first and then helped Vess. The elderly man seemed weaker than before, and wasn't exhibiting the same self-reliance he had been days earlier. As they walked up the path that led to the house, Oliver asked, "What do you suppose we're going to find in here?"

"I have no idea," said Vess, but his tone revealed concern.

Oliver opened the door, frightened of what he might see.

The home's front door was set between the living room on the left and a kitchen on the right. The television was facing towards him, set on a table on the far wall, and it was still turned on, displaying static. The volume was up, and the sound of the static crackling provided an eerie soundtrack to the scene.

Directly across from the front door, behind the kitchen, was a stairwell that led to the second floor. There were bloody handprints on the wall.

"Look," said Vess when he entered. He was pointing down to a dog cage on the floor. Oliver knelt and peered inside where he saw a mangy, unconscious dog laying on a urine-soaked towel. The smell was pungent, and he cringed as he stood back up again.

"There's blood on the wall there," said Oliver as he walked towards the stairs.

Vess followed, but he was growing weary as he went. Oliver waited at the bottom of the stairs for him, but Vess waved him on and said, "Go without me. I'll make my way up there in a minute."

Vess looked exhausted, and Oliver was stunned by the change in the formerly vivacious old man. It was as if he were suddenly feeling his age.

Oliver went upstairs as Vess took each stair slow and cautiously. There was blood everywhere. The wood floor was splattered with dry blood, and there were streaks on the wall that looked like someone's bloody fingertips had traced along it. The trail of blood led to a closed door at the end of the hall, and Oliver moved slowly towards it. He turned the knob and then paused before opening the door, steadying himself for what might be inside.

The blood in the hallway was a precursor to a far worse scene. Lying on the floor in the master bedroom of the home was a young woman that had been slaughtered. She was nude, and her skin was mottled pink and purple, with large blisters on her cheeks. Her mouth was open wide and flies were buzzing around her swollen lips. The smell was horrendous, and Oliver quickly covered his nose in the crook of his arm.

While the woman's blistered skin was bad enough, the worst sight was what had been done to her stomach. Someone had cut her open in an awful display of violence. She hadn't simply been stabbed. Whoever had murdered her had plunged the knife in so many times that her gut was split wide, causing her entrails to spill out around her. The kitchen knife that was used to murder her was standing straight up from her midsection, the tip stuck in the wood floor beneath. Flies buzzed and swirled around the scene, and Oliver turned away in disgust as he swatted at the insects.

Vess was standing behind him, staring down at the murdered girl.

"The Watcher got what he wanted," said Vess.

"What do you mean?" asked Oliver.

"He got his sacrifice."

Oliver looked away, but caught sight of something else that shocked him. There was a child sleeping in the bed, his head set on the pillow and the sheets pulled up over him as if he were just asleep. His face was horribly disfigured, and his teeth were chattering as he stared up at the ceiling.

PART THREE – And No Winners

CHAPTER 19 – Loose Ends

Chicago
March 15th, 2012

Alex knocked on the door of the apartment and waited for someone to answer. It had been a long trip, and he was looking forward to finishing his task.

When he'd met Rosemary, he had no idea how she would change his life. He'd been sent along with a couple other guards to investigate what Helen from Cada E.I.B. had seen when driving in to work. Helen warned the security team that a woman was camping out by the reservoir, so Alex and his group had been sent to look into it. That's when they discovered Rosemary.

The mysterious woman had been drawing in her sketchpad, and Alex never expected that she would be any danger at all. But when she reached into her bag, she didn't pull out a paintbrush. Instead, her bag was loaded with weapons. None of the security team were carrying real weapons, and they were forced to do as the stranger asked.

Alex had been lucky, because Rosemary had chosen him to be the bearer of her bracelet, which she explained was a rare gift. He wore it with pride.

Rosemary took his van, saying that she needed it and that he could use the car that she'd driven there. Unfortunately, she didn't leave any money for gas, and Alex wasn't supposed to use his credit cards to keep anyone from being able to track him.

The other guards that he'd been working with had some cash on them, and he stole it after murdering them. When Rosemary left, the men Alex worked with assumed they were safe, but Alex knew they had to die. They never suspected he would hurt them. They didn't know how important Rosemary was to him.

After that, he dumped the bodies off the edge of the scenic overview at the Jackson Reservoir, content to let the catfish gnaw at them until their bodies were dragged over the dam.

The cash that Alex had been able to scrounge up got him enough gas to get to Joliet, while still saving enough to purchase what he needed in Chicago, but that left him with nearly 150 miles to cover. He managed to get a ride from a truck driver that was on his way to Chicago, and he would've murdered the driver too, but he was already low on bullets. Alex had to make sure he kept enough to complete his job.

The jerry can he'd filled with gasoline was set down beside the door, and he pushed it to the side to make sure no one saw it when they opened the door.

Alex knocked again and heard a woman answer from inside, "Coming, coming."

The door finally opened, and Alex saw a short, chubby girl with glasses. She kept the chain on the door latched, and only opened it as wide as the chain would allow.

"Hello?"

"Hi," said Alex. "Are you Mindy?" He laughed, and then corrected himself, "Sorry, not Mindy. I meant Terra. Are you Terra?"

"Who's asking?" asked the woman inside.

"I'm a friend of Rosemary's." Alex showed the woman the bracelet on his wrist that Rosemary had given him. Terra looked at it in befuddlement, uncertain why that should be proof of anything.

"Okay," said the woman, uncertain of the guest. "I'll ask again, who are you?"

"My name's Alex. Rosemary sent me to bring something to you."

"I haven't talked to her in years. I heard she was living in Europe or something."

"No, she's back in Widowsfield."

Alex noted the way the woman responded. She cringed at the name of the town, and that was all Alex needed to see to know that this was definitely who he'd been sent to dispose of. This was the woman that had accompanied Rosemary to Widowsfield in 2007, and she was one of the last loose ends Rosemary had yet to deal with.

"Who are you?" asked Terra again, but Alex didn't need to talk anymore.

He raised his pistol and shot her in the head. Next he would spread the gasoline through the apartment and burn away the evidence before blowing his own brains out. That's the way this had to end. That had always been the plan.

Widowsfield
February 24th, 2007

Oliver was staring at the CORD that had been built in the basement of the Cada E.I.B. offices in Widowsfield. The room was dark, except for the glow of a single halogen lamp that was placed in front of the expensive machine. He'd spent nearly twelve years of his life preparing for what was supposed to occur in just eighteen days, but now everything had fallen apart.

Vess had wanted Oliver to perform the experiment using Nia as his sacrifice inside of the machine. Vess's health had deteriorated to the point where he rarely visited the facility anymore, and he wanted to use a new subject inside of the machine to see if that made a difference. He planned to bring Lyle along as well, but hoped to use Nia as a sacrifice instead. This would be the first time this particular CORD would be activated, and Vess wanted to make sure it was working properly before he emerged from wherever he was hiding. But Oliver had ruined that plan by having his assistant, Lee, murder the psychometric from Chicago.

The cellphone that was clipped to his belt began to vibrate, and he looked at the screen to see who was calling before flipping it open.

"This is Oliver," he said.

The voice on the other line was garbled due to the poor reception Oliver was getting in the basement.

"Alex? Say that again, I didn't hear." Oliver walked out of the CORD's room and back into the hallway where his reception improved.

"We found blood," said Alex, one of the guards that helped patrol the area. "Quite a lot of it."

"Where?"

"Right at the edge of the cliff," said Alex. "Just like you said."

Oliver placed his back against the wall and then slid down so that he was sitting in the hallway. He pressed his left hand to his forehead in frustration. "On the scenic overlook by the reservoir?"

"Yeah," said Alex. "Right next to where that lady tried to kill her daughter a while back."

"Amanda Harper," said Oliver. "And she did kill her daughter. They both died." Oliver massaged his temple as he contemplated what this meant. He and his assistant had murdered two girls to prevent them from leaking information about Widowsfield to the public. There was no doubt in his mind that they had to die, but now he couldn't remember why. He'd hoped the event on the cliff overlooking the Jackson Reservoir had just been a dream, but the two girls were missing, and now their blood had been found. He no longer had any doubt that his memory was correct. Lee had shot those two girls.

"We can hire a team to come out and dredge the reservoir if you want," said Alex. "Will The Accord be upset that we've stopped construction?"

"I'll call Vess and try to figure something out," said Oliver. "Just keep looking for Nia. But don't call anyone, Alex. No one else can know what happened out there."

"Okay," said Alex before ending the call.

Oliver closed his eyes and silently cursed as he contemplated the call he was going to have to make to Vess.

How could he explain that the psychometric that they'd been using to put Widowsfield back together was dead?

Oliver flipped his phone back open and started to scroll through his contacts in search of Lee. He needed his assistant's help now more than ever, but Lee was nowhere to be found. Oliver had even managed to accidentally erase Lee's contact information from his phone. He slapped the phone shut and screamed a curse that echoed through the empty hallway.

"Eleven fucking years," said Oliver as he pounded his fist against the wall behind him in anger. "Eleven years down the God damn drain."

After the event in 1996, The Accord and the United States military began working together on the CORD project. The Accord feigned a complete willingness to cooperate, and the Eldridge had been taken, along with the original CORD, to a military base in New Mexico where further experiments took place. However, Vess and Oliver kept silent about the theory that the entity in the Eldridge had passed to the town of Widowsfield.

Cada E.I.B. purchased the land in and around Widowsfield, and the military helped accommodate the silencing of any angry townsfolk to prevent the story from getting out. The cover-up had been easier than expected. As it turned out, people across the country were more than willing to accept that a small town like Widowsfield could be corrupted by the illegal drug trade. The marketing strategists employed by the military did the same thing with Widowsfield that they'd managed to do with several other stories that should've made the headlines world-wide. They allowed information to be disseminated to the public through false third parties, and cooked up a conspiracy that the government was trying to hide the fact that they'd put so many people into a witness protection program.

The American public will almost always dream up conspiracy theories to explain even the most mundane of government activity, and the strategists had learned that the best way to deceive the public was to cook up the conspiracy for them. The government continued to deny involvement with the Widowsfield meth-ring investigation, but the internet exploded with supposed interviews with former residents who were speaking out about how they'd been moved to a new town in Florida, or California, or some other state far from Missouri. To add fuel to the fire, these fake witnesses vanished following their statements, and conspiracy theorists were quick to insist that the government had killed them for talking. The rabid public was sated with a faked conspiracy, and the truth about what really happened in Widowsfield was known only to a few.

The Accord placated the military, and while the CORD experiment never proved fruitful for them, there were several other projects that Cada E.I.B. had funded that were handed over to the military as recompense. Everyone was happy, except Vess.

Since the experiment in 1996, Vess obsessed about duplicating the results. However, it wasn't as simple as just turning the CORD back on again. The military had taken Tesla's machine, so Vess and Oliver set out to build a new one. That process had been far more difficult and expensive than either of them had anticipated. The CORD was a delicate machine, and the addition of uranium made it much harder to complete. The Accord had access to such material, but Vess had taken over communication with them, severing Oliver's ties with his former employers. From that point forward, Vess oversaw everything.

The years following the 1996 event had not been kind to Vess. The old man's age was finally catching up to him. He became frailer as time passed, and eventually admitted to Oliver that the telomerase levels in his blood had begun to fall. While he still produced more of the valuable enzyme than the average person, his cellular structures were no longer immune to the degradation of time. He was slowly dying.

The acquisition of enough uranium to power the CORD became their largest hurdle. Oliver had expected that The Accord's ties to the military would've made the process of securing the radioactive material easier, but Vess insisted that wasn't so. Instead, they were forced to capitalize on the collapse of the Soviet Union to secure their goods. The arms race was long over, but the extent that the Soviet Union had gone to in an attempt to compete with the United States had left them with an overabundance of uranium and plutonium. By the early 2000's, their stockpile of radioactive material had made it to the black market. Vess was able to get enough uranium to power the CORD, but it had to be delivered in small amounts to avoid detection. This process ended up taking years, and during that time Oliver was left to manage Widowsfield.

In late 2004, Oliver and Vess completed the construction of a new CORD. The machine was hidden in the bowels of the Cada E.I.B. facility, but it was wired directly to the town's power grid, which was fed by the hydroelectric dam on the Jackson Reservoir. Oliver argued with Vess about the need for the Eldridge to be rebuilt in the reservoir, but Vess insisted that the ship was of no consequence any longer. The entity had moved into the town itself. Vess believed that in the original experiment, in 1943, the entity had moved from one of the sacrificial relics he was carrying and into the Eldridge. Then, in 1996, the CORD allowed it to move from the ship to the town itself.

Great care was taken to ensure that Widowsfield was isolated from neighboring towns. The electric grid was severed, and connections to outside counties destroyed. The only power coming into Widowsfield was supplied by the dam in the Jackson Reservoir, and Vess believed that this would help contain the entity once they built a new CORD and activated it.

On March 14th, 2005, they attempted to use the machine with Lyle Everman inside. It didn't work.

Vess was convinced that their new CORD had been built incorrectly, and he insisted a new one be constructed. That had been two years earlier, and now their new device was ready to be tested. Unfortunately, Vess was too ill to attend, and he asked that Oliver find a new psychic to be placed within the machine. During their last experiment, the introduction of radioactive material hadn't produced the tell-tale green electricity that meant the machine was working, and Vess wanted to know that the new CORD was functioning properly before he attended an experiment.

When Oliver found Nia in Chicago, he tried to call Vess to tell him the good news. However, Vess's illness had worsened and his communication with Oliver had been sparse. He was excited to hear that a replacement for Lyle had been found, and he told Oliver that The Accord would happily fund whatever Oliver thought was necessary to get the experiment moving in the right direction. Oliver continued his work with Nia, and never sought permission from The Accord or any other part of Cada E.I.B. for the massive expense. It wasn't until Vess's illness had passed that the old man discovered how much Oliver had spent.

Vess had lied to Oliver about The Accord's involvement with the Widowsfield project. It turned out that Vess had been funding the project on his own, and Oliver's overspending nearly bankrupted the dying man. But Oliver was convinced that what Nia had discovered at the murder scene was evidence that the entity could be placated by any sacrifice, and that they didn't need to use a psychic in the CORD to contact it.

Oliver and Vess knew that a woman named Terry had been murdered at the house on Sycamore at around the same time that the CORD had been activated. That was also where they found the catatonic child. Oliver proposed that the CORD be activated at the same moment that a new sacrifice was offered in the house, but Vess insisted that the most important part was having a psychic placed within the machine.

Unfortunately, Nia and her friend had to be killed before the experiment could come to fruition. Though Oliver couldn't have explained why, he knew it was the right decision.

He knew he would have to call Vess and explain what had happened, but he delayed the inevitable. Oliver got up and walked back into the CORD's room. He stood in the threshold and stared at the machine that had become the focus of so much of his life. He knew that if he called Vess with nothing to report other than that Nia was dead, and that all the money they'd spent over the past couple months had been for nothing, that Vess would likely shut down the entire operation. It seemed criminal that all that work would go to waste.

None-the-less, he had no choice but to close the book on the Widowsfield project for the time being. Oliver turned off the only light in the room, shrouding the CORD in darkness once again, and then locked the door on his way out.

It would be years before he went in the room again.

Inside Cada E.I.B.'s facility in Widowsfield
March 13th, 2012
Shortly after 5:30 AM

Oliver was standing in front of the CORD as its door stood wide. He'd nearly finished dragging the body of the young nurse into the machine as the silver rings began to spin on the pillars that bookended the steel box, but it was more difficult than he'd anticipated. He panted from the exertion of dragging her through the hall and to this room. He'd rerouted power to the machine, and the process of powering it up was nearing its end. The next step would be to cut the cord, and release the uranium from the stopgap to allow the CORD to be fed the radioactive material.

The handle of the butcher knife was slick, and he passed it over to his other hand so that he could wipe his right palm off on his pants. He'd never murdered someone before, but this was in the name of science. The nurse's death might facilitate the greatest discovery in the history of mankind. Just like a war general had to accept that he might be sending thousands of soldiers to their deaths in the interest of winning a battle, Oliver had sacrificed the nurse to reach a similar end.

The girl's blonde hair was wet with her blood, and a small pool had collected on the floor of the CORD's interior. Oliver rolled up his sleeves as he prepared for what he had to do.

Blue bolts of electricity crackled along the spinning rings, and Oliver flipped the final switch on the CORD's panel that allowed it to draw in the final surge it needed. Next, he went to the orange stopgap mechanism and held his finger over the red switch that would cut the cord.

"Now or never," he said to himself before taking a deep breath. He flipped the switch. He heard the stopgap's gears churning, but it sounded more lethargic than he remembered. He was terrified that something was wrong, but he could only pray that it would work properly.

He didn't have time to watch for the electricity to take on the green hue that he'd seen in 1996. This time, he was going to try and offer up the sacrifice to the entity in Widowsfield the same way that had been done by the murderer in the house on Sycamore. He was even wielding the battered kitchen knife that they'd found stabbed through Terry and stuck in the floor.

Oliver went into the CORD, ducking to avoid hitting his head, as the lightning zapped around him. He straddled the nurse and stared down at her stomach. His arms were trembling, and his eyes watered as he tried to convince himself that killing her had been the right thing to do.

Her eyes fluttered, and her head rolled. She started to raise her arms, and then she realized that someone was on top of her.

"What..."

Oliver was spurred into action. He stabbed down with all his strength, and the blade easily pierced her belly. The nurse's grogginess evaporated. She came alive to defend herself. She screamed and scratched, but Oliver continued his assault. He pulled the knife out and tried to stab her again, but she thrust her hands up at him, catching the blade between the ring and middle fingers of her right hand. His strike slit her down to her knuckle and she retracted her hand as she cried out in pain. She thrust her hips up hard enough to turn to her side, and then she gripped the threshold of the CORD as she cried out for help.

The lights in the room began to dim as the CORD utilized the majority of the building's power. Oliver saw that the reflection of the electricity shining in on him was still blue, but he didn't have time to worry about why it didn't glow green yet. He pulled at his victim, and she continued her desperate attempt to get away. He stabbed at her over and over, each strike glancing off her bones and leaving long cuts that immediately bled. Within only a few seconds, the smooth steel walls on the inside of the CORD were decorated with smears of blood as Rachel desperately tried to get away.

She continued to kick at Oliver, and was able to knock him off of her. He sliced at her calf, cutting her deep, but she was fueled by adrenaline now. Pain wouldn't slow her.

She screamed for help as she started to crawl away. Her formerly white Keds, which were now blood red, squeaked as she tried to gain traction, and her knee slammed back down as she slipped. Her foot fell near Oliver, and he took the opportunity to disable her. He aimed carefully with the knife before hacking down at her Achilles heel. She wailed in pain, and then kicked at him hard enough to send him pounding against the opposite wall. She tried again to get away, but the most recent wound was too grievous. She collapsed again, and this time the pain was intense enough to stop her. She flipped over onto her back so that she could face her murderer.

"Why?" she asked as she crawled backwards out of the CORD.

Oliver rose and followed. He wasn't a psychotic murderer, and he didn't take pleasure in this. He was horrified by what he had to do, but he wasn't going to let heaven slip away. He needed to meet The Skeleton Man that Paul had met. He needed to know the truth.

"Why?"

"I'm sorry, Rachel," said Oliver as he stalked her. He was crying as he loomed above, the knife in his hand dripping with her blood. "I wish it didn't have to be like this, but trust me…"

She cursed at him and begged for her life as she continued to try and get away. She turned back over so that she could crawl, showing her back to her attacker in her attempt to flee.

"I'm sending you to Heaven!"

Oliver lunged and pounded down on Rachel's back. The force of his landing knocked the woman's breath out, and she could only make pitiful gasps as he pulled her head up by her hair and then slit her throat.

CHAPTER 20 – Burn It All

Widowsfield
March 13th, 2012
Shortly after 5:30 AM

"Let me check her airway," said Helen as she held onto Paul's arm to get him to stop pushing the gurney along.

Rosemary's breathing had become shallow as they were moving through Cada E.I.B.'s facility, but then she started to cough and choke. Paul and Alma felt helpless and just watched as the old nurse worked.

Helen lifted the back of Rosemary's neck so that her chin was pointing straight up, and then she put her finger into the dying woman's mouth. Helen looked back in frustration, searching for something, and then said, "There's not enough light in here."

As if in wicked response to her complaint, the already sparse light in the hall grew dimmer. The red emergency lights that had blazed so bright moments earlier had begun to fade, as if the power was being drawn somewhere else.

"She needs to go to a real hospital," said Helen. "She's going to need a…"

Rosemary sputtered on the gurney. She reached out and grasped at Helen, and the nurse moved closer to help.

"Don't worry," said Helen. "We're going to get you someplace that can help."

"No," said Rosemary. "You can't. You can't." She was struggling to speak and it sounded like her mouth was filling with liquid.

"You need a CT scan," said Helen. "We can't do that here. We have to…"

"Vess will come," said Rosemary.

Helen looked up at Paul and Alma as if they might offer a better explanation. Alma looked over at Paul and then back at Helen before asking, "Who's Vess?"

"He worked with Oliver, right?" asked Paul.

Helen nodded and then said, "He's our boss."

Rosemary was holding onto Helen's arm. Alma saw that part of the psychometric's hand was touching a beaded bracelet that the nurse was wearing. Rosemary said, "He'll be here."

"Vess?" asked Helen. "I don't understand."

"He's coming. Keep me here…" Rosemary coughed, and then tried again to speak, but Helen cut her off.

"Fine. Have it your way." Helen motioned for Paul and Alma to help push the gurney again. "Let's go. I'll do what I can here, but she still needs to get to a dang hospital."

They wheeled Rosemary along as fast as they could without causing the trip to be too bumpy. The lights in the hall got dimmer as they went, and when they got to the elevator the power in the facility had grown so weak that the call-button was no longer illuminated.

"I don't know what's going on," said Paul, "but I sure the hell don't think we should be hopping on an elevator."

"The building has back-up power," said Helen as she jabbed her thumb on the 'down' button.

The elevator door squeaked, and then opened only a foot wide before the door stopped. The elevator within was pitch black.

"Well, that settles that," said Paul.

The light in the hall wavered. "I don't understand," said Helen as she looked around. "Something must be wrong."

"Let's take the stairs," said Paul.

Helen agreed, and then she showed them how to lower the gurney so that it could be carried. Paul took one end while Helen and Alma struggled to support the other, and they made their way slowly down the stairs to the level where the sleepers were kept.

"Paul," said Rosemary as they were nearing the sleepers' floor. "Listen to me."

"Just relax, dear," said Helen.

"Paul," said Rosemary again, ignoring Helen.

Paul was holding the front of the gurney and Rosemary was looking directly up at him. He gave the woman a pained smile and said, "I'm right here, Rose."

She gave him the first honest smile he'd seen from her. "My mother used to call me Rose."

"Just keep calm," said Paul. "We're almost there." He pressed his back into the bar that opened the door to the sleepers' level and then they unlatched the accordion base so that they could rest the gurney on the wheels again.

Rosemary reached out and grasped Paul's arm. "You have to save her."

"Save who?" asked Paul, although he was only humoring the addled woman. He was certain that she'd lost so much blood that she was either hallucinating or about to.

"Alma," said Rosemary, which drew Paul's attention.

He gave Alma a puzzled look and then asked Rosemary, "What do you mean?"

"The Skeleton Man," said Rosemary, although her consciousness was fading. "He'll try to use her."

"I'll keep her safe," said Paul.

"Put things back where they came from," said Rosemary. "Put The Skeleton Man back in his wall."

They pushed the gurney down the hall and past the sleepers' room. Helen explained that they needed to get into the room where Alma and the others had been kept. That was where the medical supplies that the nurse needed were located.

"But your friends locked themselves in," said Helen. "Maybe you can get them to open the doors."

"I'll see if…" Paul started to walk away from the gurney, intent on banging on the door that Stephen and Rachel were locked behind, but Rosemary panicked when she thought he was leaving.

Rosemary reached out to Paul and nearly knocked herself off the gurney as she grabbed at his arms. "Stay with me. Talk to me, Paul."

"I'll go see what's up with them," said Alma as she started to walk away from them. "You stay with her."

Paul wasn't sure what was wrong with Rosemary, or why she was so intent on Paul staying by her side, but he did as she asked. She held onto his arm and pulled him closer.

"You'll be fine, Rose," said Paul.

Rosemary looked over at Helen, and then back at Paul as she whispered, "Why'd you keep the noose?"

"What?" asked Paul. The injured woman's question shocked him.

"The noose in the closet," said Rosemary. "The one you were going to hang yourself from before your friend called."

"I don't know," said Paul as he looked over at Alma. She wasn't more than six feet away, and had just started knocking on the door that Stephen and Rachel had locked. She hadn't heard Rosemary, and Paul didn't want her to know about his near-suicide. That wasn't something he wanted her to worry about.

"You kept it as a symbol," said Rosemary.

"Sure," said Paul. "Look, I don't want to talk about that." He glanced over his shoulder as Alma called out to their friends. He could hear Rachel speaking from the other side of the door, and then the 'clack' of the lock coming undone.

"You let an object own you," said Rosemary.

"I don't want to talk about that," said Paul as he watched Rachel open the door.

"Burn it, Paul," said Rosemary. "It all has to burn."

Paul wasn't sure what she meant, but didn't risk asking as Alma came back over to help them guide the gurney into the room with Rachel and Stephen. Rachel was moving the other gurneys in the room out of the way and Paul saw that Stephen was sitting in front of a laptop.

"Sorry," said Stephen as he closed the computer and stood. "We had the doors locked because…" He looked uncertain and then shrugged. "Well…"

Rachel finished her husband's explanation, "Because this place is fucking creepy."

Helen rushed to the counter where Stephen had been working on the computer and told him to move. He stepped aside, and Helen pushed the computer out of the way. Paul noticed that one of Stephen's cameras was connected to the laptop via a USB cord, and he wondered what the two had actually been up to in the room that they needed the doors locked. He didn't have time to ponder it.

"Paul, help me," said Helen as she pointed at the top shelf of one of the cabinets over the counter. "Grab the box of gauze up there, please."

"Oh my God," said Rachel as she finally noticed that Rosemary had been stabbed. "Is that a knife? What happened?"

"She got stabbed," said Helen, obviously annoyed with the reporter.

"How?" asked Rachel.

"It's a long story," said Alma.

"Did you guys get Michael and Ben?" asked Stephen.

"Yes," said Alma as she walked around to the other side of Rosemary's gurney so that she could hold the woman's hand. "They're outside with Jacker."

The building's power finally cut out after a sudden, loud bang. They were left in darkness and Rachel succinctly expressed everyone's thoughts, "Well that's fucking perfect."

"I've got a flashlight app," said Stephen as he dug out his phone.

"There're some flashlights in the bottom cabinet," said Helen and Paul went to retrieve them. He pushed aside a box that had a label with the contents handwritten on it: Muriate of Potash. He didn't know what that was, but pushed the box aside and heard glass bottles clink within it. He found two flashlights and got them both out.

Stephen used his phone's app to provide a surprising amount of light. Helen instructed Stephen to hold the phone over Rosemary, and he complied as the nurse worked. He grimaced and looked away, and Helen saw his queasiness.

She grunted disapproval and then asked for Alma's help applying pressure to the wound.

Rosemary screamed out in pain as Helen began to search the extent of her injury. Helen promised that it would be okay, and then walked Rosemary through the process, explaining every detail to help keep the victim calm.

"Stephen," said Rosemary, surprising everyone. "Listen to me. I need you to do something."

"Sure, sure," said Stephen, but his tone didn't inspire trust. "Whatever you need."

"You have to find Oliver."

"Rachel already went looking for him," said Helen.

"No I didn't," said Rachel from beside her husband.

"Not you," said Helen. "The nurse I worked with. She went looking for Oliver, but never came back. I don't know if she got scared and took off or what happened to her."

"Oliver's got her," said Rosemary.

"I doubt it," said Helen. She was humoring Rosemary, but wasn't taking the wounded woman seriously. "There's no way you could know that."

"She knows all sorts of shit she shouldn't," said Paul. "She's psychic."

"He has her down below us," said Rosemary. "He's the reason the power went out. He's trying to use the device…" she was overcome by pain and clenched her teeth until it passed. "You have to go find him."

"No," said Stephen with a laugh as he looked around at the others. He expected them to sympathize with his refusal, but both Alma and Paul glared at him. "You can't be serious. You want me to go traipsing around this place looking for some lunatic? Are you nuts?"

"Someone's got to do it," said Paul. "I'll go if you won't."

"No," said Rosemary. "I need you and Alma here with me. Stephen, you have to trust me. I'll tell you how to get to him. Just go down there and tell him that Nia is back. Tell him you're friends with Nia, and he'll do whatever you say. Get him to come back up here with you."

"I'll go with you," said Rachel.

Stephen looked around at the others and then cursed before saying, "Fine. We'll take the camera with us. We can use the night vision on it."

"Be careful," said Alma, and Stephen groaned an unenthusiastic response.

CHAPTER 21 – Beneath the Cords

Inside of The Watcher's Widowsfield

Raymond was sitting alone at the Salt and Pepper Diner, staring out the window at the desolate town. A storm had come in, darkening the pavement as the wind kicked up and sent a Styrofoam cup bouncing along the curb until it got stuck in a storm drain.

"Dad?" asked Raymond as he glanced around the empty restaurant.

He heard a woman's moan from somewhere in the building. Raymond scooted out of the bench seat and called again, "Dad?"

Lightning flashed outside, illuminating the restaurant before the crash of thunder arrived. The large windows of the diner rattled and the faint bulbs above flickered as Raymond cringed in fear. He looked outside and watched as the street got darker still. The wind was blowing strong enough to rattle the street lamps and cause the sign on the bank across the street to shake.

"Do it again," said the woman's breathy voice from the back of the restaurant.

"Hello?" Raymond called out to the woman, but he didn't get an answer.

"Yes. Oh God yes. Just like that," said the woman as she breathed sharply between each sentence. Raymond wasn't too young or naïve to know what was happening. He'd watched his sister have sex while he was hiding in her closet, and the noises the woman in the back of the restaurant was making were nearly identical.

He heard the sound of wet penetration.

"Harder," said the woman in a throat expulsion of pleasure.

Raymond looked at the door that led outside, wondering if he should leave, but the storm was only getting worse. He considered hiding in the bathroom, and wondered if that was where his father had gone, but he was surprised to see a sign dangling from the handle that read, 'Out of Order.' Not only was the bathroom broken, but a wooden plank had been nailed across the threshold as if ensuring that no one could go in, or that nothing could get out.

The woman continued to moan in pleasure, and Raymond could hear the distinct sound of flesh slapping against flesh. Who was having sex?

Raymond felt ashamed and intrigued all at once. Some of the boys that lived near him were in their early teens, but they still palled around with Raymond's younger crowd because there weren't many other kids in the area. While the kids Raymond's age were content playing hide-and-go-seek, the older boys always had other activities in mind. They talked endlessly about sex, and flaunted the dirty magazines and movies that they'd stolen from their fathers. Raymond always kept quiet about what he'd seen his sister doing, although he thought of it often. Despite the shame he felt, he was undeniably aroused. The burgeoning sexuality of young boys is a force of nature, and Raymond often fantasized about what he'd seen his sister doing.

Now he had a chance to witness it again.

His heart raced as the sexual act continued in the back of the restaurant. Part of him wanted nothing more than to flee, but a stronger impulse led him to creep behind the counter and towards the two-way door that led to the kitchen. He just wanted to peek.

The woman continued to command, "Harder," as Raymond got to the door. He set his hand on the metal kick-plate on the bottom half of the door and gently eased the door back a few inches so that he could peer in. The hinges squeaked, but not enough to alert the people in the kitchen.

He saw a large man standing with his back to the door. He was still wearing his clothes, and he had shaggy black hair that bounced as he thrust himself forward. Raymond heard the slap of wet flesh again, and he was confused by what he was looking at. The man's girth nearly hid the woman in front of him, but then the man stepped back slightly, allowing Raymond to see the girl better.

She was much smaller than the man, with short blonde hair and silver studs in the dimples of her cheeks. An ornate, colorful tattoo was emblazoned across both arms and down across her chest, and he caught a glimpse of her right breast as the man moved further back.

Raymond's heart was thundering in his chest as he watched, hoping to see more.

"Again," said the woman. "Harder."

The man surged forward, once again blocking Raymond's view of the woman's body. The husky man's arm thrust forward and the woman's head fell back as she gasped in pleasure. Raymond wasn't sure what he was witnessing, and guessed that the man was using a sex toy of some sort on the woman, like the ones Raymond had seen in his friend's pornography movie.

Something dripped down from between the two and splashed in a pool of liquid on the floor. Whatever the two were doing, it was creating a mess that was falling to the floor between them. It was too dark to see the color of the fluid, but then the man stepped back again, revealing even more of the woman's body for Raymond to see.

Suddenly, the eroticism ended. Raymond's perversion turned horrific as he saw that the woman's stomach had been stabbed multiple times. The man was holding a butcher knife, and had cut the woman open enough that her innards were spilling out to the floor beneath them.

Raymond clasped his hands over his mouth and fell backward. He wanted to run, but the door swung open further before he could get away. Michael Harper was standing behind the door, and had been there the whole time. He held the door open and smiled down at Raymond as he asked, "Do you like what you see?"

Raymond tried to move backward, but something was holding him where he was. He pushed harder, but it didn't help. He was caught on the floor like a fly in a spider web.

Michael Harper was free of the trap, and he smirked down at the young boy the same way that he had when he'd discovered him hiding in Terry's closet.

Michael closed his eyes and raised his head slightly, as if smelling the pleasant aroma of fresh bread. He smiled back down at Raymond and said, "I love your fear."

Behind Michael, the massacre in the kitchen continued. The man never turned to see Raymond, but the girl was staring directly at him. She licked her lips just before her assailant stabbed the knife back into her gut. The damage to her stomach was extreme, but she continued to act as if the assault pleased her.

Raymond wanted to scream. He wanted to leave this nightmare behind, but his body was trapped on the floor. Below him swirled the fog that had blighted Widowsfield for sixteen years. As the frigid vapor rose around him, he was reminded of the awful memories he'd gratefully forgotten moments ago. Green lightning flashed around them, crackling through the fog as it seeped across the restaurant, carrying with it the souls of the others that were trapped here.

Michael's hand was still on the door, but Raymond could see that it was changing shape. The skin on his hand was undulating, like a flesh-colored glove that was filled with worms. Black wires stretched out from the tips of his fingers and disappeared within the door. Michael knelt down to get closer to Raymond, and at first his hand seemed tied to the door, but then the wires stretched and snapped, freeing him. The black cords writhed and shrank, eventually pulling themselves back into the door and disappearing.

Michael Harper leaned in closer to Raymond, and the fog avoided his touch, shrinking away as if repelled by his body. Michael was looking down at Raymond, and he set his hand on the boy's left thigh. Raymond could feel the cords grinding within Michael's palm, as if the entire innards of the man were just a mass of coiled, writhing snakes. Michael's head was at Raymond's level, and he stared into the boy's eyes as he got closer.

The man's eyes had turned wholly black, and as he approached, Raymond was forced to stare into them. Within Michael Harper was an endless mass of twisting cords, and the blackness seemed to stretch into infinity. But then, deep within the black, he caught sight of an even larger shape, and the realization that there was more than just the cords terrified him even more than he already was. Raymond wished he could close his eyes and never see into the darkness again, but he was trapped in The Watcher's web.

"Let's play," said Michael, though his voice had become deeper and echoed as if they'd been transported to the innards of a steel box.

The Watcher's hands burst, revealing the mass of black cords within as the skin ripped away. The cords pierced Raymond's thigh and started to course through his body, tearing through muscle and flesh, causing the child immense agony. Cords began to seep from the corners of Michael's eyes as if they were tears.

When the Watcher was in the midst of tearing the boy apart, the world resounded with a new noise. It wasn't the crack of thunder, but a more metallic sound that shook the walls. The silverware beneath the counter shuddered in their plastic cups, and a napkin holder fell and bounced on the rubber mat.

"Did you hear that?" asked The Watcher as he rose up from his victim. The cords that had been snaking out of his shattered hand snapped free of the creature and wormed their way into Raymond to continue their torture, independent of their master's will.

Again, the pounding of metal shook the earth, and The Watcher nearly lost his balance. The cords within him quivered. Raymond saw The Watcher's true form revealed. His false skin cracked and split, revealing the wires within him twisting and writhing about. The pounding of metal that dominated their world was causing the wires to vibrate, and his skin suit was torn apart by the motion. The grinding wires swallowed up strips of skin as other pieces of flesh fell to the floor with a wet splash.

The creature spoke, although his voice no longer mimicked Michael Harper. Now the monster sounded more like two pieces of metal sliding across one another, but the noise formed a hiss of a word, "Vess."

All the walls around them began to quiver the same as the wires beneath The Watcher's skin suit. His illusion fell away, and the façade of the Salt and Pepper Diner began to crumble away, like strips of wallpaper or chips of paint coming loose. Beneath everything was the mess of cords, like maggots beneath dead skin. Raymond felt the floor beneath him moving, but the fog still held him down. He tried to push down on the floor, but felt his fingers slid into wires there, and then the grinding cords pinched his skin. Within moments, he was being torn apart, caught in The Watcher's world like a piece of meat being grinded into hamburger. He felt every agonizing second as his body was transformed into pulp, but his soul refused to leave. It wasn't until he felt the icy grip of the fog cover his face that he finally felt peace. But he knew, just as all the others in the fog did, that his peace was fleeting. It would all begin again, and he would suffer just as much, if not more, than he had this time. The only thing he could look forward to were the few short, blissful minutes where he would be alone in the diner, and ignorant of The Watcher's plan for him.

In Cada E.I.B.'s parking lot
March 13th, 2012
Shortly before 6:00 AM

Jacker was waiting beside the security van with his arms crossed. He watched the caged light that was above the entrance as it flickered. It would grow dim, and then flash bright, threatening to break at any moment.

The moths' enticement by the light was unfazed, and they continued to spin around and around, thwacking into the metal bars in their fervor. The combination of his weariness and the pulsing light made the moths' dance nearly hypnotic.

The crook of his arm itched.

He scratched at the place where he used to put the needle in when he was shooting heroin. He could feel the vein beneath his skin, thick and plump, and just the sensation of pressing against the vein gave him pleasure. He closed his eyes and imagined his finger was a needle, tapping into the vein, delivering euphoria. He felt his lips grow wet at the thought, and he wiped at his mouth after a long sigh.

He reached to his pocket in search of the coin that Paul had given him, but remembered that he'd given it to Rosemary. Even though the symbolic coin didn't belong to him, he still longed for the strength it would give him. Addiction was a never-ending curse, and one that required a large reservoir of will to overcome. His will had faded since learning of Debbie's betrayal.

His five year relationship with Debbie had never been easy. She was bombastic, commanding, and quick to anger, but Jacker's mother had been the same way, and he learned that behind the hardest exterior often lay the kindest heart. Debbie's outward hostility was a defense mechanism, and Jacker was able to break it down and reach the kind-hearted woman within.

But that was all over now.

Her decision to sleep with her co-worker had been exactly what Jacker needed to fall back into old habits. At first, he'd only planned on taking a single hit, but any addict could attest to how falling for that same old lie almost guaranteed a binge. The next one always promised to be the last moments before succumbing, and it rarely ever was.

Jacker's binge had eased his anger over what Debbie had done, but only while he was high. Each time his high lost its edge, his anger returned, and it always seemed more intense than it had been before. By the time his binge was reaching its end, his sober moments were filled with blind rage. He'd been staying with his dealer, and hadn't returned home since discovering what Debbie had done. But during a break between doses, his rage grew to the point that he began punching holes in his dealer's walls. That signaled a forced end to his binge, and left him dealing with his anger without any respite. He exploded at work, and was promptly fired, and that's when he began to plan his revenge.

He never hit Debbie, and would never allow himself to, but he needed an outlet for his rage. He wasn't even sure how he ended up at Debbie's work, or by what luck, or lack thereof, he found her partner in the alley behind the grocery store, but the confluence of events led him to confront the young man, leading to a violent altercation that sent Jacker fleeing and Debbie's lover bleeding and unconscious.

Jacker had been Paul's sponsor in their support group, but the two had developed a close friendship over the past few months. Paul promised to help in any way he could, but he was dealing with his own issues at the moment after being fired from his job. They spent a long evening drinking and ruminating on their bad luck. Jacker had lost his job, his girlfriend, and was on the run from the law. Paul had also lost his job, fought endlessly with his girlfriend, and pined for an old girlfriend that wanted nothing to do with him. They drowned their sorrow in alcohol that night, and laughed at how bleak each of their future's looked. Little did they know how things were just about to get so much worse.

Except that Paul had Alma now.

A twinge of jealousy shot through Jacker at the thought. He hated himself for it, but Jacker had enjoyed knowing that Paul was just as down and out as he was. Now that Paul had Alma again, things were looking up for his friend. Meanwhile, Jacker was continuing his downward spiral.

"Fuck me," said Jacker as he stared at the spinning moths around the fading light.

He was so tired that the walls looked like they were moving, and as he leaned against the van it started to feel like he was sinking into it. He was reminded of being on acid, where solid objects could suddenly take on the appearance of a sheet with snakes slithering beneath. As he stared at the moths, the wall around the flickering light began to quiver. The shadows of the moths were growing larger and longer than they should be, as if they were also being affected by the wavering wall.

"What in the hell?"

Jacker took a step closer as the shadows on the wall grew. It looked like the moths were drawing black lines on the walls with their shadows, but then the path they carved began to move on their own. The twisting shadows struck terror in Jacker and he rubbed his eyes to see if this was an illusion. Was he experiencing a flashback? He'd often heard legends of drug-users being struck by flashbacks days or even weeks after using. Was that what was happening?

The black shadows twisted and grew, but then the light finally faded away, failing like it had been threatening to do for a long time. Now the whole wall was merely a shadow, but he could still see movement within it, as if there was something darker than the shadows moving in front of him.

CHAPTER 22 –This Might Hurt

Inside Cada E.I.B.'s facility
March 13th, 2012
Shortly before 6:00 AM

Stephen was walking in front of his wife, and he was using the viewfinder on his camera, utilizing the night vision to get a better view of what lie ahead. Rachel had a flashlight, but was using it to watch behind them.

Rosemary had given them directions to Oliver's lab, and explained that the emergency doors in the facility were temporarily disabled. However, they would have to take the stairs down because the elevator required a key to access the bottom floor. Paul explained that it wouldn't do any good to argue with Rosemary about how she could know so much about the building, and that she'd been using her ability to 'know' things during their entire trip out to Branson.

The Cada E.I.B. facility was as quiet as a tomb, and the clack of Rachel's shoes echoed through the halls. Stephen stopped and said, "Take off those shoes. We sound about as subtle as a drum line."

Rachel groaned, but did as he asked. Without her shoes on she barely reached up to Stephen's shoulders as she stayed close behind him.

"How the fuck did we get roped into this?" asked Rachel.

"Babe, this whole thing might suck now, but when we get this story out…" he shook his head and whistled. "It's going to be huge."

"It won't do us a hell of a lot of good if we're dead."

Stephen didn't offer a retort. He just nodded and said, "True. So let's not go dying. Rosemary said the stairs were by the elevators. Do you see them?"

"Yes," said Rachel as she used the flashlight to point over to a nearby door. "Right there."

They went over to the door and Stephen turned the camera to Rachel so that she was looking at the lens. She stared at him, her eyes showing as large, green globes in the viewfinder, and he asked her, "Are you ready, Mrs. Knight?"

She glowered and shook her head. "No, not really."

"Are you scared?"

"Of course I am. Why? What's with you? Why are you asking stupid questions?"

"I'm just trying to help the people that watch this get a better idea of how we're feeling."

"You're taping?" asked Rachel, surprised and annoyed.

"Of course I'm taping. I've been taping everything. I'm not letting any of this get lost."

"I thought a red light or something would blink when you were taping."

"Not if you shut it off," said Stephen. "I'm not risking Rosemary or any of the others freaking out on us and making us shut it off. Fuck that. This is too important."

"Great," said Rachel. "I'm sure they'll be super happy when they find out you've been recording so much."

Stephen had his hand on the door's bar when he lowered the camera and sneered at his wife. They could see each other faintly by the light of her flashlight as she scanned the area. "Babe, this whole thing is too big a story to worry about what they think. Forgive me, but if they try to stop us from getting this story out there..." He laughed and said bluntly, "Fuck them. I'm not even thinking about money, or our website, or anything else other than how fucking huge this is. People need to know what happened in this town."

"What happened?" asked Rachel. "Do you know? Because I sure as hell don't. I'm still trying to sort out what was real and what was a dream. I'm not even sure I know anymore. And plus, I'm exhausted. I'm not even sleepy, but totally exhausted. My hands are shaking, and my stomach is upset. I just want to get out of this place."

"I offered you my pills. You're the one that didn't want to take them."

"Are we seriously going to start fighting about that again?" asked Rachel. She pointed her flashlight at the door to the stairs and said, "Let's just get a move on."

Stephen raised the camera again and started recording as they opened the door to the stairwell and headed down. Rachel was about to follow when she caught sight of something on the floor.

"Hey, look," she said as she shined the light at the tile.

Stephen looked down with the camera, but the glare from the flashlight muddied the picture. When he looked past the viewfinder and directly at the floor he saw that Rachel had noticed a smear of what might be mud, or blood, or both.

"Is that blood?" asked Rachel.

"Some of it looks like mud," said Stephen. "But that's blood," he pointed at a reddish-brown streak. "Paul shot the dude in the foot, so we can probably follow the trail to him."

"Rosemary was pretty confident this guy would be in his lab," said Rachel.

"Yeah, well, maybe the blood leads there. Only one way to find out." Stephen smiled and raised his eyebrows.

Rachel sighed and said, "You're enjoying this way too much."

"Of course I am," said Stephen. "Don't get me wrong, I'm freaked out too, but our trip out here has been better than I could've ever hoped. We're not just proving that supernatural beings exist, we made contact with them."

"Yeah, and I don't want to do it again," said Rachel. "I don't want any of this. I don't want the site. I don't want the show. I don't want any of it. I just want to go back to how things were before we came here."

"Are you insane?" asked Stephen. "You want to go back to being a local news reporter making thirty grand a year? With what we've found out here, we're going to be millionaires."

"I liked my job," said Rachel. "Sure, the pay wasn't great, but people around town were getting to know me, and who knows what might've happened if I'd stayed there. All of the anchors at the station started as field reporters."

"Come on, babe," said Stephen with a dismissive roll of his eyes. "They fed all you reporters that same line of bullshit. It's how they get you to put up with all of their crap. They tell you that if you ever want to be an anchor, you've got to go through the field reporter duty, but what they don't tell you is that the anchors keep their jobs for decades, and when it comes time to hire a new one, experience isn't what counts. They'll give that job to anyone that's good looking and can read a teleprompter. They chew up and spit out girls like you by the dozen. They make you think you're destined for the anchor's seat, and then send you out on bullshit assignments over and over so the viewers can gawk at your tits."

"Nice," said Rachel. "Real nice, asshole."

"Hey, I'm just telling the truth. I saved you from years of dealing with bullshit and false promises from those people."

"You can be a real piece of shit sometimes. You know that?" asked Rachel as she walked past her husband and started to head down the stairs.

"How so?" asked Stephen as he followed behind his wife. "Because I'm always looking out for you? Because I'm always looking out for our future?"

"No," said Rachel as she stopped on the stairs and turned to face him. She shined her flashlight in his eyes. He cringed and held his arm up to block the light. "Because you're always trying to manipulate people into doing what's good for you, and not necessarily what's good for them. You never even once asked me if I wanted to stay at the station. You always just talked about how stupid I was for staying there, and how I could make so much more money if I did this stupid fucking paranormal site with you."

"And I was right," said Stephen, flabbergasted by his wife's anger.

"But I don't want this. I don't want any of this. I was happy with my job. And, like an idiot, I let you convince me to quit."

Stephen nodded as he calmly said, "I get it. I get what's up. You're just tired and freaked out about everything. That's understandable. But you've got to see that we made the right choice. This story is going to change our lives."

"Did you make the right choice for Aubrey?" asked Rachel.

"It's a shame what happened to that girl, but that's not my fault."

"It's not?" asked Rachel with a snort and a laugh. "You're the one that convinced her to come, and now she's dead. She's fucking dead, Stephen. How can you be so glib about all of this when a girl died because of us?"

"She chose to come along," said Stephen. "No one forced her."

"No, you never have to force anyone," said Rachel. "That's just it. You manipulate everyone into getting what you want out of them. And while we're on the subject, you and Aubrey might've fooled Alma, and you damn near fooled me too, but after I realized that you paid Aubrey to have sex with Jacker, everything clicked into place for me."

"What are you talking about?" asked Stephen with a high pitched whine.

"You just happened to run into a hooker that looks like all of your old girlfriends, and she just happens to know all about Widowsfield. How fucking lucky. Right? What're the chances?"

"Rachel, come on," said Stephen as he started to walk down the stairs again. "Do you hear yourself? You sound crazy now. The girl lived around here all her life. It's no mystery that she knew about Widowsfield. You're just trying to convince yourself that something's going on when it's not. You've always been like that; always looking for the secrets other people are hiding. That's what makes you such a good reporter."

Stephen tried to put his arm around his wife, but she moved away from him. She glared up at him and asked, "Why don't you just tell me the truth. No more lies."

"I am telling the truth," said Stephen.

"Bullshit."

"Rachel, listen to me," said Stephen in a last ditch effort to calm her. "I knew Aubrey was an escort, it was pretty damn obvious, but Jacker didn't figure it out. The dude's not the sharpest crayon in the box. You know? But the poor guy's been dealing with his breakup, and he was feeling pretty down on himself, so I struck up a conversation with Aubrey to try and get her to give Jacker some attention. You know, to boost up the guy's self-confidence a little. I never intended for it to go as far as it did, but while Jacker was talking to her he mentioned Widowsfield and she told us how she used to come here. That's when I offered to pay her for a few days of her time. That's the whole story, I swear."

"And she just happened to look like all your ex-girlfriends?"

"That's all in the past. I had a lot of girlfriends before you," he said with a snide grin. He could see that she was beginning to trust him again.

"And they were all blonde, petite, and with tattoos."

"And then I met you, and I realized that you were the girl I was looking for my whole life. That's why I gave you that ring."

Rachel raised her naked ring finger, the indent still visible, and said, "I don't have it anymore. Rosemary's got it."

"Oh right," said Stephen as he looked at his own ring-less wedding finger. "I forgot about that. But you get the point. I love you, babe. And the only reason I convinced you to leave your job is because I know you're better than that. You deserve to be a star."

"I don't want to be a star," said Rachel. "I just want to go home."

"We'll make it there," said Stephen. "I promise. Let's just get this guy that Rosemary wants, and we can start figuring out how to get home. But first, are you and I okay?" asked Stephen as he again tried to put his arm around his wife's shoulders. This time she didn't move away. "Do you trust me?"

"No, but I guess I still love you."

"I'll take it," said Stephen with a wide grin.

"But you'd better not be lying to me."

"Never, babe."

They kissed, and then continued down the stairs.

In Cada E.I.B.'s parking lot
March 13th, 2012
6:00 AM

Jacker heard Ben Harper cackling inside the van. The twisting shadows on the wall of the facility transfixed Jacker, but he managed to reach for the van's sliding side door and open it to find out what the frail man inside was laughing about. "What's going on?" he asked without turning to look at the two men in the back of the van. He just continued to watch as the shadows formed tentacles that snaked across the wall.

"He's coming," said Ben, his voice was no longer maligned by his weakness like it had been before. He wasn't coughing and sputtering as he spoke.

"Who's coming?" asked Jacker.

"The one that knows us. The one they call The Watcher in the Walls."

Jacker finally looked away from the twisting shadows and into the van. "What do you mean by that? How is he coming here? I thought we were in the real world now."

"They've turned the machine back on," said Ben. "I can feel it. The Watcher's coming."

Jacker felt himself beginning to panic. The shifting shadows on the wall terrified him, and he wanted nothing more than to get in the van and drive as far away as the gas tank would take him, but that would require abandoning the only people in his life he could honestly call friends, and he wasn't willing to do that.

"I've got to save them," said Jacker.

"You can't," said Ben. "You'll die in there. He'll tear you to pieces. And if he doesn't, then the witch will see you dead before this is over."

"Go to hell, you twisted little fuck," said Jacker as he slid the door shut again. He decided that his friends' safety was more important than watching over Michael and Ben. He held the salt-pellet shotgun tight as he approached the door. It was dark out, but he could still see even darker shapes slithering on the wall, but they retreated as he approached, as if frightened of him.

"This is crazy, man," said Jacker to himself as he prepared to open the door. "Paul, you'd better fucking appreciate this, bro." He gripped the handle and pulled the door open. It was pitch black in the hall beyond, but he stepped in anyhow. He placed his foot against the door to keep it open so that the sparse moonlight could shine in. The door was on the side of the hallway, and he knew that Paul and the others had gone to the right. They'd been headed downstairs, but he hoped that he could scream loud enough for them to hear. He called out Paul's name, and then Alma's, but got no answer.

The hall was pitch black, and he couldn't see the end of it, but the darkness was shifting. He squinted to try and see, and he thought he discerned movement coming his way. His eyes adjusted, and he finally caught a glimpse of what was coming his way. Hundreds of thin, black wires were sliding across the floor, headed towards him like a nest of snakes fleeing a flood.

Jacker leapt out of the door and back towards the van as he cursed. The door was closing slowly, but then the black wires reached out and wrapped around the door's bar handle. They pulled and the door shut with a thunderous bang. Jacker continued to back away until he collided with the van, cursing in fright the entire time. His hands were shaking, and his heart was beating so hard that he could feel its fast rhythm in eardrums.

"Paul," said Jacker as he gripped the shotgun close against his belly. "I'm not going to give up on you, brother."

Despite what he said, Jacker ran to the driver's side of the van while fishing the keys out of his pocket. When he opened the door, Ben was quick to say, "Good, Hank. Get us away from here. Don't let The Watcher find us."

"You can go ahead and shut the fuck up, weirdo," said Jacker as he turned the van on. "I'm not running this time." He put the van in reverse and sped backward into a quick, jarring two-point turn. Then he drove out of the parking lot on the side of the building.

"Get us out of Widowsfield," said Ben. "You have to get us away from The Watcher."

"I thought I told you to shut the fuck up."

Jacker drove along the front of the Cada E.I.B. building and then slowed down. The front of the facility had a small courtyard area that preceded the flat, glass entrance. It was a fairly standard looking edifice, and didn't even have the company's name on the front of it. To anyone passing by it would look like a generic office building, and certainly didn't hint at its expansive size.

Jacker drove up over the curb so that the van was facing the glass entryway.

"What are you doing?" asked Ben.

"You've gotta figure a place like this has got some sort of an alarm system on a back-up generator. Right?" He looked in the rear-view and winked at Ben. "We're about to find out."

Jacker moved his seat's base back as far as it would go, and then pulled the lever that would let him recline. He leaned back until his seat was pressing into Ben, who squawked a protest.

"Get ready," said Jacker, "cause this might hurt."

He stepped on the gas with the van pointed directly at the entrance to the Cada E.I.B. building.

CHAPTER 23 – Wherever That Takes Us

Widowsfield
February 23rd, 2007

Rosemary was standing on the cliff overlooking the Jackson Reservoir with her friend, Terra, who'd come with her to assist in rebuilding the town. When they'd first left Chicago to come to this town in the Ozarks, neither of them had expected to be gone for more than a couple days. Rosemary had always known that she possessed a unique gift, but she'd always wondered if it was more of a curse. Now she was sure of it.

"What are we doing here?" asked Terra. She was still upset with Rosemary about a trick that her friend had pulled by infusing false memories into a ring and then giving it to her.

Rosemary was knelt near the edge, beside a guard rail that had been broken and was bent outward. The rail was rusted from where the accident had peeled away its protective coating, and Rosemary set her finger on the jagged, rough metal. She was trying to concentrate as Terra stood behind her, complaining about the chilly air that swept up over the cliff.

"Can we go?" asked Terra. "I just want to go home."

"I don't think we should go home," said Rosemary.

"What? Why the hell not?"

"Because they're going to be looking for us."

"I thought you said you took care of all that," said Terra.

"I did my best, but I'm not sure how long it'll work. I'm new at this stuff."

"Then where the hell are we supposed to go?"

"We can cash our checks and just go…" Rosemary paused and shook her head. "I don't know. We can go to Vegas for a few weeks or something. I don't care where. Give me a minute here, I need to concentrate."

"On what?" asked Terra. "What in the hell are you doing?"

Rosemary pressed her hand against the railing and closed her eyes again. "I'm trying to protect Alma Harper."

"Who?" asked Terra.

"The girl that this town wants back. The whole time we've been here, I could tell that that creature, The Skeleton Man, has been trying to find her. He lost her, and he wants her back. So I'm going to try and make him think she's dead. If he thinks she went over this cliff and died with her mother, then maybe he'll stop looking for her. Then, after I'm done with this, we're going to cut ourselves and spread our blood all over the place."

"What the fuck?" asked Terra with comical shock. "I'm not cutting myself up. What the hell's wrong with you?"

"We have to make it look like two people got shot in the head here, Terra. Come on, work with me. I'm trying to save our lives."

"All you've been trying to do is ruin mine. You can cut the shit out of yourself. I'm through letting you fuck with me." Terra walked away, and headed back to the car they'd stolen from the Cada E.I.B. parking lot.

Rosemary knew her friendship with Terra had been frayed, and would likely never recover. She wasn't that upset about it, and would be content parting ways once this was over. Rosemary's abilities had become so strong over the past month that she wondered if she would ever be able to have friendships again. Now that memories constantly flowed into her head, it would be difficult to ever trust anyone. Rosemary hoped that when they left Widowsfield, her ability would fade. She hoped that the reason she'd become so powerful was because the town itself was trying to speak to her. If that wasn't the case, then she would be tortured by these memories until they finally drove her insane.

She was terrified of what might happen if her powers didn't fade and she was forced to suffer with this curse forever.

Inside Cada E.I.B.'s facility

March 13th, 2012
Shortly before 6:00 AM

"It hurts," said Rosemary, but her voice was barely a whisper as she lay on the gurney. She was holding Alma's hand, but her grip was growing weaker as her hand turned cold.

"It's okay," said Helen as she continued to dress the woman's wound. She'd pulled the knife out, and they'd done their best to clean Rosemary off after Helen stitched her up, but the old nurse insisted it was best not to move her too much. "You're going to be all right."

"Is she really?" Paul's tone revealed that he wasn't sure Helen was right.

"Let's hope. She's lost a lot of blood," said Helen.

"Maybe we should call an ambulance," said Alma.

"No ambulance," said Rosemary. "Don't bring anyone else into this. When Oliver gets here, we can leave. Is he here?" She was dazed as she looked around the room.

"Stephen and Rachel went to find him," said Alma. "They'll be back soon."

"Why is she so insistent on not going to a hospital?" asked Paul.

"Don't bring anyone else into this," said Rosemary as her eyes fluttered. "No one can know what happened here. We have to stop it from happening again. Alma, listen to me." She gripped Alma's hand tight. "Take Ben back to Terry's house, and at 3:14 you have to perform the same ritual on him that your mother did on you. In my bag you'll find the same type of candles that she used. You don't have to wait until tomorrow afternoon. Just go ahead and do it at 3:14 in the morning. That should still work."

"Wait," said Alma. "You don't expect me to..."

Rosemary squeezed Alma's hand as she tried to sit up. Helen was quick to settle the wounded woman back down again, but Rosemary's insistence was evident as she spoke, "You're the only one that can end this, Alma. You have to send The Skeleton Man back to where he came from, and then we can finally end this whole nightmare."

"How will forcing him to look at that stupid number do that?" asked Paul.

"I don't know why it works, but it does," said Rosemary. "You tapped into something powerful the last time you did it. The ritual that your mother performed brought The Watcher out again. He thinks that date and time are important, but I'm not sure why. If you take Ben there, and do the ritual again, then I think The Watcher will take him back."

"And what about us?" asked Paul. "The last time Alma stared at that damn number, we ended up in a nightmare."

"And I'm the one that got you out," said Rosemary, her anger obvious. "Alma followed my lead and got everyone out of The Watcher's prison. I'm not going to let you get trapped there. That's part of the reason I took your things from you. The things you gave me are in my bag along with the candles. Right before you perform the ritual, take those things back, but not before. It's important that you don't have them until right before you start the ritual. Those things will protect you, just like the bear when you were stuck in The Watcher's web, Alma. It'll work the same way. Just keep those things close, and his lies won't affect you."

"Just keep calm," said Alma. "You're going to be all right."

Rosemary shook her head and tried to smile, but the agony of her wound was too intense and she grimaced before taking several sharp breaths. "It's okay if I don't make it out of here. I never planned to."

"Don't talk like that," said Alma.

"Go," said Rosemary as she closed her eyes. "Hide at the cabin until tomorrow. Helen can take care of me."

"We have to get Stephen and Rachel," said Alma. "We can't leave without them."

"They'll be fine," said Rosemary. "When they get back, I'll send them to the cabin to meet up with you."

"No," said Alma. "I'm not going to just leave them here."

"You have to trust me," said Rosemary. "I've spent the last five years of my life trying to protect you, and trying to put a stop to whatever Oliver and his company were up to in this town. Do you trust me, Alma?"

Alma was quiet for a moment, but then relented and said, "Yes, I trust you."

"Good," said Rosemary. "Then do as I ask. Take Ben back to the cabin, and wait there until tomorrow. Stay away from Ben if you can, and don't all go to sleep at once. I don't know what he's capable of, but I don't think he can control all of you. At least not yet."

"Not yet?" asked Paul.

"He doesn't know what he's capable of yet, and you can't let him find out. You have to trap him again."

"He's my brother," said Alma.

"No he's not," said Rosemary. "He's a weapon."

Both Alma and Paul looked at one another in shared confusion, and then Alma asked, "What do you mean?"

"That's what this has been about since it started," said Rosemary. "It's a weapon experiment that went wrong. But if they know The Skeleton Man got out, then they're going to try and figure out a way to use him. You can't let that happen. Ever since I left this place, I've come back here every March to try and make sure Oliver doesn't figure out how to get The Watcher or The Skeleton Man out of their prison. You're the only one that can put an end to it, Alma. You have to finish this. You have to trust me."

Alma looked up at Paul for answers, but he just stared plaintively at her. He raised his brow and took a heavy breath before saying, "Your call, babe. I'm in it till the end with you, wherever that takes us."

Alma nodded and said, "Okay, let's go."

"Thank you," said Rosemary. "You're making the right decision."

The injured woman laid her head down on the gurney with a content smile as she closed her eyes, appearing finally at peace. Alma looked at Helen as the nurse began to check Rosemary's pulse.

"She's alive," said Helen. "But she's fading fast. I'm not sure she's going to make it."

"I'm not sure she wants to," said Paul.

On the bottom floor of Cada E.I.B.'s building
March 13th, 2012
Shortly before 6:00 AM

Stephen and Rachel had followed the trail of blood to the bottom of the stairs, and they carefully opened the door and peered into the hall beyond. The trail continued on, and they silently followed, too scared to speak as they delved deeper into the building.

Stephen was using the viewfinder on the camera to see, and Rachel was watching behind them with her flashlight. When she shined her light forward, the night vision on Stephen's camera was useless, so she kept the flashlight pointed behind them and let him lead.

"Oh shit," said Stephen in a loud whisper.

"What?" asked Rachel as she tried to look into his viewfinder to see what had frightened him.

"Shine your light out that way," said Stephen as he pointed forward, down the hall ahead.

Rachel did as he asked and saw what looked like a fire extinguisher lying in a pool of liquid.

"Is that blood?" asked Stephen.

"I think so," said Rachel. "Oh fuck me. We need to get out of here."

Stephen shushed her, and started walking forward again.

"What are you doing?" asked Rachel. "Are you out of your mind?"

"We have to find him," said Stephen with odd determination.

"No we don't." Rachel grabbed his arm and pulled him back. "We don't have to do anything but get the hell out of here. I'm through with this place."

"We have to stop him," said Stephen. "We're the only ones who can. If he attacked that other nurse, then we've got to help her."

"I'm scared," said Rachel.

"It's okay," said Stephen as he took out the pistol that he'd taken from Rosemary's bag. "If that fucker's whacking people with fire extinguishers in the dark, he's going to have trouble taking me out. I've got a gun and a night-vision camera."

"When have you ever fired a gun in your life?" asked Rachel.

"I play Call of Duty," said Stephen, but his joke went unappreciated.

"I swear to God, Stephen, if you get me killed I am going to haunt the fuck out of you."

"Cool," said Stephen as he started to follow the trail of blood again. Rachel smacked him, but followed along.

A massive trail of blood tracked back from where the fire extinguisher was laying and then around a corner and down another long hall. Rachel and Stephen agreed that the marks were left by a dragged body, but they stayed silent after that. As they got deeper into the facility, they could hear what sounded like whips snapping in the distance.

"What is that?" asked Rachel in a whisper.

"I don't know."

"It's making the hair on my neck stand up," said Rachel.

"Look at my arm," said Stephen and Rachel shined the flashlight on his arm to reveal that his hair was standing straight up.

"What the fuck?" asked Rachel.

"We must be getting close," said Stephen as he continued on.

Rachel followed, although Stephen knew she didn't want to. He understood her fear, but at the same time he was angered by it. They were so close to having the answer they'd been seeking ever since first considering coming to Widowsfield. Nothing could sway him from soldiering on. This would be the story that would define his career.

"The trail leads to there," said Stephen as he stared ahead at a closed door at the end of the hall.

"Is there any way in hell I can convince you not to go in there?" asked Rachel.

Stephen shook his head and said, "Nope. Come on, babe. Don't chicken out now." He moved to the door at the end of the hall and the sound of electricity got louder each step he took. He could feel the energy, and it was exhilarating.

"Stephen, don't," said Rachel as he reached out for the handle. Her plea for him to stop was practically unheard. There was nothing she could do to stop him now.

The door should've been locked, but in Oliver's haste he hadn't secured it. As Stephen opened the door, the sound of electricity intensified. His night-vision camera caught the burst of orbs that spewed forth from the opened door and quickly lit up the viewfinder with green light. He lowered the camera, and opened the door further.

"Oh my God," said Rachel.

They saw the machine that had been the origin for Widowsfield's nightmares. The pillars on either side of the metal box were crackling with blue electricity as rings spun around them. The arcs of lightning reached high into the air, zapping the beams above and causing them to release white puffs of smoke. The motion of the machine's rings was causing the ground to shudder, and Stephen could feel the vibration hitting him.

The man they'd come to find was straddling the nurse that Helen had sent down first. He had a knife gripped with both hands, and he was stabbing down into the woman's belly. Her body was a mess of blood, and she was clearly already dead, but his maniacal slaughtered continued unabated.

"Oliver," said Stephen, halting the man before he stabbed down again. Stephen clicked off the night-vision on his camera to allow it to record what was happening in the room. "Get off of her."

Oliver looked up, his face splattered with the girl's blood, and raised his hands slowly. He said something, but the zapping electricity muted him.

"Put down the knife," said Stephen.

Oliver stepped towards them.

"Put down the knife!"

Oliver continued walking forward.

"Shoot him," said Rachel from behind Stephen.

Stephen pulled the trigger, but was holding the gun in one hand and wasn't prepared for how strong it kicked. The gun nearly sailed out of his hand as it jerked back.

Stephen's aim had been off, and the bullet sailed past Oliver. It struck the machine behind him, causing the bullet to ricochet off somewhere else in the room. The gunshot prompted Oliver to stop and glance back at what Stephen had hit. He glared at Stephen and Rachel and said, "You're going to ruin everything. Get out. You can't be here."

"Put the knife down," said Stephen again.

"You have to get out," said Oliver as he used the blade to point at them. He continued to move forward.

Stephen dropped his camera and held the pistol with both hands. He pleaded, "Stop," but Oliver continued to come at them. Stephen pulled the trigger, and this time he didn't miss.

CHAPTER 24 – Are They All Dead?

Widowsfield
March 14th, 2011
One year before Alma's return

Rosemary was in her usual spot, on the cliff overlooking the Jackson Reservoir, and was continuing to spread her lies about Alma Harper by infecting the area with a false memory about the girl's death. Despite her effort, she still got the sense that the town was longing for Alma's return, and Rosemary often debated if she should try to seek out Alma first. She decided against it, and hoped that the young woman would never return, and would leave the town always longing for the final piece of the puzzle that it was searching for.

The most important thing, and the reason for these annual trips, was that Rosemary wanted to make sure Oliver never succeeded in his attempt to contact the creature that was hiding in the walls of Widowsfield. Furthermore, she knew that Oliver hadn't worked alone. If she could track down Oliver's boss, then she might have a chance at putting an end to the Widowsfield experiments once and for all.

She was considering this possibility when she heard a loud pop. The sound passed easily across the still water of the reservoir, making it sound as if it had occurred closer to Rosemary than it actually had. She moved to the edge of the cliff and scanned the area below, searching for the source of the noise.

Far below, across the reservoir, she saw a car stopped on the side of the road. A woman was getting out of the car and Rosemary reached into her satchel to retrieve a pair of binoculars to get a better look. She watched as a familiar looking woman inspected her blown-out tire.

"Who are you?" asked Rosemary to herself as she watched the frustrated woman open her trunk to get her spare.

Rosemary watched for several minutes before she remembered who it was that she was spying on. "Helen," she said as she watched. It was one of the nurses that worked for Cada E.I.B. while Rosemary and Terra had been there. She remembered Helen coming in for the evening shift, and a thought occurred to Rosemary about how she might be able to finally end the Widowsfield experiments. It would require manipulating this woman's memories, but it could lead to finally figuring out who was funding Oliver's project.

Inside Cada E.I.B.'s facility
March 13th, 2012

Paul held Alma's hand tightly as they made their way through the dark recesses of the Cada E.I.B. facility. He felt guilty for leaving without Stephen and Rachel, but Rosemary had been insistent that they get out as soon as possible. Rosemary was a persuasive personality, and Paul wondered if his reluctance to disobey her had something to do with her psychometric ability.

"Alma, wait," said Paul as they got to the stairs that they were going to take up to the ground level. He shined his light down at the tracks of blood and mud that led through the door. "Are you sure we should leave Rachel and Stephen?"

"We have to," said Alma, and she sounded sure of herself. Then her expression changed and she asked, "Don't we?"

"Why?" asked Paul. "Just because that chick says so?"

Alma was holding Rosemary's satchel and she adjusted its strap on her shoulder as she thought about it. "She's been right about everything else."

"Yeah, but are we the type of people that leave friends behind? I mean, I know we don't know Rachel and Stephen all that well, but I'm not sure I'm okay with just leaving them here."

"You're right," said Alma before she moved closer to give him a kiss. "That's why I love you, babe."

"I love you too," said Paul as he opened the door to the staircase. "And about that Lacey stuff; I hope you know I'm going to break things off with..."

Alma hushed him with another kiss. Then she smiled up at him and said, "Don't worry, I know. I almost let myself get upset about that, but I came to a realization about it that calmed me down."

"Oh yeah, what's that?" asked Paul.

"I love you enough that I want you to be happy. Hopefully that means you and I get to be happy together, but if not, then I just want to know you're happy, wherever you are and whoever you're with."

"I'm your guy for as long as you'll have me, babe," said Paul.

"Damn straight you are," said Alma, making Paul laugh as they headed down the stairs together.

They'd both heard Rosemary give Stephen the directions to Oliver's lab, but it wasn't hard to find. The blood trail led them along, and as they got closer they could hear the crackle of electricity. Then the distinct sound of a gunshot echoed through the halls and they quickened their pace. They turned the corner and could see bright blue light emitting from a room at the end of the hall. The cacophonous noise of the electricity got louder as they approached, and they could feel the hair on their arms standing on end. Rachel and Stephen were ahead, but the electric zaps drowned out anything they were saying before another shot rang out.

Paul and Alma rushed to the room, but stopped in shock once they saw what had happened. Oliver was on his knees, a butcher knife clutched against his chest, the tip resting just under his chin. He was already splattered with the blood of the nurse that was lying on the ground behind him, but it was clear that he'd been the victim of the gunshot. The amount of blood that was pumping from his chest was startling.

Stephen stood in shock, his arms still held forward with the smoking gun gripped in his hands. His shadow danced behind him from the wavering light of the machine that dominated the space. Alma and Paul got to Rachel, and asked what happened, but the reporter just shook her head and explained, "He had to. He had to shoot."

"Help me figure out how to shut this thing off," said Paul as he pulled Alma along. He looked at Stephen, thinking he would ask for his help as well, but it was clear he was in shock. Stephen just stared at the ground where the nurse lay.

"Rachel's dead," said Stephen as he stared at the nurse. "Rachel's dead."

Rachel tried to console Stephen as Paul and Alma approached the machine that was producing the electricity that crackled above. Alma and Paul examined the various gauges and levers on the machine, and Paul picked the one that looked the most like it would power the thing. It was a wide-bar lever with orange and black stripes on the arms, and he pulled it down to see what would happen. It worked, and they heard the motors within the spires on the side begin to slow. The rings grinded to a stop and the blue electricity finally stopped arcing forth.

As the noise went away, they heard Oliver saying something. He was on the floor now, staring at the ceiling with the knife still clutched to his chest. Beneath his hands, the gunshot continued to produce a fountain of blood that was seeping out through his clothes.

"I won't make it…"

Paul assumed Oliver was talking about surviving the gunshot, but then he continued.

"…make it past." Oliver wasn't speaking for the benefit of anyone else in the room but himself. He was staring at the ceiling as he held the knife to his wound. "There's no light ahead. Only fog. There's only fog."

His hand lost its grip on the blade, and the weapon fell to the wet floor. Oliver died there, staring up with unblinking eyes, just like the myriad of sleepers he'd hidden for so many years.

"Stephen," said Rachel as she took the pistol away from her dazed husband. "Look at me."

Stephen looked at his wife with glassy eyes. "I'm a murderer."

"You had to, honey. He didn't give you any choice. You did what you had to."

"Are they all dead?" asked Stephen.

"Yeah, buddy," said Paul. "He's dead. Come on, let's get the hell out of here."

Inside Cada E.I.B.'s facility
March 13th, 2012

"Rosemary," said Helen after watching the others leave. She approached the psychometric cautiously, like a child sneaking into a sleeping parent's room. "Honey, are you okay?"

"No," said Rosemary with an attempt at humor. "I got stabbed."

"You really should get to a hospital," said Helen.

"You know I can't do that," said Rosemary. "You know what we have to do." She looked over at the portly nurse and grinned. "Did you send the message to Vess?"

Helen nodded. They could see each other by the glow of a single flashlight that was sitting on the counter. "I went to Oliver's office earlier and sent Vess an email."

"Good," said Rosemary. "Hopefully that'll draw the old snake out of his hole."

Helen's hands were trembling, and she gripped them together as she paced. "I'm scared. I don't know if I can do this."

"Yes you can, Helen," said Rosemary. She was having an easier time speaking now, and Helen realized that her previous weakness and agony had been largely an act. Rosemary had certainly been stabbed, and she was far from healthy, but her near-death pantomime had been for Alma and Paul's benefit. "We've been working on this for too long to let it fall apart now."

"But this isn't how it was supposed to happen," said Helen. "I didn't know so many innocent people would be involved."

"And if we don't do something about this now, then a lot more people are going to get hurt before this is over. Helen, listen to me, we're the only ones that can put a stop to what's going on here."

"I know, you're right."

"Do you have the shots ready?" asked Rosemary.

Helen nodded.

"You should get started on that as soon as possible," said Rosemary.

"But some of the sleepers woke up," said Helen. "They don't have to die, do they?"

Rosemary nodded and said, "All of them. They all have to die."

"But, why?" asked Helen, rattled by what she was being asked to do. "They can't tell anyone anything. They don't know what happened here."

"They met The Watcher," said Rosemary. "They're better off dead. We all are."

Helen turned away and closed her eyes.

"You know I'm right," said Rosemary.

"I know," said Helen, defeated. "I just wish it didn't have to be this way."

Helen reached into the cabinets below the counter and retrieved the box labeled, 'Muriate of Potash.' She set the small box on the counter and the glass vials inside clanked together. Next, she got a syringe from one of the drawers and pulled off the plastic wrapper.

Helen took the box with her as she left Rosemary and went into the sleepers' room. The women were still tied down to their beds, and were moaning in pain and fear. Their bodies were victimized by sixteen years spent lying in the same spot, only moving when the nurses turned them or changed the sheets. Now, for the first time since Helen started working for Cada E.I.B., the sleepers watched her.

The men were still catatonic, and staring up as their tongues licked at the inside of their jaws, but something had happened inside of The Watcher's world that allowed many of the women to wake up. Helen thought it would be best to inject the women with the Potassium Chloride first, but couldn't bring herself to do it. She decided to start on the ones that were still sleeping.

As she was preparing the needle, the lights in the facility came back on. The fluorescent lights above clicked on one by one, starting at the far end of the room. They clicked and buzzed, and then flickered before coming to life. One by one, the rows of lights came on, and the sound of nearby machines resetting caused the room to come alive with blips and beeps as Helen stood in the center of the sea of sleepers.

She cursed at the timing, upset that she would have to kill these people while seeing their faces. She knew this had to happen. She'd been trying to prepare herself for it ever since meeting Rosemary a year earlier. Helen looked at the bracelet that Rosemary had given her, and she felt a renewed sense of purpose that stilled her. This had to be done.

Helen injected the needle into the first sleeper and pushed on the plunger until the pinkish liquid within the canister flooded into his veins. When she first learned that she would have to murder the sleepers, she looked into what would be the most efficient way. She studied Dr. Kevorkian's suicide machines, and decided upon using the same Potassium Chloride solution that he employed. While this compound is found at most pharmacies, it was important to prevent anyone from getting concerned about such large quantities being purchased. Fortunately, Potassium Chloride can be made at home. Over the past year, she'd worked hard perfecting the process of dissolving ash and using hydrochloric acid to neutralize it. The box she was carrying was the result of her work, and she was confident that it would kill the sleepers.

Her first victim began convulsing within a minute of being injected. His eyes rolled back and his teeth clenched as he began to shake. His fingers clawed at the sheet beneath him and his legs did their best to kick. Soon, the convulsions subsided, and the first sleeper died.

She looked around at the room full of victims she had to make her way to. All of the women watched her, but they seemed calmer now, as if patiently waiting their turn.

In The Watcher's Widowsfield

Jeremy Tapper was at home, in his bed, as he called out for his father. There was no response. The only noise in the house was from the tree branches outside scratching at the roof.

He looked at the clock and saw that it was almost 3:14, and he felt a sense of dread as he looked out the window. A storm darkened the sky, and he could see the tree in their front yard being whipped around by the wind. The scant new buds of growth on the limbs were being torn away as the storm raged. There was no rain, but the dark clouds blotting out the sun promised a downpour at any moment.

Jeremy got out of bed and started to walk down the hall. He glanced into the bathroom and saw the straight razor resting on the edge of the sink. Then he looked at the tub and thought he saw movement behind the drawn, opaque shower curtain. He heard what sounded like a nail scratching against the inside of the plastic.

"Dad?"

No answer.

He crept in, and thought about grabbing the razor to protect himself, but he knew that his father would be mad if he caught Jeremy with the dangerous weapon. Jeremy moved to the curtain and kept telling himself that there would be nothing behind it. There was nothing to be scared of.

The wind outside shook the windows of the house, and the tree's limbs continued to scratch at the roof. It sounded like a creature was trying to burrow its way into the home.

Jeremy gripped the shower curtain and prepared to pull it aside. He took a breath, and finally worked up the courage. He yanked the curtain to the left and the metal rings above scratched along the rod as he did. Jeremy let go of the curtain and moved back at the same moment that he'd opened it, just in case he was wrong and something was in the tub, waiting to attack him.

Thankfully, the tub was empty. He stepped forward so that he could see in fully, but there was no sign of anything inside. He was about to leave the bathroom when he heard a hiss coming from the drain. He stared down, but didn't dare get any closer than he already was. The hiss grew louder, and was accompanied by a gurgle of liquid. Steam began to rise from the drain, and soon after water bubbled up. The water was murky, and it seemed to be boiling as it started to rise from the drain.

Jeremy cried out, "Dad!" He backed away from the tub, but didn't turn. He was too enthralled by the spectacle not to watch.

The boiling water spewed forth from the drain, creating a miniature geyser that sent some of the water splashing on the floor at Jeremy's feet. When the boiling water struck his toes, Jeremy finally retreated from the bathroom. The room was filling with steam, and he could see shapes within the geyser that looked like strands of long hair, or wire, rising up and clinging to the walls. He slammed the door shut and saw water leaking out from beneath it.

He continued to scream for his father as he ran down the stairs. He saw a phone lying on the kitchen floor, and could hear the dial tone as he approached. The storm outside had gotten worse. The wind was tearing the tree in their front lawn apart, and a felled branch struck the picture window in the living room, causing the glass to crack but not break.

Jeremy stared at the glass in shock, and saw that the cracks in the glass looked black, like someone had drawn them on. The wind gusted again, and the branch finally pushed its way through the glass, causing broken pieces to fall to the floor. The cracks that had been there before revealed themselves as black wires that shuddered in the wind that blew in through the gap. The wires pulled themselves back into the frame of the broken window, disappearing once again.

The noise from the wind blowing into the house was deafening as it whistled. Jeremy could feel the air rushing past him, but it wasn't pushing out from the broken windows. Instead, it felt like he was being pulled outside.

He heard banging coming from upstairs, as if someone was hitting a door. At the same time, Jeremy heard the screams of a child coming from outside. He didn't know what to do, but before he could consider an escape he heard a crack of what sounded like thunder coming from upstairs. Suddenly, boiling water began to flow down the stairs and into the living room, forcing Jeremy to flee to the kitchen. The water was steaming and bubbling, and it hissed as it collided with the couch.

"Over here," said a woman's voice that Jeremy didn't recognize. He looked through the kitchen, towards the back door, and saw a red-haired woman beckoning him. "Hurry."

"Where's the fog?" asked Jeremy. He wanted to disappear into the fog, but all he saw outside was the raging storm.

"You can't go to the fog," said the woman.

Jeremy had no choice but to go to her. The boiling water was filling the living room, and he had no other escape.

"Where can I go? Where is it safe?"

"Run past the storm," said the stranger. "Look for the sunrise. Okay? Just keep running until you see the sunrise, and then head towards it."

Jeremy went through the kitchen and reached the back door where the woman was waiting for him. He was leery of her, and thought she might try to grab him as he came closer.

She answered his unease as if conscious of his fear. "I'm not going to hurt you. I'm only trying to help."

Jeremy got to the door and looked back at the woman. "Are you coming?"

She shook her head. "No, not yet."

Jeremy was beginning to remember the truth about Widowsfield. He remembered how The Skeleton Man had been there before, and how he'd tried to protect the children from The Watcher. He knew that the fog was safe, and that The Skeleton Man only wanted to kill the daddies. But he also knew that The Skeleton Man, who'd been Jeremy's only friend in this nightmare, was frightened of the red-haired woman.

"He's scared of you," said Jeremy as he looked at the woman that he'd been running from for what felt like years.

"I know," she said as she nodded. "He doesn't have to be afraid anymore. Now go. Look for the sunrise. It's coming. It'll burn away the fog."

Jeremy left, and ran into the storm. He searched for any sign of sunlight, but there was none to be found. The black clouds above were swirling, as if he were staring down at the top of a tornado. The crack of tree limbs being pulled from their trunks could be heard everywhere, and the frequent flashes of lightning created a dance of shadows all around him.

He went around to the fence at the side of the yard and ran out to the street. There, far in the distance, he saw a beam of sunlight breaking through the clouds. He raced towards it, but felt the ground beneath him falling away, as if he were running through gravel instead of on pavement. He looked at his feet and saw the sidewalk was cracking beneath him. As the gaps grew wider he could see what looked like worms below, interlacing with one another and struggling to keep the concrete together. The cords were snapping, and the ground was falling apart, making it nearly impossible to traverse.

Jeremy knew he couldn't reach the light before the world fell apart beneath him, but ahead he saw that the sunrise was blooming faster, and the crepuscular rays were breaking through the black clouds above. Finally, just as the sidewalk was giving way beneath Jeremy and promising to swallow him into the grinding wires below, a ray of light caught him.

The second the warmth graced his skin, Jeremy knew his nightmare had ended. He watched as the world collapsed beneath him, but he no longer cared. The wires were driven back by the light, and he felt solace at last.

Sparks of light emerged from his skin, and he felt himself evaporating and being pulled upward. Ahead, merely a silhouette in the bloom of heaven, he saw his father waiting for him.

CHAPTER 25 – At the End

Inside Cada E.I.B.'s facility
March 13th, 2012

Alma and Paul led the way as Stephen and Rachel followed. They were eager to get out of the building, but they all knew their time in Widowsfield wasn't over yet. Alma explained to Rachel and Stephen why they had to go to the cabin and wait until the following day. Rachel was hesitant, but agreed that now wasn't the best time to argue about it. They could discuss their plans at the cabin, but they had to get out of the Cada E.I.B. facility first.

Stephen was shook up about what he'd been forced to do, and was quieter than usual. Rachel was similarly stunned, and she asked Paul to take the gun from Stephen. He did, and Stephen didn't offer any resistance. He was happy to be rid of the weapon for the time being. Paul put the gun back in Rosemary's satchel where it clinked against the glass candles within.

Power had returned to the facility after they turned off Oliver's machine, and as they climbed the stairs to the main level they could hear an alarm ringing. They opened the door to the first floor and the shrill alarm struck them as they exited the stairwell.

"What the hell is that?" asked Paul.

No one had a chance to respond before they heard a familiar voice screaming their names. Alma looked at Paul and said, "It's Jacker."

They followed the sound of their friend's voice and found him near the front of the building. His head was bleeding from a gash above his left eye, and he'd taken his glasses off. He squinted as they approached from down the hall, and then waved to them, "Guys, come on!"

"What the hell happened?" asked Paul as they rejoined Jacker.

"I'm here to rescue you."

"From what?" asked Paul.

Jacker was flustered and looked at each of them before saying, "I don't know, from the fucking devil-thing in the walls. I could see it."

"You saw it?" asked Rachel.

Jacker nodded. "Yeah, I was in the parking lot and the walls started shifting and shit. Ben told me The Watcher was coming, and that we should try and get the fuck out of town, but I told him to shut up because I wasn't leaving my friends behind."

"Thanks," said Paul, "but why the hell are you bleeding?"

"I drove the van through the entrance of the building."

"You what?" asked Alma in astonishment.

"I figured it would trip an alarm, and it did, and now I found you guys, so it worked. Sort of."

"Is the van still drivable?" asked Rachel.

"I don't know," said Jacker with a shrug.

"Are my dad and Ben still in the van?"

Jacker nodded and pointed back the way he'd come. "They're in there. Let's stop talking and get the fuck out of here."

"Amen to that," said Stephen. It was the first thing he'd said since leaving Oliver's lab.

The group agreed and followed Jacker to the entrance where he'd plowed the van through the glass doorway. The van had broken all of the glass, and bent the frame of the entrance inward so that it contoured to the shape of the van's hood. The radiator was cracked, and fluid was dripping out onto the floor. One of the headlights was shattered, and the driver's side door was open. Ben and Michael were still in the van, and Jacker told the others to wait as he tried to back the van out.

They watched as he got in, adjusted his seat, and then managed to back the van out of the hole he'd made in the entrance. Chunks of glass and metal fell away from the frame as he moved. The security van's front tires ground the glass beneath them as he went, and it was clear that one of the tires was quickly losing air. None-the-less, Jacker managed to get the van out, and he leaned out the window as he waved them in. "Come on, let's go."

"This thing's going to overheat," said Paul as he looked at the steaming radiator.

"It doesn't have to get us far," said Alma.

"We should dump it somewhere away from the cabin," said Rachel. "There's a good chance they're going to send someone out looking for us."

"Good point," said Alma. The group lingered near the shattered entrance to Cada E.I.B. for a moment before Alma said, "Are we ready?"

"Ready as we'll ever be," said Paul. "Let's finish this."

In The Watcher's Widowsfield

Widowsfield was falling apart. Desmond had watched buildings coming apart to reveal the wires behind the walls. He saw how the raging storm tore the world asunder, cracking edifices and uprooting trees. He witnessed the way the blooming glow of heaven began to wash away the lies that had been erected here. The storm was receding. He ran as the clouds shrank, and he followed their shade, always staying out of the rays of the sun.

Every time he tried to traverse the town, he eventually fell back into the maelstrom of wires churning below, and they devoured him. The grinding cords tore him apart, but he had to suffer the torture to remain in The Watcher's web. He couldn't allow himself the safety of heaven. Not until he found his son.

At first, Desmond continued to wake up inside of the Salt and Pepper Diner, and from there he would make his journey out to the street and north from there, towards where the storm seemed to be centered. However, each time he reappeared, the diner seemed a bit more disheveled. At first, it seemed that the food was rotting, and he recalled seeing a dilapidated cake on the counter. But each time he awoke again, he noticed other parts of the building had fallen away as well. The bathroom had been boarded up, and one of the tables was missing. Next, a crack in the wall was present that had never been there before. Eventually, the building was a shell of what it had been. The recreation of the scene was flawed, and each time it became worse. The Watcher was losing track of his lies, and his world was falling to pieces.

The pavement was cracking as Desmond ran. He screamed out Raymond's name over and over, desperately searching for the boy he knew was still trapped here.

He avoided the light, and stuck to the cold shadows as he made his way to a familiar street. It became clear that the storm was centered around a house on Sycamore, and he knew which one. The house he'd bought for his daughter was ahead, and he understood that this hellish world revolved around whatever was hidden within those walls.

Terry's cabin was the only building in Widowsfield that wasn't falling apart. He approached the house, and the door opened as if someone inside was expecting him. He heard a familiar voice say, "Hi, Dad."

"Terry?"

He recognized his daughter's voice, but didn't see her. Within the cabin he heard the distinct bark of Terry's dog, Killer. The barks echoed, as if they were coming from far away.

"Why are you here?" asked Terry from somewhere inside.

Desmond walked in and saw the house as it had been when he first purchased it for his daughter. There was no furniture, and the home looked like it had been well cared for by its former owner. He remembered helping his daughter move in, and thinking that she might be able to have a good life here. Above all else, he'd wanted her to be happy, but simply buying her a house hadn't been enough to change her life. In fact, it only seemed to make things worse. Without the incentive to pay rent or a mortgage, Terry had fallen deeper into the drug world that she'd dabbled in before. Over the years, he'd watched as this once nice house had fallen into disrepair.

"Terry, where are you?"

"I'm here," said his daughter as she revealed herself by coming down the stairs. He saw her bare feet as they padded gently down the wooden staircase that was partially hidden behind the kitchen. She was wearing a white dress that he recognized as having once belonged to her mother. Her skin was pale, but had a healthy glow to it, like it had before she'd started using meth.

"Terry," said Desmond as his heart swelled with emotion. "You look so pretty."

She stood on the bottom step and gave him a pained grin. "I'm sorry I made you hate me."

"Oh, honey," said Desmond as he took a step closer to her. She backed away, taking a step up the stairs again as he approached. "Terry, I never hated you. Never."

"Then why aren't you here looking for me? Why are you here looking for Raymond?"

"Because he's my son," said Desmond, his voice heavy with guilt. "I love you both."

"Don't worry, I don't blame you."

"Terry, I don't hate you. I love you." Emotion caused his voice to quake as he took a step closer to his daughter. "I've always loved you."

"Don't come up here, Dad," said Terry as she took another step up the stairs. "You should just leave."

"Terry, help me find your brother. Let's all leave together. Okay? I want you to come with me."

"I can't," said Terry. "And neither can Ray. He's with The Watcher now, and we all have to play our roles." She reached the top of the stairs as Desmond followed her up. Terry was walking backwards, towards the bedroom at the end of the hall. As Desmond followed, he saw the home changing back into the way it had looked after Terry owned it. The walls became darker, and cobwebs grew in the corners. The stench of drugs became prevalent as he watched his daughter back her way into the bedroom.

Terry's glowing skin turned paler and the dark circles under her eyes returned. She no longer looked like the cherub-faced girl he once knew, but now resembled the addict she'd become near the end of her life. Her teeth began to fall out, and they tapped on the wood floor.

Desmond saw that there were scratches on the floor of her bedroom, and blood began to seep from them to form a pool. Terry walked into the growing blood and began to lie down on it. The center of her dress, over her stomach, bloomed red with blood as if she'd been wounded, and then the cloth began to melt away until she was left nude. Her gut was open, and Desmond could see her intestines within as she lay back. The skin on her face began to turn bright red and blister, and white foam began to coat her lips as she looked up at him and said, "Don't look at me. I don't want you to see…"

She choked and a gush of the white foam and blood surged over her lips.

"Terry!" Desmond screamed his daughter's name over and over as he tried to reach out to her. As he grasped, she faded away. All that was left was the blood where she'd died. He knelt over where his daughter had been murdered and wailed in agony.

"I'm so sorry, baby. I love you. I love you so much. Don't go away again."

Her blood began to seep back into the stab wounds on the floor. Terry was lost again, and the cabin began to crumble, just like the rest of the world. The Watcher was starting over, and Desmond was caught in the walls as the cords swallowed him once again.

"Daddy," said Terry. "Go home. Raymond's hiding there."

CHAPTER 26 – Hidden Truth

Widowsfield
March 13th, 2012

"Are you telling me we have to wait in this fucking haunted ass house for a day?" asked Jacker as they walked back into the house that none of them ever wanted to be inside of again.

"Not a full day. Just until 3:14 in the morning," said Alma as she looked at the tile in the kitchen where she'd scrawled '314' with her own blood. There was no number on the floor there anymore. She looked at her palm and realized that she'd never actually been cut. The realization made her question which parts of her memory were true, and which were fabrications. She glanced over at the window and saw that a pane was still broken out of it from where her mother had forced her to crawl through so many years earlier.

Paul was carrying Ben in his arms. "Where do we want him?"

"Upstairs," said Alma. "Put him on the bed."

Ben did his best to speak, but he was still only able to croak out a few words at a time. "Alma, please… Kill…"

"He was talking earlier," said Jacker. "Back in the van he was talking just fine."

"Maybe he was fucking with your head," said Rachel. "You said he was trying to get you to drive away, right? Maybe he was the one creating the visions you were seeing."

"He can do that?" asked Jacker.

"Rosemary said she didn't know what he was capable of," said Alma.

"And we're going to have to stay in the same house with him?" asked Stephen.

"Not just any house, either," said Rachel as she pointed at the floor. "This damn house."

"Guys, if you don't want to stay I'd understand," said Alma.

"Didn't we just have this exact same conversation a day ago?" asked Jacker with a weak grin.

"Yep," said Rachel. "And I wanted to take off back then too. But, I'm not going to abandon you guys. You didn't have to come looking for Stephen and me in the basement of that place, so I'm not going to leave you guys either. As much of an idiot as that makes me." She shook her head and looked out the window.

"Well, thanks," said Alma. "Although, I don't know what to expect tomorrow."

"No one knows," said Jacker. "But I sure the hell know a couple things for certain: I'm starving and exhausted."

"Same here," said Stephen.

"I can drive the security van out by where we first arrived and see if my van's still there," said Jacker. "If it is, then I can take it and swing out to a fast food joint around here and get some food for our slumber party in Creepsville."

"Stephen," said Rachel, "go with him."

Alma sensed that Rachel wanted Stephen to go along not only to help, but to make sure Jacker didn't take off. Rachel still didn't trust Jacker after she discovered that he was wanted by the police back in Chicago.

Stephen agreed, and soon he was headed out with Jacker. Paul took Ben upstairs, and they put Michael on the couch. Alma's father had become lethargic after leaving Cada E.I.B., and Alma suspected that whatever drugs he'd been taking that gave him so much energy had finally begun to wear off.

"I'm so tired it feels like the floor's moving," said Rachel after Jacker and Stephen had left.

"We should try and get some sleep," said Alma. "We can do it in shifts, that way someone can watch Ben and my dad."

They were standing in the kitchen, near where Alma had scrawled the number '314' in her own blood on the floor. It was the same spot where Alma's mother had performed the ritual that had re-ignited Alma's memory of Ben.

"I'm so sorry we convinced you to come back here, Alma," said Rachel.

"It's not your fault," said Alma as she looked around the room. Oliver and Rosemary had done a good job recreating the cabin to look like it had sixteen years ago. "I think I needed to come back. There're so many things about my past that got wiped out of my memory. When we were getting my dad from Branson, Rosemary told me that my mother tried to kill me."

"Are you serious?" asked Rachel.

Alma nodded and explained, "She drove me off the cliff. The same one I drove you guys off of in our dream, or whatever the hell that was. She tried to kill me, but I don't have any memory of it at all. It's just like how I couldn't remember Ben. There're just whole parts of my life that were stolen from me."

"Maybe that's for the best," said Rachel. "Remembering how your mother tried to kill you might screw with your head."

They heard Paul coming back down the stairs, and Alma noted how it sounded as his footsteps thumped on the carpet. She looked quizzically at him as he approached.

"Ben's in the bed," said Paul. He saw Alma's odd stare and asked, "Is everything okay?"

Alma could distinctly recall the sound of her father coming down the stairs. The couch that Ben and Alma always sat on was faced away from the stairs, and whenever they heard the loud sound of their father's footsteps she recalled feeling tense and nervous. "There wasn't carpet," she said as she walked past Paul and to the stairs. She studied the way the carpet on the stairs stopped at the bottom floor, and she looked up in confusion.

"What are you talking about?" asked Paul.

"There wasn't carpet here before," said Alma. "Someone put that here after what happened."

"Maybe it was part of how Rosemary was lying to Oliver," said Paul.

Alma nodded in agreement, but wasn't satisfied. She went to the kitchen and reached for one of the knives in the butcher block. She noticed how the butcher knife was already missing, so she took a smaller blade and headed for the stairs.

"What are you doing?" asked Rachel.

"Checking on something," said Alma. Paul and Rachel followed her up the stairs as she walked quickly down the hall. She stopped just before entering the bedroom and set her hand against the wall to steady herself.

"Alma," said Paul as he walked up behind her to provide support. "You okay?"

"Yeah, sorry," said Alma. "Just a little dizzy. I think it's from not sleeping."

"What are we doing up here?" asked Rachel.

Alma walked slowly into the bedroom where Ben was lying. Paul had placed him beneath the covers, but the invalid was writhing where he'd been left. He was agitated by their intrusion, and called out his sister's name over and over.

Alma knelt down near the foot of the bed and set the tip of the knife into the dirty carpet. She dug the blade in and used it to force the carpet up before sawing into it. She gripped the flap that she'd cut free and then pulled up on it before asking Paul to hold it. He did as he was asked and Alma continued to cut a hole in the carpet. Eventually, she finished the circle and Paul pulled the cut portion away. The wood beneath bore a deep, brown stain. Chunks of the wood had been cut away, and Alma pointed the tip of her knife at them.

"There," said Alma as she made a stabbing motion with the knife at the gouges that were already in the wood. "That's where he killed her. That's where my dad kept stabbing her over and over." She stabbed the knife down hard, revealing the extent of her pent up anger. The blade stuck easily in the wood and wobbled in place as she let it go.

"They covered it up," said Alma as she watched the blade waver. "They covered it up for him, but this is where he killed Terry."

At the Harper Residence
June, 1995

Ben knocked on the bathroom door. It was late, well past midnight, but he could hear his sister crying and he wanted to make sure she was okay. "Alma?"

"Don't come in," she said. "I'm taking a shower."

She hadn't been, but she quickly turned on the shower to drown out her weeping. He could hear her trying to hum, but she kept breaking into sobs.

Ben glanced across the hall at their parents' closed door. Their father had returned from one of his frequent business trips, and had been in a foul mood most of the day. Ben and Alma had learned how best to deal with him during these times, although it was impossible to completely avoid his frequent outbursts. Their mother almost always sided with Michael, and explained to Ben and Alma how they needed to obey their father so that he would come home and spend more time with the family. Ben wasn't certain he wanted that.

Michael Harper had a quick temper, and Ben had earned more than a few lashings for things he never knew warranted punishment. Sometimes it was because he was talking back, or had tracked mud in on the carpet, and sometimes it was just because of the way he'd looked at his father that caused Michael to whip his belt out of its loops. Ben's mother had explained that the best way to deal with a whipping was just to grin and bear it, and if the pain got to be too bad, then they should hum until it was over.

Just hum a pleasant tune until the pain stopped.

Alma had been trying to hum in the bathroom, but she was crying too hard to keep a tune.

"Did he hit you?" asked Ben. "Did Daddy hit you again?"

Usually Alma avoided their father's wrath more deftly than Ben managed to. He preferred it that way, and had taken the blame for things Alma had done more than a few times to save her. He didn't mind doing it. He loved his sister, and he hated nothing more than hearing her cry. He always felt like he needed to protect her.

"I'm okay," said Alma from behind the door.

"I'm coming in," said Ben as he started to open the door.

"No, don't," said Alma from inside the bathroom, but Ben was already going in.

He closed the door behind him and saw that Alma hadn't turned the light on yet. He flicked on the light, and the multiple bulbs over the mirror blazed to life, revealing that Alma was hiding behind the shower curtain. Her hand was clutching the curtain, and there was blood on her fingers.

"Alma," said Ben as he approached. "What happened?"

"It's okay," said Alma as the shower got hot enough that steam began to fill the bathroom. "I'll be okay. Mommy said that I should hum until it stops hurting. But it hurts so bad."

"Did he whip you?" asked Ben.

Alma didn't answer, and Ben assumed that his sister had been the victim of their father's rage once again. Perhaps she'd talked back to him, or she'd woken him up while going to the kitchen for something to eat when she was supposed to be in bed. He didn't know what she'd done, but whatever it had been, she didn't deserve the punishment she'd received.

Ben sat on the toilet, affording his sister privacy as she took a shower. "Do you want to talk?"

Alma didn't answer, and Ben didn't pester her anymore. He listened as she hummed and cried, and he began to cry with her. He wished there was a way he could get rid of her pain forever.

To make her forget what Daddy did.

CHAPTER 27 - Lambs to the Slaughter

Widowsfield
March 13th, 2012

The Skeleton Man was trapped. He was back in the place where he'd desperately tried to flee, lying on the same bed where The Watcher had first appeared and taken Ben's soul as a sacrifice. He knew that his father was asleep downstairs, and he wanted to infect his dreams and finally murder the bastard that had been the cause of so much of Ben's torture through the years. But he also knew that The Watcher would be quick to find him here, and that stepping into Michael's head would invite The Watcher in as well.

When they were at the facility, The Skeleton Man had felt The Watcher's attention brought back from its web to the real world. He'd felt the approach of the cords, and heard the grinding of the creature that owned him. The Skeleton Man's power grew once The Watcher approached, just as it always had, and he tried to infect Hank Waxman's mind, but the big man fought off Ben's suggestions, exerting a willpower that he wouldn't have owned had they met in a dream. The Skeleton Man worried that he was trying to do too much, and that it was a mistake to leave a portion of his influence behind at the facility, but he needed to take every opportunity he could to have the revenge he craved.

Now Ben was forced to lie and wait. He had to stay quiet and hope that The Watcher's attention was pulled elsewhere as Ben Harper's body slowly gained strength. The Skeleton Man felt like he was in a prison as he looked around the familiar setting.

Then he heard a bubble plop nearby. He tried to look to the right, towards the bathroom, but he could barely move his head. He heard another bubble, and then a splash. Drops of water started to plop onto a wood floor as he listened to wet footsteps approaching. Finally, a figure came into view.

Terry was there, as she had been sixteen years earlier. Her skin was blistering and brilliant red and her eyes were wide and bloodshot. She was nude and dripping with water, cleaner, and blood. A strip of flesh was missing from her arm and her teeth had fallen out, revealing purple, inflamed gums.

"Ben," said Terry as she approached the bed. "Look what you did."

The Skeleton Man wanted to flee, but he was trapped inside of Ben's body. He'd been running from the red-haired woman for sixteen years, doing everything he could to avoid her grasp. Ben remembered how she'd reached out from the tub and pulled him down in with her, and he knew that she could do it again. She was here to torture him; to burn him and rip away his skin. She would finally have her revenge.

Terry reached out to him. Her arm dripped with a syrupy mix of melting skin and blood, and her hand was shaking as if she was in pain. She set her hand on his head, and he could feel the caustic burn of the chemicals that had ravaged her body. He could smell the stench of bleach mixed with the heavy, metallic scent of blood. He wanted to scream out, but he knew that the horrors she could inflict on him would pale in comparison to The Watcher's retribution.

Terry leaned in closer and she stared down at The Skeleton Man with her wide, bloodshot eyes. He could smell the decay coming from her open mouth, caused by her severely inflamed and rotting gums. He braced himself for the torture she'd dreamed up for him, and he closed his eyes in expectation of pain.

She kissed his forehead, and then moved back again.

He opened his eyes and saw Terry as he'd never seen her before. She was young and beautiful, with bright red hair that seemed to glow even in the sparse light coming into the bedroom. Her face was no longer burned, but only colored by the light blush of her cheeks. She smiled and said, "I'm sorry for what I did to you and your sister. I wish I could take it all back."

"Terry?" asked The Skeleton Man with Ben's quivering voice.

She nodded and set her hand on his forehead again. This time her touch didn't cause his skin to burn, and she stroked his hair as she grinned. "Your sister helped me."

"Alma…"

"She helped me move on, but I didn't want to leave without you. I owe you that much. I'll help you get out. We'll play our parts, just like he wants, but then we'll escape. Okay?"

Ben nodded, and felt his eyes begin to tear up. She leaned down and kissed his forehead again, and stroked his hair one more time. Then she got up and moved backward. Her expression became marred by pain again, and he saw her skin begin to blister. Her eyes grew wide and bloodshot. White foam and blood began to flow from the corners of her mouth as she said, "Play your part, Ben. Our lies will set us free."

She backed up, out of Ben's line of sight, and into the bathroom. He heard her scream in pain as she stepped back into the tub. He could smell her skin cooking in the chemicals and boiling water as she played the role expected of her.

Inside Cada E.I.B.'s facility
March 13th, 2012

Rosemary watched as Helen committed suicide. The old nurse had done her job well, and the final injection was for her. The Potassium Chloride caused the old nurse to begin to convulse almost immediately, and she slid out of her seat as her body shook. She fell to the floor beside Rosemary's bed and foam began to rise from her mouth. Rosemary looked away, and focused on the ceiling of the room again. The end of Widowsfield was fast approaching.

A year earlier, Rosemary had managed to earn Helen's trust by altering the woman's memories. Since then,

Rosemary had perfected the use of her psychometric ability to implant memories into objects, and quickly learned how to tailor those memories to get people to do just about anything she wanted.

At first, Rosemary had planned on sending Helen into Cada E.I.B. with the sole purpose of murdering Oliver. However, Rosemary learned that Oliver wasn't the one in charge of the facility, and that another man named Vess was the one that funded the project.

Vess had been in hiding for years, and despite everything that Rosemary and Helen tried, the old man never came to Widowsfield and Helen was never able to discover where he was hiding, although she suspected it was close by.

Everything fell into place right before the sixteenth anniversary of the Widowsfield experiment. The group that founded Cada E.I.B. decided to start to shut down the project for reasons that neither Helen nor Rosemary knew, but the fervor that the decision caused meant that this year would be the last chance Vess would have of completing his experiment. Then the appearance of Alma Harper meant that the only other person to ever contact the entity in Widowsfield was now within their grasp.

Helen snuck off to use Oliver's computer during the commotion, and she sent an email to Vess explaining how Alma, Ben, and Michael Harper had all been caught and would be at the house on Sycamore, performing the ritual, at 3:14 in the morning on March 14th. If this didn't draw the reclusive old man out, then nothing would.

Rosemary knew what she had to do next. She forced herself off the bed, and the debilitating pain from her injury nearly caused her to fall to her knees. She cringed and gripped her stomach, hoping her movement hadn't ripped the stitches Helen had given her. She had to make it down to the basement, and to the lab where the experimental machine was kept that had caused all of this to occur. She planned on waiting for Vess there so that she could put an end to this nightmare.

Each step was arduous as she made her way slowly through the facility and to the elevator. Rosemary knew that when Vess arrived, he would find the dead sleepers, but she couldn't risk leaving them awake and alive. She wasn't just trying to kill Vess, she was also working on destroying The Watcher in the Walls as well. The entity that ruled Widowsfield had to be stopped, and she knew that he was using the souls of the sleepers to keep his world together. He was using, and abusing, their memories to craft his lies.

After Vess was dead, Rosemary could finally end her own nightmare. She'd been plagued with nightmares about Widowsfield for the past five years. Every waking moment was filled with dread about the coming night's sleep, when the dreams about cords and chattering teeth would come again.

No more.

Within a day, it would all be over.

Rosemary limped along, using the wall for support as she passed a fire extinguisher that was lying in pool of blood. She knelt and touched the red canister, and learned that Oliver had used it to attack Helen's assistant. Then she proceeded to follow the trail of blood to reach the room where Vess's monstrosity had been built.

She discovered Oliver's body lying only a few feet away from the nurse he'd murdered. She didn't need to touch anything nearby to understand what happened. It felt like the room wanted her to know everything. It had expected her to come. It was welcoming her in.

She saw the yawning door of the machine that they'd used to contact The Watcher, and she saw the blood splattered everywhere around it. Such a perfect tomb.

Rosemary's head was spinning, and she wasn't sure why. Everything was as it was meant to be, and she was nearing the end of her journey. This was as good a place as any to die.

This was how it was meant to be.

Rosemary got to the door of the machine, took a deep breath, and stepped inside. She sat down in the blood of the murdered nurse, and she let herself rest. Vess would come. She was certain of it.

Her legs felt stiff, and her arms fell to her side. She was stuck in the corner of the machine, barely able to move.

The sacrificial lamb had climbed atop its own altar.

Terry's cabin
March 13th, 2012

"Yep, that's it," said Rachel as she held up her phone for the others to see. "My phone is officially dead." It was nearing dusk, and the group had been trying to amuse themselves in any way they could, but none of them were willing to play games on their phones. They'd hoped their charges would last, but none had.

"Mine's been dead for hours," said Stephen. The others agreed that the batteries on their phones had died off as well.

"I guess we're officially stuck here now," said Rachel. "No calling for help." She looked into a bag of chips from the haul that Stephen and Jacker had brought back when they went for food, but the bag was already empty.

"I don't think anyone could help us anyhow," said Jacker.

They were sitting in the living room, behind the couch where Michael was still sleeping. Each of them had taken turns napping, and the day had passed uneventfully. They spent some time reviewing what had happened, and trying to piece together the nightmare they'd shared about The Watcher's Widowsfield.

Alma was still confused about if The Skeleton Man was really her brother, and Paul explained that he believed The Skeleton Man wasn't made up of just one soul. He thought that The Watcher used the fears of some people to create the monster that they'd come to know as The Skeleton Man, and that was the reason it seemed like it was Ben sometimes. Alma wasn't sure, and explained that she thought there was more to it than that. She felt like the man sleeping in the bed upstairs was her brother, but that he'd been twisted into a monster by the awful things that had happened to him. The group went round and round in circles on the subject, but none of them knew anything for certain. It was all just theories.

Occasionally, one of them would go upstairs to check on Ben, and he always looked the same. He was staring up at the ceiling, quiet and still, as if terrified of disturbing the ghosts that lived here. It was a feeling they all shared.

"Have you looked in Rosemary's bag at all?" asked Rachel as she glanced at the satchel that was leaning against the wall by the door.

"Yeah," said Alma. "It's got the things we gave her, and the candles for the ritual tomorrow. It's also got her sketchpad and paint brushes."

Rachel got up and went to retrieve the bag. "Well, let's take a look and see how good of a painter she is."

Rachel brought the bag back over to their circle and sat back down. Before she took out the sketchpad, she pulled out a watch and showed it to everyone. "I guess we're going to need this now that we can't check the clocks on our phones." She set the watch on the floor and then pulled out the sketchpad. She placed the pad on the floor and opened it to the first page. Each of them gawked at the picture, and fell silent as they stared at it.

Rosemary had filled the book with pictures of awful scenes of murder and torture. Each page was gorier than the last, with depictions of people being flayed, boiled, and hung by black cords that reached out from the walls. There was a picture of the Salt and Pepper Diner on Main Street, but the front window had been broken and a corpse was on the ground, surrounded by shattered glass. His eyes had been plucked out and a bloody spoon was near his head.

"What the fuck?" asked Rachel as she continued to flip through the pages. "What is wrong with this bitch?" The last several pages depicted fires consuming corpses, and Rachel closed it in disgust.

"She spent too much time in this place, that's what," said Jacker as he sat back. He'd had enough of the gory scenes.

"That's the hell we might be headed back into," said Alma. "Tomorrow, when we write that number on the floor, we might get pulled right back into his world."

"Are you sure we ever got out?" asked Paul and everyone looked at him with quizzical, almost accusatory gazes. "Think about it. Maybe we never got out. I don't understand how any of this works, or what the hell happened. How did you guys get pulled into that dream in the first place? And why was I kicked out of it? The whole damn thing's a mystery to me."

"Well, trust me," said Jacker, "sitting around here is a hell of a lot different than what it was like in those dreams. When we were jumping back and forth in time, and watching Aubrey come apart like that..." he shivered and crossed his arms. "We're not in The Watcher's world right now. I can promise you that."

"Sure, we're not in the nightmare he created," said Paul. "But who the fuck knows anymore? This whole ordeal's got me questioning all sorts of shit. I don't know, it screws with your head if you spend too much time thinking about it."

"That's all we've got right now is time," said Stephen.

"Well, I for one am counting down the hours until I get to hop on my bike and get the fuck out of here," said Paul. "I want to leave this town far behind me."

"Hear, hear," said Jacker as he raised a two-liter of soda in agreement before taking a swig.

"We should've picked up some beers," said Stephen.

"No, you shouldn't have," said Paul. Stephen cast a confounded glance in his direction and Paul explained, "Jacker and I are off the sauce. Right buddy?"

"Doing my best, man. Of course, it's times like these when getting wasted sounds like a damn good plan."

"What are you going to do when you get back, Jacker?" asked Rachel. "Are you planning on turning yourself in?"

Jacker sighed, raised his brow, and then finally nodded. "I don't think I've got any other choice. I'm not going to try and run from this forever."

"What about your priors?" asked Paul.

Jacker shrugged and said, "They'll toss me in the joint. But fuck it, after going through this shit, prison sounds like a luxury vacation."

The group chuckled and agreed, except for Stephen who shook his head. "I don't think so man. I think in a few days, all of our lives are going to get a whole lot better."

"Why do you say that?" asked Alma.

"Because this story's going to get out there," said Stephen. "People are going to find out what happened here, and everything's going to change for us. This story's going to be huge."

"Whoa," said Paul. "We never signed off on shit. Don't forget, you gave Alma the final say on all of the footage here."

"Well, yeah, sure…" Stephen was flustered. "Right, I know, but come on. Guys, this is different. None of us expected any of this to happen."

"Still though, Alma's got the final say on everything," said Paul.

"Of course, of course," said Stephen.

Rachel looked at her husband, and then back at the others. She was clearly upset, and waited for Stephen to say something else, but he stayed silent. "Stephen," she said his name as fair warning that he needed to be honest with them.

"What?" he asked, perturbed.

"If you're not going to say something, then I will."

"Say something about what?" asked Alma.

"No, Rachel," said Stephen. "They don't have any right to that. They weren't in it."

"Weren't in what?" asked Paul, his anger growing.

"We filmed something when we were at the facility, while you guys were gone. The younger nurse took off to go find Oliver, and Helen went upstairs for something, so we took the camera into the room with all of the sleeping people and filmed them. Then we shot a bit of me explaining what had happened. We posted it on our site."

"You what?" asked Alma in shock at the betrayal.

"It's not live," said Stephen. "It won't post until around this time on the fifteenth. Chill out."

"When were you planning on telling us about this, you slimy fucker?" asked Paul.

"We're telling you now," said Stephen.

Jacker shook his head in disgust. "Dude, you're really a slimeball. You know that?"

"Me? Fuck you. You're the one that bashed some kid's head against a wall. What I did was smart. It was fucking smart, you guys. None of us know if we're going to make it out of this alive, and if something happens to us then there's a record of it."

"And if Rachel hadn't forced you to say something, then you would've posted that video with or without our consent," said Paul. "Right?"

"There's no point in arguing about hypotheticals," said Stephen.

"Well stop the video from posting," said Alma. "At least until we get a chance to think over whether or not we want it to get out there."

"I can't," said Stephen. "Even if I wanted to, there's no way to do it. We don't have any electricity, and my laptop's in the van. Plus, it's not like this town is set up with Wi-Fi to get online. Right? Look, guys, chill out. The post isn't set to go live for a couple of days. You'll have plenty of time to decide if you want to let the story get out about what happened here or if you want to play right into the hands of the people responsible for all of this and bury the story. Okay?"

"You're such a weasel," said Jacker.

"Go fuck yourself, man," said Stephen.

"Don't have to," said Jacker. "You paid one of your old hookers to do it for me."

Stephen cursed back at Jacker, but Rachel didn't let the remark pass without focusing on it. "What do you mean by that?" she asked of Jacker.

"Nothing, forget it," said Jacker as he started to stand up.

"No, I'm not going to forget it," said Rachel as she stood up with him.

"Babe, just sit down," said Stephen as he reached up and took his wife's hand.

She jerked her hand away from Stephen's grip. "No, I want to know the truth. I want to know who Aubrey really was."

"I'm staying out of it," said Jacker as he started to walk towards the front door. "I'm getting some fresh air."

"No you're not," said Rachel as she grabbed his arm and held him back. Her hysteria was becoming apparent as she screamed, "Tell me the truth!"

"Okay," said Stephen. He waited for a long moment before continuing. He stood up, closed his eyes, and took a deep breath. Finally, he admitted the truth, "Aubrey and I slept together about a year ago."

"You piece of shit," said Rachel. "You miserable fucking piece of shit." She went to grab at her ring to take it off and throw it at him, but she remembered that she'd already taken it off to give to Rosemary.

"Rachel, honey, let's not do this…"

Rachel screeched a curse at him and then headed for the door. She pushed past Jacker, flung the door open, and went outside. Before anyone had a chance to react, Rachel was coming back in. She quickly shut the door and shushed the group.

"What's wrong?" asked Alma.

"There're people out there."

CHAPTER 28 – Cogs in the Machine

Terry's cabin
March 13th, 2012

"People?" asked Alma as she approached the door.

"Man, this is just like last time," said Jacker as he shook his head.

"I saw headlights up the road," said Rachel. "A lot of them."

"You've got to be kidding me," said Stephen as he went to the window to peer out. It was late, and the sun had gone down several hours earlier, making seeing the approaching headlights easier. "She's right," he said as he ducked down.

"Of course I'm right," said Rachel. "I might be blind to how big of a piece of shit you are, but I'm not actually fucking blind."

Paul hushed them both as they all got down on the ground to avoid being spotted as the vehicles passed. The living room lit up as the vehicles drove down the street, and the group sighed in collective relief as the intruders kept driving. After being certain they were safe, they got back up and looked out the window to see where the cars were headed.

"Do you think they're going to Cada E.I.B.?" asked Paul.

"I think that's a safe bet," said Stephen in a mocking tone.

"This is happening just like it did before," said Jacker. "Next thing you know, we're going to get shot with salt pellets or something."

"Not me," said Rachel. "I'm getting the fuck out of here."

"No," said Jacker as he grabbed her arm. "Don't you remember what happened last time? I left and I got caught."

"That was different," said Rachel. "You were with my husband's whore at the time."

"It's not different," said Jacker. "Look, I don't know if this is just a coincidence or what, but this whole thing feels like we've done it before, just like how everything felt in that dream, or whatever the hell it was. Here we all are, and we're fighting, and there are people out there driving around, and Alma's going to do her weird ritual again. It's all the same. It's like what Paul said earlier, like how maybe we're all just still stuck in that creature's web."

"That's bullshit," said Rachel.

"Is it?" asked Jacker. "Are you sure? Because if you are, then convince me, because I'm losing my damn mind here."

"What are you trying to say?" asked Rachel. "What do you propose we do? Because I think we should all just pack our shit, count our losses, and get the hell out of here."

"How much longer do we have to wait?" asked Jacker.

"Just over three hours," said Stephen as he looked at the watch they'd found in Rosemary's bag. He'd decided to wear the watch in preparation of the coming ritual. "It's just about to be midnight."

"Okay then," said Jacker. "Here's what I think, and bear with me because I'm still trying to figure all this out myself. I think we need to wait here, and give Alma a chance to use her Chaos Magick shit to fix this, otherwise we're all going to be stuck going around in circles like this. I can't be the only one that thinks that us ending up back here, in this same damn situation, is eerie."

Alma was quick to agree. "No, you're right. My whole life I've felt like I've been getting pulled back here. If we don't fix this now, then I think we're going to find ourselves getting dragged back again at some point in the future. We're just a few hours away from getting it over with. I don't want to risk screwing it up now."

"I agree," said Stephen. "Let's see this to the end."

"Well, I don't agree," said Rachel. "I just want to get away from here."

"And go where?" asked Jacker. "Out there where you're going to get spotted and hauled back to that facility?"

"It's better than being here, where they're probably going to come looking for us because this is where they found us last time," said Rachel.

"Then let's go across the street," said Paul. "We can wait there, and once it gets close to 3:14, we'll come back over. That sounds like a smart plan to me. And I'm all for getting out of this creepy house for a little while."

"Are you sure the other house will be unlocked?" asked Stephen.

"If it's not, then we've got the doorbuster himself to break it down," said Alma as she pat Jacker on the back. "I swear, this guy's always busting down doors everywhere he goes." Paul and Jacker appreciated Alma's joke, but neither Stephen nor Rachel offered even a hint of a smile.

"Fine," said Rachel as she shook her head. "God damn it. Fucking fine. Let's go over there and hide, but as soon as we're done I'm out of here. Stephen, I never want to see you again. We're done."

She opened the door, looked to make sure it was safe, and then started to walk across the street. Stephen stood at the threshold and watched her go as the others began to gather their things. Paul went over to the couch, past the mannequins that they'd set on the floor, and prodded Michael. Alma's father jostled, but didn't wake up.

"Christ," said Paul as he poked at the man a second time. He was familiar with how meth users often slept for long stretches after a binge. Michael's face was facing the couch, and the belt was still strapped around his face, holding the t-shirt in his mouth. When Paul rolled Michael onto his back, he saw why the man hadn't responded.

Michael wasn't dead, which they all knew because of the constant, sharp breaths he'd been taking, but he was staring straight up, with shrunken pupils that didn't move. At some point during the day, Michael Harper had become a sleeper.

Inside Cada E.I.B.'s facility
March 14th, 2012
12:01 AM

Vess was confined to an electric wheelchair, and he had to be helped through the debris at the entrance of the facility. The guards that accompanied him performed a search of the building, and reported back to Vess about the bodies they'd discovered. Tom had been shot dead in the mess hall, and Helen was found adjacent to the sleepers' room. Unsurprisingly, all of the sleepers were dead as well, victims of lethal injection administered by the nurse before she'd committed suicide.

Vess had expected this to happen.

The guards wanted permission to access the lowest floor, but Vess denied them. He insisted on going down first. They tried to explain that the building hadn't been cleared, and that whoever had shot Tom might still be in the building. Vess told them that he hoped the murderer was, which was why Vess needed to go alone.

No one argued with him, and he was allowed to go by himself to the elevator. Over the past sixteen years, the telomerase levels in Vess's bloodstream had all but vanished. His former immortality had faded, and his desire to successfully activate the CORD had become more than just a passion of his. He firmly believed that his life depended on it.

He used the key that would allow access to the bottom floor of the facility. His trusted guards watched helplessly as the doors closed, leaving them separated from their boss for the first time in several months.

Many members of The Accord would be happy to learn of Vess's death. It was no secret that they'd been hoping to get their hands on Vess's notes about his successes with the CORD, but he'd been careful to avoid their grasp after the event in Widowsfield, sixteen years earlier. Unlike Tesla, who fell victim to the government thugs that stole his research, Vess had hidden himself from the prying eyes and hands of the greediest members of The Accord. He knew that his research was valuable, and he'd been able to win the support of a few of the more prominent members of The Accord by releasing bits and pieces of what he'd discovered.

This would be his last chance to successfully activate the CORD, and he'd been forced to make several concessions to get everything to work out exactly as needed. The Accord allowed him this one, final opportunity to be the man that opened the door to Heaven.

Vess wheeled through the basement of the facility, and he paused to look at the mess left behind where someone had been attacked with a fire extinguisher. He'd hoped to avoid this sort of violence, but the entire CORD project had been mired by such horrors. The sacrificial altar craved blood.

The trail of blood led to the lab, as Vess had expected. The assassin would be inside, waiting for Vess to arrive.

He saw Oliver's body and cringed at the sight. He'd hoped his former assistant would survive, although he'd been prepared to find him dead. The message that he'd been sent earlier had clearly not been sent by Oliver. It had been the coded message that Vess had been told by The Accord that he should expect to receive.

Vess studied the body of the dead nurse that had been dragged here, and he realized that Oliver had been foolishly trying to activate the CORD on his own, clinging to the belief that sacrificing any human might be the key to activating the machine as opposed to using a psychic. Oliver also didn't realize that the CORD's stopgap mechanism was programmed to refuse delivery of radioactive material into the machine except at exactly 3:14 on March 14th. The Accord was still set upon using that date and time specifically.

"You can open the door," said Vess loudly as he stared at the partially closed door of the CORD. "I know you're in there."

The assassin didn't obey immediately. But after a few moments of silence, the metal door finally creaked open slowly to reveal Rosemary Arborton sitting inside. She was clutching her belly, and Vess saw that she'd been hurt.

"You were shot?" asked Vess, surprised.

"Stabbed," said Rosemary weakly.

"I'm sorry to hear that," said Vess. "I hope it's not fatal."

"What do you care?" asked Rosemary. She was weak, and Vess knew that she was having trouble using her limbs. This was the state he'd been told he should expect to find her in, after her mission was complete.

"I care a great deal, my dear," said Vess. "I'm counting on you living another few hours at least."

"How did you know I'd be here?" asked Rosemary.

"The same way I knew you couldn't kill me once I got here, even though you've been planning on my death for ages already."

"I don't understand," said Rosemary.

"The people I work for are very interested in people like you, Rosemary," said Vess. His voice was frail, as was his body, and he wheeled his chair closer to the CORD so that he could speak to the wounded assassin easier. "They aren't the type of people that would simply shrug off the discovery of someone with a talent like yours."

"What are you saying?" asked Rosemary.

Vess grinned at her and said, "Those are nice necklaces you're wearing. You use those to control people, don't you? You infect that jewelry with your will, and then hand them out as gifts. Do you remember where you first got the idea to do that? Who was it that handed you your very first necklace?"

"My mother," said Rosemary with a rising anger. "Are you saying my mother works with you?" asked Rosemary, clearly not believing him.

"No, not her, but the lady who gave her that necklace did. Right after Oliver told me about your supposed death, The Accord had someone pay a visit to your mother, just in case you showed up with a bunch of money that you'd earned from cashing all of those checks Oliver wrote to you."

"You manipulated me," said Rosemary.

"Don't feel bad, we're all being manipulated by somebody. It's human nature to be guided by someone else's strings. If it's any consolation, you did a fabulous job."

"That's why I kept thinking about all of those experiments," said Rosemary. "I kept writing about them in my journal. You and your company planted those things in my head?"

"No, not on purpose at least. It's no surprise that the person who implanted that necklace with your new agenda would've accidentally imparted some of their own thoughts into them. That comes with the territory."

"And the reason you've had me doing all of this is to get me here? Why go to all that trouble?"

"It wasn't much trouble, really," said Vess. "The reason everything became so convoluted is because there were multiple forces at work trying to sway things in their direction. There are parts of The Accord that want me dead, and other parts that think giving me one last shot at turning on this machine would be worth it. Luckily, the people that want to give me one last chance prevailed, otherwise you'd be aiming a smoking gun at me right now and we wouldn't be having this conversation."

"It's all been a lie," said Rosemary as she struggled with the truth.

"Says the consummate liar," said Vess with a smirk. "Come now, Rosemary, you of all people shouldn't be surprised that you've been lied to. If only poor Alma knew all the ways you've lied to her."

"You people just look at me as another tool. Is that right?" asked Rosemary as she watched Vess begin to rise up from his wheelchair.

He struggled to stand, but eventually walked forward and approached the CORD. He reached up and grabbed the latch on the door. Then he smiled and said, "Just a cog in the machine," before closing her in.

CHAPTER 29 – 3:14 on March 14th

Michael Harper woke up in a bed that he didn't immediately recognize. It looked like the room of a young woman, but he couldn't fathom how he'd gotten there. There was a dresser against the wall with a mirror over it and a pink, lacey bra hanging off the knob of one of the drawers.

"What the hell did I get myself into this time?" he asked as he looked around.

There was a closet beside the bed with an accordion style door, and he faintly recalled seeing that door somewhere before. But Michael had made a habit of sleeping with a variety of women during his time working on the road. Waking up in a stranger's bed wasn't that big of a shock to him.

He saw an old watch of his on the nightstand that he hadn't seen in years, and he grabbed it in surprise. "What the hell do you know about that," he said as he slipped the watch on. He checked the time and cringed when he saw that the watch had stopped at 3:14.

It had to be a coincidence.

Michael went to the door of the room and peered down the hall. There was another bedroom door beside the one he was walking out of, and he eased the door open to find that it belonged to a messy young boy. The room was littered with toys and Michael was reminded of his son, Ben.

He paused and thought about his son. It had been a long time since he'd seen the boy. How long had he been out on the road on business?

Michael started to get confused, and he blamed it on the aftereffects of what must've been a long, drug-fueled night. He walked past the boy's bedroom and to the bathroom just beyond. He stepped in, urinated, and then examined himself in the mirror. He looked younger than he had in years, and he felt great. He smirked at himself, and then looked at his watch as he started to wind the gear to get it started again. Despite his efforts, the watch didn't work.

"Wait a second," said Michael as he looked at the watch and tried to remember the last place he'd seen it. That's when he suddenly realized where he was.

Michael marched back into the girl's bedroom, his feet thumping on the carpet as he went. He walked in and went to the closet. He gripped the handle and threw the door open.

Inside, clutching his knees as he sat on the floor, was Terry's little brother, Raymond.

"You little shit," said Michael as he glared at the frightened boy. "You fucking pervert."

"Hit him," said a female voice from somewhere in the house.

Michael glanced around and then asked, "Who's there?" He'd expected to see Terry, but it didn't sound like his girlfriend's voice. Whoever was speaking sounded familiar, but he couldn't place the voice. It was as if the voice didn't belong here, at this time.

"If you want, you could make him watch," said the woman as her voice grew nearer. He saw a person's shadow cast into the room from a figure in the hall.

"Who is that?" asked Michael.

His daughter walked into the room. She was wearing Terry's clothes: A short skirt, pink boots, and a tight t-shirt. She sauntered in and sat on the corner of the bed. She was wearing more make-up than he'd ever seen Alma wear before, and she was grinning seductively.

"Alma, what are you doing here?" asked Michael.

"Isn't this what you want?" asked Alma. "Would it be better if I closed my eyes and hummed a little?"

"Jesus Christ," said Michael as he clasped his hands to his head and closed his eyes. "What the fuck is going on? What sort of sick fucking joke is this?"

"Michael," said Alma seductively. He refused to open his eyes, but he could hear his daughter rustling on the bed.

"Daddy," said Alma again, but this time she had the voice of the child that Michael remembered from so long ago.

He finally opened his eyes to see.

Alma was on the bed, but she was no longer the adult that she'd been moments earlier. Now she looked to be only eight years old, if not younger. She was lying flat on the bed and her eyes were bulging and wide. Her mouth was open, and it was clear she was choking. White foam bubbled up and dripped from the corners of her mouth.

Michael screamed and ran. He ran across the hallway and to the front door as he kept an eye on the room behind him. He was terrified of what had happened and wanted to get away. He needed to get out as fast as possible. He grabbed the handle of the door and tried to open it, but the door wouldn't budge. He looked to see if it was locked, but found that the door was fused to the wall itself. There was no gap between the door and the threshold, and he pounded on it in anger and fear.

He looked back down the hall and saw that Alma was standing in Terry's doorway. The foam and vomit was cascading down her chin and dripping to the floor. She had her hands reached out to either side of her, gripping the doorframe as she watched her father try to escape.

The room around him seemed to shrink. At first he thought it was an illusion, but then the walls began to groan and shudder. Pictures of Desmond's family fell to the floor and shattered as the walls cracked and shifted. The entire house was becoming smaller, and despite his best efforts, Michael was being pulled closer to Alma. She didn't even have to move for him to be drawn to her. The walls were crumbling around him, and as the plaster fell away he saw wires within the wall that were pulling everything tighter.

"Oh Daddy," said Alma, though her voice had become twisted and deep. When she spoke, it sounded like the world was coming apart at the seams. "We're going to have so much fun together."

Widowsfield
March 14th, 2012

2:45 AM

"It's almost time," said Paul as he looked out the window at the cabin across the street. "We should probably start bringing everything back over there.

"Last chance to back out of this," said Rachel.

"Not me," said Alma. "I'm looking forward to getting it over with."

"Okay then," said Stephen as he picked up Rosemary's bag. "Let's do this."

Jacker carried Ben, and everyone agreed again that Paul would have the easiest time carrying Michael. He'd carried the sleeper over to this house when they came across, and he was angry that he had to do it again, but he eventually relented.

They'd taken Michael's gag out, and now his tongue was lashing around inside of his mouth. His eyes stared straight up, and Paul avoided their gaze as he walked as fast as he could across the street.

"Put him upstairs," said Alma when Paul came in with Michael in his arms. Paul grumbled, but did as he was asked. Michael wasn't a heavy man, but the dead weight of a grown man is still hard to carry. He took each step slowly as he ascended and then saw that Jacker had laid Ben out on the bed.

"Where am I putting him?" asked Paul as he strained to keep a grip on the sleeper.

"I don't know," said Alma. "Maybe on the floor, right where he killed Terry."

Paul got to the spot and unceremoniously dropped Michael to the floor. Alma's father thumped down hard and Jacker grimaced as Paul shrugged.

"Fuck it man," said Paul. "That guy can rot in hell for all I care."

"Cool by me, brother," said Jacker as he pat Paul's shoulder on his way out of the room.

Stephen was setting up the circle of candles in the kitchen like Rosemary had instructed. As he was laying them out, Alma picked one up. "What's wrong?" asked Stephen.

"This is the same candle," said Alma as she inspected the glass, pillar candle. The wax inside was white and rose up along one side where it had once spilled out. On the opposite side the glass was marred by smoke from when it had tipped over with the flame still burning inside. She studied the picture of Saint Francis of Assisi standing beside a lamb that was licking at a wound on his leg.

"She must've done her homework," said Stephen.

"No," said Alma. "This is the exact same one that my mother used. I remember when it tipped over. How did she get this?"

"Who knows?" said Stephen as he took the candle back and set it in its spot on the floor.

"Mark that down as number one thousand five hundred and seventy of creepy ass things about this town," said Jacker, making a joke of the seemingly random number.

"Should we take our stuff back now?" asked Stephen as he took Alma's teddy bear keychain out of the bag. She saw that he was holding the gun that Rosemary had left them.

"I guess so," said Alma as she took the bear from him. She rubbed her thumb over the soft fur belly of the memento, and she smiled. She was happy to have it back. Stephen handed Paul his keys, and gave Jacker the purple sobriety coin. Then he retrieved his wedding band and slipped it on. He got up and brought Rachel her ring, but she frowned and shook her head.

"Keep it," said Rachel.

"No, you've got to put it on," said Stephen. "At least for now. At least until this is over."

Rachel snatched the ring from him and paused before putting it on. She grimaced, but relented, and pushed the tight ring over her finger. It didn't seem to fit easily now.

"Should I put the mannequins back on the couch?" asked Rachel as she regarded the two figures they'd placed on the floor.

Alma shook her head. "No need. We're both really here this time."

"Oh crap," said Jacker. "That just made my stomach drop when you said that. Guys, do I need to say that I've got a bad feeling about this, or is that just a given at this point?"

"It's a given," said Paul.

Stephen pulled a red, felt-tipped marker from Rosemary's bag and handed it to Alma. "Do you want to do the honor?"

Alma took the marker, and then uncapped it as she scooted closer to the circle of candles that Stephen had set out. She took a deep breath and then looked up in confusion. "I don't remember if she wrote the number or the symbol for pi."

"Does it matter?" asked Jacker.

"I think you wrote the number last time," said Paul.

"Hold on, let me get the camera ready," said Stephen, but then he glanced around at everyone. "Is that okay?"

"Go fuck yourself," said Rachel.

Stephen ignored her and asked the others. "Do you mind if I film this?"

"No, go ahead," said Alma when no one else offered any answer. "It's fine by me." Her hand was trembling as she held the marker.

"It's almost time," said Paul.

Alma set the tip of the marker on the tile and heard the familiar squeak as she began to write '314' for what she hoped would be the last time.

Beneath Cada E.I.B.'s facility
March 14th, 2012
2:50 AM

Vess was getting ready to start the CORD when two of his guards came in with Lyle Everman on a gurney. They wheeled the decrepit sleeper in and approached the machine.

"Do you want him inside?" asked one of the guards.

"No, you can leave him there," said Vess. "He was just a backup in case our new psychic didn't do as she'd been told. Luckily, she's a good listener." He grinned back at them and then waved them off. "You can leave us. Shut the door on your way out."

He waited for them to leave before he wheeled himself over to Lyle's side. His chair put his head at the same level as Lyle's, and he sat there staring at the sleeper for a few moments. Lyle had suffered the same aging curse that Vess had, and their temporary immortality had failed following the 1996 experiment.

Lyle's body had suffered worse that Vess's. The elasticity in both of their skin had been challenged by gravity, but Lyle was confined to the bed, meaning that his skin had always been pulled backward, causing his skull to become pronounced. His eyes had sunk back into his skull, seeming to shrink even though they were always open, and lips had grown wider, now revealing the extent of his upper and lower jaws as his tongue flicked within.

"It'll all be over soon," said Vess as he touched Lyle's head with compassion. "We'll find our way to Heaven one way or another."

Vess wheeled himself over to the CORD and waited until his watch struck 3:00 before he pulled the lever that would begin drawing power from the hydroelectric dam straight to the machine. The lights in the lab began to dim immediately, and the old, familiar grind of the silver rings started. This would be the end. This would be when Vess finally answered the questions that plagued him.

Blue arcs of lightning cascaded up through the spinning rings and over the orb atop each pillar. The electricity crossed the width of the CORD and seemed to compete with the other side. The crooked lines of blue zapped at one another before finally meeting in a single dance that undulated up and down, but kept a central beam intact.

With every minute that passed, the electric current seemed to grow stronger. Vess watched in agonizing impatience as time slowly inched onward until finally the time to cut the cord had arrived. First, he flipped the final switch on the base of the machine that allowed it to draw in the maximum amount of power. Then he got out of his chair and carefully knelt in front of the stopgap mechanism.

Vess set his finger on the switch that would send the uranium into the machine. He gazed at the watch on his left wrist as his right index finger was poised to flip the switch.

"There's no barrier that man's ingenuity can't break down."

The minute hand clicked over.

3:14 had arrived.

Vess flipped the switch.

CHAPTER 30 – I Want to Watch

3:14

Paul woke up in a haze of smoke. He got to his knees and tried to search for Alma, but there was no one beside him. He cried out her name, but his voice echoed through the nothingness that was hidden by the white smoke. Or was it fog?

As he reached out, his hand touched something cold and hard. He flattened his palm against the object and realized that it was a metal wall. He could see his hand pressed firmly against the surface, but it appeared as if all he was touching was the fog itself. Paul searched his prison, and discovered that he was inside of a metal box of some sort that was barely more than five feet across in either direction. He continued to search the space, but then the corners seemed to vanish. It was as if the room had become circular; as if it was shifting while Paul stood within it.

Electricity crackled within the fog, and Paul saw a darkness emerge above. The shade grew thicker, and he began to see shapes sliding through the mass. The black cords began to slither across the invisible walls that trapped Paul in, and then a new shape came into view. Globes of white began to emerge from the mass of wires, and then they turned to reveal pupils staring down. There were hundreds of them, like stars in the sky that were focused solely on him.

That's when The Watcher finally revealed itself.

From within the tangle of cords a shape began to emerge. An arch curled through the mass of wires, like the spine of a mythical sea creature rising above the waves. It had spines and it slithered through the cords before disappearing behind them again. The space that Paul was trapped in resounded with the sudden explosive noise of metal screeching as it was torn apart. He covered his ears and got on his knees to stay far from the lashing cords above.

The small cords that had writhed above now began to retreat, and when they pulled back, the shape of The Watcher was revealed. The large form that had been slithering within the cords was one of eight similar appendages, and each of them was reaching out to gather up the loose cords. The eyes watched from within the mass of smaller cords as the larger arms gathered them up.

The Watcher was enormous, and towered above Paul's prison. The fog began to dissipate, and the scope of what he was looking at became apparent. The mass of collected cords that hung above him was just one part of an enormous collection of similar appendages. It was as if the whole sky was suddenly revealed to be one, single, living entity. The eight larger arms clasped the mass of cords, and the eyes continued to watch from the space between. It looked like an eight-fingered hand had reached down and gathered up a ball of twine, and the eyes were watching from between the strings. The fingers of the creature were scaled and adorned with spikes, and they connected above to a singular base. Paul was reminded of a tree, except the trunk was made of the earth instead of rooted in it.

Seeing the extent of the creature caused Paul to finally understand the futility of what they'd been trying to do. This wasn't an entity that could be defeated. It was like staring at the Earth itself and hoping to destroy it. The appendages sprouted from the pulsing land above like trees, and he could see hundreds of them across the horizon. The other arms were splayed, and the wires that the eight arms had set free were striking down at the same plain where Paul was trapped, but far from where he was. Echoing through the void were the screams of tortured souls. It seemed as if each of the arms that sprouted from the singular mass high above was focused on one soul, and for some reason the one above Paul had released him for long enough to allow him to see the truth of where he was.

Somewhere, far through the fog, was the glow of light, but Paul was too close to The Watcher's world to see past it. The fog clustered around the illumination, and it was growing thicker each second, blotting out the glow.

"Paul," said a woman's voice from nearby. "This way."

He turned and saw a sliver of light appear beside him. It was a doorway that he hadn't been able to find before, and someone was opening it for him. The world seemed to spin, as if he'd been floating one second and was now lying on the ground again. The tumult caused his stomach to lurch and he felt dizzy as he reached out for the exit.

Someone grabbed his hand and pulled. He gripped the stranger's hand with both of his own and reoriented himself to the truth of where he was. Above, The Watcher screeched, its voice the sound of grinding metal, and its arms opened to allow the cords to descend again. They lashed out at Paul, and some tied themselves into nooses that hung down around him.

He was nearly free, but then one of the cords wrapped around his neck. The Watcher caught him, and he felt the rope scratch his flesh as it constricted. He felt the world kicked out from beneath him and suddenly he was hanging from a noose in his own apartment.

He knew where he was, and how this had happened. The noose was hanging from one of the rafters that made up the ceiling of his studio apartment. He could hear the steady beat of the music being played in the tattoo parlor below, and his mind was muddied by the drugs he'd consumed that evening. It was the high that had finally driven him to commit suicide.

Paul had struggled to stay sober since Alma left. He wanted to become a new man for her, so that he could win back her heart, but every day was a struggle that he wasn't prepared for. He'd assumed sobriety would be easy, and that making the decision would signal a change in his life that would make everything better. That's how it had been at first, but the malaise of sobriety was something he hadn't been prepared for. The slow creep of depression came back, and temptation haunted every waking moment. When he finally succumbed, it seemed easier to just end it.

The rope choked him as he struggled and kicked. He tried to worm his fingers between his flesh and the cord, but it was too tight. He could feel it crushing his windpipe, and no air reached his lungs as he felt his eyes begin to bulge.

Paul reached for his pocket in desperation. He found the key that Rosemary had given him and pulled it out. He held it tightly in his hand as he closed his eyes. He concentrated on Alma, and how much he wanted to hold her in his arms again.

The rope lost its grip. Paul fell to the floor, but when he opened his eyes he was no longer in his apartment above the tattoo parlor. Instead, he was lying halfway out of the machine they'd discovered in the basement of the Cada E.I.B. facility.

He felt safe, but that feeling was lost when he heard The Watcher screech from behind him. Paul crawled away from the machine and through the blood that covered the floor. He looked behind and saw black cords snapping from within the door of Oliver's machine. They reached out of the doorway and gripped the edges as if using it for leverage to draw forth an even larger shape. The eyes began to peer through the tangle, and they focused on Paul as The Watcher came forth.

"Go," said Rosemary, although Paul didn't know where she was. "Get to Alma."

Paul tried to get up, but the slick blood nearly felled him. He saw the nurse's body on the floor, but noticed that she wasn't dead. She was staring at him as he got up, although she didn't move anything but her eyes. Oliver was lying just past the nurse, and he was awake and staring as well. He started to move, but Paul was faster. Paul got to his feet and headed out of the room. He kicked Oliver hard in the face as he passed, and then looked back in time to see the cords lashing out from the machine. He never turned back again, and ran as fast as he could to get out of the lab.

He had to make it back to the cabin.
He had to get to Alma.
Paul got to the door of Oliver's lab, opened it, and ran through without hesitation. However, he stalled as he found himself running through an alley instead of a hallway. He looked up and saw a starry sky above, and he could smell the distinct scent of laundry nearby. In the distance he heard the steady rhythm of traffic going by. He was somewhere in the city again, although he didn't understand how he'd gotten there.
"Fuck you, Kyle," said Jacker from somewhere nearby.
Paul looked ahead and saw his friend standing on the stoop outside of what looked like a loading bay for a grocery store. Jacker was standing over the body of a young man that he'd beaten nearly to death.
"Jacker," said Paul as he approached from behind.
Jacker turned, startled, and asked, "Paul? What are you doing here?"
"This isn't real," said Paul. "Jacker, none of this is real."
Jacker looked at the blood on his hands, and then back at his friend in confusion. He shook his head and said, "No, I did this, Paul. This is real. I did this."
"Reach in your pocket," said Paul as he took cautious steps toward his friend. "Look for the coin I gave you."
"What coin?" asked Jacker.
"The purple sobriety coin. It's in your pocket. Trust me."
Jacker trusted his friend, and he reached into his pocket. He pulled the coin out and marveled at it. "How did you know?"
Paul got to his friend and said, "You're just going to have to trust me. We've got to get to Alma."
"Your ex?" asked Jacker, his recollection of the past few days was muddied by The Watcher's lies.
Paul wasn't sure where to go next, but he remembered transitioning from the lab to this alley after opening a door. He grabbed Jacker's arm and pulled him up the steps, and over the body of Debbie's lover. He gripped the handle of

the back door of the grocery store where Debbie worked and opened it, hoping to again pass through The Watcher's illusion.

Beyond the doorway they could see Sycamore Street, across which was Terry's cabin. Paul was sure Alma would be there, and he pulled Jacker along with him. "Come on, we've got to finish this."

3:14

Vess saw the formerly blue electricity turn green. He raised his hands in jubilation and cried out in joy. He'd won. After all this time, he was finally going to uncover the secret that had been lost to him for so many years.

"Vess," said a voice behind him. He turned his wheelchair to see who had spoken and saw a familiar figure standing near the door.

"Lyle?" asked Vess as he saw the younger version of the man he'd taken on as an assistant so many years ago. "Is that you?"

Lyle Everman nodded as he approached. "Yes, it's me. It's the man you sacrificed almost seventy years ago."

Vess gazed at the young man, and then over at the sleeper on the gurney. Lyle walked closer, and stopped beside the husk that he'd once resided within. He set his hand over the sleeper's eyes, and pulled the lids closed. The sleeper shook, and his weak arms tried to reach out, but Lyle kept his hands over the skeletal man's eyes. The sleeper reacted as if being suffocated, and his writhing eased until he finally stopped. Lyle retracted his hand, and then focused his attention back on Vess.

"I sent you to meet God," said Vess. "What did you find? Tell me what you saw."

"I'll do better than that," said Lyle. "I'll let you see for yourself."

Black cords snaked their way out of Lyle's sleeves, whipping and snapping below his fingers as he grinned. He stepped forward, but parts of his body were stuck where they'd been, as if he were a man stepping forth from a cast of himself. His skin pulled away, ripping as the bones protruded. He didn't bleed as he broke free of the skinsuit he'd worn. From the shape of Lyle Everman stepped the creature that had been warped by The Watcher. A skull with chattering teeth emerged, and Lyle's eyes stayed in their sockets as they stared down, lidless, at Vess. He grew taller than he'd been, and the cords that had been hiding under his clothes now swirled around his form, keeping his bones in place as he approached.

The Skeleton Man spoke, and the walls seemed to tremble with his words.

"Suffer with me."

Cords shot out from The Skeleton Man's extended arm. They pierced Vess as the old man wailed in agony.

Then the metal walls of the CORD began to groan, and the door burst open as white fog poured out. The cords that had attacked Vess now pulled back, releasing the old man.

A figure emerged from the mist. Her silhouette in the fog was splayed and broken, but the cords quickly collected to form The Watcher's new guardian. Rosemary Arborton emerged from the fog within the CORD, and The Skeleton Man backed away from her in uncertain fear.

"Lyle," said Rosemary, although her voice had taken on the mechanical grind that of The Watchers. "You're time is at an end."

"No," said The Skeleton Man. "I'm not finished yet. I haven't had a chance to torture him."

"He's not yours to torture," said Rosemary. "Lyle, I'm giving you a gift. I'm letting you leave. I've taken your place here."

The door of the lab was open, and there was light coming in from the hallway. The glow intensified, and the source seemed to be drawing nearer. The shadow cast by the doorway was receding, and soon Lyle Everman was caught by the beam. He turned and put his arm over his eyes, but he couldn't avoid the blinding light. The door slammed shut, blocking out the blooming glow, and Lyle Everman was no longer standing in the room.

Vess was beginning to remember. The shroud of lies that had made him forget meeting The Watcher before was lifted, and he tried to pull on the joystick of his chair to make it wheel away. The motor grinded, but the wheels were caught in a mess of wires that had risen from the ground. Rosemary turned her attention to him.

"You need me," said Vess. "I'm the only one that knows how to reach you. Without me, you'll never get more sacrifices."

"But we took care of that, didn't we?" asked Rosemary.

"No." Vess shook his head in a panic to convince The Watcher's new pet that it needed to keep him alive. "You need me. I'm the only one that knows how to turn the CORD on."

"We don't need you," said Rosemary. "Your friends are making these machines as we speak. They've got Tesla's notes, and now they'll have yours as well. Vess, your time has come."

Vess knew that his chair was trapped, and he tried to get out, but the cords slung themselves up and over his arms, tying him down. Then they slithered around his neck as others reached over the back of his head and hooked into his eyelids before pulling back so hard that he felt the lids tear back. Blood cascaded down over his eyes, and he couldn't blink the liquid away. He was forced to see through the red haze as Rosemary advanced.

"You were right about one thing though," said Rosemary. Cords were descending from the ceiling and connecting to Rosemary's arms as she held them out in a Christ pose. She looked like a marionette, just a puppet dangling from its wires. Her voice was cacophonous, like the sound of a crumbling building that somehow formed into words. "It's human nature to be guided by someone else's strings."

Vess cried out in agony as the wires pierced him.

3:14

Raymond was hiding in his sister's closet and praying that he wouldn't be found. He knew that he was trapped in this hell, but he didn't know why. The Watcher had been exploiting Raymond's fears, but he continued to focus more on Michael Harper, often forgetting all about Raymond as the boy hid. The Watcher was fascinated with the man, and seemed to be using Raymond as bait.

The nightmares kept starting similarly, with Raymond hiding in the closet as Michael searched the house. Eventually, The Watcher would arrive, sometimes in the form of Raymond's sister, Terry, and other times as a woman that Raymond recognized as an older version of Michael's daughter.

This time, however, Michael never came. It was as if both The Watcher and Michael had forgotten where Raymond was hiding, but he was wary of believing that was possible. He kept hiding, certain that if he opened the door The Watcher would be there waiting for him. He knew he was doomed.

"Ray?"

He heard his father's voice, but it felt like it had been years since he'd heard it. He didn't want to fall for what was certainly a trick.

"Raymond, are you here?"

Raymond eased the door open. He was scared to reveal himself, but the chance of seeing his father again seemed worth the torture he might have to endure. Just the promise of being held in the safety of his father's arms was worth the risk.

"Daddy?"

Desmond came running down the hall, yelling his son's name. He burst through the bedroom door and stopped in sudden shock and joy as he saw his son standing there. He fell to his knees and pulled Raymond in for a hug before beginning to inspect him. "Are you okay? Raymond? Oh my God, Raymond. I love you so much. Are you okay?"

"I'm scared."

"I know, buddy," said Desmond. "But you don't have to be scared anymore. I'm here for you."

"I did something bad," said Raymond as he felt his eyes begin to tear up. "I watched Terry…"

Desmond hushed his son and pulled him back in for another hug. He cradled the back of the boy's head as he said, "It doesn't matter, buddy. None of that matters anymore. We're free now."

Desmond stood and took his son's hand. "Come with me. I'll show you."

Raymond and his father walked through the hall and to the front door. A storm was raging outside, but it sounded as if it were passing. The thunder took its time following the flashes of green lightning.

Sunlight was cascading through the storm clouds, and reflecting off the dew on the grass in their yard. Raymond lifted his arm to shade his eyes from the light, but his father pulled him forward. They went out into the yard and approached the beam of light.

"Come on, Ray," said Desmond. "It's time to go."

Together, Desmond and Raymond walked into the warmth of the sun that pierced The Watcher's storm.

3:14

"Is it boiling yet?" asked Ben of his little sister.

Alma looked in the pot on the stove and nodded. "Yes."

"Okay, good," said Ben as he slipped on the oven mitts. He pointed over to the butcher's block and said, "Get the big knife out, and wait until you hear me call you. Then come up and do your part."

Alma nodded as she watched Ben gingerly lifting the overflowing pot of water. Ben had filled the pot too high before putting it on the stove, and the water had been bubbling over the side and hissing as it hit the stovetop. He cringed as some of the water sloshed over the side and hit his arm.

"Do you want help?" asked Alma.

"No," said Ben. "Just do what I told you. Okay?"

Alma agreed, and watched as Ben took slow, steady steps towards the stairs with the pot held carefully with both hands. She could hear a dog growling, but Killer's cage wasn't where it was supposed to be. She looked around the room, and noticed that it looked different. The window was broken, and she wasn't sure how that had happened. There was carpet on the stairs, and she was certain that it hadn't been there before. And the loveseat that had been under the window was now moved across to the other side of the room. It was as if she was in a dream and the sleeper hadn't gotten the details of reality right.

She felt something in her pocket, and reached down to see what it was that was jabbing into her thigh. She pulled forth a teddy bear keychain, and then she heard a woman's voice call her name.

"Alma," said the familiar voice. "You have to stop him."

"Who is that?" asked Alma as she searched the room. "Terry, is that you?"

"Yes," said Alma's father's mistress. "You have to stop Ben. He's not doing what he's supposed to. He's going to let The Watcher keep him here if he doesn't stop."

"I don't understand," said Alma as she searched for the source of the ethereal voice.

"Ben's giving in to hate. He's going to fall right back into The Watcher's web. You have to stop him."

Alma rushed to the stairs, the knife in one hand and her keychain in the other. She could feel the wet carpet beneath her bare feet as she climbed, and she was reminded of the time she'd arrived home to discover her father naked in her bed. Her stomach lurched and she fell to her knees as the memory addled her.

She could hear her father's voice beckoning her, "Alma, come here. Sit down with me."

She began to wretch, and then vomit. Bile and white foam spewed out over her hands as she crouched on the stairs and heaved. All the pain that Michael Harper had caused came rushing back, causing worse damage to her than any weapon ever could. She was assaulted with the memory of his hand pressed over her mouth as she tried to hum like mommy had told her to. She tried to hum, but it didn't help.

"Alma," said Terry. Alma looked up and saw Terry leaning down and trying to help her stand. Terry looked different than Alma remembered her, healthier and younger than she'd been. Her visage faded as Alma got to her feet. "Don't let him make you hate Michael. I can help. Bring Ben to me."

The hall way was shifting. The floor was carpeted, but then it was wood, as if Alma was flashing between time periods, caught in a dizzying display of reality. She placed her right hand against the wall as she kept the knife tightly in her grip.

"He deserves this," said Alma as she remembered everything that her father had done.

Ben was ahead, and had walked through the door that led to the master bedroom. Alma was taller than he was now, and she realized that she was no longer the child that she'd been in the kitchen moments before. She was an adult again, and she was watching the scene unfold as it had sixteen years earlier.

This would be her chance to pay Michael back for everything that he'd done. This would be her chance for revenge.

Ben was walking slowly to the bathroom, the pot of boiling water held steady in his hands. Alma walked up behind him, and he looked back when he heard her coming.

"Alma, no," said Ben. "You have to play your part."

"Is that for him?" asked Alma. "Is he in the tub? Did you boil that water to pour on Dad?"

Ben was hesitant to answer. Then he finally nodded and said, "Yes."

"Good," said Alma. "I want to watch."

CHAPTER 31 – It Begins Again

Four fires already raged in Widowsfield, and Stephen was moving on to set the next. He was splattered with blood, but that didn't matter. He had to finish the job that Rosemary had set out for him.

Widowsfield had to burn.

Rosemary and Helen had spent the past year filling the buildings of Widowsfield with flammable items. The decrepit town was already dry and suitable to burn, but the psychometric needed to make sure there would be nothing left of The Watcher's favorite spots by the time anyone in a neighboring town saw the glow of the flames.

He entered the Salt and Pepper Diner on Main Street and walked around the counter. This would be the last fire he had to set. This place had been the focus of many of The Watcher and The Skeleton Man's worst atrocities, and it had to be consumed by flame.

Stephen went to the bathroom that was boarded up. He grabbed one of the boards and pulled until he was finally able to wiggle it free. He took the 'Out of Order' sign off the handle and tossed it aside. He opened the door and saw the tinder within. A gas can was on the floor.

He uncapped the can, and then splashed the tinder with a generous amount of gasoline. Then he moved out into the dining area to draw a line of gas across the counter. By the time he reached the dessert case near the register, the can was empty. He tossed it aside and then pulled out the lighter Rosemary had left in the bag for him.

Stephen ignited the fire and then ran out of the diner as the gas quickly ignited.

From the center of Main Street, Stephen Knight watched the town burn. He marveled at the scene, and watched the sky fill with smoke that was thick enough to blot out the stars. His mission was nearly complete. There was just one thing left to do.

He took the pistol out of his waistband. He knew there was at least one bullet left. His legs felt like they were losing strength, and he wobbled as he finished his journey. Stephen got on his knees and placed the barrel of the gun in his mouth.

Widowsfield claimed its final victim as the shot that ended Stephen's life echoed through the empty streets.

3:14

Paul and Jacker ran across the street and into the house on Sycamore.

Rachel was inside, and she was startled by their entrance. She'd been crying, and her mascara was streaked across her cheeks. "Who are you?"

"Rachel, it's me, Paul."

"Who?" She was confounded and frightened by their intrusion.

"Where's your ring?" asked Paul. "Put your wedding ring on."

"No, I took it off," said Rachel. "As far as I'm concerned, I'm not married anymore. My piece of shit husband is upstairs right now, fucking some whore."

"No, Rachel," said Paul. "You've got to trust me. You've got to put the ring on."

"Trust you? I don't even know you."

"Yes you do," said Paul. "I know you and Stephen have been having problems, but you've got to trust me and put your ring back on. You're falling into The Watcher's trap."

"I'm not putting that ring back on," said Rachel as she looked at the ring that was sitting on the counter.

"Fine, then just hold it," said Paul. "I don't have time to argue with you about it. Jacker, get her to hold the ring. I've got to go upstairs and find Alma."

Paul left them behind as he bounded up the stairs two at a time. He could hear moaning coming from the closed door ahead and he tried to run the length of the hallway to get there, but the walls stretched, and no matter how fast he ran he never seemed to get any closer. He screamed out to Alma, and a woman's moans of pleasure grew louder each second. The Watcher or The Skeleton Man were trying hard to keep Paul trapped in Rachel's nightmare, and he couldn't break free.

"Rachel," screamed Paul, "put the ring on!"

"Fine, God damn it," she yelled back.

Paul knew the moment she'd picked the ring back up. The hallway snapped back into shape and the sounds of people having sex behind the bedroom door ceased. Paul was able to grip the handle and open the door.

Alma was standing across the room beside a young boy that was carrying a pot of something that was steaming. Paul called out to her and she turned in surprise.

"Paul? What are you doing here?"

"Get out of here," said the boy that Paul recognized as Alma's brother.

"You have to stop," said Paul. "You're going to fall into his trap again."

"Whose trap?" asked Alma.

"The Watcher in the Walls."

"Shut up," said Ben as he tried to walk faster towards the bathroom. The boiling water in the pot splashed over his arm and he cried out in pain before dropping it to the floor. The metal pot banged hard against the carpet as water splashed out at the boy's feet.

"Look what you did," said Ben in fury as he leapt away from the boiling liquid. Ben's expression contorted in anger, and he screamed out as he began to shudder. His bones crackled, and his skin split. Blood seeped from his wounds as he began to convulse. The bones in his right arm grew suddenly long, carving their way through the skin they'd been hiding within. The Skeleton Man emerged from what had once been Alma's brother, leaving the shredded skin behind as he grew and shook. His teeth chattered as the black wires rose from the floor and wrapped themselves around his legs like vines around the trunk of a tree.

Alma stood beside The Skeleton Man, either unafraid or unaware of what her brother had become. "I don't want you here, Paul," she said. "We have to pay him back for what he did."

"Pay who back?" asked Paul.

"The daddies," answered The Skeleton Man.

"He deserves this," said Alma. "Don't try to save him."

Paul saw a hand reach up over the edge of the tub in the bathroom. Michael Harper rose from the bath, naked, wet, and shivering. The belt gag that they'd tied on him in the hotel room in Branson had been placed back over his mouth, and he was crying tears of blood as he stared out at the children that meant to torture him.

"Alma, you can't do this. You're better than this."

"No I'm not," said Alma. "Don't you get it? This is why I had to come back. This is what Ben was trying to help me do before. The only reason he had to trick us was to try and get out and get to Daddy. He knew that I would never be safe until Daddy was dead. Ben's the only one that's ever loved me." She moved closer to the shambling mass of bones and wire that was standing beside her. The Skeleton Man's teeth chattered as his sister put her arm around him.

"That's not true," said Paul. "I love you, Alma. And I know that…"

"You don't know anything!" Alma's sudden fury shocked Paul into silence. "You don't know what he did." She pointed back at the shivering man in the tub behind her. "You don't know what sort of things I've had to live through. If you really loved me, then you'd be standing here with me, helping me torture this piece of shit. You'd be the one sticking the knife in and cutting him open. You'd be the one pouring the water in."

"No I wouldn't," said Paul. "Because I know you're better than that. Alma, you're better than me. You're better than him," he pointed at The Skeleton Man. "You've always been a good person, and there's no way I'll ever believe that you want to torture someone, no matter what they did. That's not the type of person you are."

Paul stepped forward and felt his boot hit wood instead of carpet. He looked down and saw the hole that Alma had cut away in the carpet, revealing the spot where Michael had stabbed Terry to death. The gouges in the wood were healing themselves, and he stepped back, uncertain what was happening.

"Alma, where's the keychain I gave you?" asked Paul while still staring at the floorboards.

"Here," said Alma as she lifted her left hand.

Paul looked up and saw that she was holding the keychain in one hand and a butcher knife in the other. "Okay, then drop the knife. You don't need it. Drop the knife and just concentrate on the keychain."

"What are you trying to do?" asked The Skeleton Man as he took a step forward. "Just leave. She doesn't want you here."

"Please put down the knife," said Paul as he backed away another step. The Skeleton Man drew nearer, and he was growing larger with each step. The cords had now begun to cover his entire frame, and were weaving between his bones to craft a mockery of a human being.

"The daddies have to die," said The Skeleton Man.

Alma watched The Skeleton Man as he approached Paul, and despite how much she wanted to punish her father for what he'd done, she wanted to save Paul more. She loved him, and so she dropped the knife.

As the butcher knife hit the floor, a woman's arm grew forth from the spot where Terry had been murdered. Paul saw the ghost of Michael's mistress rise from the floorboards and reach out to try and grab Ben.

The Skeleton Man reeled back and avoided the ghost's grasp. He backed into Alma, and she held him steady as the ghost of Terry continued to try and crawl free.

"We have to run," said The Skeleton Man, although his voice sounded more like Ben's now. "We have to get away."

Alma looked at Paul as she gripped the keychain. She understood what she had to do.

"No, Ben," said Alma. "It's over."

The Skeleton Man turned on her and yelled in fury. The walls shook and began to crumble, revealing the wires within. Alma pushed at The Skeleton Man, but the cords shot out from the walls and tied themselves to their demon, refusing to let him fall into the grip of the red-haired woman.

Paul rushed over to help. He wrapped his arm around The Skeleton Man's neck and felt the twisting cords pinching the flesh on his arm as he pulled backward. The cords snapped free as The Skeleton Man cried out in anger and fear. One by one, the cords seemed to abandon Ben. They broke away from The Skeleton Man and shrank back into the deteriorating walls, making it easier to drag the creature closer to Terry.

"Alma, no," pleaded Ben's voice as they pulled the creature down to the floor.

Terry's arms reached out and gripped The Skeleton Man. She pulled him down with her, and golden light burned in the space where the carpet had been cut. Terry continued to drag him down until the only thing sitting above the pool of gold was The Skeleton Man's chattering jaw. Then Terry's hand reached up and covered his mouth before dragging him down, silencing The Skeleton Man for good.

There was no peace after Ben vanished beneath the floor. As soon as he was gone, Michael screamed out in pain from the bathroom. They looked up to see that he was being attacked by the wires that were breaking forth from the walls around them. His skin was being lacerated, and the weapons of The Watcher were snaking into the wounds.

"Come on," said Paul as he took Alma's hand. They ran to the hall and slammed the door shut behind them. It sounded like the lid of a coffin, heavy and final.

Widowsfield
March 14th, 2012

Alma woke up, cold and shivering on the kitchen floor of the house on Sycamore. Nothing made sense to her anymore, and she gazed up at what looked like fog floating near the ceiling. Her heart sank as she feared that she was still stuck within The Watcher's fog; lost somewhere in his nightmare.

Then she smelled the smoke.

"Fire," said Alma with a groggy croak as she sat up. She coughed and then yelled louder, "Fire!"

Paul was beside her, and she pushed at his arm to wake him. She was beginning to panic as she saw what was happening, and realized that she might not be able to wake Paul up. She could see Jacker and Rachel lying nearby, but Stephen was missing.

Paul groaned and muttered, "Let me sleep."

Alma slapped him hard on the cheek and yelled, "Get up."

"Jesus, Alma," said Paul as he opened his eyes. At first, he seemed annoyed with her, but then he quickly realized what was going on.

"Help me get Jacker and Rachel up," said Alma before the smoke caused her to begin coughing.

Paul wasn't concerned with being gentle. He slapped Jacker much harder than Alma had hit him, and Jacker yelled out in protest, "What the fuck?"

"Get your ass up," said Paul. "The house is burning."

Alma was able to get Rachel up without striking her, and she guided her to the door as Paul and Jacker followed. She tried to open the door, but then discovered it wouldn't budge.

"There's something blocking the door," said Alma.

"Let's go through the window," said Rachel.

"Hold up," said Jacker as he moved the others out of the way. "This is my specialty."

Jacker charged the door and bashed his shoulder into it hard enough to crack the threshold and send the door swinging wide. He fell hard to his side outside and the others quickly followed behind. Rachel helped Jacker to his feet as Paul inspected what had sealed them in.

"Someone nailed boards over the door," said Paul.

"Where's Stephen?" asked Rachel.

"He wasn't in there," said Alma as she backed away from the house. She saw that the roof was on fire. It looked like whoever had tried to kill them had set the fire outside, probably after boarding up the door. The far side of the house was engulfed, as was part of the yard that separated Terry's cabin from her neighbor. As Alma watched, part of the roof collapsed over where Terry's bedroom had been. The windows shattered and a spout of flame erupted forth as the house began to collapse.

"Holy shit," said Jacker as they all moved out towards the street.

"Look over there," said Rachel as she pointed in the direction of the school. They all looked and saw that there was a fire there as well. It seemed that several buildings in Widowsfield had erupted in flames.

"Come on," said Jacker. "The van's parked up the street. Let's get the fuck out of here once and for all."

They ran up the street, but Jacker slowed down and finally stopped. He was patting his pockets as if searching for something before he cursed.

"What's wrong?" asked Rachel.

"My keys are gone. I must've left them in the cabin."

"Well, fuck it," said Rachel. "There's no going back now." They all looked down the hill at the raging fire that was consuming Widowsfield.

"I might be able to jump the van," said Paul.

Jacker groaned in disapproval, but they didn't have any other option. They knew that if the keys were in the cabin that they would never be able to get them.

Shortly after, as they made their way up the street, Jacker stopped and cursed again.

"What's wrong now?" asked Paul.

"This is where we parked," said Jacker as he spun in a circle. "That mother fucker."

"What?" asked Alma.

"Stephen stole my van, that's what. That's why my keys aren't in my damn pocket, because that piece of shit stole them off me and took off."

"Where's the security van? Can we take that?" asked Alma.

Jacker pointed in the direction of the burning town. "It's back at the field where we first came in. I don't think we can get there from here without going through the fires."

"Great," said Rachel. "What the hell are we supposed to do now?"

"Keep walking," said Alma. "That's what. We're going to keep walking until we get out of this town, and I'm never looking back."

They all agreed. Each of them was eager to leave Widowsfield behind for good.

Sycamore Street proved to be an arduous walk. It was steep, and didn't level out until it t-boned at the road that curved a path around the Jackson Reservoir. If they turned right, they would end up headed back down into the town they were escaping, and if they turned left they would make their way up to the rest stop where Amanda Harper had driven off the cliff.

They turned left, and Alma mentioned that they could rest at the scenic overlook that peered down on the hydroelectric dam. She felt like it would be an appropriate place to ruminate on what they'd been through, and Jacker was panting hard enough that they were all concerned he might pass out if they didn't rest soon.

Night was giving itself slowly over to dawn, and the emerging light revealed that the area was beset by more than just smoke. Heavy, cold fog blanketed the area, masking the woods that surrounded them.

Alma led them to the parking lot of the scenic overlook and Jacker sat heavily upon a rock near the entrance. He panted and scratched at his shaggy hair. Rachel stayed beside him, and only glanced back at Widowsfield once as she toyed with the wedding ring she was still wearing, certainly wondering if she should just take it off for good.

Paul walked with Alma as she crossed the lot. They approached the broken, rusted railing where Alma's mother had driven their car off the cliff in an attempt to murder her daughter. She looked down, but the fog was too thick to see the water below. Alma walked to the edge and sat down with her legs dangling over the side. Paul sat beside her and held her hand.

"It's all over," said Alma. "I can't believe it's finally over."

"Are you okay?" asked Paul.

Alma smiled and leaned over to peck him on the cheek. "Better now that I'm with you."

Paul put his arm around Alma's shoulder and pulled her close. Together, they watched the bloom of sunrise burn away the fog.

THE END

AUTHOR'S NOTE

And so ends the Widowsfield trilogy, with the bloom of sunrise burning away the fog.

In the Author's Notes of my books, I usually like to look back and reflect on the book's plot, and discuss some of the themes and hidden information that I tried to weave into it. However, this time I'm going to shut my mouth and let the story do that work for me. In this particular book, I feel like any puzzlement someone might have after finishing the final page is part of the fun, and I don't want to steal that away.

I tried hard to make sure that the most pertinent questions about the Widowsfield mystery were answered, and any new question that might be burning their way through the fog in the reader's head once the book is over can be answered within the text of the book itself. I'm being super vague here on purpose, because putting the puzzle pieces together about Widowsfield was part of the fun.

My hope is that some readers walk away from this book pleased, but then pause a few days later and say, "Wait a minute!" If that happens, and a reader starts tearing through the book a second time, picking up on clues that they didn't see the first time, then I'll feel like the book was a resounding success.

The original inspiration for the 314 series came from reading urban myths about The Philadelphia Experiment. The myths about the green fog and bodies fused to the walls was just too rich a subject not to tinker with. Take all those old stories about the USS Eldridge however you want, but I tried to incorporate a lot of true events and figures into this book. Major Leslie Groves (later on he became a general) was a real person, and headed up the Manhattan Project with Oppenheimer. The USS Eldridge was really sold to Greece and turned into the Leon, and it actually did get scrapped in 1996, but not before disappearing mysteriously for a little while. There are also areas where it would appear from above that a ship had been built on dry land for some unexplainable reason. And Einstein's birthday is really March 14th. Sticking these little nuggets of truth into a work of fiction helps to make it all feel so much more intense and real, at least to me.

After finishing this trilogy, I'm going to be working on the final book in the Deadlocked series, so this time in my life has suddenly become dramatically transitional. To wave goodbye to Alma and Paul, and then to have to go and wave goodbye to the characters of Deadlocked, is at times depressing, but oddly joyous. With the 314 trilogy, I'm extremely happy with the ending. It stays true to the story, and can be fodder for discussion for people for a long time. That's exactly what I want, because these books have always been a puzzle for the reader to try and decipher.

Once I close the book on the final Deadlocked, I'm going to be continuing with the Bathory series, but there's a good chance that I'll be delving into something else as well, and starting a whole new world to rip into. Hopefully the 314 series has been a good enough read that you'll follow along with me on the next journeys, to wherever horrific places it takes us.

Please come in visit me at arwisebooks.com, and on the ARWise fan page on Facebook. I also try my best to respond to everyone that emails me over at aaron@arwisebooks.com, although I have to warn you, there are certain answers to puzzles in the 314 series that I don't want to divulge to anyone because it might take the fun out of debates people have.

Finally, you shouldn't be shocked if your ever reading a book of mine in the future and run across a shadowy organization known simple as, The Accord.

SPECIAL THANKS!!!

Before I take off, I want to give special thanks to a few people. First off, thanks to Lauren Patrick, who helped create the cover for this book. I think that the cover she did for this book is beyond my favorite cover of any that have ever graced my books. I find it eerie, gorgeous, and absolutely haunting. Lauren, I think you're insanely talented, and I hope hope hope HOPE we do more covers together in the future.

Also, thanks to my wonderful beta readers, who put up with my insane get-the-book-done time schedules right before a book gets released. I promise ladies, one of these days I'm going to try to be calm and relaxed when a book is about to be put out!

And finally, to all of the fans that have stuck with me through my various books. I'm in your debt, and I'll do everything I can to continue putting out books that curl your toes and make you a little more anxious when flipping off the light before bed.

After all, who knows what might be watching from the walls?

Made in the USA
Middletown, DE
03 August 2023